"You going to kill me?"

She was young. Her long ponytail swished to one side as she spoke and I saw what I hadn't before. She'd orchestrated this whole thing. Without thinking, I shook my head.

"I knew it," she said, thumping her fist against her thigh. "I knew you could be turned. The others said you never would, but I knew."

"I'm not turned. He was a Shadow agent, so I killed him."

"I'm a Shadow agent," she said. I raised a brow, and she dropped her eyes. "Well, I will be soon. And you didn't kill me."

I nodded slowly.

I really should kill her.

I *would* kill her. But there were things I needed to know first. "How'd you find me?"

She shrugged nonchalantly, but there was pride in the movement. "I saw you leave the bachelorette auction."

That wasn't what I meant and she knew it. I didn't press.

I'd find out what I needed to know . . . one way or another.

Books by Vicki Pettersson

THE SCENT OF SHADOWS
The First Sign of the Zodiac

THE TASTE OF NIGHT
The Second Sign of the Zodiac

THE
TASTE OF NIGHT

THE SECOND SIGN OF THE ZODIAC

VICKI
PETTERSSON

AVON BOOKS

An Imprint of HarperCollins Publishers

This is a work of fiction. Names, characters, places, and incidents are products of the author's imagination or are used fictitiously and are not to be construed as real. Any resemblance to actual events, locales, organizations, or persons, living or dead, is entirely coincidental.

AVON BOOKS
An Imprint of HarperCollins*Publishers*
10 East 53rd Street
New York, New York 10022-5299

Copyright © 2007 by Vicki Pettersson
Author photo by Derik Klein
ISBN: 978-0-06-089892-2
ISBN-10: 0-06-089892-5
www.avonbooks.com

First Avon Books paperback printing: April 2007

Avon Trademark Reg. U.S. Pat. Off. and in Other Countries, Marca Registrada, Hecho en U.S.A.
HarperCollins® is a registered trademark of HarperCollins Publishers.

Printed in the U.S.A.

10 9 8 7 6 5 4 3 2 1

For Becky Brahma—
sister, confidante, friend.

Acknowledgments

Thanks be to the usual suspects—Roger Pettersson, Ellen Daniel, Linda Grimes, Kris Reekie—for early readings, and to Suzanne Frank for both holding me accountable and holding my hand. To those in the KWC forum for ensuring it lives up to its name, and my family for putting up with my mutterings and moods. To Miriam Kriss, without whom this book would have no title, no representation, and no home (you know, the little things). Special thanks to my child's caregivers, Paula Peck and Dennis Stephenson, for enabling me to confidently leave this world for another. And to Diana Gill, who makes the other world a better place to be.

1

It's funny how a name can change the world's perception of you. Your perception of yourself. My mother used to stroke my cheek with her fingertips, calling me her Jo-baby—my earliest identity; a child both loved and cherished—though obviously that was before she abandoned me. And while the man I'd once thought was my father just called me Joanna, the way he said it was telling as well, all the syllables crisply clipped and pronounced, like he was biting them off between his teeth before spitting them out. Like being Joanna, like being me, was a bad thing. And then there was the love of my life. He'd called me Jo-Jo, and that was the name I missed most of all.

Because for the past six months everyone had called me by my sister's name, and it was the one I used on myself now, fluffing my blond hair as I stood in a makeshift dressing room in one of Las Vegas's most opulent resorts, the Valhalla Hotel and Casino.

"Olivia Archer," I muttered as I straightened my Chanel pencil skirt, my feet screaming in heels as high as flagpoles. "What the hell were you thinking?"

Of course, she couldn't answer. The real Olivia was six

months dead, and while I still mourned her every day and every minute, even if she'd been here I doubt her answer would've made sense to me. I mean, how did one even come up with the idea of selling women to raise money for charity? Much less entering herself in the bidding?

I'd been asking myself this ever since I received the phone call from City of Light Charities two months earlier, asking if the bachelorette auction was still on in spite of "recent events." I'd then scrambled to make sure it was, as Olivia would've done. Because that was one thing I needed to do.

Be Olivia Archer. Or be dead.

And so I stood, staring in the mirror at skin that was supposed to be mine, buffed, fluffed, and shellacked to aesthetic perfection, about to auction myself off to the highest bidder.

"Livvy-girl!" The screech—another of my new names—could be heard above the emcee's cheery voice as yet another debutante was sold out front. "Olivia! No, no! Get away!"

I whirled, images of honed blades and demon faces assailing me, but there was only Cher, Olivia's best friend—now mine—waving frantically as she danced from foot to foot. She breathed a theatrical sigh as I picked up my Dior handbag and clicked over to her in my medieval torture devices. Yanking me to her side, she whispered harshly, "That's the suicide mirror, remember? Leave that for the other hags . . . er, contestants."

She batted her thickened lashes when I glared at her. I needed this event to be a success. Which meant cheering on all the other hags. Er, contestants.

"It's true," added Madeleine Cross airily, mistaking my annoyance for disbelief. I recognized her from her photo in Vegas's equivalent of Page Six, and it turned out she was just as vain and self-absorbed as reported. She flipped back a lock of recently streaked auburn hair and ran her finger across a perfectly waxed brow. "Two socialites, sharing that mirror, were brought down by bad press after last year's event."

"Social homicide," Cher said, and both women shuddered.

I wanted to say, *But it was for a good cause,* and only just managed to keep my mouth shut and face straight. "Oh. Well . . . thanks. For saving me, I mean."

"'Course, darlin'! We're BFFs!" Cher gave my shoulders a squeeze before her gaze strayed over my shoulder and she gasped. "Oh my God! Don't look!"

We turned, and a squeaky sound from Cher whipped us back around. Madeleine leaned forward to peer at the offending contestant through the critical lens of our mirror.

"She's using M·A·C lipstick in . . ." She squinted before drawing back, chin lifted. "Vegas Volt. At least two coats. The whore."

I leaned over and joined her in study of the woman now perched obliviously in front of the suicide mirror. She was dressed in high-class hooker wear and dripping diamonds, just like the rest of us. "I think she looks good."

"Olivia!" Cher looked at me like I'd just told her I wore press-on nails. "Priscilla Chambers is her own object of desire!"

"Truly," said Madeleine, applying more mascara as she rolled her eyes, nearly stabbing herself in the eyeball. "Watch, she'll bid on herself."

Olivia had lined up the bachelorettes months before—thank God—and clearly I was missing out on some social nuances. So under the guise of polite inquisitiveness, I probed for more information. "Well, what about her? In blue?"

Cher and Madeleine jostled for mirror time, but neither glanced in the direction of the woman about to take to the stage. "Lena Carradine. Puh-lease."

Madeleine executed another perfect eye roll. "Queen of the facelift tribe."

"See where her brows are tattooed? Those used to be her cheeks."

Tough crowd.

"Ladies?" Oh, thank God, I knew that voice. We all turned to find a reporter standing so close she'd easily copped every word. She smiled. "Could I get a couple quotes for the *Las Vegas Sentinel*?"

Cher and Madeleine launched into a litany of clichés about charity, peace on earth, and the quest for a good man, and the reporter pretended to jot it all down, an expression of carefully vacuous cheerfulness on her honeyed face. Meanwhile I studied Vanessa Valen; naturally bronzed, exotic as a hothouse orchid, and a woman who had the art of camouflage down to a science. Though I'd seen her do it a hundred times now, it was still mystifying how easily she disappeared in a crowd. She was beautiful, but more than that, she had a rock-solid presence and a will to match. She also had a steel fan with viciously curved claws resting somewhere beneath her tidy reporter's guise, and was my only real ally at this whole bubble-brained affair. It was all I could do not to latch on to her leg and hang there.

When Cher and Madeleine unexpectedly took a breath at the same time, Vanessa managed to shoehorn in a request. "Perhaps I could have a one-on-one with the chair of the"—here she glanced down at her pad—"Cheesecake for Charity Auction?"

The smirk was slight, but it was there, and I discreetly shot her the bird as I pretended to brush back my hair. Then Cher pushed me forward, amusing Vanessa all the more, and we waited in silence until we were alone.

"Tell me I'm your hero," Vanessa finally said, tawny eyes twinkling when I turned back to her. "That's all the thanks I need."

A heroine's hero. Yeah, that's funny. I reached down and rubbed the sole of one foot, wincing. "I'll repay you with backstage gossip from Vegas's most famous glitterati. You wouldn't believe how catty this crowd can get."

"Please. I may be a superhero, but I'm still a woman." She glanced around the room with distaste before arrowing back in on me. "Nice shoes, by the way. And quite an event. Even the mighty Henshalls are here. Didn't they snub last year's affair as 'too gauche for words'?"

"Did they?" I too had snubbed last year's fleshfest.

"And looks like your so-called father is working the room for you. He never even shows up for his own functions. Maybe he's growing a charitable spirit."

I snorted. "I could write a doctoral dissertation on his 'charitable spirit.'"

She twirled a strand of hair around her finger as Cher had and said airily, "Yeah, if you were, like, a doctor."

"Hey, don't pick on her. She said you have nice toe cleavage."

"Really?" Vanessa looked down hopefully, then caught my smug look and straightened, clearing her throat. "Anyway, Daddy Dearest just provided me with a rare quote. He said you're the kindest, most generous person he knows."

I considered what I knew of Xavier Archer's business, personal, and—most importantly—*otherworldly* contacts, and could believe it. Then again, Olivia had been the best person I'd known too. Even with her predilection for overpriced shoes.

"Shows how well he knows me, huh?"

Vanessa cocked a hand on her hip. "Right. I mean, if he knew his supposed daughter was really a member of Zodiac troop 175, charged with promoting peace and cosmic balance in the Universe—"

"Or at least in the greater Las Vegas valley—"

"And that taking over Olivia Archer's identity was really a crafty plot to infiltrate our enemy's most profitable mortal-run corporation . . . he'd shit bricks."

"Yeah," I said wryly, and motioned down my cartoon character body. "Crafty."

Vanessa pursed her lips. "Hey, it's a great cover. You're like Diana Prince and Wonder Woman. Or Clark Kent and Superman. Bruce Wayne and Batman."

I drew back, Olivia's most haughty expression on my face. "Excuse me, but I have nothing in common with that . . . bat."

"Sure you do. He was a billionaire philanthropist and playboy. You're a—"

"Millionaire heiress and Playmate?" I quipped, as the emcee sold another woman out front. "Sure, rub it in."

Vanessa's amusement returned. "Okay, so instead of a loyal butler you have a bubble-brained socialite as your closest confidante. But your tactical support ain't so bad"—and here she took a bow—"and I bet you have all the martial assistance you need tucked between your legs."

"Don't be crude."

She smirked. "You know what I mean."

I did know, but I hadn't been able to squeeze anything else beneath this pencil skirt, so I clipped open my handbag and showed her the conduit I'd stashed there. It was a palm-sized bow and arrow, weighty, but made just for me. I never left home, much less hosted a charity auction, without it.

The polished slide of the metal beneath my fingers was soothing, and I shot Vanessa a wry grin as I snapped the bag shut again. She was right. It could be worse. "So what are you going to write about this time, Vanessa?"

"The usual. I'll use this event to recap how the beautiful and wealthy Olivia Archer has bounced back from an attack on her life—that killed her sister—to become this city's premiere philanthropic icon."

I winced at the nutshell version of "Olivia's" recent past, though anyone who'd been in the Las Vegas valley more than a minute would've already heard all the gory details. They'd dominated headlines for weeks.

CASINO HEIRESS PLUMMETS TO DEATH WHILE SISTER WATCHES.

Only thing, it'd been Olivia plummeting and me watching. Not the reverse.

"So, where've you been lately?" Vanessa asked abruptly.

I shifted uncomfortably. Apparently she was here to do

more than polish her pristine reporter's persona. "Is that your not-so-subtle way of telling me I'm wanted back at the sanctuary?"

"Wow, beauty and brains," she quipped, then shrugged, returning to the topic. "You haven't been back in weeks."

"I'm taking the scenic route to superherodom." I joked, but this time she didn't smile. Well, she was right. It *had* been a while. "Okay. Dawn or dusk?"

She blew out a breath, obviously relieved to be able to give our troop leader good news. "Dusk tomorrow is fine. The training field should be ready by then."

I lifted a brow. Training field?

"Oh yeah," she said, seeing my expression. "Tekla's set up a new lesson for us. Everyone is going to be there."

Great, I thought wryly. Heropalooza.

Vanessa looked over my shoulder. "I think you're being paged."

I turned to find the stage manager waving at me frantically. Apparently I was up next. "Oh God. I wonder what exactly these people think they're buying."

"Whatever it is, tell them you'll throw in the knife set for free."

"I don't think they know I'm the kind of girl who plays with knives," I said, and couldn't help but return her grin.

I joined Cher huddled next to the runway ramp, peering through the gold lamé curtain as the emcee announced Lena Carradine. She pivoted and twirled her way down the catwalk, lifted her surgically enhanced face into the blazing spotlight, and blew air kisses with a mouth stretched so tight she could barely pucker. Cher hissed at Lena through her peephole. "Go on, girl. Hurl yourself down the walk of shame."

"I'm trying to raise money here," I reminded Cher.

She turned to me, placed one palm on each of my cheeks, and said encouragingly, "And you will, honey. The second you set foot on that stage, you'll have more to give to charity than Warren Buffett."

I looked at her.

"Before the Gates Foundation got to him, I mean. Now go."

Pushing my handbag up to my elbow, I lined up, took a deep breath, and when I heard my new name called, stepped onto the stage and into my personal hell.

A soft, sensuous tune from the live orchestra accompanied my stride down the catwalk, and I fought the impulse to look down, hide my face, and rush through the torture of being so blatantly stared at, knowing Olivia would do none of those things. So I forced myself to make eye contact with those seated at the numbered tables—both the men who eyed me with appreciative speculation, and the women who sought out flaws where there were none—and shot them all Olivia's most blinding smile. There were only a handful of faces I recognized, dozens I didn't, and one in particular I wish I hadn't: Olivia's father, Xavier—owner of Valhalla, human lackey to the most evil man on the planet, and the man who'd made my teen years a living hell.

He probably thought selling off his daughter for charity was a good investment. I snarled inwardly as I shot him a saccharine smile. He nodded back.

Could this get any worse?

It could—and did—as soon as the bidding began. I held my breath until the first paddle was lifted in the air, sending a relieved smile out to number 15, but the emcee's voice quickly acknowledged a second bidder, then a third . . . then a stream of numbers in such quick succession I lost count. I concentrated on keeping a look of cheery interest plastered on my face, feeling sweat trickle down my spine as the bidding, and minutes, went on.

Finally, after what felt like light years, the bidding was narrowed to four. Number 15 was still in it, but he lifted his paddle more slowly now, and it shook slightly in the air, which meant his funds couldn't match the heart practically pulsing on his sleeve. The three other bidders saw it and doubled the pace. One, surprisingly, was a young woman—blond, tidy, her good looks understated in unrelieved black—but the emcee didn't question her right to bid, nor did anyone else. This was Vegas, after all. Money didn't just talk here, it screamed for attention.

One of her rivals was a well-dressed gentleman standing next to Xavier, probably a business associate, and I wondered how much he was willing to drop on me just to ingratiate himself to my "father." Finally, there was a blond man who looked as out of place as I felt. Number 56 reminded me of a construction worker despite his double-breasted suit, but he wielded his paddle with a careless flick of his wrists, so I let the observation pass. Looks, as I well knew, were deceiving.

As expected, number 15 didn't last much longer. The woman, closest to him, shot him a haughty glance, but she was the next to fall. Now it was between Xavier's sycophant and the blond giant. I was hoping the latter would win, anything to put a hitch in Xavier's stride, so I shot the man a smile so encouraging a murmur went up from the audience.

That smile, and his responding bid, was enough to finish off Xavier's man. Applause rolled through the room, and I acknowledged the winning bidder with a tilt of my head, and pivoted, glancing sideways at Xavier as I left the stage. He only rolled his eyes, turning his back as his companion's paddle fell, and walked away.

"How the fuck am I supposed to follow that?" the next bachelorette grumbled, trudging reluctantly up the stairs as Cher and Madeleine swallowed me in a group bear hug.

"You were awesome! Incredible! Inspiring!"

"Guys . . . I just stood there," I fought for breath through the assault of lotion, perfume, hairspray, and breath mints.

"Oh no . . . Priscilla just stood there."

"Stood there so long her use-by date expired!"

They gave each other an air high-five and squealed.

"Ladies." The emcee, an anchorman for one of the local channels, poked his head through the curtain. "Time to meet your bidders. Congratulations on a job well done . . .

and make sure they know we take cash, check, or money order."

Number 56 made me come to him. There was no meeting me halfway; he just stood as before—watching me skirt around tables, smile at people I was supposed to know, and dodge the woman who'd also been bidding on me—arms folded over his chest expectantly. On second thought, he fit right in with this pretentious crowd. And, I decided, he fit in especially well at Valhalla. Larger up close than he'd appeared from the stage, he had one of those overdefined builds that makes one wonder what exactly he was compensating for, and with the blond hair and gold winking in one earlobe, he was a modern-day Viking . . . right down to the suddenly avaricious glint in his eyes.

"Congratulations on a fine bid," I said, shifting my handbag to my left arm as I held out my right. The giant accepted it, dwarfing my palm in his, and drew me in close like it was his right. Tension immediately sprang up in me.

Relax, Jo, I told myself, flashing him a tight smile. Hidden identity or no, I didn't want to be one of those women who let one little near-death experience scar her forever. Okay, two near-death experiences.

Well, five . . . but who was counting?

"I'm Olivia," I said, pulling my hand away. He let it slide from his reluctantly.

"Oh, I know exactly who you are." And though he smiled, he said it like he really did.

I tilted my head and sniffed. Smell was the strongest of my senses—and for both my allies and my enemies—but right now I scented nothing.

"And you are?" I asked, raising a brow.

"Liam," he answered, and though I waited for more, that was apparently it.

"Okay," I said, as cheerily as I could manage. "Well, you have three weeks to claim your . . ." God, I could barely say it. "Prize. After that the bid is void. You can pay at the front before you leave, and the attendant there will provide my contact information."

Liam just nodded, that amused expression still touching his face. I mirrored him, nodding back, now straining to keep my smile in place. Time to extricate myself from this social train wreck, and let Mr. Chatty get back to polishing his biceps. I'd just cross my fingers that the next three weeks would pass uneventfully.

"All righty, then. See ya later, Liam." I turned to head back to the dressing area.

"Good-bye . . . Archer."

I froze. Slowly turned. Sniffed again.

And there it was; faint, just a smudge across the pane of my temporal lobe—like memory, but thicker—with edges and hooks that snagged my attention. He let his natural scent intensify, growing so densely cloying I had to breathe through my mouth, and even then the oxygen was round and full, like I could bite it.

My heart thudded in my chest, and I had to fight to keep my own nerves, and scent, from rising to permeate the room. "What do you want?"

Liam's mouth widened into a full grin. "I want you to want me."

I thought of the weapon nestled in my bag. Believe me, I wanted him.

"Uh-uh," he warned, shaking his head as he sensed the direction of my thought. And why not? He was a Shadow. I was an agent of Light. It was only natural to want to kill each other. "Look at all the people, Joanna. Look at the press. 'Bachelorette Auction Turns into Bloodbath' would make a terrific headline."

"You know who I really am." Though surprised at his use of my real name, I stated it as fact . . . because the real question was *How?*

He smiled in mock sympathy and began that slow head nod again. "Kinda puts a hitch in your five-year plan, doesn't it?"

I clenched my jaw, but said nothing. Shadows were braggarts, down to the last, and while annoying, it was something I might be able to use to my advantage. Keep him talking, buy enough time to signal Vanessa, and we could corner him and escort him outside to his death. If that failed? I'd shoot him where he stood.

"You're the first real Shadow I've seen face-to-face in a long time," I began conversationally, though the taunt was spot-on. For some reason our enemies had been lying low for the past six months, a move that spoke of a blanket command. I knew that couldn't sit well with all the Shadows, and was right in suspecting Liam was one of them. His eyes narrowed, and the air around us warmed, peppery cinders bleeding from his pores. "I mean . . . you are a real Shadow, aren't you? Not just some rogue agent looking to score brownie points with the local troop?"

His face tightened. Rogue agents were outcasts looking to usurp their counterparts in a city's established troop, and nobody on either side of the Zodiac liked to be mistaken for what essentially amounted to a paranormal mutt. "I'm more real," he said through clenched teeth, "than most of the breasts in this room."

"Prove it," I said, shooting an unconcerned glance around the room. I didn't see Vanessa anywhere. "What raids have you led lately?"

As expected, he was anxious to brag. "I was responsible for the showgirls held hostage at the top of the Trop at the beginning of the year."

"That was you?" I feigned interest, having caught sight of Vanessa near a tray of crab cakes, and he nodded while I waited for her to turn. "Not very original."

The smile dropped. "I also devised the implosion of the new Cirque showroom."

That'd been two months earlier, a paranormal prank that'd spilled hundreds of gallons of water out and onto the Strip. "We should've let that one go." I shrugged philosophically.

"Cleanup was a bitch, was it?" he said, referring to the lengths we'd had to go to keep the entire event from mortal notice.

"Not really," I said, shrugging. Vanessa had turned my way to grab a champagne flute from a passing waiter. Now all I had to do was catch her eye. "But we don't need another fucking Cirque show in this town."

"Okay, then." He licked his lips, provoked. "How about the theft of the mayor's gin back in March?"

He smiled when an involuntary twinge shuddered up my spine. The mayor and his damned martinis. The entire city's coffers had nearly gone to the first person to come up with a bottle of Tanqueray. "That was a close one," I had to admit.

His arrogance returned. "So. Been taking many photographs lately, Joanna? 'Raising awareness of the homeless and displaced through your art,'" he quoted, and it was my turn to stiffen. Those words had been in my obituary six months earlier. "But Olivia doesn't take photos, does she? Though plenty are taken of her."

I feigned a yawn, like his words—and knowledge—didn't matter. "I've been kinda busy lately. You know. Saving Las Vegas from evil beings bent on chaos and destruction."

"You mean tourists?" Liam grinned at my unamused stare. "Wouldn't it be so much easier to protect these mortals if it weren't for the whole 'free will' thing?"

"Forgive me if I don't get into the moral responsibility of promoting individual choice with a guy who takes his orders from an evil overlord."

"An overlord, I should remind you, who's also your father."

People just loved to throw that in my face.

"So is that why you're here? Dear ol' Dad send you to convince me to turn to the dark side of the force?" I rolled my eyes and caught Vanessa heading toward the Henshalls. Damn.

"Actually I wanted to see for myself what all the excitement was about." And he looked me up and down, doing just that.

His curiosity didn't surprise me. I was something new, after all. Something spoken about in the superhero mythology and written about in our texts, but that no one on either side of the Zodiac had ever seen before. I was the first star sign who'd ever been both Shadow *and* Light, the person our mythology called the *Kairos*, and the fulcrum upon which the supernatural fates hinged. Basically I could tip the metaphysical scales in the favor of whatever side I chose, Shadow or Light, which made me a valuable commodity in the paranormal world.

"And?" I finally said, resisting the urge to cross my arms over my chest.

Liam leaned close in a way that must have looked intimate and wolfish from afar. "I think you're the biggest joke I've ever seen. I think you've as much chance of being the Kairos as my dirty socks. And I think you should die for even breathing the same air as I am right now."

"Then it's a good thing," I said slowly, "that I don't give a fuck what you think."

And now my paternal heritage pushed itself to the forefront, soot and dust overpowering his own scent as my vision went red at the edges, telling me my eyes had gone tar black.

If Liam was startled, he didn't show it. He just reached out very slowly and put a hand to my face, resting it on the side of my cheek. I let him, just to show I truly felt no fear just then. I could reach up and snap his wrist before anyone in the room blinked, but I let him touch me. I was feeling philosophical about the whole thing. I'd touch him back soon enough.

He let his hand rest before patting my cheek hard enough to sting, and probably leave a red mark as well. "You've got the balls of your father, I'll give you that. Do you know he was actually proud of the way you took care of Ajax and Butch? A Shadow, proud of the Light." He shook his head and scoffed. "But I want to see what you've learned since then. I wonder, do you know how to do more than just fight?"

"Like what?"

He let his gaze wander off over my shoulder, as if he was pondering the eternal question, and when his eyes returned to mine, he smiled. "Like . . . run."

He was gone before I could take a breath. I swiveled as the air rushed past me, caught myself before I darted after him. People were watching. Plus it was already too late. Liam was already halfway to his destination; a normal door with a red-lettered EXIT sign fixed above it, but with another symbol above that, one noticeable only to those who knew how to look.

I cursed inwardly and bit my lip as I stared at the tiny winking star that marked a portal. Once Liam opened it, he shot a final victorious glance back at me, then slammed it so hard the room's chandeliers rocked and the champagne flutes shook on their trays. I sighed inwardly. Even the mortals had noticed that.

More importantly, the star above the doorway flickered, then blinked out. Portals disappeared as soon as they were accessed, a paranormal precaution against mortals accidentally getting through . . . and proof positive the Universe had a twisted sense of humor.

Run, Liam had said. But what he meant was follow. And even though my instincts told me not to, that a trap awaited me on the other side of reality, I didn't have much of a choice. Either I stopped Liam before he got too far, or my hidden identity would spread across the supernatural world like napalm across the rain forest.

And if that happened, Kairos or not, my troop would place me in a secured holding cell to wake up a week from now with an entirely new identity, and alias, to get used to. That'd be the end of the relationships I'd been working on so hard these last six months. Good-bye to Cher. Good-bye to the life I'd built.

Good-bye to Olivia.

And that wasn't going to happen. So I said nothing to Vanessa, who was staring hard at Lena Carradine's lip implants, and slipped out of the room when no one was looking. And once outside I did as Liam wanted, even in skyscraper heels. I ran.

2

Portals are to the supernatural realm what dreams are to the subconscious, ways to access an alternate reality. Everyone encounters these supernatural gateways at one time or another, usually in the form of an elevator skipping the floor of a button you know you just pushed, or the feeling of being watched out of a window that is, by all accounts, empty. Small things, mostly, but ones hiding an entire world behind their impenetrable cores.

Needless to say, humans were personae non grata in the supernatural realm. Portals were . . . unstable. Even an agent didn't always know what lurked on the other side. Sometimes you didn't want to know.

In this case, however, I needed to get to the danger awaiting me on that side of reality, and to do so I climbed the stairwell to the roof, disconnected the alarm, and exited there. Sure, there were active portals inside the casino, but I didn't have time to look for one now, and there was always one located at the apex of a giant building—something having to do with the mechanics of superstrings—so that was the one I beelined for.

The lights of Vegas were on full throttle, but I ignored the sight and pulled my conduit from my bag. The flathead of the crossbow shone like polished onyx in the reflected light, and the wire string gleamed thin and dangerous as I thumbed off the safety. Its weight in my palm warmed me even more than the balmy late-spring night, and I quickly located the tiny variable star winking like a diamond chip above a maintenance hatch and reentered the building.

The greatest difference between the real world and this alternate one was the silver-gray tint smearing the entire landscape, obscuring everything that wasn't an agent's aura in a dull, hazy, shroud. Texture and weight played a factor in the depth of color, so buildings were denser than cars, and birds and butterflies were only the lightest shade of smoke. People could be ashen or silvered, depending on their mood: this was a mirrored world, the earth in negative, a place that divided light and shadow down to its most basic structure. Even the air carried that clouded tint into your lungs, the ions and electrodes laid bare so that each breath tasted metallic.

Yet all the natural rules still applied, which was why I still had to run when chased by Shadows, and I still had to dodge people and objects, and basically avoid those who operated in the real world. We could still be seen by mortals, though perhaps a better word was *sensed*. It wasn't an entirely comfortable feeling to brush up against an agent operating in the supernatural realm, rather like biting down on a wad of tinfoil, and feeling that ache in every limb, pore, and soaring cell of your body. Without even realizing they were doing it, mortals would step aside when I brushed too close, or quickly look away if we happened to make eye contact. Because I had no pigment to attract the eye, they seemed to feel a touch of vertigo if I was too near, and—to the amusement of some of our more immature agents—were easily unbalanced.

Once I was back in the main casino, I inhaled sharply, searching out the skein of scent Liam had so thoughtfully provided. Now that I was on the negative side of reality, I had a visual tell too: here an agent's aura could be read like a psychic map, a bright splash of color amid all the shades of gray.

Weeks ago I'd had the ability to read the moods and temperaments of agents and mortals alike, and I'd thought it was a part of my nifty hey-look-it's-the-Kairos package. But apparently my powers were more of the use-it-or-lose-it variety. Outside the portals now I could view only the auras of those agents with the strongest and most inflexible wills, and I couldn't discern human auras at all.

So I searched throughout the achromatic gloom for something similar to the rosy Technicolor streaming behind and around my body and moved quickly through the casino, the mortals around me unaware of my presence, though the zombies feeding cash into the slot machines probably wouldn't have looked up anyway.

I'd just passed the main casino cage when the air reverberated around me, the stench of decay strong enough to prickle my skin. I swung around and spotted a zephyrous streak of blood orange rounding a far corner, followed by a stark white void erasing the silvery light. It was like a bright spattering of paint next to an empty space on a contemporary artist's fresh canvas, and the scent of mold hit me as a giggle floated my way.

I raced around the corner to find Liam's shadow splayed on an adjoining wall, backlit and straining forward. Then the shadow retracted, elongating and snapping, before disappearing entirely from view. I began running again.

I followed Liam's scent past the empty sports book and packed poker room. I wasn't worried about the casino's security cameras tracking my movements—they couldn't on this side of reality—but I did start worrying when the tangerine aura vanished under a doorway situated beneath a bank of escalators. Damn. He'd crossed back over into the mortal realm, taking his visual tell with him. If I wanted to pick up his olfactory trail again, I'd have to do the same.

"C'mon, there has to be another one," I muttered, and

began scanning the casino's perimeter. Hoping I wouldn't have to go back outside to find another portal, I moved quickly among the slot banks, keeping to the walls as much as possible. I was scouring the buffet line, which was doing a surprisingly brisk business for ten o'clock at night, when I ran into a security guard. Literally.

"Ow," I said, rubbing my forehead with one hand while I discreetly slipped my conduit behind my back with the other.

"The fuck you doin' here?" he said, mouth barely moving. I smiled up at him, more relieved than I cared to admit to see a familiar—if not altogether friendly—face.

Hunter Lorenzo was one of ours, and as close to an ideal image of a superhero as one could get. Thing was, he wasn't a cartoon, and it wasn't an act. He was the troop's weaponeer and head tactician, and had artistic hands—though he practiced a violent art—and a hooded, if sure, intelligence. I could still see his aura on this side of reality; banners of gold and white splaying out around him—typical superhero fare. He wore his clothing like armor, and moved so effortlessly he made a cat look clumsy. His thick, shoulder-length hair had recently been shorn into a severe military cut, a move I'd privately lamented, but it made his brooding brown eyes even more intense.

Hunter and I had butted heads from the first—I had the scars from his conduit to prove it—and a bit of that friction still remained . . . but then something else had happened. We'd briefly shared a power that had made us temporarily invincible—the aureole—but doing so had left us knowing more of each other than either of us was comfortable with because it was an unearned intimacy. I didn't know his middle name or his favorite color, but I knew how his thoughts felt caressing my mind. The bright tang of his adrenaline coursing under my skin. The force of his heart, strong and rhythmic and a bit sad, pumping within my own chest.

We'd been in the same room only a handful of times in

the ensuing months, a mutual choice, and never alone. Fact was, I was attracted to Hunter when I didn't want to be. My heart belonged to another, and always would. Besides, paranormal Boy Scout that he was, if I had only one word to sum up Hunter, it would be *feral*.

"You shouldn't stand around talking to yourself, Hunter," I told him, motioning to the cameras mounted like shining black half moons on the ceiling above us. "It might look suspicious."

"Warren's going to be pissed when he finds out you slipped through a portal without permission."

"It was an accident. I was looking for the bathroom." He glanced at me sharply, then looked away, obviously scouring the walls for a portal, which made my pulse trip faster. Sure, that's what I was doing too, and I could probably use the help, but if Hunter knew the Shadows had found out who I really was, my identity would be altered so fast I wouldn't even have time to say, *Good-bye Olivia*.

Besides, I hated all that domineering alpha male shit . . . even if Hunter did wear it well.

I crossed my arms over my chest and gave him a wry look. "What's the big deal, Hunter? Only agents can see me, and when was the last time you saw a Shadow agent wandering these sacred halls, huh? It's been weeks, months." Minutes.

He did look at me then, dead on, his eyes cool and hard on my face. "Your aura's bleeding into this reality, Olivia."

"What?" I looked around me, swallowing hard when I spotted a Kool-Aid stain pooling onto the carpet. "How?"

From the way Hunter was shielding my body, I could tell the color was visible to the mortal eye. Yes, we existed to protect them . . . but they weren't supposed to know it.

Hunter pulled his radio from his belt, looked around, and pretended to speak into it. "I don't know. The Tulpa must have installed a new security system on that side. We have to get you back through a portal, and quick."

"Which is what I was trying to do when you pulled the whole rent-a-cop routine." I lifted my arm, watched color waft beneath my left pit. "Shit."

"This way."

We pushed past the crowd gathered around the blackjack tables, skirted the baccarat lounge, and barely escaped an excited throng gathering for a slot tournament. All this took a full minute, a minute in which I was aware of my aura slowly oozing into the mortal plane like a leaky tire. Thank God the carpeting in Vegas casinos was made to stand such things. Though the same couldn't be said for the cream-colored walls around me.

"Hurry," I told Hunter, my voice quavering involuntarily. Hunter feinted right suddenly, arm snaking back to grab my wrist, yanking me behind him. From behind a slot bank I spotted two other security guards. Hunter followed them with his eyes until they passed.

"They see us?" I asked, straining around him.

"Every time you speak, color spews from your mouth. Shut up."

He started moving again, and I followed. Quietly.

We finally made it to a recessed doorway where a gently pulsing star marked a portal's entry. No shout of alarm rose behind us, no Shadows were ahead to greet us. I'd deliberately slowed my breathing to try and minimize the seepage, and I was feeling a bit like I'd been under water too long. Crouching low, I let out the breath I'd been holding before sucking in another. When I stood again, I found myself two inches away from Hunter's chest.

"Sorry," I muttered feebly. I'd put him in danger. Again.

"Go," he said, blocking a visual of the doorway with his body. "Then get out of Valhalla."

It wasn't the steel in his voice that propelled me through the archway, or the risk of detection a few seconds more would have cost me. It was the look on his face just before he tore his gaze away; his eyes searching mine before lowering to linger on my mouth, then dropping to my throat, which forced me to swallow hard, and then lower still. *Feral*. We turned away from each other at the same time, the air crackling between us like charred satin, and I dove through the portal. It was safer, I thought, in the shadows.

I found myself thrust into a pitch-black room. Always comforting. At least Hunter couldn't just open the door I'd entered and find me back in living color, aura-less, waiting on the other side. He'd probably have thrown me out of Valhalla himself. I tried to gain my bearings, edging forward, my footsteps echoing on linoleum. A fairly large room, then, probably storage. I felt along the wall, reaching a second doorway before long, and ran my palm along the right side until I found a switch. I didn't flip it on immediately, instead yanking my conduit from my bag again, crouching low in a readied stance. Then I flipped it on.

Two liquid brown eyes stared at me through the crosshairs of my weapon.

The owner of the eyes screamed, and I screamed back.

"Oh shit. Shit!" Heart pounding, I fell back against the wall. The beast across from me began shaking its cage, the sound lost in a cacophony of agitated screeches and cage rattling by the room's other inhabitants. I took a quick look around—obviously a lab of some sort—then did the only thing I could think of when faced with a roomful of shrieking chimpanzees. I flipped the light back off, felt for the door handle, and got out of primate hell.

I'd entered a softly lit anteroom, the middle cleared for foot traffic, with a U-shaped reception desk off to one side and a sofa and coffee table opposite that. The beasts continued their muffled screeches behind me while I tried to figure out where to go next, wondering what the hell monkeys were doing in a casino, when I heard the pounding of footsteps. I sniffed—two mortals—and ducked behind the couch just before they appeared.

I watched them launch themselves down the staircase, dressed in civilian wear, but athletically trim, sporting buzz cuts . . . and military-issue guns trained on the door before them. They communicated in sign language and entered the door in tandem, a well-practiced team. Not, I thought, regular security guards hired off the street. The monkeys went crazy once again, and I could've used the opportunity to escape up the stairs, but something held me back. Curiosity, perhaps. Stupidity, more likely.

"Fuckin' chimps," one of the men muttered as he slammed the door behind him a few moments later, muting the cries circulating from inside . . . though not much. I palmed my conduit in case they decided to search this room too, but relaxed marginally as I scented annoyance and laziness overtake the martial interest that had propelled them down here. "We can't come running every time those fuckers have a coronary over their own shadows."

"Actually, chimpanzees are the smartest primates alive, besides humans. Their closest relation is to us, not gorillas or orangutans, so they can make tools, be taught to communicate, and they possess similar emotions to our own."

"What are you, a fuckin' encyclopedia?" I heard a smack, and a pained exclamation from the smaller man before he came into view, rubbing the back of his head.

"I'm just sayin'. I've been reading the books the professor gave us—"

"*Chimpanzees for Dummies*," the first man scoffed.

"—and it's really interesting. Did you know they enjoy lifelong bonds with their mothers?"

"Yeah, well, I shoot mine a card on Christmas and her birthday. Guess we're not all that closely related after all. Let's go."

"Shouldn't we look around a bit more?"

"Be my guest, Dr. Dolittle, but I'm not missing the playoffs for no fuckin' monkey."

Dolittle, seeing his point, sighed and followed.

I remained where I was a few minutes after their boot-clad steps faded away, more alarmed by this than I would've been a few months ago. I'd watched enough of the Discovery

Channel to know that labs and chimps meant experiments. Experiments meant science. And science was what the supernaturals used to augment their magic to more easily manipulate the mortal world. So what was a lab full of primates—primates that most closely resembled humans, I now knew—doing in a casino on the Las Vegas Strip? And why were soldiers—mortals, sure, but armed nonetheless—guarding them? Somehow I thought I could rule out coincidence as a viable option, but maybe Hunter would know what was going on. I'd ask him later . . . or perhaps I'd come back again on my own.

For now, however, both guards and monkeys had to wait. I was in search of a Shadow.

3

Once I was sure the guards had gone, I bounded up the empty stairwell, straightening my clothes as I walked and tucking my conduit back out of sight.

It didn't take long before my presence was known, and reported, among the employees. The Valhalla Hotel and Casino was one of the newest and most extravagant resorts in Las Vegas, and Xavier Archer the savviest, most respected, and feared entrepreneur in town. Thus walking around in Olivia Archer's skin was akin to the queen of England strutting around Buckingham. Employees practically genuflected in front of the woman they assumed was the sole heiress to the Archer family fortune.

Yet I knew something they didn't. Xavier might have held the title of president and CEO of Valhalla, but he did so by my true father's will and whim. Though we had yet to prove it, the agents of Light believed this was where the Shadow organization was headquartered, and where their conspiracies—operating under the guise of a little innocent gaming—were plotted and set into motion. That my biological father tried to kill me here last winter was proof enough for me.

I shut out the memories of that last encounter as I strode

through the pit. Sure, I was walking around the lion's den, but this time I was doing so with claws and fangs of my own.

Dozens of gazes weighed on me as I crossed the casino floor, and I could practically hear the whirring of machinery as every eye in the monitor room followed my progress. If I'd ever in my life considered striving for fame and fortune, my time spent in Olivia's skin would've had me reconsidering that career goal.

I plastered an expression of vacuous cheerfulness on my face, moving as quickly as I could without looking hurried, and added an extra bit of sway to my hips as I walked. Meanwhile I searched for the olfactory thread I'd memorized while racing down the streets. I was like a voluptuous, blond bloodhound.

Twenty feet later my eyes fastened on a sectioned-off area of the casino. Bingo. If I'd had a tail, I'd be on point. Renovations were ongoing in most Strip properties, and I skirted the craps pit to edge along the curtained area, scanning the signs updating tourists on the latest and greatest improvements. The Great Hall of the Gods was, apparently, getting an aquarium. One that, I recalled Xavier saying, would make Monterey look like a wading pool. At two hundred million, it had better.

And though it was new, it smelled like a few fish had been rotting too long in the tide pool. Another specimen Monterey didn't possess, I thought, wrinkling my nose. Shadows.

I exited through the main entrance before I could be stopped by some solicitous casino host, knowing the Eye in the Sky was still trained on me as I strode through the porte cochere. Once on the Boulevard, I circled the block, ducked behind a line of perfectly edged shrubs, jumped an eight-foot wall, and approached again from the back.

Everyone thinks Las Vegas casinos are impenetrable, that any place with security cameras, trained personnel, and mountains of hard cash would be as hard to get into as Fort Knox. Mostly, they're right. You can't walk right into a stripfront property and wander any way your fancy dictates. That's a given.

But what's also a given is human error. Not to mention sheer boredom. You spend forty-plus hours a week, year after year, in the same smoke-filled, sensory-overloaded environment for an unimpressive hourly wage, and try to maintain a semblance of genuine interest. It'd be hard to feign curiosity under those circumstances, never mind a state of urgency. This was what I was counting on when I approached the aquarium's guarded back door, and I wasn't disappointed.

It was nearly midnight, probably about five hours into the guard's shift, and he was slumped next to the door, near catatonic. As a bonus, he had a prohibited MP3 player that I could hear pumping gangsta rap from ten feet away. I slipped in the door half a foot away from him, and he never knew I was there.

The aquarium's main room was cool and humid, silent but for the humming white noise of the tanks. Concrete walls were bathed in an eerie blue glow from the exhibit's thick acrylic windows, and sea life from jellies to sharks floated obliviously content through beds of fresh seawater. Most of the tanks lined the walls, but a few transparent cylinders spiked through the center of the room, holding the more delicate fish. I turned around myself, thinking of those action movies where the thick glass cracks to send stingrays and water and kelp and plankton over the hapless hero as the bad guys get away. That thought in mind, I pulled out my weapon, as well as a mask that I slipped over my head. Then I dropped my bag in the corner.

"Too late for that, Archer of Light," came a woman's voice, and then bell-like laughter came at me from everywhere. "We already know who you are."

"Know it," Liam's voice boomed out at me from the opposite side so that I turned toward it, "but can't believe it."

Shit. There were two of them.

"I told you she'd follow." The woman again, but closer. I

whirled again. How had I missed the second aura? And why was I still scenting only one Shadow?

"I thought she'd be harder to catch."

"You haven't caught me yet," I said, getting more and more nervous as the calm banter continued. Where the fuck were they?

"Patience, Olivia . . . or can I call you Joanna?"

My jaw clenched as I slid toward the center of the room, back against a circular tank housing glowing pink jellies. I was confused; they were obviously close, but the glyph on my chest had yet to engage. I tapped at my cleavage, wondering if the thing was working. In movies and comic books, glyphs were represented by large lettering on the superhero's clothing. In reality it was like a brand under the skin, undetectable until it started glowing, and only then in the presence of enemy agents, a sort of preternatural alarm system.

So if the Shadows were so close that Liam's scent was clogging my pores, why wasn't my glyph glowing now?

"Are you okay, Archer?" the woman said, this time from my right. "You look a little confused."

I frowned, edging around the cylinder. How were they seeing me?

"Don't have this place mapped out, do you? Of course, once we knew you were posing as Xavier Archer's daughter, we knew you'd have studied Valhalla's floor plan. That's why we picked the aquarium. That's why we waited until it was nearly completed to lure you here."

Alarm skirted through me. They'd known who I'd become, and they'd waited. And I, walking around in Olivia's skin, hadn't known that they'd known. The woman, feeling the bump in my adrenaline, laughed.

"What's wrong? Wondering if the Tulpa is going to show up and finish what he started?"

Liam chuckled now too. God, he sounded like he was practically on top of me. "It's a sad day when a father tries to kill his own daughter."

"He stopped when he found out I was his daughter," I said, and bolted across the room to another tank.

"Which is why we haven't told him about your new identity, or that you'd be here tonight. The place is soundproof, and the security cameras won't be installed until next week."

"And you'll be long dead by then," the woman added, her laughter ringing out again.

Oh good. They'd given this some thought. I swallowed hard and tried to soften my gaze, see shapes rather than colors. Maybe they'd found another portal and were stalking me from the other side. We could still reach each other that way. We could still kill each other. "And you think the Tulpa will be fine with that? With you killing his only child, his heir? The one he believes is the Kairos?"

"You're not the Kairos," Liam said, his tone falling sharply. "And the Tulpa will never know."

I thought about that for a moment, and decided he was bluffing. My death would leave a kill spot, noticeable by any supernatural, same as anyone else's. And kill spots didn't only leave the psychic imprint of the person who'd died, they identified those who'd done the killing as well. It was a supernatural calling card, bragging rights, and a history lesson all rolled into one.

Except in one way, I thought, and swallowed hard, gripping my conduit more tightly. No agent could heal from the blow of his own conduit. If you were killed by your own paranormal weapon, your aura was negated, your scent obliterated, and your death would be blighted from the mythology. It was as if you'd never existed.

"Over my cold, dead body," I murmured, just as my glyph began to glow. I looked around frantically.

"Pleasure," came the woman's voice from above.

I looked up to see her already falling. There was no time to clear my bow for a direct shot, though the impact of her body landing on mine caused my trigger finger to tense, and an arrow was released into space. I heard a surprised yelp and an angry "Watch it!"

I head-butted the woman, and she cried out, falling back, but by that time Liam had dropped from the rafters and had my weapon hand secured in both of his. He lifted it, using pure brute strength to angle my conduit toward my chest. I held tight, but he had power and leverage on his side, and he angled the arrow toward my core, ripping through my left bicep as he pushed the arrow lower and closer to my heart.

I rammed him with my knee, but felt the jarring sensation of my kneecap meeting with a cup—what the hell was it made of, steel?—and my leg crumpled beneath me upon its return to the ground.

Halfway to the floor, weapon hand still trapped in his, I anticipated his reach. I released my conduit, latched on to his forearms, and pulled him with me as I rolled back, propelling him with my good leg so he went flying over my head. There were more cries as he collided with the woman, and I was up again, stretching for my conduit. Inches away, a black boot connected with my weapon, sending it skittering across the concrete floor. A second boot plowed into my face. Another pair landed on my back. Something popped like corn, and numbness sped along my limbs.

Please, God. Don't let whatever that was have been important.

"Jesus, that was easy!" Liam gasped, stomping on my neck for good measure before kneeling in front of me.

It was, I thought, disgusted with myself as he sat me upright. My back was spasming in pain, but knowing I'd heal, I pushed away the agony and looked up at him through watering eyes. I was surprised—though I shouldn't have been—to find he was dressed as the security guard I'd passed on the way in. Even without my ability to see auras anymore, I should've at least scented him. And I hadn't.

I deserved to die for that alone.

"Speak for yourself," the woman told him, rubbing at her forehead as she came around to stand in front of me. And there was the second surprise. It was the same woman who'd been bidding on me at the bachelorette auction. I closed my eyes and let my head drop back. Okay, I deserved to die twice.

I opened my eyes when I heard the scrape of my conduit being lifted from the floor. The woman was inspecting it carefully, and the sight of it in someone else's hands was unsettling, like she was carrying around a piece of me.

The woman was dwarfed next to Liam, even though she was taller than average, and fit despite being small boned. Though not as blindingly blond, she was serviceably pretty, with eyes that were less greedy than assessing. Of the two, she alarmed me more. I glanced at her hands. It could've been the easy way she was palming my weapon. Damn.

She knelt, grabbed my arm—stronger than she looked, even for a nonmortal—and torqued it until I was angled awkwardly against a glass cylinder. Her other hand was busy pressing an arrow against my temple, and I got the picture, and held very still. She took a surprising, steadying breath . . . then leaned forward and kissed me on the lips.

Soft, I thought, as shock buzzed through me. That's why guys liked us. I understood this as her tongue gently flitted in my mouth, touching mine, bringing with it the taste of the exotic; ground ginger and warm apples and something undeniably female. Had I been born a different type of woman I might have enjoyed that softness, but to me it was an earthworm sort of soft. The softness of slugs. The tenderness of raw meat. She withdrew her tongue before I could bite it off. I cleared my mouth and spit as she fell back.

"What are you doing?" Liam asked, sounding more horrified about two chicks locking lips than most men would be. We both ignored him.

She pulled back, gazing intently into my eyes. "Just an experiment," she murmured.

"Sorry." I rubbed my mouth against the back of my hand, fighting back rage at being manhandled. "But I'm not into girl-on-girl."

She stared at me another moment, assessing; running her tongue over her lips, tasting. Then the speculation cleared from her eyes and she smiled playfully. "What? No final wishes? No regrets?"

"Not in that regard." Though that wasn't exactly true if we were speaking about my love life in broad terms. I allowed one word to float through my brain—*Ben*—then banished it before the accompanying scent leaked out. I'd hate to lead her on.

"Well, I've had enough with experiments," Liam said, glancing suspiciously around the aquarium. "Let's just do this and get out of here."

The woman smiled apologetically at me. "No sense of foreplay."

"Bet he always has to be on top too."

Liam rammed his forearm across my neck, cutting off my words and my breath as he leaned in close. His scent was one of moldering skin, dusty bone, and the bitter tang of bile. I'd gag if he kissed me. "You want to find out?"

"Oh God, Liam. That's so caveman," the smaller Shadow said, pushing him away. "Have it your way."

She stepped back, readying my conduit as Liam lifted me to my feet. Oh God. They were really going to do it. I was going to die, and I realized a part of me hadn't thought I would. The Tulpa hadn't been able to kill me . . . and that had made me careless.

"I wish you'd let me do it," Liam said, holding me in place.

"You lost the toss," she replied, motioning him aside. He grunted and backed away.

"You guys tossed for me?" I grimaced. Now not only was I humiliated, I was insulted.

The female Shadow smiled and raised my conduit so the arrow was centered between my eyes. I could see the other arrows lined in the small chamber, and the shiny onyx metal glinted at me in the short distance. "I got heads."

I closed my eyes, tensed for the impact, and wondered so many things in quick succession, I felt dizzy. What was it going to feel like to die? Would it hurt? Would there be a bright light at the end of a dark tunnel?

Would Olivia be there with outstretched arms, forgiving me for not being able to save her?

Senses primed, I flinched when the spring action on the bow caught, though it almost sounded like it was done in slow motion. The arrow was nocked, and the string sang as the bow reached full draw. I held my breath, not wanting my last emotion on earth to be fear.

Behind me, Liam screamed. His hold on me gave suddenly, and I opened my eyes.

"Fuck!" he hollered through gritted teeth. He was clasping his right shoulder, fingers wrapped around the shaft of an arrow. "You have bad aim, you stupid bitch!"

The woman tilted her head. "Now why would you say something like that to a woman with a weapon?" She shifted and shot out his other shoulder, then looked directly at me and jerked her head, the universal signal for *Get the fuck out of the way*. I did.

She shot out his knees in quick succession, barely pausing to aim. Then the chamber was empty. "This thing have any more ammo?" she asked me. I shook my head. She glanced from me to my abandoned bag, smelling the lie but ignoring it anyway. "Oh well," she said. "I guess we'll have to use something else."

Whistling the theme song to *Peter Gunn* she strolled over to Liam, now writhing on the ground like a landed bass. My heartbeat slowed marginally, but quickened again as she turned back to me. Liam's conduit was in her hand, but she didn't point it at me. Instead she handed it to me.

I glanced down, took it by the knobbed handle, and felt the heft of hinged titanium. It was a weapon meant for an agent larger than me, but the length of a forearm when folded, small enough to carry concealed in a large cargo pocket, which was where Liam had stashed it in his appropriated uniform. I grasped the knob, whipped it out in front of me, and it elongated with a biting snap. It was a bata, or shillelagh—an Irish fighting stick—and I glanced back at Liam with some surprise. I hadn't pegged him as a Mick.

"Why?" Liam and I asked at the same time. She answered me.

"Because I can't kill one of my own. Even if I use his own weapon against him, the kill spot will still identify me as the slayer."

I hadn't known that. I'd only used a conduit against its owner once, but he had been an enemy. Unlike the woman next to me, I'd never even thought about killing one of my own. Well . . . except Warren. But it'd been a fleeting thought, and only that once.

Okay, twice.

"Because it's unnatural," Liam spat, his shock still evident in the scent of rancid lemon rising from his pores. But he was angry too, and who could blame him? He'd probably thought he was needed to protect her in this operation. By some arbitrary whim, however, he was the one who needed protection. He wasn't going to get it from me, and his partner—former—looked away.

I hefted his conduit, holding it about a third of the way from the butt, and his eyes widened when he saw I knew what I was doing. "You can't do this, Regan! We were seen leaving together! The Tulpa will find out!"

"Nobody saw, Liam. I made sure of it." Her voice was flat, but a wisp of regret flickered over her face, slithering across her features like a ripple over a pond, disappearing as soon as she realized I was watching. "Just do it," she said, and turned away.

I stepped forward before that shadowy regret could turn into full-blown repentance.

I didn't make him suffer. It wasn't my style, though I'd kind of overlooked that when I'd tortured and killed the Shadow who'd taken Olivia's life. This wasn't personal, though—if murder can be termed an impersonal thing—just as I knew his wish to kill me was nothing personal. He was doing his job, Shadow versus Light, and I would do my job now. Still, I liked to think there was some difference between us.

"Your full name?" I asked, resting my thumb along the bata's shaft.

He squinted up at me through pain-hazed eyes. "Why?"

"For the records," I said in a voice that was merciless despite my words.

He hesitated, knowing I wasn't talking about the Shadow manuals. A kill spot was normally recorded in written form for both Shadow and Light, but by killing him with his own weapon, I'd erase his death and his life from the Shadows manuals forever. I gave him time, and at length he came to the same conclusion I would've. It was better to be remembered by your enemies than to leave no legacy at all. "Liam Burke, the Piscean Shadow."

I nodded to show I'd heard. Then, before any gratitude could enter his eyes, I lifted the bata over my head, and with one hand brought the knob crashing down between his eyes.

The air exploded with the stench of the Shadow, the decay of his rotted core spilling from the deadly wound, before recoiling invisibly and imploding upon itself. I stood perfectly still as the air wavered around me, letting curls of evanescent energy roll over my body in little shock waves, chills popping up over my limbs and core before enveloping my face, cool and light and tickling, like a thousand bees swarming gently to their hive. My mind began to hum with it, and I swayed, dizzy, suddenly aware of myself as if from the outside; a bright torch of a woman with her eyes closed as she rocked on an unseen wind, one hand clasped tight around a stick dripping with blood as the light slowly drained from her cautionary glyph.

This was the aureole. The dictionary defines it as a circle of light that surrounds the representation of a holy person, like the halos emanating from an angel or the Madonna or a saint. There also happens to be a great restaurant in Vegas by that name. But none of those definitions applied here. Here it meant being infused with the ability to walk through the world for twelve hours, imperceptible by Shadows or Light, unscented and untouchable. Now I could stand inches away from the Tulpa, and he wouldn't know I was there. And even if he did, there wasn't a damned thing he could do about it.

When it was over—or at least when the droning had lessened to a point where I could once again hear my own thoughts—I inhaled deeply, exhaled slowly. There was nothing of Liam in the air. I glanced down at the weapon in my hand. His conduit possessed no scent marking it as belonging to him either. It was just a stick now. I'd erased his olfactory impression wholly.

I threw the stick aside, almost at the woman's feet, and glanced down. The arm Liam had cut with the tip of my conduit had mended, a mere scar now, and my injured knee was solid beneath my weight. My spine was straight and healed. I could be pierced by a thousand weapons now, even my own, and deflect them all like unwanted kisses.

I glanced over to find the remaining Shadow eyeing me nervously. Released from the fetters of fear and certain death, I saw what I hadn't before. She'd orchestrated this whole thing. No wonder my glyph hadn't kicked into gear. I'd been in no danger from her. And, I saw, she was young. Her long ponytail swished to one side as she asked, "You going to kill me?"

Without thinking, I shook my head.

A smile began its upward climb on her face. "I knew it," she said, thumping her fist against her thigh. "I knew you could be turned. The others said you never would, but I knew."

"I'm not turned," I said, holding out my hand. She returned my conduit, and I tucked it back behind me. "I killed him, didn't I?"

"You gave him Last Rites," she pointed out. "You allowed him remembrance in your mythos."

I shrugged. "It's what I'd have wanted."

"And if he'd refused to tell you his name?" she asked, tilting her head the other way.

"He was a Shadow agent," I said, meaning I'd have killed him anyway.

"I'm a Shadow agent," she said. I raised a brow, and she dropped her eyes. "Well, I will be soon. And you didn't kill me."

I really should kill her, I thought, nodding slowly. I *would* kill her. But there were things I needed to know first. "How'd you find me?"

She shrugged nonchalantly, but there was pride in the movement. "I saw you leave the bachelorette auction. I saw you enter the portal after that."

That wasn't what I meant, and she knew it. I'd faked my death, disengaged from family and friends, and I had been careful to steer clear of my old habits and haunts. So even if Regan had been studying the life I'd left behind, she shouldn't have been able to find me. "You see a lot," I murmured, but didn't press. I'd find out what I needed to know . . . one way or another.

"Including your fingers. Like mine." She offered me a small smile, and wiggled her fingers. The marblelike smoothness of the tips reflected unnaturally in the aquarium's soft light. She saw this too, and her smile widened as she tapped on the wall of glass housing sea turtles. Mortal fingers would thrum dully on the great water-filled tank, but hers clinked like glass on glass. She glanced back at me from the corner of her eye with a look that could almost be described as shy. "In fact, if you take a closer look, *Olivia*, I bet you'd find we have a lot in common."

I felt my own hands fist in my lap at the way she sang my not-name—it'd been sly, not shy—and the place where there should have been prints on my fingers pressed hard into my palms. "Did the Tulpa send you?"

"You mean your father?"

"Don't," I said, jerking reflexively. "Don't call him that."

"Well he is, isn't he?" She walked toward me, eyes hungry on my face, fingers trailing over the glass like nails over a chalkboard. I imagined the turtles cringing in their shells. "You have his eyes, you know."

I gritted my teeth, and a flash of light sparked through the room, along with my anger. It was like a light switch had been flicked on, only for the bulb to burn out. I saw my reflection flash in the tank opposite me, and wished I hadn't. My face was drawn, skeletal, with a humorless grin, and those eyes she had mentioned were opaque black marbles sunk deep in their sockets. The scent of singed hair rose up around us, and I knew if I opened my mouth, smoke would pour out.

"Oh look . . . his cheekbones too." She took a step back, but it wasn't fearfully. It was to regard me. She was young, yes, but dauntless. "Anyway, no, he didn't send me. He'd kill me if he knew I was here."

When I thought I had control enough, when my reflection off the glass was mine once again, and red didn't tinge everything around me, I asked, "Why?"

"Because I came to warn you." And even though we were alone, her voice dropped to a whisper. "My name is Regan DuPree. My mother was the Cancerian Shadow until she was killed by your Cancerian Light nine years ago. We've had an interim agent acting as the Shadows' Cancer since then, but I'm to take up the sign on my birthday."

"So you're twenty-four." Would be twenty-five, and undergo metamorphosis into a full-fledged Zodiac member by the end of the summer. I filed that information away as she nodded, and crossed my arms. A young initiate, helping out one of the agents whose troop was responsible for her mother's death nine years earlier. That didn't compute . . . though I suppose it depended on what kind of relationship she'd had with her mother. But she was also defying the Tulpa, who was still very much alive. There had to be a good reason for that.

"So what did you have against Liam? He was a Shadow"—I jerked my head at him, then her—"you're a

Shadow initiate. You're all still on the same side, aren't you?"

"As far as I know there are still only two sides. Black or white. Bright or dark. Light or Shadow." Her voice had gone cold, and I could tell she didn't like being talked down to. Maybe that had caused some friction between her and Mommy Dearest. "Do I look like Light to you?"

She didn't. As blond and pretty as she was, there was a merciless stoicism about her, the same as in a sociopath's mugshot. But all her sociopathic outbursts lay latent in her future.

I shook my head. "I don't get it."

She sighed, like the story bored her but she'd indulge me anyway. "Look, I figured out who you were, and a few weeks later Liam followed me following you. The only way to keep him quiet was to tell him about your Olivia Archer identity. He said he'd let me kill you if he could take the credit." She screwed up her face. "Liam was a sturdy agent, but he had absolutely no imagination whatsoever."

She sounded like she was defending herself, and for a moment I couldn't tell if she was talking to me or herself. Then the coy look returned, but this time it had an edge. "I understand his reasoning, of course. You're slumming with the agents of Light right now, and fair game for anyone who finds you, but you're also the Tulpa's heir apparent, a woman who can walk both sides of the Zodiac with more freedom than the rest of us will ever know. You're the reason all of us act, or lately don't act. You consume the Tulpa's every waking moment, did you know? You guide his every action and thought."

She looked me over again, like she was trying to understand what the big deal was. Good luck. I'd been trying to figure out the same thing for the last six months. "You killed Liam because he didn't want me on the Shadow side?"

"What better way to show you that I do?" she rejoined.

Boy, they trained these Shadows young.

"Well, good for you," I said as she beamed. I shook my

head. "No, I mean really. It's good for you. He'd have killed you right after he did me."

Regan looked startled at that.

"What?" I asked, tilting my head now. "You think Liam trusted you not to tell the Tulpa what he'd done? Or at least tell someone about your part in it?"

She started to say, "He wouldn't . . ." but trailed off, knowing he would. He had trusted her just as much as she did him . . . which was why she'd taken the first shot. She looked away, fumbled for a cigarette, and lit it right beneath a NO SMOKING sign. I said nothing, knowing I'd given her a good shake.

"How long have you known?" I finally asked.

"What?" she asked, blowing out a long stream of smoke. "That Olivia Archer died six months ago, and Joanna Archer, her half-sister and the black sheep of the Archer family dynasty, has been living in her apartment, driving her car, and squatting in her skin ever since?"

She was just saying it to regain her footing, to feel more in control and appear less rattled about the thought of Liam killing her, but I swallowed hard. She really did know it all.

"I found out shortly after you became an agent of Light," she continued, propping one foot behind her, against the pillar. "After Butch killed Olivia, and before you killed Ajax."

My jaw clenched at the mention of Ajax, but I gave a stiff nod. It was what she wanted—a gold star for figuring out what no one else had—and it cost me nothing to give it to her. After all, I'd made sure neither Ajax nor Butch would ever harm me again.

Satisfied, Regan flicked some ash on the floor and smiled. "It wasn't that difficult. I knew the agents of Light were trained to stay away from those they'd been close to in life. So are we. But the way I figured it, nothing about you was normal. You changed all the rules on us. I didn't have to use supersensory powers or even be a full-fledged agent to figure it out. All I did was put myself in your place, then ask myself, 'What would I do?'"

She was once again drawing parallels between her and me in a bald effort to forge some sort of tenuous link, one that was destined to fail . . . though she couldn't know that.

"We thought no one knew," I said, to encourage her further . . . and because it was the truth. There were only three others in my troop who did, and my heart sank as I thought of what this meant. I'd have to change my identity again. I'd have to invent a new life for myself.

I'd have to say good-bye to Olivia . . .

"No one else does," Regan said.

I looked up at her sharply.

"Think about it and you'll know it's true. Half the Shadow Zodiac is like this guy." She flicked her cigarette butt at Liam's corpse. "They want to kill you just because you're of the Light. The other half are looking out for their own interests, so they'd kill you anyway. That's why your fa— the Tulpa, hasn't pushed very hard for you to come to our side. He wants you to make your own decision, and he wants to give the rest of us time to get used to the idea."

"And what about you, Regan? What do you want?"

"You." The truth of her answer sat like acid on my tongue. "It's been prophesied that your arrival on the Shadow side will usher in an era the likes of which have never been seen before. Our mythology tells us the second sign of the Zodiac will soon be fulfilled. I want to sit at your right-hand side when you rule this city. I want to tell my children and grandchildren I was born in the generation of the Kairos."

I looked at her and smiled wryly. When most people heard of the zodiac signs they thought of the sun signs, the positions each of the twelve houses held on the horoscopic wheel. What Regan was talking about, though, was an actual portent signaling one side of the Zodiac's ascendancy over our enemies. The signs were revealed only as the one before them was fulfilled, and the first sign had been the rise of the Kairos. That was me, and my discovery six months ago. Once I'd satisfactorily proven myself to be the Kairos—causing mayhem, destruction, and ultimate victory for my chosen allies, in that order—the second sign was revealed.

A curse upon the Zodiac's battlefield.

Cheery, huh? Regan obviously thought this obscure riddle meant the Shadows would come out the victor, and therefore I, the Kairos, would have to switch sides. I could only assume this belief had been passed down from the Tulpa. Why else would he be content to sit back and let me come to him? Especially when the second sign indicated a battle had to be fought and won?

But there were two problems I could see with Regan's theory. First of all, it just plain wasn't going to happen. I'd shoot myself with my own conduit before becoming a Shadow. And second, even if I did want to switch sides, I doubted it'd be as simple as just waltzing into the Tulpa's house and announcing my intentions. Nothing in this world ever was.

"You guys kill innocent people for fun and profit," I told Regan, not caring if I sounded prudish. Murder just kind of niggled me that way.

"I haven't killed anyone," she said, ignoring Liam's death. "See, that's what I'm trying to tell you. You think we're wired differently than you, but it's not true. We have a job to do, and do it to the best of our abilities. Like you."

I looked at her like she was a toddler with a fork and a light socket. This from the girl who'd just sacrificed a senior troop member to be part of the most wicked era in Shadow history. Yeah, I thought, unable to keep my eyes from rolling, she was just like me. "But there's another reason you're keeping my identity a secret, isn't there, Regan? If you befriend and convince me to become your troop's Kairos, you incur the debt of the Tulpa. And it'll be your name that's passed down for generations to come."

Her jaw clenched, and she returned her hard gaze to mine, as if to say, *So what?*

"So what if I don't play along?" I continued. "What if I just keep hunting Shadows?"

"Then after I become a full-fledged star sign—"

"You come after me yourself," I finished for her. "You kill me—"

"And still go down as one of the most celebrated Shadows in history."

"Perhaps the most."

She inclined her head, and her pretty blond ponytail swung slightly. "Perhaps."

I nodded slowly. "Quite a coup. It would've been easier all around to kill me while you still could."

"If you're into short-term gratification." She shrugged. "As satisfying as it would be to know I was the one who'd killed you, I'd rather wait until the world could know it too."

"All the world's a stage, huh?"

"And I could've killed you at any time in act one," she said, and paused so I could think about it. "You may die yet if you foolishly stick with your current allies. The Tulpa has plans for them, and it doesn't matter to him that you've been filling your star signs. It's a—what did he say?—a *nonissue*." She shot me a sly smile. "He's found a way to wipe you all out in one fell swoop."

"And that's what you were going to warn me about?"

Regan nodded, and though it still felt like there was something missing, it made a sketchy sort of sense. "It'd be more helpful if you told me exactly how he's planning to do this."

She rolled her eyes. "You must not have heard me earlier. I said, Do I look like I'm Light?"

I crossed my arms, tapping my fingers impatiently. "So what can you tell me?"

She lit another cigarette, then angled her head up and to the right, blowing smoke that spiraled prettily in the blue light. "You can't go back to your sanctuary, Archer. We've got something big planned for the agents of Light."

"But you won't tell me what."

She lifted a shoulder. "What if I'm wrong? What if you stay with those goody-goody losers? Though I don't think you will. You have two fates spiraling before you, but only one will lead you to true greatness. Eventually you'll see that."

"Don't count on it."

"You're not even a little curious?" she asked, light brows furrowing. "Don't you want to know where we live, what it's like? How we train?"

"If I knew any of that you'd all be dead."

She crossed her feet at the ankles, took a long drag, and blew smoke in my direction. "What about your father? Don't you want to know what he's really like?"

"Uh-uh. You're not going to tempt me with that shiny red apple."

"Oh, a biblical reference. Thanks," she said, and smiled, serpent-sweet.

"It wasn't a compliment," I said, and I raised my bow, aimed for her heart.

"I know where Joaquin is," she said quickly, hands flying up in front of her as if to ward me off. After a few moments of neither of us moving I lowered my conduit. Regan swallowed hard, then licked her lips, eyes still on my weapon. "I'm not going to tell you everything because you just might raise that bow again, but I'll give you enough to catch him. You have my word."

"You are smarter than Butch and Ajax were combined," I said, unable to keep the admiration out of my voice. Because if there was one thing I'd stop, drop, and roll for, it was information about the man who'd assaulted me when I was just a mortal teen.

"I know," she said, relaxing a fraction. "Just think what a team we'd make if we were on the same side."

I started to lift my hand again.

"Okay, okay. No more trying to convince you. It doesn't matter. You'll come to the same conclusion soon enough. You'll see."

"About Joaquin?" I prompted.

"He'll be at Master Comics tomorrow at four P.M. He likes to be the first to read the Zodiac manuals, and Zane will sometimes put them out a day early if you go right before the shop closes."

"That's it?"

"It's more than you have now," she pointed out. "And it's enough. Once you see him you'll know I'm telling the truth, that I'm really on your side. Then I'll tell you more."

"More about Joaquin?" I asked stiffly. I wanted to know his habits, his haunts, his schedule, down to the food he had for breakfast every morning.

"More about everything."

I sighed. She was right, it was more than I had now. And while it could be a trap, I didn't think so. As Regan said before, she could have killed me at any time in the past six months . . . shit, she could've handed me over to Joaquin if she'd been inclined. For some reason she wanted me alive—though I doubted that reason was as simple as hope that I'd become the Shadow Kairos.

Besides, slaying Joaquin was worth the risk.

I glanced back at Regan, knowing I was walking a moral tightrope here. If Warren was here she'd already be a pretty corpse. But I possessed the aureole. Nothing I did could be tracked, none of my actions would be recorded in the manuals, and this decision was mine alone to make; kill this initiate, or let her live in exchange for intel on my greatest enemy.

Regan was silent, letting me work all this out for myself, and sensing I'd made a decision, she glanced up, looking almost innocent bathed in the aqua light of the tanks, leaning there next to sharks.

"Make one move from that spot, and I'll pin you through your heart and yank it back out of your chest. Got it?"

One corner of her mouth lifted, and she blinked slowly, inclining her head.

"Don't follow me, and swear to stay away from my . . . Olivia's house. No tailing me, no contacting me, no trying to convince me to come to your side. Any of that, and I'll kill you."

"Okay." She waited for me to leave. "But where will you go?" she asked, then held up her hands when I half turned on her. "Not that I'd follow. But I can't help wondering . . . where does a woman belonging equally to the sun and moon escape to when she can't be followed? Where does Joanna Archer go in a world that no longer believes she exists?"

I wanted to tell her there was no escape, and that being a superhero wasn't something you shed like clothing, or that just because I was alone didn't mean I could be and do what I really wanted in this life. But I was afraid that answer would reveal even more of myself than she already knew. Besides, she'd be a full-fledged Shadow agent within months. She'd find out for herself.

For now, though, I left her reclining against the shark tank, thinking she'd won something tonight just because she was still alive.

"Nice shoes," she called as I left the aquarium, and though she didn't move, her bell-like laughter followed me down the Boulevard.

4

I was too antsy to return to the auction, and knew if I made myself sit down in a confined space I'd just spend the night berating myself, replaying the events that'd led me to the aquarium, near death, and Regan. So ignoring the nightly bacchanalia of the Las Vegas Strip, I took a succession of rights on the gridlike streets and climbed into the city's gritty underlife, where I truly felt at home.

When I'd been me, Joanna, I'd canvassed these streets religiously, snapping pictures and documenting the welfare of Sin City's displaced and forgotten. Back then I'd been tough, a student of a fighting system called Krav Maga, but these days I was practically immortal, and I didn't have to worry about my safety while handing out sandwiches to the men and women pooled in the city's darkest crevices, or while helping the runaways I found cowering beneath the possessive arm of someone bigger and meaner and more predatory than themselves. I'd be lying if I said I didn't get off on that. Now I could protect people without worrying about getting hit or stabbed or shot, and how cool was that?

Tonight I had the additional protection of the aureole, which meant I could climb into bed with my greatest enemy if I desired, and he'd never even know I was there. I was like a ghost in both the paranormal and the mortal world, and right now that suited me fine.

About a block away from a run-down strip club I spotted a man watching the building's back door. Actually I scented him first. He was breathing hard and smelled like wild game and curdled desire. So I began to stalk him, the spikes of my heels ticking like a time bomb as I snuck up behind him. He was already jittery with ignoble intentions and fled easily, even as one of his prey slipped out the back door.

By the time we hit Carlisle Street, the sweat rolling down his neck had nothing to do with the evening's warmth, and he was breathing harder still. If there was one thing I hated, it was a human predator. And after a night in which I'd been on both sides of the hunt, his ill intent struck me like a punch to the gut. Finally he swerved down an alley filled with large green metal Dumpsters, weaving his way past stripped tires, broken bottles, and the carcass of something that used to be small and furry and living. Scenting that his desire to stalk had been blunted, I let him escape over a fence topped with cyclone wire, whimpering under his breath as the scent of fresh urine joined the stale urine already staining the alley walls.

I know what you're thinking. Big, bad supernatural chick picking on the poor little human, but I didn't do it just for sport. A decade earlier I'd been attacked, raped, and nearly killed by a man who'd smelled a lot like this one, and I'd be damned if I was going to let some other woman fall prey to the same fate. And yet I didn't know if that drive came from the heroine in me, or if it was—as I really suspected—my father's genes asserting themselves.

My father. The Shadow Archer. The Tulpa.

I sighed and leaned against the rusty metal fence. It was easier to face that here, in the dark, surrounded by refuse. Easier too to admit that I'd lied to Regan about not being curious about my father.

Why wouldn't I be? I'd been born on his birthday—exact

date, exact time—yet another herald of the Kairos legend. But what *he* was—other than the darkest of the Shadows— was another legend entirely. Because the very definition of the word Tulpa was rooted in Tibetan mysticism: it meant materialized thought. And it meant my birth father was a being who'd been created rather than born.

Created, I thought, pushing off from the fence, by some- one with a profound amount of energy, perseverance, pa- tience . . . and, if you asked me, too much time on his hands.

So how do you wrap your brain around the idea that your birth father first existed as a thought form? Well, first you had to get on board with the idea that thought was just an- other form of energy; same as desire, belief, love. But en- ergy was a powerful, volatile thing, and if a person—and not just a supernatural, but a mortal too—could visualize something so completely even their own mind was fooled into believing it existed, they could generate that thing in their life. If they were adept enough, they could even create a separate being. A Tulpa.

But if what I knew about the Tulpa was enough to fill a thimble, his knowledge of me was even smaller. At first he'd only known that I was the new Archer of Light, his opposite on the paranormal Zodiac, and that alone would've been enough to make him wish for my destruction. But as our lineage was matriarchal, he also knew my mother was Zoe Archer, once his greatest love, now his greatest enemy. With her in hiding for the past decade, he was all too willing to take her betrayal out on me.

And then he discovered I was *his* daughter as well, and the tactics had changed. He was now trying to recruit me to the Shadow side, an approach that obviously wasn't sitting well with all his evil, stank-ass minions.

I was jolted from my thoughts by Bananarama's "Cruel Summer" pealing from my handbag. "Not now, Cher," I muttered, peering down at the glowing face of my cell phone. But duty had me answering anyway.

"Where did you go?" she asked without preamble. "One minute you were there, the belle of the ball, and then next you were gone."

"I got . . . sick." I mustered up a cough as I left the alley. "Decided to head home early."

"Oh, honey! Do you want me to come over and play nurse? I have a great product to loosen up congestion. It contains pig placenta and no preservatives!"

"No!" I swallowed, softened my tone, and said, "No, Cher. But thanks. I'm just going to work on the computer for a bit, and then go to bed."

Which was as big a lie as any I'd ever told. While Olivia had been a closet geek beneath all the peroxide, gloss, and L'eau d'Issey, the computer guru bit was something I'd had to drop as soon as I took over her identity. I could impersonate a bubble-brained socialite, but a self-taught computer genius was a bit beyond my second-rate dramatic skills. Luckily, most people who knew her in real life, as opposed to cyberspace, didn't know about her surprising, and sometimes illicit, little hobby.

Another pause, this time with Cher mentally ciphering what I meant by this. "Starting up your business again?" she asked carefully.

As if, I thought, rolling my eyes. I'd never even gotten Olivia's blasted machine to work, even after inputting every word I thought she might use as a password—Archer, her birth date, Prada. Nothing worked.

"No, I . . . I forgot my stupid password."

"Oh. Want your backup disks?"

Backup disks? I blinked as I slipped past a stray dog, unnoticed. "Uh . . . you still have them?"

"Of course. Locked in the floor safe just like you told me. Momma tried to move them into the safety deposit box, but I told her you needed easy access for times like this, you know?"

I did a quick mental calculation. Dusk set at seven-fifty tomorrow. Joaquin would allegedly be at the shop four hours before that. So I could feasibly squeeze in a visit to Cher, grab the disks, kill my arch nemesis, and still manage to cross over to my troop's headquarters no later than mid-dusk. And that brought the first true smile to my face since I'd found out about the bachelorette auction.

So Cher agreed to meet the next afternoon and made me promise to rub vapors over my chest for my cold, but as we hung up I'd never felt better. There were secrets stored on those disks that had to do with me. My past.

Maybe even my mother.

Because I had questions for Zoe Archer, and they weren't just of the where-ya-been? variety either. She was the only agent who'd ever gotten close enough to the Tulpa to try and ferret out a weakness to be used against him, to sleep with him. To make him vulnerable.

And that was what I was *most* curious about. How to find him, hurt him, kill him. I'd vowed on our first and only meeting that I'd do all those things. Ruin anything with the Archer insignia on it—which included all of Xavier Archer's businesses—and commit my every waking moment to destroying him and the Shadow organization. He'd suffer for all the cruel deeds he brokered in this valley, and more importantly, for authorizing the attack that had devastated me a decade earlier.

So I left the abandoned streets behind me, heading home as I thought of death and destruction. Wanting to cause it all myself.

Sometimes I was such a daddy's girl.

5

The greatest benefit in taking over Olivia's identity was not having to learn a whole new set of mores,
thoughts, and values. We'd essentially held the same worldview and basic ideals, and though our approaches to life dif-
fered in many ways, our bond had been a tight one. I'd sworn
to her that I'd never leave her, that I'd guard her from anyone
who wanted to harm her in either word or deed or thought,
and I had.

Except once.

Thus, the downside in taking over Olivia's identity was
having to look at her beautiful face in the mirror every day
since I broke that promise, and meet the blaming eyes
framed by all that blond, burnished glory.

It was also ironic that her appearance—so delicate, so con-
spicuous, so laughably clichéd—was what protected me now.
The dichotomy between how I looked and how I felt was one
of the greatest jokes I'd ever seen played out in life, and the
worst of it wasn't even that I'd been turned into every hetero
male's wet dream . . . though it had once seemed that way.
No, the worst part was knowing Olivia had kept the promise I
had broken—she was now protecting me—and that was

something I was going to have to live with for the rest of my life.

So the next day I turned into a gated community, pulled in front of a sprawling single-story home, and gamely headed up the long, sloped drive to face the second hardest part about being Olivia.

Her friends.

If people were food, Cher and her mother would be dessert. Their thought processes were about as dense as powdered sugar, their lives as airy as angel food cake. Fortunately, beneath all the peroxide, M·A·C makeup, and designer clothes were two hearts that had truly loved Olivia. And, apart from a mystifying penchant for Brazilian waxing, they weren't too bad themselves. I was grateful Olivia had known such true friendship while alive and did my best to keep both Cher and Suzanne from ever suspecting the truth.

"Hello!" I called out as I opened the door to Suzanne's ranch-style house, having learned long ago not to knock. I passed directly through the tiled foyer to land in a combined living and dining area that stretched across the middle of the house. The place had surprised me at first. I'd expected something flashier from Suzanne, whose "More is more" motto had practically been branded onto my eardrums within the first hour of meeting her, but the beige rugs and cream couches were offset only by textures; silk, chenille, cotton—and patterns; weaves, brocades, and cross-stitchings. An entire wall of black and white photographs, matted in beige, served as the home's focal point. There was a montage clearly detailing Suzanne's family and friends—her early life, her late husband, and countless depictions of Cher and, of course, Olivia. I turned from the wall and called out again.

"In here, Livvy-girl," came the answer from the back hall. Dropping my bag on the couch, I followed the murmur of dulcet tones and feminine giggles until I rounded the corner into Suzanne's bedroom.

"Oh, for fuck's sake," I said, quickly turning away. The

two women—the two *naked* women—laughed behind me, and after a moment, I felt a hand on my shoulder. I shook it away and focused on the heap of discarded clothing scattered across the king-sized bed. Did I mention it was like a sorority house in here? "I'm afraid to ask," I started.

"You won't have to if you'd just turn around," Cher said.

"Uh-uh," I said, shaking my head. "There are some piercings there I did not need to know about."

"Come, dear. Let's put on some clothing so we can preserve Olivia's modesty, bless her heart."

I'd have been grateful to Suzanne if it weren't for the distinct teasing note in her voice.

"Momma," Cher protested, "we can't do the pencil test with clothes on, you know that."

"Undergarments won't hurt anything. Besides, I have to get ready for my date."

Cher sighed dramatically, but the rustling behind me, the sound of clasps clicking home, and a bit more stifled laughter told me she was doing as told.

"What am I doing here?" I muttered under my breath.

"What was that, honey?" Suzanne asked, her voice muffled.

"I said, what should I do with my hair?" and closed my eyes, shaking my head slightly. Of course, I knew the answer to my original question. Being Olivia meant being with her friends as much as possible. But my mind was still reeling from the previous evening's events, and in the morning light, away from the eerie glow of the aquarium and the heady odors of fear and adrenaline and hate, it seemed foolish to have let Regan live. She was still a Shadow, even if only an initiate.

Who had spared my life. Who had helped me kill one of her own. Who had gifted me with the greatest shield in our universe, the aureole, and put her own life into my hands.

Okay, so maybe in light of all that it wasn't so foolish . . . but should I really be wasting my time finding out if this pencil test had anything to do with higher education?

"Pencil test?" I asked, managing to sound cheery as I turned around. In answer, Cher picked up a trusty number two and used it in a way my elementary teachers had never envisioned.

"The pencil test," said Cher, standing as straight as possible and tucking it between her left breast and the skin of her rib cage. The pencil fell to the floor. She smiled victoriously. I smiled back thinly. Another small victory in the battle against gravity. "Want to try?"

"Uh . . . no, thanks."

They both looked at me, blinking.

"I mean, I did it last night. At home."

Cher frowned. "I thought you were going to work on the computer?"

"Oh, are you embezzling again, dear?" Suzanne looked surprised. "Good for you."

I ignored the moral ambiguity of that statement and answered Cher. "I did it on my breaks," I told her. "You know what they say about all work and no play . . ."

"Makes for a saggy ass," Cher said, nodding, and turned to her mother. "Livvy needs the disks she stored in our vault. She's havin' trouble with her computer."

"My friend Ian is a computer programmer," Suzanne put in. "Maybe you can ask him for help."

"Momma!" Cher snapped. "Stop pushing your loser running pals on Olivia."

"I'm not pushin'," Suzanne tossed her head, piqued. "I'm just sayin' if there's a computer anywhere in sight Ian's the best man for the job."

"And Olivia's the best woman," Cher said, in a show of sisterly pride. *Bless her heart.* "Now here, Momma. You try."

Suzanne daintily plucked the proffered pencil from her stepdaughter's hands and turned her perfect, and thankfully covered, backside to the mirror. She tucked it between a non-existent crease between cheek and thigh, and took a well-deserved bow when the pencil fell to the floor. Even I clapped. Suzanne's masochistic love for running had certainly paid off. And the unforeseen core of discipline and inner strength in a woman I'd took to be nothing more than an older version of Cher—all silicone and pinks and whites—had surprised me. Enough so that I'd asked her about it once. Her explanation was simple. "Cellulite waits for no ass."

Cher said it was her motto, or something.

My thoughts were interrupted by dual gasps of horror. Cher, buttocks clenched fiercely, was whirling from one side to the other, straining to see into the mirror behind her. The pencil, firmly planted beneath one butt cheek, tilted this way and that, like a chopstick that had missed its mark. Uh-oh, I thought, swallowing hard. Cher gasped again.

"I've failed!" she yelled, and bolted from the mirror. There wasn't far to run as I was still blocking the door, and Suzanne was standing—hand covering her mouth—at the entrance to the bathroom. Cher ended up running circles around herself. "Oh my God! I've failed the pencil test!"

Halfway into her flight around the room, the pencil fell.

"No, look!" I said. "It dropped."

Cher screeched.

"Keep doing that, though," Suzanne said, as Cher completed another lap around the room. "It'll help."

"But I don't think the yelling does anything," I said.

Cher shrieked louder.

It was touch and go for the next ten minutes, but we finally calmed her down enough to get her dressed, and were hiding the horrors gravity had wrought on her body beneath a size two Diane Von Fursten-someone wrap dress when the doorbell rang.

"Oh, honey," Suzanne turned to me, eyes wide and pleading. "Would you mind getting that while I tidy myself? Cher's in no state to be entertaining."

We both glanced over at Cher. She was seated at the vanity, applying lip gloss, small mewling noises coming from her throat.

"Sure. Who is it, that guy from the sexual sign language seminar?"

Suzanne actually had to think a moment. "Oh no. This one's from Austin. Spent time as a guitarist on Sixth Street, and hitchhiked here to become a lounge star. His name's Troy Stone. Can you remember that?"

"Troy," I repeated, like I was participating in a spelling bee. "Like Brad Pitt's city. Got it."

Troy was actually more like Brad Pitt's twin. Same hair, same eyes, same lips . . . and I was hoping—for Brad's sake—the resemblance stopped there, because he was leaning against the entry wall like he'd been posed there by a fashion photographer. Slick in blue jeans made to look worn before they'd left the manufacturer, he had a face lined in the way ad agencies had decided made men look mature and worldly, and made women just look old. His profile was rugged and proud, sloping down to a pointed chin that just begged to be punched. With a lift of that chin, he turned a startling blue gaze on me.

"You must be Cher," he said, and before I could correct him, he reached forward and brought my hand to his lips. His mouth lingered over my knuckles as his eyes went dark and seductive. "Like mother, like daughter, I see." And his tongue actually flashed out for a quick taste.

My knuckles fisted instinctively. Suzanne might have a great ass, but she apparently had absolutely no asshole radar. Forcing a smile, I relaxed my hand and returned him Olivia's most saccharine smile. "I'm Olivia, actually. Cher's bestest-ever friend. And you must be Jeffrey. Suzanne's told us all about you," I said, dragging a now faltering Troy into the foyer. I shut the door and turned to him, pressing closer. "You simply must show me that thing you can do with your tongue. She's been talking about it for weeks."

He was saved from having to answer—and I was saved from the assault of his cologne—by Suzanne's arrival.

"Troy, darling!" she said, sweeping in like a modern-day Scarlett descending the staircase at Tara. She was dressed in bejeweled sandals, white jeans, and a bright coral top showcasing the rest of her gravity-defying assets. Her light blond curls had been swiftly pulled back in a style only confident older women could pull off, and not for the first time I wondered how old she really was. She looked anywhere from twenty-eight to forty-two, the high side fathomable only because Cher had told me she was "ages" older than us.

Eyes glazed, Troy began spewing sexual pheromones so potent I got dizzy. Suzanne's eight-mile-a-day runs must have paid off in ways never fathomed by a superhero. Or maybe it had something to do with that piercing I'd seen earlier.

"I'm going to go check on Cher. You kids have fun," I said, breathing shallowly, wanting to get out of there before Troy started humping her leg. Yet Cher appeared just then, looking like a newborn Bambi, legs not quite steady, but clearly determined.

"Are you okay, baby?" Suzanne asked, rushing to her side.

"You should sit down, Cher," I said, doing the same. "Let me get you a cool washcloth or something."

Troy shook himself from his lust-saturated state. "What's wrong with her?"

"She was hit by a piece of lead," I said. And who knew a number two could pack such a wallop?

"Don't worry, honey," Suzanne said, drawing Cher across the room to a chenille-covered armchair. "You'll be fine. Nothing a glass of wine won't fix."

"I'll get it," I said quickly.

As I headed to the bar tucked just around the corner, Troy started in on a story about how he'd once rescued a girlfriend from a homicidal rodeo clown who'd used the pro circuit to stalk women in five different states. I scooped some ice into a steel shaker and rolled my eyes. Taking care of innocents was rewarding, but sometimes it was also a pain in the ass. After all, innocent really meant human, and humans were flawed, capricious creatures, and sometimes downright mean. Taking down a rapist or molester was easily the best part of my job.

The worst? Standing by, like now, and watching the petty slights, the sleazy intentions, and the domestic dramas . . . things we had no obligation, and indeed no right to interfere with. People had to make their own mistakes, but that didn't make it any easier to stand aside and watch bad choices and shortsightedness play havoc with lives.

"Here you go," I said, returning to Cher with the cocktail. I offered an encouraging smile at her puzzled look. "Vodka instead of wine," I told her, before lowering my voice to a whisper. "Fewer calories."

Cher teared up before accepting the drink with shaking hands. "I love you."

A quarter of an hour later Cher was revived enough to kneel with me in her mother's hangar-sized closet, where we shoved aside enough evening gowns to supply Suzanne with a new car, if she wanted one. These disks, I thought, leaning back on my heels, changed everything. At the least they meant I no longer had to pick Cher's brain about things I should know, risk raising her suspicions, or hope she'd slip up and deliver salient bits of information in an unguarded moment.

A moment like now.

"So if you're not starting up your business again," she said, exposing the floor safe, concealed stylishly beneath an Hermès scarf, "I guess that means you're still trying to find Ashlyn?"

Ashlyn.

My exuberance over the backups died. *Dammit, Olivia.*

"Olivia?"

I swallowed hard, not entirely trusting my voice. "It's just . . . Joanna didn't want me to do that, you know?"

She scoffed. "You used to say that was all the more reason to do a thing."

"Well, that was before she died trying to save my life," I retorted, and had to bite my tongue before I said more. I had died in a way, I thought. Died in trying. Died in failing.

Cher took a moment before answering. "And that means you can't continue looking for her daughter?"

It was an effort, but I kept my voice even. "Joanna didn't have a daughter."

"Your niece?"

"I don't have—"

"A child that's a part of your family no matter the circumstances under which she entered this world? No matter who the father—"

"Stop!" I yelled, then winced, squeezing my eyes shut. "Please . . . stop."

I remained unmoving until my breathing had evened out again, but it was too late. My mind had opened. The scented memories of blood and new life slipped out like water leaking from fissures in a dam, slight cracks I'd been patching up for a decade, hoping they wouldn't expand and give. I was afraid if they did I'd be swallowed up, ferried away on them like a piece of driftwood. I shook my head, told myself they were unimportant, and cemented them away tight.

Cher fumbled with the combination in the elongated silence, and I reached out to steady the martini tipping in her left hand. She shot me a thankful smile—and an apologetic one—then reached inside and pulled out three disks. "Here you are."

"Thanks," I said quietly, accepting them.

Cher closed up the safe and sat back on her heels. Biting her lip, she tried to put on a happy face. She and Olivia argued so rarely that the smell of her discomfort overpowered even the leather from all the shoes lining the closet. "We still on for a mint mudbath tomorrow?"

Shit. I'd forgotten about that. "Uh, Cher? I'm going to have to pass."

"Why? Are you ill? Injured? Is it fatal?" She was joking, but I could tell it was strained. I laughed brightly like I knew Olivia would, and watched some of the strain ease away.

"No, but something came up," I said, which was true. "I have to go out of town for a bit," I added, which wasn't.

But it wasn't like I could say, *Hey, I have the chance to kill the man who's haunted my dreams for a decade. After that I need to hang at my superhero hideout for a bit. Try to find out what plans my evil birth father has concocted for our demise.*

"You've been going out of town a lot lately," she said, and I bit my lip at her suspicious tone. Cher would never suspect the truth—at least not without finger puppets to explain it—but she wasn't supposed to be suspicious of Olivia. And any deviation from normal could tip off the Shadows to my real identity.

Those who didn't already know it, I thought wryly.

I decided to play the sympathy card . . . though I'd done it so much recently it was a bit worn at the edges. "Sometimes I just have to get away, Cher. You know . . . from the apartment, from this town." A vision of Olivia plummeting to her death came to me unbidden, and I swallowed hard. "From this life."

"Your life isn't so bad," Cher said, softly encouraging. "I mean, you could have dark roots."

I smiled as a sigh shuddered out of her. "Or wear a shoe size so large Manolo doesn't make it," I said, having studied up for an occasion such as this.

"Or have been born in an age where men abducted women and sold them into slavery."

"And pulled them around by their hair," I said, getting into it.

"What?" Cher paused. "You don't like that?"

I laughed. I hadn't always liked Cher; we'd had a fierce, if unspoken, competition for Olivia's attention while she'd still been alive, but she'd grown on me these past months. Like a fungus. But the good kind.

Now that things were easy between us again, she passed me her martini, watching as I took a small sip. "You'll miss the Valhalla party. Some are saying it'll be the party of the year."

I shrugged. It couldn't be helped. I'd be tucked safely into the sanctuary by then, and who knew what Warren had planned for me there.

"We're on the VIP list, of course," she said, taking back her drink. "So's Troy."

I grimaced, unable to help myself. "What does she see in him, anyway?"

"Who, Momma?" Cher rolled her eyes expressively. "The same thing she sees in all of them. An unwillingness to commit, a predilection for lies, and a supertoned bod."

"So why bother?"

"Because she likes to go out. She likes dinner and dancing." She rose to move the gowns back into place, straining with the effort, before plopping back down next to me. "And because ever since Daddy died she's been afraid to allow herself to love again."

I knew Suzanne and Cher's father had been a surprise love match, a May-December romance that'd bloomed quickly and been the object of great speculation within their social circle, especially after his death only nine months later. What I didn't know was how they'd met or how Suzanne had dealt with his death, and I'd never found a way to ask her or Cher about it that wouldn't incur suspicion. I couldn't find one now either, so let the moment pass.

"I hate it when you're gone," Cher said, pouting a little.

"I really need to get away for a while," I said, itching to do so now. I had what I came for.

"I do too!" she said earnestly. "But wherever I go this ass will follow!"

"It's not that bad." At her horrified look I amended my statement. "I mean, it's lovely."

"I'm just worried about you. I don't want to see you turning into your sister, you know?" And before I could work up affront at that, she continued, motioning with her drink. "She was so alone. Like one of those heroines you read about in a book, sad—without the slightest sense of fashion or personal style—but a heroine no less. I guess she was kind of like Momma in that way."

I drew back. I'd been like Suzanne in *what* way?

Cher, noting my surprise, nodded. "It's true. Momma may seem like she's living life fully, but look at the way she keeps men at arm's length. And the way she runs." She shook her head, eyes softening sadly. "You know that she's running *from*, not *to*, don't you?"

"From what?" I asked, genuinely curious.

Cher shrugged. "She's never said, and I can't ask, but there's a need boiling deep inside her. And that's what Joanna was like, except instead of running she used her fists to keep her memories from catching up."

I hugged my knees, pulling them in tight to squeeze out the hollowness that'd suddenly popped up in my chest, and looked around at beaded gowns and pressed suits and a wall of shoes for feet that never stopped moving. It was true. I had been that way; angry and bitter and trying to turn back time with my fists. "Cher. Can I ask you a hypothetical question?"

"Okay, but you know I'm no good at math."

"Let's say Joanna was still alive," I said, toying with my nails, not looking at her. "Do you think we all could've stopped fighting and just been friends?"

Cher placed her palm over my restless hands. I stilled and looked up to find her as sober as I'd ever seen her. "That's not a sensible question, Livvy-girl."

"Why?"

"Because that's like askin', *What if Momma stopped running?*" Her brows furrowed and she shook her head. "Women like that? Broken women? With pasts that wake them up screaming at night? They don't ever stop. They can't."

"Because the day they stop," I said, feeling stripped bare, even kneeling in the corner of a closet full of designer clothes, "is the day they die."

And for a moment the scent of tuberose and freesia seemed to drift through the air as a Shadow's laughter growled through the closet. A scream, Olivia's, sounded in the night. And a *thud,* a body crashing through an arching wall of glass, resonated in my mind. I closed my eyes and knew she was right. I would never stop. Not until Joaquin, and all the Shadow agents—the Tulpa included—were six feet under, toes pointed up.

When I opened my eyes again, Cher was holding her martini out to me. I took it because last night I'd killed a man, and today I'd been reminded of a daughter I didn't want to have. A toast to senseless questions and unlived lives wasn't entirely out of order. So my sister's best friend and I finished off that cocktail in silence, sitting on the floor of a broken woman's closet.

6

Ever since Steve Wynn single-handedly revital-
ized the casino industry with the 1989 opening of the
Mirage Hotel, Las Vegas had experienced a growth like that
of a pygmy into a sumo wrestler. The stretch marks could be
seen in beltways and housing tracts spreading throughout
the valley, and navigating these thoroughfares—though they
were always in construction so could never truly be called
thorough—really did resemble a combat sport. One made
that much more challenging when you added in 110-degree
heat.

This afternoon Mother Nature was taking a test drive at
summer. The wide sky screamed with sun, and the heat ra-
diating against my Porsche—a recent gift from Xavier—was
felt even from within the confines of its air-conditioned
cabin. It wasn't the full frontal beating the valley would take
under a midsummer sun, but soon. Very soon.

I'd dressed casually for the day, throwing on summer-
weight jeans that cost just under two hundred bucks but
looked like they'd spent some serious floor time down at the
Salvation Army. I added slide-on sneakers and a fitted top,

switched out the bag I'd been carrying the night before, and pulled my blond mane back into a high ponytail that shone and swished when I walked. I left my face bare but for sunscreen, but the effect was still dizzying. I swear, sometimes I felt like I was dressing a life-sized Barbie.

I pulled into a nondescript strip mall—the kind that could've sprouted up in any town, anywhere—swerving sharply in front of the blare of oncoming traffic, and narrowly missing a teenage skateboarder who'd decided to use the shopping center's paint-chipped handrails as a training facility for the X Games. *Miscreant*, I wanted to yell, but didn't because I was afraid I'd sound like my mother. Or, rather, an approximation of somebody else's mother. Mine was a miscreant too.

I turned off the car and stared up at the building that housed Master Comics. It looked innocuous enough from the outside, just another comic book and card shop for angsty teens and shifty-eyed adults. But this was where the manuals depicting the actions of both Shadow and Light were sold, and, I'd discovered, where they were created. The store's owner, Zane Silver, wrote both lines of comics, recording the two sides' quest for dominance over city politics, community mores, and personal power, though technically we—the valley's heroes and villains—were the creators. We fought our very real battles between good and evil, and the next week our derring-dos ended up on the pages of graphic novels to thrill the voracious reading appetites of gullible preteens everywhere.

There was no way to tell if Joaquin was already here or not. Mine was the only car in the lot, and other than the aforementioned teen—currently riding a storefront railing the way a pro surfer would ride a wave—there was nobody else in sight. But I was early. I stepped from the car, thinking I'd settle in and have a deadly little surprise waiting for Joaquin when he swung in the door.

Entering the shop, I let the glass door jangle shut behind

me, the air-conditioning muting the sounds of traffic, as well as the gratifying yelp of the skateboarder as he took a hard tumble. It took a moment for my eyes to adjust from the outdoor glare to the dim interior, but when they did I saw a handful of teens scattered about the shop, all looking my way.

There was an Asian girl I didn't recognize looking up at me with eyes as wide as the heroine on the manga she was holding, a threesome of boys who couldn't have been more than ten poring over some sensational find in the store's far corner, and the rest were the usual suspects. As one of them trotted toward me, I shot Zane—the only adult—a half wave. He grunted in response and turned back to the paperwork splayed next to the register.

"Hey, Archer." Carl Kenyon was a shrewd-eyed boy verging on gangly, and just strange enough that every time I saw him I felt like saying, *Take me to your leader*. He was also the penciler for the Zodiac series, a seriously talented kid with a dubious sense of humor and an astounding knowledge of the complex ethos behind every comic series ever made. For some reason he'd taken a liking to me. I looked him over, from his black Converse high-tops, striped pants, and white T-shirt declaring I'M A LOVER. NOT A FIGHTER. His hair was plastered in yesteryear's faux-hawk, a fashion miscue I forgave since he'd given it his own twist, forming two rows of spikes along his skull instead of one.

At least, I noted, he'd grown out of his fondness for excessive body hair. And, as wary as I was about Joaquin's imminent arrival, I was happy to see Carl. I guess he'd grown on me too.

"Hey, Carl. What's up with the 'do?"

"Thought I'd try something new," he said, touching the spike tips gently with inkstained fingers. "What do you think?"

"I think you look like the spawn of Satan."

"Yeah, and you still look like my brother's favorite blow-up doll."

"Speaking of, what's the deal with the size of my breasts

in last month's manual?" He'd drawn me so top heavy a stiff wind could have knocked me off balance.

"Creative license," he said with a shrug.

"A little too creative."

"Well, I have to do something. Ever since your side and the Shadows called this unspoken truce—which is totally lame, by the way—it's been hell to keep reader interest."

"Can't you just make something up?"

"Like what?"

I thought for a moment. "Give the Shadow Aries a strange itching sensation down there. While you're at it, make their Gemini accidentally chop off her own hair with her machete. Mangle it too. She'll really have to do it for continuity's sake."

Carl grinned and held up a hand to high-five me, but when I responded in kind, he drew back, frowning. "What's that?"

I glanced down and spotted the scar on my left bicep. Damn. It was the wound Liam had given me before I'd killed him. I covered it up without answering.

"How'd you get a new scar?" Carl persisted.

"It's not a scar," I said.

Carl turned to Zane. "Is it a scar, Zane?"

Zane didn't look up. "Yep."

I glared at him.

Carl looked back at me. "How'd you get it?"

I clenched my teeth. "I cut myself on one of my arrows."

Carl wrinkled his nose in disbelief and glanced back over his shoulder. "How'd she get it, Zane?"

Zane, bulbous body still hunched over his work, did look up this time, and he met my eyes with malicious glee. "She crossed over into an alternate reality, chased a Shadow agent throughout Valhalla, where she was ambushed, cut, and somehow still managed to survive."

The other kids, who'd been inching forward during this telling, started throwing questions at me all at once. They were like prepubescent rioters. I felt the urge to retreat as their stinky little bodies pressed up against mine.

"You gonna give them milk and cookies before you put them down for their naps too?" I asked Zane. Actually I snarled. Didn't faze him, though. He just shrugged, reached for his work so I could see the sweat stains circling his pits, and kept writing. Which left me to deal with the Lost Boys.

I felt a tentative tug on my arms, and looked down to find the small Asian girl looking up at me, concern brimming in her large eyes. "You were injured?"

One of the older boys shoved her out of the way. "She was almost killed, dude. Nothing can scar an agent except a conduit."

"That's cool," his bald twin added.

"I wish I could cross into other realities," one of the ten-year-olds threw in, and I rolled my eyes.

"I can't believe you weren't going to tell me," Carl said over them all, his voice filled with hurt as he shook his head. He lifted up my sleeve to get a better look. "How'm I supposed to draw you accurately if you don't tell me these things?"

I slapped his hand away. "You'd find out from Zane's storyline soon enough, anyway."

They all looked to Zane. He sighed and put down his pen, leaning back so his substantial weight was propped against a glass case. I feared for the case. "Actually, he wouldn't have. Everything that happened from the time you entered the aquarium to the time you woke up this morning . . . never happened."

"I don't understand," the girl said softly, tilting her head.

"I don't either," the twins said together, then grinned at each other.

Carl scratched his head.

"I do."

We all turned to the back of the shop, where a lone figure rose from his chair, thin and pale and wavering like a snake under a charmer's spell. Sebastian, I thought, my lips curling. The little freak. Actually the big freak now. He'd grown a whole foot in the months I'd known him, and his bones seemed to rattle in his skin as he stepped toward us, eyes never leaving mine. For some reason the kid had never liked me.

"What do you know, Sebastian?" Zane asked him. I glared at him, but he only shrugged back, a half smile lifting one fat cheek.

"She," Sebastian yelled, pointing a finger at me, "is hiding something! She doesn't want anyone to know how she got the scar because she doesn't want anyone to know what she was doing in the aquarium last night!"

"But you're an agent of Light," said one of the bald twins. "What could you have to hide?"

"Did you fulfill the second sign of the Zodiac? Will all the Shadows die on a cursed battlefield?"

Obviously a reader of the manuals of Light.

"Or did you finally jump to the Shadow side?"

"Dude! I told you she would! You owe me five trading cards!"

"Or did you find your mother?" the girl asked, peering up at me sweetly.

"Did you get it on with one of the underwater divers in the kelp forest?" Carl asked, nudging me in the side.

I looked at him.

He grinned. "A boy can dream."

"No!" Sebastian yelled, slamming his fist down so hard on a glass case I thought I heard the top crack. "You idiots! There's only one way to wipe out an entire block of time so it can't be recorded in the manuals. Only one way you can disappear for twelve straight hours and nobody know where you are, who you are, or what you're—"

He didn't get to finish. The others had all turned back to me, and Carl's fist shot into the air. "The aureole!" they all yelled together.

The twins started hopping around, I think they were trying to dance, and the girl began clapping madly, her face a mixture of delight and hero worship as she gazed up at me.

"Man, the aureole," Carl said, shaking his head. "Good

job, Archer. Two times in six months. That must be some sort of record, huh, Zane?"

"The aureole," Zane repeated in a whisper, nodding to himself as he turned back to his work. I should have known I couldn't keep it a secret.

"How long do I have?" I said, crossing to stand in front of him, a half-dozen kids trailing me like I was the Pied Piper.

"Before this issue comes out?" he asked, pointing to the pages in front of him. He was writing it already? "Two weeks Wednesday. I might be able to delay it until Thursday, but that's all."

Two weeks before the entire Zodiac found out I'd killed Liam with his own weapon . . . when I wasn't supposed to be chasing the Shadows at all. And once the Shadows found out—which might be any minute if these little brats kept yelling their heads off—it would totally jack up the cosmic balance. Warren would not be pleased.

"So who'd you kill, Archer? Was it Zell? Or Dawn? Or Sloane, the Shadow Goat?"

"Oh yeah. That Capricorn bitch totally needs to die." The boys high-fived one another.

I agreed, but shot them a hard look anyway. "Guess you just have to wait and read the book."

A chorus of protests met this announcement, but I ignored them and headed to the back of the shop. There was an alcove next to the manuals that was the perfect spot to lie in wait for Joaquin.

Sebastian had returned to his usual chair, and was using a newspaper to shield his face from my view. I flicked it as I passed, which made him jump and fling a few F-bombs my way, but I just smirked and kept on walking.

The shop was elongated, each wall filled with floor-to-ceiling comics, with an entire section devoted solely to manga. The collectibles, action figures, and model kits were grouped together, and there was an extensive DVD collection filling the back wall. I stopped in front of a wooden cabinet with glass doors and studied the two carousels of comic books locked inside. The only other books that were locked up this tight were the collectibles, and Zane kept those near the register, right under his nose. Carl pulled up behind me with the key he'd fetched from behind the counter.

"You want the newest manuals?" he asked, unlocking the case. "I don't think you've seen *Shadow Sanctuary: Portal to Hell* or *The Might of Light: Warren's Return*."

"Sure," I said, "I'll take those, and . . ." I hesitated, sneaking a peek at my watch. I was still five minutes early. Joaquin would be here, or he wouldn't, but I could kill two birds with one stone . . . if I was quick about it.

"And?" he prompted.

"And I'm looking for some back issues too."

He chuckled darkly. "The classics are going to cost ya."

"Not that far back. I just want to find out about the last Cancerian star sign."

"Shadow or Light?" I had the feeling Carl got off on asking me that question. I hated being reminded of my Shadow side—as if I could ever forget—but as the only agent who was both, I was also the only one who could touch both series of manuals. Try to pick up a manual that didn't belong to your troop, and you'd get a shock that made sticking a finger in a light socket . . . well, child's play.

Anyway, the inability to read our enemies' actions kept the playing ground relatively even, Warren's beloved "cosmic balance." The manuals also had a kind of fail-safe mode, a way of depicting an agent's life and actions while excluding details that might compromise that balance.

For example, in my case they revealed what the interior of my home looked like, but not where it was, or that it was located in a high-rise. They also referred to me as either Joanna, or The Archer, but they didn't use my full name, and never, ever my hidden one. This protected the mortals, the children who read these books, as much as it protected us. None could be tricked by an agent into revealing the secrets of the opposing Zodiac signs because they simply lacked all the pieces of the puzzle. Besides, by the time the manuals were released, the events each contained were already ancient history.

But now I could read the Shadow manuals, report my findings to the other agents of Light, and we could anticipate their actions from the information gleaned there. Cosmic balance or not, Warren had no problem listening as I recounted *The Shadow Chronicles: Under the Cover of Darkness*. I suspected this was another reason the Shadows had been lying low as of late.

"Shadow," I replied in a low voice. There was nothing to be ashamed of, but I didn't exactly relish the world knowing my business, and I was all too aware of Sebastian lurking just behind me.

"Ohhh, they're sucking you in, aren't they?" Carl said loudly. "You're inching over to the dark side."

I gritted my teeth and silently counted to three. "I just want to know a bit about this agent's history. How she lived, how she died." I couldn't find out about Regan directly; her first and second life cycles—from birth to puberty, then from puberty to age twenty-five—weren't depicted in the manuals. The third life cycle was the only one recorded, so her history, strengths, and identity would remain veiled until she metamorphosized. Studying the actions of Regan's mother, however, might give me an idea of what I'd someday be up against . . . and possibly her true motivations in seeking me out.

A voice popped up at my other side. "I can show you where they are."

The young girl again. I smiled, amused by the way her eyes kept darting to my smooth fingertips, and flattered by her obvious infatuation. She had glossy black hair cut in a sharp bob, with a long fringe overrunning her brows. Long lashes fluttered above deep-colored orbs, and she wore a schoolgirl's uniform, complete with knee-high socks and polished Mary Janes. I hadn't seen anyone this cute since Shirley Temple last graced the screen, and I wondered why she was hanging out with these losers.

"I'm sorry," I said, bending so I was eye level with her. "I don't think we've been introduced. I'm—"

"The Archer," she said quickly. "I know."

"Jasmine's a big Zodiac fan," Carl said, patting her on her head. They had to be about the same age, but he was at least a half-foot taller.

"Just the Light series," Jasmine clarified. "When I grow up I want to be an agent of Light too."

Sebastian gagged behind us. I ignored him and smiled at Jasmine. She was like a little pixie, and I couldn't easily envision her conking Shadow agents over the head with billy clubs like I had the night before. "Well. Eat your veggies."

She nodded vigorously and took my hand. I straightened and headed in the direction Carl was pointing. "In the storeroom, all the way to the back, right-hand side, fifth shelf from the bottom. Let me know if you need any help."

I'd need help all right, I thought, letting Jasmine lead the way. Help explaining, justifying, and ever being allowed out of the sanctuary once Warren found out what I'd done. If I wanted to find Joaquin before then, I had to get busy. Two weeks felt like a mere ten minutes away. Then again, if I was lucky, I thought, looking at my watch, five more minutes was all I'd need.

Jasmine and I had to pass single-file along a dark hallway before getting to the storeroom, which was strange in itself. The building didn't appear that long from the outside, though I hadn't been around the back. Not only that, the air was growing colder as we progressed, until the warmest thing around me was Jasmine's hand clutching my own. Rubbing one arm with the other hand, I kept my eyes focused on a light directly ahead, shivering as I thought of hot toddies and furry slippers. Odd for late May in Vegas.

Finally we crossed the threshold from darkness into light. I blinked a few times so my eyes could acclimate, then blinked again to be sure what I was seeing. And feeling. The cold was gone, replaced by a warmth as welcoming as a wool blanket falling over my shoulders.

For a moment I thought I'd entered another portal rather than a storeroom, but that wasn't possible. Jasmine was with me; and though she was an oddly cute kid with a startling awareness of supernatural phenomena—prepubescent teens had an acceptance of the extraordinary that adults had long lost—she was no agent. Yet here we were, in a room more befitting the manor house of an English lord than the storage room of some caustic counter jockey. Sure, there were comics stored along every inch of the wall, but the shelves were made of thick mahogany planks, and matching crown molding arched toward a cavernous ceiling soaring over a room the size of a small theater.

While there was space enough for multiple aisle dividers in the center of the room, it was already clustered with leather easy chairs, each with an overstuffed ottoman, and mismatched side tables piled high with comics, texts, and what looked like a teetering cup of forgotten coffee. At the room's core was a square stone fireplace lit and jumping with orange flames, its flue suspended yards above, but still able to capture the smoke as it rose lazily from the ash. Hence the warmth. I turned a circle around myself, taking it all in.

Observing my reaction, Jasmine pointed to a tight circular staircase in the back corner of the room, which wound up into a rectangular platform, leading to what I assumed was an attic. "Zane's living quarters are upstairs, but he spends most of his time writing and researching down here. He says the fire keeps his third eye open, and the dance of the smoke lends inspiration."

"Geez," I said, whistling as I ran my hand over a stack of titles dating back to the eighties. "He must have every comic written for the past fifty years."

Jasmine shook her head earnestly. "Oh no, these are all manuals. Zane wouldn't waste valuable storage space on regular comics."

"All manuals?" But there were thousands of them, tens of thousands. "How far back do they go?"

"All the way to the beginning," she said, pulling me toward a tottering stack of sleeved comics pushed up against a corner shelf. "Back to when the first troops settled in the valley."

"Really?" I'd never thought to ask before. I'd been too concerned with the present to worry or wonder much about the past, but I knew that Las Vegas was only a hundred years old, and the troops wouldn't have formed here until there was a large enough population to merit notice. That's when agents moved in, staked out their places on the city's star charts, and began the whole good-battling-evil-for-the-sake-of-mankind bit. This same scenario had played itself out for centuries in every major metropolis, though the suburbs were the domain of the independents. Too many representatives of the same star sign—even Light—tended to destabilize things, so rogue agents weren't tolerated within city boundaries. I knew all this, but nothing about where the agents originally came from, or how far back the beginning really was.

I asked Jasmine just that and she eyed me with a small frown, though more out of concern that I didn't already know than suspicion as to why I wanted to. "You mean back to the original manual?"

"Is there such a thing?" I asked, watching as she knelt, hair swinging to obscure her china doll face, and began picking through the stack. I mean, I knew there had to be at one time, but what shape or language or location it was in was anyone's guess. But the idea was compelling.

"Well, you know originally legends on both sides of the Zodiac were passed on orally, right?"

I nodded like I had, and leaned against a bookcase as Jasmine handed me a manual with an agent of Light running through an alley, a shadow looming on the brick behind him. "Well, the first manual was put to paper—or papyrus—as oral storytelling was becoming obsolete. It documented

the original division between Shadow and Light, and fore-
told everything from the spread of troops to the new world,
the proliferation of cities throughout North America, to the
migration westward. It also predicted the creation and rise
of the Tulpa."

I blinked. The little girl-turned-walking-encyclopedia
blinked back. I said, "I'd love to see that."

Jasmine scoffed, looking back down to blindly pass me
another comic. "Yeah, you and the rest of the paranormal
world."

"What do you mean?"

"Legend has it that it also contains the so-called recipe
for killing the Tulpa, but each metropolis possesses one
copy only. Our city's original manual is lost. Or destroyed.
Nobody really knows. Maybe the Tulpa got ahold of it and
destroyed it himself. Still, the knowledge buried in that one
manual is so complete, so powerful, it'll forever tip the balance to the side of the Zodiac troop that possesses it, so the
search goes on. That's Zane's quest, you know. He's given
his life over to finding the original manual, or die trying."

"Yeah, but . . . how?" Nobody knew if the manual even
existed. Where did you start the search for something
nobody could account for? "Might as well be searching for
the Holy Grail."

Jasmine shook her head, sending smooth sheets of hair
swinging. "There are supposed to be clues planted throughout the earliest manuals that reveal its location. Alone they're
nothing more than simple parables and entertaining anec-
dotes. But together they form a comprehensive map leading
directly to the master manual."

"So somebody should assemble them," I said, accepting
two more manuals, and wondering—with not a little
irritation—why Warren hadn't told me any of this. "Someone should patch together the clues and start tracking it
down."

"Well, duh," Jasmine said, causing me to blink in affront.
Hard to stay mad, though, looking at her wide-eyed inno-

cence. Besides, she was right. Surely I wasn't the first troop member to think of it. She stood and began studying another shelf. "But the earliest manuals were created before the widespread use of the printing press. One edition only, handwritten."

And I bet private collectors had snapped those up like priceless Monets. My heart sank. "So they're all gone. Spread out so thinly that no one collector can piece together the whole."

At the disappointment in my voice, Jasmine turned her attention from the shelf she was scanning, fingers pausing over a section marker to hold her place. "But the trick is to keep looking, and people do. Agents die, remember? Manuals are bequeathed, won, stolen, bought. That's what keeps Zane in business. Not only does he trade out and up with every agent interested, but he thinks because he's the record keeper he has the best chance of finding the original."

"And you believe him?"

Jasmine shrugged. "One thing's sure. The Tulpa is endlessly sending agents to troll this place."

"Then he's worried," I said, following Jasmine along the near wall of stretching bookcases. "I didn't know the Tulpa could be made to worry."

She stopped beneath a leaning ladder of polished mahogany, adroitly plucking a manual from the dozens buried on the third shelf. She handed it to me as she turned around. "Zoe knew."

I froze, and the jolt wound through my body like a live wire, making my printless fingertips tingle as I grasped the manual.

"Do you have that one?" she asked innocently, tilting her head.

I shook mine, unable to tear my eyes from the cover. *The Archer,* it said, *Agent of Light.* Beneath the emblazoned caption was a photo of my mother.

She couldn't have been any older than I was now, dressed in short-shorts and go-go boots that were made for more than walking—it was an outfit guaranteed to get her in the creator's door. But there was blood on her thigh, her conduit—now mine—was clutched in both hands, and she was gritting her teeth, staring into shadows, bent-kneed as she backed away toward an opened door. I flipped open the manual, and caught a flash of color as a howl of rage splintered the silent room. The word *nooo-o-o!* bubbled up from the page before popping in a angry red spark.

"This is the one where she killed him, isn't it?" I asked Jasmine, flipping to the back. "The Tulpa's originator. When she thought killing Wyatt Neelson would weaken the Tulpa." It hadn't though, I thought, scanning another page where she escaped through a sewer lid portal. Instead it had loosed Neelson's hold on him, the creator's death doubling back to make the Tulpa stronger.

Jasmine nodded, rising to her tiptoes to flip back to the beginning with me, revealing the panels that showed my mother using manipulation, patience, her body, and pure chutzpah to gain that information from the Tulpa. She was already pregnant, I saw. And she was worried that with the hormone shift that came with pregnancy, the Tulpa would soon smell it on her. It would give her Light identity away.

I would give her away.

"This is my favorite," Jasmine breathed, as we watched Zoe sneak from the Tulpa's bedroom, him sleeping peacefully— face only partially revealed in black and white—while she stood framed in the doorway, her silhouette backlit, fists clenched, glyph fired. "She was wonderful."

But she had failed. Killing the Tulpa's creator had only freed him from the power of the original mind. From then on he'd been free to think and feel and act as he wished. And what did he wish for more than anything? To kill the woman who'd betrayed him.

The very last page showed her returning to the sanctuary, being wheeled into the sick ward by an impossibly young Micah, who told her not to worry. He was going to change her identity so the Tulpa and his agents would never find her.

And they hadn't, I thought wryly, closing the book. They'd found me instead.

"There are others," Jasmine said softly, watching my face with those giant doe eyes. "Lots. Would you like me to find them for you?"

"I don't know." Which surprised me. I wanted to find my mother, right? I wanted to exact revenge on the Tulpa for forcing her to run, leaving Olivia and me. So why was I so conflicted now? Why did it feel like watching events that had profound impact on my life through my mother's eyes would somehow be a betrayal to my younger self? "I don't know," I said again.

I looked around the room, wondering how many of these books had the power to forever change my impression of myself, and how many times that perception would flip-flop. Where I would end up when I finally knew all. I looked back at the schoolgirl in front of me. "How long have you known all this, Jasmine?"

A half smile flashed, a question she could answer, and a dimple flickered with it. "I was born knowing. Just like Carl, and Sebastian, and the twins. We're changelings."

"Changelings?" I asked, recognizing the word from one of Warren's lectures, but not what it meant.

The embarrassment in my voice touched her. She took my hand and swung it back and forth in hers, like we were schoolgirls on a playground. "We keep the secrets of the Zodiac and make sure the knowledge is passed on to the next generation. We need the agents to continue the battle of good versus evil, of course, so that the legends are put into print, but you need us just as much. Here, read this." She passed me another manual, then waved for me to follow.

I glanced down as I did. "Why?"

"Because it's the story of your troop's emergence," she said, facing me as she continued walking backward. "Your genealogy is in there. It's a good place to start."

"No . . . er, thanks," I said, tucking it under my arm. "But I meant why do agents need you?"

She halted so suddenly I almost ran her down, but looked more amused by the question than annoyed. "Because we think about you. We read your stories and believe in you. Were Zane to stop writing them down, or die without passing the craft on to another, or were we to enter puberty without recruiting new changelings from the six and seven age group, your stories would cease to be told. Your alternate realities would fade, your portals would close forever. You would cease to exist."

"Impossible," I said, on a half laugh. "I exist whether you believe it or not. One thing has nothing to do with the other." Though I thought about the Tulpa—how someone else's thoughts had created him, how a group's belief had strengthened him—and had to suppress a shudder.

Jasmine half laughed back. "You have an immunity to mortal harm and a chest that lights up like a Christmas tree whenever danger is near. Who're you to say what's possible or not?"

Shit. She had a point. I motioned for her to go on. The dimples flashed again. "All I know is belief in something is what makes it real, and not just paranormal episodes but regular things too. Love, hate, fear. Perception colors all our experiences." She gestured back the way we came, to the shop front and those still there. "For instance, Sebastian believes the Shadows are going to win the fight for the valley, and it's his job to convince other mortal children to believe along with him. They go home, read the manuals he's given them, and begin to dream about a world where evil rules the day. Those dreams become energy that feeds and fuels the Tulpa, giving strength and purpose to his troop's deeds."

"Can't disappoint their fans, eh?" I said wryly. At least I had a clear explanation as to why the kid couldn't stand me. "Maybe we should lock Sebastian up in a cabinet until he reaches puberty. Then, poof! He's gone. And no more Shadows either."

I was surprised no one had thought of it earlier.

She gave me a smile a parent would give to a pouting two-year-old, and handed me a comic depicting a man being mutilated on the cover by an unseen assailant, body parts tossed into an abandoned freezer after they were carved up. Nice. "But then you'd have to lock me away too. I'm Sebastian's opposite. I approach all the mortal children who are inclined to believe in the Light and I tell them the story of the Archer, how she not only survived, but overcame an attack that would have killed any other agent, how she made herself into something stronger, and how she's the Kairos, fated to bring down the Shadow side in our fair city forever."

Sheesh. The hyperbolic prose was bad enough. Now I had to worry about ruining some rugrat's bedtime story. "Thanks . . . I think."

"No problem," she said sweetly, dimples flashing. "Like I said, I'm a changeling. It's my . . ."

Jasmine's gaze left mine as a look of astonishment passed over her face, and she looked through me, as if seeing something just on the other side of my bones. The manuals she'd plucked from the shelves fell to the floor, and she stiffened.

"Jasmine?" I said, putting a hand on her arm. She trembled beneath my touch, small warning shudders before a greater quaking overtook her. It was some sort of seizure, I realized, as her eyes rolled to white, her little mouth opening soundlessly. I didn't know what to do. I knew CPR, but had no idea what to do with a seizure victim. Lay her down? Stick something in her mouth to keep her from biting her own tongue? I couldn't even decide if I should try and help her, or if I should leave her and run for help.

What happened next decided it for me.

Her smooth skin began to shimmer, just around the edges at first, like she was backlit, but it soon spread to the center of her frame, like wind rippling over water, except that this was a human being. I felt the texture of her skin alter beneath my hands, softening like putty, and quickly let go when I saw what looked like bruises popping up beneath my thumbs. But the bruises lifted also, like they were attached to my hands, and I jerked away. Her skin, like rubber, snapped back into place. It must have hurt because Jasmine's wide, rolling eyes seemed to fix on mine. Her open mouth shifted, like something had come unhinged inside, and her jaw extended into a gaping yawn. By the time I realized her teeth had grown unnaturally pointed and deadly sharp, her misshapen jaw was as long as my forearm and growing longer.

God help me, I thought, backing into the shelves with a startled crash. I was going to get eaten by a preteen!

Jasmine—or what used to be Jasmine—reached out to me with her hand, and I noticed the bruises I'd accidentally inflicted had spread. Her whole arm was that deep, shimmery color . . . and that hand had grown speared claws. I jerked away, dodged another swipe, and began to run across the great room, back into the tunnel leading to the shop, back to where little girls didn't turn into voracious monsters.

Jasmine roared behind me.

I hurtled through the dark passageway blindly, banging like a pinball against the narrow walls, but keeping my eyes fixed on the pinprick of light at the other end. Was it me, or was this tunnel getting longer? And was the panted breathing behind me getting closer?

"Zane!" I yelled, picking up speed. "Help!"

I'd have stopped to fumble for my conduit, but the-child-formerly-known-as-Jasmine was closer now. I could hear the report of little feet slapping behind me, needy growls erupting from her elongated throat, and knew if I stopped she'd be on me before I could draw and aim. Besides, shimmering spawn of Dracula or not, did I really want to kill her?

Finally, as the light grew larger and the hallway shorter, I could make out the shop beyond the doorway. There were chairs and shelves and—far, far off—the front door. I ran faster. Jasmine roared again. A figure stepped into the doorway of the passage, and I heard a gasp before Carl came barreling toward me as well.

"Carl, no!" He must not have seen the monster on my ass. "Move!"

He did . . . just enough to send his shoulder barreling into me. My breath left me in a whoosh, and I ended up on my back, Carl on top of me . . . Jasmine poised for attack at the tip of my head. But she wasn't looking at me. Carl was yelling, telling me to calm down and let Jasmine get in front of me. His other instructions were hurried, mumbled, panted—something about mask, identity, hide—but I got the gist of it.

"What, Carl? What is it?" I asked as Jasmine squeezed past us with feline grace, limbs blackened to the point of opaqueness, stretching, elongating, and retracting as needed. No wonder she'd been gaining on me. She was a life-sized Gumby! So fixed was I on the sight of her gelatinous legs, I almost missed what Carl said next.

"Joaquin."

Jasmine roared again, and ahead of me a shadow moved to block the light from the shop. All the breath left my body on a shaky exhale. My conduit was out of reach, dumped on the floor when Carl tackled me, and my glyph had failed to fire in warning. But Carl was right. Joaquin had arrived. And Master Comics had just turned into the little shop of horrors.

7

He wore no mask, though I'd have known who he was beneath it anyway. Silhouetted in the doorway where Carl had been moments earlier, he wore a suit that accentuated his frame, making his shoulders as broad as a linebacker's, but narrow at the hips. Sugar-coated heat rose in roasting waves from his body, and the air in the hallway gave way to a cloying sweetness that clung to my nostrils, coating my throat. The scent was unmistakable, as was the man. He took a determined step forward.

Still down, I began backpedaling madly, knowing just how Linda Hamilton had felt against the Terminator.

"Stop, Archer. Stop!" Carl tugged on one of my legs. I shook him free and struggled to my feet, still backpedaling. Carl grabbed one of my arms and dug in. "Just let Jasmine stay in front of you. You'll be fine."

From a half crouch I looked again. And slowly straightened. Joaquin was still there, outlined in the doorway with one hand cocked on his hip, head tilted as he tried to peer around Jasmine. But she had grown, stretching to a cut-out form that eerily echoed mine, a shadowy barrier between him and me. I straightened, and she did too, my mirror image but tinged in a vibrant shade of violet that pulsed from her body with each beat of her heart.

"She won't let you come to harm. That's her job. Your identity's protected as long as she's between you."

I turned my head toward Carl, to show I was listening, but kept my eyes on Joaquin. "So, what's he seeing?"

"Nothing but your outline right now. And I do mean *your* outline. The real you. As you were before."

I glanced at Carl. Jasmine, in front of me, mirrored the movement. "Really?"

He nodded. "If you want to be fully seen as you were before, then just step through her. She'll try to echo the movement, but move a little faster and her aura will become attached to your own. It'll mold and shape this body into your original frame. Right now it's just like using a medium to reveal who you are. Step through her and you actually become the medium."

I swallowed hard, but my heartbeat was slowing. Joaquin didn't come any closer, and Jasmine didn't look like she'd let him. "I don't get it."

"She's the frame," Carl said, motioning ahead, "you're simply what's being mirrored."

It made sense in some unbelievable way I no longer questioned. Still. Step *through* another person so their aura could stick to my own? "I don't think so."

I did take a step forward, though, and when nothing happened—other than Jasmine mimicking the movement—took another. Reaching my bag, and the comics I'd dropped when Carl had plowed into me, I gathered them together and sought out my conduit, trying to ignore my shaking hands. Jasmine mirrored my movements exactly, keeping my Olivia identity hidden from Joaquin on the other side. A changeling, I thought, shaking my head slightly. And here I thought she was going to eat me.

Just as I began to compose myself, Jasmine roared. It sounded like the earth quaking at its core, and I realized too late that she was backing up as Joaquin charged forward. As wind rushed ruthlessly down the hallway, the pages of the manuals flipped madly before they were wrenched away from my grasp, and Carl's voice faded as he flew backward.

"Hold still!" he yelled, his voice trailing off as he tumbled away. I held still. Jasmine backed into me. And like the slamming of a storm cellar door, the wind abruptly died. Rolling to my back, I hit the floor, and was looking up at a man who'd cleared twenty-five yards in less than a breath. My arm whipped up; I sighted his chest between the crosshairs of my conduit and fired.

Nothing happened.

"Worth a try," Joaquin said, his smile shining in the light of my glyph, finally lit. He shrugged. "For both of us."

And he turned and sauntered back into the shop. I watched until he disappeared before I breathed again. Then I looked down. My hands, I realized, wiggling my fingers. And my arms. I felt my chest . . . wonderfully unimpressive. My hand flitted to my hair. Mine—short, bobbed, brown—wonderfully mine. And other than everything being tinted in a deep violet hue, I looked like me. Me, Joanna. Me, me.

Then, letting my head loll to the side, I saw her. "Oh my God! Jasmine, no!"

She was her normal size again, curled in the fetal position, legs drawn tightly up to her little chest, eyes squeezed shut, a wince of pain on her frozen face. She wasn't breathing.

"Don't touch her!"

I let my hand fall short of her too-white skin as Carl skidded to a stop next to me, breathing hard. His dual faux hawk had divided and multiplied into a dozen different styles, and he stepped between me and Jasmine as if to protect her.

"We have to help—" I began.

"She's fine," he said, holding up his hands. I strained to get around him. "Archer! She's fine."

I licked my lips nervously as I glanced back down the hallway—no sign of Joaquin—then back at Jasmine. "She doesn't look fine."

"Well, she will be," he clarified, looking down at her. "As soon as you give her aura back to her. She can't move without it, of course. And she won't live if you keep it beyond a twenty-four-hour period . . . oh, and if you happen to be injured or die while wearing it. But other than that, she's pretty much just sleeping."

Just a few little contingencies then. I swallowed hard. "She looks . . . waxy."

"She's fragile," he admitted softly. "Like an egg with the yolk blown from the center. She gifted you with her vitality, her life force. Without it, she's just a shell."

Great. No pressure. My greatest enemy was one room away, and not only did I have to watch out for my life, but another that was connected to it.

"You look just like I pictured you," Carl said, sizing me up, squinting one eye. "God, I'm good."

I rubbed a hand over my face. "What the fuck just happened?"

"Jasmine did her job, that's what. Changelings always protect their agents . . . even if the agent is too stupid to protect themselves."

"Hey!" I snapped. "How was I supposed to know he'd rush me?"

"Joaquin. Enemy. Duh." I grimaced because he had a point. "Now, are you just going to stand there, or are you going to go out and face your mortal enemy like a true heroine of Light?"

"What about her?"

"She'll be fine. Probably more comfortable on a lounge chair in the back, but no one will disturb her here."

I glanced at him dubiously, then down at the conduit still clenched in my hand. "Why couldn't I kill him?"

"The shop is neutral territory. Both sides of the Zodiac come here to study, so it's considered a safe zone, even for those on the Shadow side. Neither of you can touch the other."

Which Regan had known when she gave me Joaquin's

location, I thought wryly. But the rest of her information was good. Joaquin was here. As unprepared as I was for my conduit not to work and my glyph not to fire—not to mention having my own demon-child protectress—Regan hadn't put me in danger. She'd even said she'd give me enough information to catch him . . . when the time came. Smart girl, I thought again.

"Are you sure?" I asked Carl. The last thing I needed was to waltz into the shop front and face another surprise attack.

He nodded. "Jasmine will preserve your identity as long as her aura is molding your true frame. Just don't make any jerky movements. Limbs sometimes disengage—it's gross— so if he lunges at you just ignore it."

Easy for you to say, I thought, but nodded as I took a step forward. It was a strange feeling at first, like hearing my footsteps fall a second after I felt them land, but there was a sense and rhythm to it, and after steeling myself with a steadying breath, I entered the shop.

He was seated at a gaming table in a chair that was too small for him, one long leg crossed over the other, hands linked at his knee. Sebastian, as slate-colored, slack-jawed, and long of tooth as Jasmine had been, was stationed at his right side. The twins had also morphed into onyx-colored changelings, and were standing guard on each side of the door, though whether they were keeping us in or everyone else out, I had no idea.

And right now I didn't care. I only had eyes for Joaquin. He shifted, and I glanced down, expecting to find a weapon in his hands. I was actually surprised to find them empty. It was something he carried around inside him, I then realized, a sort of vigilance that made him look ever-armed. He was one of the few agents who didn't have a conduit fashioned just for him. His body was his weapon, and it was all he'd ever needed.

Sebastian tried to shield him from me, but Joaquin brushed him aside with a flick of his wrist. As he did, his hand passed behind the changeling's form, and I got a glimpse of the real Joaquin. Blackened bone, cracked nails, and charred flesh hung from his frame. My nose was right. He was as corrupted and rotted on the inside as he smelled. He watched me watching him, and after a long pause, slowly licked his lips. My jaw clenched reflexively as I fought the urge to gag.

"Back off, changeling," he told Sebastian. "Nobody in here frightens me."

I was half insulted, half relieved. I didn't really want to view the rot lying beneath that composed exterior. I should've realized long ago that his disguise was that he was alive. Human.

"Nobody?" I asked, and let the darkness living inside me temporarily rise to the surface. It was little more than a parlor trick, but Joaquin swallowed hard, which gave me a glow of satisfaction. I increased the effect, and Sebastian hissed. I grinned at him and let my father's face fade.

"Neat trick . . . if you weren't hiding behind a child's aura while you did it." He'd recovered well, and motioned to the chair across from him. "Have a seat."

I didn't move. "Sitting would indicate an interest in talking with you."

"Refusing would imply you're afraid to do so."

Which, from my mad scramble back in the hallway, he already knew. I crossed my arms and remained where I was.

He shrugged. "Back in the archives, eh? What were you searching for? Clues to your past? Some link to Mommy? Buried treasure, perhaps?"

I didn't answer. He didn't expect me to.

"Carl, you should get the Archer manuals number 3543 and 4721. They document Zoe Archer's failure, as well as the many innocent lives she cost in her quest for notoriety. Amusing reads, both."

"Forget it, Carl," I said, my eyes never leaving Joaquin. "The Shadow manuals don't interest me. Except as a tool for hunting their agents."

"But how else will you keep from repeating history's mistakes? Your troop leader obviously tells you nothing." He was talking about my reaction to Jasmine, and how I hadn't known her function as a changeling.

"Warren tells me what I need to know, when I need to know it," I replied coolly, because Warren had actually mentioned it. It had just slipped my mind while staring into Jasmine's sharp, elongated jaw.

"He lies to you," Joaquin said flippantly, examining his fingernails like he was just making conversation. My eyes fastened on those fingers, and though I tried not to stare I couldn't help it. I'd have known those hands anywhere. I'd felt the knuckles pummeling my bones, the fingers scraping my throat, the tensile strength in those palms pinning me to the desert floor. I had to force my gaze from his hands to concentrate on his words. When I met his eyes, he smiled, knowing what I'd been thinking. Dammit. "He doesn't want you to know the extent of your powers. The truth is, he thinks you'll turn on him."

"That's not true." I shook my head, not allowing the thought, like a fly, to settle. "Besides, Warren saved me."

And that was the truth as I knew it. I used it to anchor me while my nerves settled.

"But for what purpose?" Joaquin said, one brow raised in question. "To be a puppet for his whim? To string you along just so he can say you belong to him?"

That rattled me—I'd never thought of it that way before—but I put on a good front leaning against the wall of comics behind me. "You know what purpose, Joaquin. He believes I'm the Kairos. They all do."

"Then why do they fear you?"

Zane, who'd been scribbling furiously throughout this whole exchange, looked up. I felt all the kids' eyes on me, including the Sebastian-thing, and Carl next to me, who'd exclaimed softly at Joaquin's words.

"They're training me and teaching me to grow in power," I said stiffly.

Zane's pencil was flying again, scratching against a yellow pad, his tongue stuck out between his chubby lips in an obviously unconscious habit. He glanced hurriedly from us to his pad, back and forth, and I wondered which series this exchange would show up in—Shadow or Light.

Joaquin, following my gaze, glanced over his shoulder, then turned his face back to me. "Ah, the record keeper. A tedious job, if a necessary one." He smiled at Zane apologetically. Insincerely. "He's bound by two laws: to tell the truth, and to resist favoring either side of the Zodiac. But when you think about it, it's not such a hard line to walk. He has the power to color our stories. He chooses the words and verbiage to describe our realities, our existence. Without him, we wouldn't exist. Now that, my dear, is power."

"What about me?" Carl muttered under his breath. "I'm the friggin' penciler."

"Power isn't about inflicting your will upon other people's lives," I told Joaquin. "It's the ability to control the impulse to do so."

Joaquin clucked softly, shaking his head. "Spoken like someone who has none."

"That's not true," I said softly. "Simply being alive is power."

He blanched at the reminder that he'd failed to kill me, and it was my turn to smile. As I did, he tilted his chair back. "And snuffing out a life is all that power amplified."

I felt my eyes grow empty and flat. It was arrogant to engage him in conversation, I realized, and we were both all too aware our words were being recorded. So I thought for a moment and abruptly changed the subject. "And is that what you have planned for the agents of Light? You think it'll be easy to wipe us all out in one fell swoop?"

For the first time Joaquin looked unsure. He opened his mouth to speak, but I held up a manual of Light, one of the ones he couldn't touch or read, and could only fathom what was inside. It was a red herring, contained nothing pertinent to this conversation, but he didn't know that.

"Well, that's a secret, isn't it? Though it looks like you have some secrets of your own." He tipped his chair forward and leaned his elbows on the table as he studied me. "Where is the rest of your troop, anyway? All still holed up underground? Did the revelation of the second sign scare them that much? Or don't they know you're acting *independently*?" Just in case I didn't catch the inflection in his voice, he mouthed the word *rogue* to me.

"They're biding their time," I shot back, assuring him . . . and perhaps myself. "As for the second sign, a battlefield's only cursed for those destined to die there."

"And you're so unconcerned that you can while away your hours looking for buried treasure?"

Again, that buried treasure remark. I tilted my head, thought, and went with my instincts. "Like you, you mean?"

He scoffed, but I saw the way his jaw tensed first. Interesting. "I admit, I enjoy slumming here every once in a while. I find the neutrality of this place intoxicating. It's a fresh slate, a blank page, if you will," he said, motioning again to Zane. "A void where anything is possible."

But I could tell from the way he dismissed it that there was more to it than that. "But that's not why you're here today."

"No, it's not," he said, surprising me with the ease of his admission. His fingers began winding themselves around each other again, like little snakes coiling to strike. "One of my friends has been missing since last night. I lost his trail after he disappeared through a portal and never returned."

"And you think he stopped by for a little game of Dungeons and Dragons with your flunky over there?" I said, causing Sebastian to snarl again.

"I think a place that caters to both sides of the Zodiac is a good place to start looking when your friends vanish without a trace." He tilted his head as if he'd just had an idea. "Strange that you're here today, of all days. You haven't recently seen a male Shadow with blinding blue eyes, about yea tall, have you?"

"Zane's the record keeper," I said, wanting to keep last night's events to myself for as long as possible. "Ask him."

"You're the only agent of Light who's been trying to unbalance the Zodiac," he said flatly. "So I'm asking you."

"Well, I don't make it a habit of kibitzing with the Shadow side. As you know."

"So is that a no, little Archer?"

My jaw clenched. "A resounding one."

"Liar."

"I'm not. I didn't kill your Shadow agent."

Joaquin leaned back in the tiny chair, somehow managing to give an air of dignified composure. It had to be challenging for a walking corpse. Steepling his fingers, he stared at me over the top of his hands. "Funny, but I don't remember mentioning he was dead."

I froze and began cursing my stupidity before realizing I could just tell him. I could reveal Regan's identity, tell Joaquin about her betrayal of Liam, and she'd be dead before the sun set this evening. The problem was, she'd either offer my Olivia identity in return for her life, or be tortured into revealing it, and that'd put me in a worse spot than I was now. As it was, I still had two weeks to kill Joaquin, find Regan, and to get it all done before Warren really pulled the rug out from under me. I glanced across at Joaquin. Between the two, I'd take my chances with Regan.

Besides, baiting the man in front of me was a pleasure. "Well, admittedly, that big ol' shillelagh was too mighty a weapon for a 'little Archer' like myself . . . but I used both hands when I bashed that Irish bastard's skull in, and he didn't seem to know the difference at all."

Joaquin sat up so fast I think he surprised himself. Everyone else had gone unnaturally still, and that's when I realized he hadn't been joking about Liam being a friend. His face slackened and paled, and that brought a pure, genuine smile to mine.

I leaned forward and rubbed salt into the wound. "He

screamed like a baby when I shattered all his limbs. Between the blood and snot and tears, I could barely make out what he was saying, but I have to confess. His begging made me feel so"—I took in a deep breath—"powerful."

Joaquin had lowered his head, and I watched the rise and fall of his chest, saw when it finally slowed and he looked up at me from beneath his brows. His eyes were as hard and cold as I remembered them, and his hands weren't exactly shaking on the card table, but they were twitching. This, I realized, was Joaquin in a fury.

"Come on outside, Archer," he said in a voice soft as a viper's. "You can even bring your little bow and arrow, as we already know what happens when you try to fight without it." He made a motion, and I knew he was stroking himself under the table. He waited for my reaction, and though I wanted to swallow the bile that had risen reflexively in my gorge, I shook my head slowly, mindful of Jasmine's protective aura. "Not here. Not now."

I'd like to say that Regan's promise to lead me to him—that old ace in the hole—had no effect on my decision. But even as I told myself that, I knew it wasn't true. Without that, I'd be out the door already. This was the man who'd taken my innocence from me. Who'd taken Ben from me. For the latter alone he deserved to die.

But it also looked supremely confident for me to turn down an opportunity to fight in broad daylight, and I knew how such confidence could play on a person's mind in the darkest hours of night, when they were alone but for the sharklike questions circling in their own mind. I wanted to poison Joaquin's mind like that. I wanted uncertainty to seep into that rotted brain and slow his movements, jumble his thoughts, and make him fear the worst-case scenario.

So it wasn't that I didn't want to battle Joaquin right then, in broad daylight, with children pressed against the shop windows behind me, because I did. But I had Regan's promise to help me further, and now I had Joaquin pissed enough to look for me himself. I'd use both those things to my advantage, and then he'd do more than die at my hands. He'd suffer first.

Right now it was enough that his smile had faltered, and his stroking had stopped. He knew why I was saying no. He recognized the Shadow in me as clearly as if he were looking in a mirror. I dropped my fists on the card table, and leaned so close I made his eye twitch. "I made a vow to run your rancid, decaying body down, and I'm renewing that vow now."

He stood, perhaps more comfortable with a small distance between us, or maybe he just wanted to be taller. His lip curled as he looked down at me, and he ran a hand over his perfectly coiffed hair, either unimpressed by my words or giving a very good impression of it. "Your passion will be your downfall."

I smirked. "Passion would imply that I give a shit about your presence on this earth. It's much simpler than that," I said, though it wasn't. "I just want to *hunt*."

And now I was speaking a language he understood.

"Agent of Light," I said, in response to his stiffening posture. "Enemy. Duh."

Carl snickered beside me.

Joaquin straightened his suit, pulling at the cuffs with those dangerous hands like he was an eighteenth-century dandy instead of a twenty-first-century supervillain. "Even the Tulpa can't keep me from defending myself under such a bald threat, Joanna. You've opened the floodgates." He jerked his head at Zane, recording our words. "I'll give you your war."

I shrugged. "Would you like a little tactical advice, then?"

"Sure," he said, stepping closer to me, invading my space this time. "I'm not beyond stealing secrets from the enemy."

"All right. Just one hint." I looked up into his face, past the thin lips, into those empty eyes, and held my ground.

"Look behind you, Joaquin. Even when you think you're alone, even when you feel safe and secure in your lair, even when you sleep. Don't ever stop looking behind you."

"A little tip for you as well, then," Joaquin said, lips curling into a cruel sneer. "Try number 5142. It's the record of the night we first met. I'm sure you'll find it fascinating."

Some may have taken it for weakness, but I let him have the last word. I watched him back away from me, only watched as he blew me a parting kiss, and stood where I was even when the door chimes split the air, severing the tension linking us together. Besides, I was too busy smiling to respond. He *had* glanced back over his shoulder, just before the door shut behind him, just as I wanted. And damn if it didn't make me feel powerful.

I should have known better than to try and follow. I thought if I could at least get a good look at the kind of car he drove I could add it to my growing trove of information about him, and the Shadows in general: a lab in the basement of Valhalla, an original manual with the facts needed to destroy the Tulpa, an initiate gone bad. Badder. Whatever.

So I pulled down the edge of an Aquaman poster, half expecting to see the Batmobile parked outside. My hand was slapped away, though, and one of the twins snarled, his elongated teeth dripping with saliva as he leered in my direction.

"Oh, back off, Beavis," I said, and slapped him upside his sooty gelatinous head.

"Ow-w," he whined, his features shrinking, skin losing its dark color, like leaking ink, until he regained his ruddy mien. His jaw snapped back into shape with an audible pop.

"You can't watch him leave, Archer," Carl said. "It's part of the rules—"

"Yeah, yeah," I said, turning away from the window. I'd figured as much. "How do I get her off me?"

"Who, Jas?" he asked, and I thought, *No, the other pre-*

teen affixed to me like Cling Wrap. "Just return to her shell and touch her. She'll take over from there."

I did, and Jasmine peeled from my frame like a Band-Aid, color rushing along her limbs like it'd been released from a dam; no more pale skin, and no more scary monster fangs. Waking as though from a dream, she blinked up at me, wide-eyed and expectant. "Are you okay?"

"Of course," she answered sweetly as I helped her to her feet. "How did we get into the hallway?"

I picked up my belongings and turned to Carl, who'd come with me after the other kids had morphed back into pockmarked pubescents. "She really remembers nothing?"

He started walking backward, keeping an eye on us as we all headed back into the shop. "Memory is unnecessary for changelings, and would actually inhibit function in their own lives. Besides, if they remembered these events as adults they'd have to be institutionalized." Carl slumped against the back wall and gave me an appreciative once-over. "You handled yourself well, Archer. That last nose-to-nose bit is going to be a beaut to draw."

"What did we miss?" one of the twins asked.

His brother hit him. "Dude, they never tell us. We'll have to wait and read the manual."

"Man, I hate that!" he replied, slapping his thigh. "Carl, we should at least get a discount if we're in the fucking thing!"

"Language! There's a lady in the house," Carl said, and the boys began looking about.

I rolled my eyes and turned back to Carl. "Thanks for your help back there. I didn't know . . ." I trailed off, thinking of all the things I didn't know. Carl, reading my thoughts, waved the appreciation away.

"Anytime. Joaquin's right about one thing, though," he said, leading to obnoxious cries of "Joaquin? The Shadow agent? Where? When?," and had to raise his voice to be heard. "You need to grow in power before you take him on. If you acted in the outside world the way you did in the hallway, you'd be dead right now."

"I know," I muttered as I headed to the register. But *that* was going to change.

"You all right?" Zane asked when I reached him.

You care? was the first retort to come to mind, but it wasn't really his job to care, and it was nice of him to ask. Still, when I nodded, I didn't meet his eye. I didn't want him to see the frustration there. I'd hate for him to write about it in the Shadow manuals. Then Joaquin would really know he'd gotten to me.

So I fumbled with my wallet instead, hunting for the cash to pay for my purchases, pausing when my eyes fell on the papers in front of him. The pages to the left were filled with dialogue, a shorthand version of Joaquin's and my conversation minutes before, but the one to the right—the one he'd been working on when I entered the shop—was blank. But for two words.

Liam Burke.

"It was nice of you, you know," Zane said, seeing the direction of my gaze as he slipped the manuals into a plastic bag. "You allowed his name to be recorded in the manuals of Light."

I shrugged. "It's what I would have wanted." I took the bag and handed him the money.

"He'd have snuffed you out without a second thought," he said, the corner of his mouth twitching slightly.

"Always a pleasure, Zane." I pocketed the change, took my receipt, and turned to leave.

"It's strange, though."

I turned back, warily. "What is?"

He tapped his pencil against his man-boobs. "Well, these events, your actions . . . they come to me in visions, bubbling up suddenly in my consciousness, and they come in color. The agents of Light are always bathed in a golden iridescent glow, the Shadows always silver."

So it was some sort of psychic energy manifesting itself, the same as mortal dreams. I'd wondered. Curious to hear more, I took a step back toward the counter. I believed in energy, that we were all created by it and created it in turn. Shit, these days it was practically the only thing I believed in. Nevertheless, I tried to hide that I was impressed. "So?"

"So, before you snagged the aureole, before my mind went blank and all I saw were those two words," he said, annoyance flickering over his face as if I'd flipped the channel while he was watching his favorite program. Voyeur. "I could have sworn there were two entities in that aquarium."

"You mean you saw another Shadow agent?" I asked innocently.

"No. The vision wasn't strong enough for that," he admitted, and I let out the breath I'd been holding. "But I know I saw something. I saw someone."

He couldn't see initiates, I realized. And the aureole had blunted my capture and conversation with Regan. So while he might have intuited Regan's presence, he couldn't prove it. "Well," I finally said, shooting him Olivia's brightest smile. "Good luck with that."

He snorted in disgust and turned his attention back to his work as I walked away. I'd find out in two weeks what he was writing. For now I peered outside, glancing left and right before stepping into the day's full sun. The only person in sight was the skateboarder from before, and he rolled directly over to my car, flipped up his board, and tucked it under his arm, while squinting at me through the bright afternoon rays.

"It's okay," he said. "He's gone."

I nodded at him—another changeling, I gathered—though he was only partly right. Joaquin was gone. On the other hand, I thought, turning the Porsche's engine over, things were far from being okay.

8

After my confrontation with Joaquin, after I'd watched a little girl turn into a monster—and ultimately my savior—and after running through a drive-through to pick up a cheeseburger, and wishing it came with a shot of Chivas, I was ready for sanctuary. Dusk was closing in fast, and the time of crossing from this reality to the other was less than an hour away. Crossing wasn't like walking through a portal. Any old agent could do that at any time, but crossing had to be undertaken at exactly the time when day and night were split evenly in the air, when the veil between the mortal world and ours was thinnest, if it was to be done at all. One second late and the door would be shut until twelve hours later, and the next split second day and night fought over the skyline.

Our sanctuary was located on the other side of this reality, in the Neon Boneyard, a place where the old signs and lettering left over from imploded hotels were stored, gathering dust and rusting, until enough money could be gathered to turn the place into a historical museum. This being Vegas, any signage older than a decade qualified as historical, but for now the boneyard had a relatively quiet life, much like any boneyard, with only the occasional private tour given by appointment in the daytime.

At night, though, it belonged to us.

Unfortunately, accessing the boneyard's second reality wasn't as easy as booking an appointment. Cleaving the curtain between two realities was a messy and sometimes violent business, and not for the faint of heart. I didn't know what Shadows used to access their alternate reality—none of us even knew where their sanctuary was—but we used fearlessness, impeccable timing, and the city's Star cabs.

What? If anyone can fight through the most impossible mess, it's a Vegas cabdriver.

Masquerading as a cabbie was a great way to glean information about the Shadow side, and that's exactly what Gregor—the Cancerian member of our Zodiac, and our liaison between this reality and the next—did. Between fares he scanned the papers and local magazines for news, obits, and reports that might be supernatural in nature. He had a police scanner, EMS scanner, and traffic cam all crammed into his front seat. It was a great cover for him, and the best way to cross over for the rest of us, and every dawn and dusk, without fail, found Gregor parked in an alley behind the Peppermill.

As for the Peppermill itself, well, it was the original Vegas ultra-lounge. With all the new clubs and bars backed by casinos with millions to invest in a little spot of nightlife, the Peppermill was somewhat dated by comparison. Yet I considered the seventies decor, the old-fashioned cocktails, and the unapologetic kitsch all part of its charm. It was a throwback to an era when all casino bosses were Italian and women dressed up to go out for a night on the town; a great place for nostalgia right in the center of the modern-day Strip.

Sometimes I went there just to sit in the bar where blue flames leaped from a firepit of boiling water, dancing off the mirrored tiles of tables and walls, reflecting myself back at me in tiny quarter-inch squares. Cocktail waitresses in long black gowns served me fruity drinks while I watched darkly from a secluded corner, observing the human jetsam and flotsam that washed in from the Strip, while ignoring couples making out in pockets of obscurity similar to my own. There was something about the Peppermill that brought out the voyeur in me, and if the clientele was any indication, I wasn't alone.

I grabbed the bag I'd packed that morning from the trunk—containing clothing, toiletries, and the disks from Cher's—and after a quick check in the alley confirmed Gregor was here, though not in his cab, I hurried through smoked glass doors to join him inside. It'd be good to catch up, just the two of us. He was extremely superstitious—known to knock wood at least once a day; never stepped on cracks or walked under ladders—but he had a sense of humor about it, and so was good company. The one exception to his numerous superstitions was that he owned a black warden . . . though perhaps it was more accurate to say the jewel-eyed feline owned him. When he was in the sanctuary she was an ubiquitous presence in his one arm.

So I scanned the lounge, eyes skimming over the neon bands lining the mirrored ceiling, the faux foliage sporting bright blossoms eternally in bloom, and the bubbling firepit, looking for a stocky man with a four-leaf clover tattooed at the base of his skull. Instead my gaze found another person I knew.

"The hell you doing here?" Chandra asked, scowling back at me as I plopped myself next to her in a red velvet booth.

"Where's Gregor?" I asked, holding up a finger to call the waitress over, ignoring her question. Chandra, in turn, ignored mine.

Chandra was my colleague, but not my friend. She was of an age to undergo metamorphosis and become an agent of Light, her one lifelong ambition. She'd been born in the sanctuary, raised expecting to take up a star sign and join the ranks of warriors patrolling Vegas's streets. But Chandra's birth sign was already occupied. By me. My mother had been the last to hold the Archer sign, and because you had to inherit your star sign, once I came into the picture Chandra was bumped to the back of the line. Now she was stuck in a sort of limbo. She had the ability, knowledge and desire to become an agent of Light, but not the lineage or the right. That alone would've been enough to make her hate me.

My mistaking her for a man the first time we'd met had sealed the deal.

I glanced at her after I'd ordered my drink, and she ignored the countless mirrors reflecting me doing so. Her dark hair was longer than it'd been six months ago, though still layered and choppy and looking a lot like a grunge rocker's idea of cleaning up. She'd lost weight, though, and was more curvaceous, her waist now slimming slightly before flaring into wide hips, her breasts round and uplifted instead of blending into a boxy T-shirt. It helped that she'd begun wearing tailored clothing instead of sweats and flannels, and I was surprised to note she had pretty eyes, long-lashed and the color of warmed cider . . . even if they were always as hard as frozen pebbles when trained on me.

My drink arrived, I paid up immediately—not wanting to prolong this tortuous silence—and watched the door for other agents. Chandra, obviously feeling the same, checked her watch and sighed heavily.

"Anyone else coming?" I asked, just to fill the uncomfortable silence.

Chandra shrugged and went back to ignoring me. I didn't bother asking her anything more, but from the looks of it she was taking Gregor's place on this trip. My turn to sigh. Saying that Chandra was a shit driver was like saying Schumacher was just so-so. She drove like a teenage boy on crack cocaine, especially when I was in the car. I began downing my drink, thinking mild intoxication might help things a bit, but slowed when Chandra looked over.

"I smell nerves," she said, a knowing smile twitching her lips.

"It's my masking agent," I replied, crossing my legs. "It goes bad after a few hours."

Her expression hardened. "Bullshit."

"It does. I could go to The Body Shop and buy a better compound."

Chandra glared, and it was my turn to smirk. She'd found solace after my unexpected appearance, and a place to contribute, in the sanctuary's lab, where she and Micah came up with scents designed to mask and alter agents' natural pheromones. Insulting her scientific abilities was like insulting her existence, but if she was going to sling mud, I had no problem dirtying my hands too.

"If you're so concerned about your masking agent, you probably shouldn't be bounding through portals when you don't know what lies in wait on the other side."

Damn Hunter. He just couldn't keep his big mouth shut.

"I was practicing," I said in my defense. "Warren's been working with me in the alternate realm."

"He tests you." And she said it like I'd failed.

"He trains me."

"He *knows* you," she said, stabbing at her drink with her straw. "We all know any time the scent of danger is in the air, the Archer will follow, no matter where it leads." She gave my title an ugly twist . . . and kept twisting. "They know it too." She meant the Shadows.

"Are you insinuating I intentionally put myself in danger?"

"I'm insinuating nothing," she said, and I almost relaxed. Her chin shot up. "I'm saying straight up that your little vendetta could get us all killed."

Little vendetta? Tracking down the man who attacked, raped, and left me for dead when I was an innocent teen was what she called a little vendetta? I felt every muscle in my body tense, even knowing I shouldn't take the bait.

"If you're so worried about your safety, perhaps you should hole up in the sanctuary permanently. Where you belong."

It was a low blow, but satisfaction still spread through me when her face drained of color. She stood stiffly, knocking into the table with her knees.

"I'm going to the bathroom. Be ready to leave when I get back."

I sent her a mock salute and sipped through my straw, watching as she walked ramrod straight, a sturdy soldier disappearing around the corner. Then I allowed myself a small sigh. Leave it to Chandra to turn a simple crossing into a pissing contest, I thought, whirling my stirring straw around in my drink. I didn't even need to be able to read her aura any longer. She practically spewed bile and malevolence whenever I walked into a room. Even now, I thought, sniffing, a thread of soured milk and citrus lingered, though only a trace amount trailed behind since she'd gotten up and left . . .

Since she left.

"Bitch!" I leaped from the couch, knocking over my empty glass, and grabbed my overnight bag as I chased after her. One of the waitresses twisted her ankle trying to lunge from my path, and another customer cursed as I barreled into his shoulder, but I wasted no time on apologies.

Clearing the front doors at full speed, I spotted the cab screeching from the lot, and as I yelled again, Chandra's smile was reflected in the rearview mirror, her left hand waving at me in a one-finger salute.

I quickly discarded the idea of running after her. I might be able to catch the cab if it got stuck in traffic, but I knew she wouldn't unlock the doors to let me in . . . and it might raise some mortal brows to see a buxom blond being dragged down the Strip on the back of a Star cab.

Fumbling for my keys, I unlocked Olivia's Porsche by remote and tossed my bag into the passenger seat. It was a beautiful car. It looked lovely cruising down the Boulevard at night, fluorescent and neon reflected in its tinted windows and off its silky body of silver paint. It whipped around corners like it was caressing them, and shot from zero to sixty in three-point-nine seconds.

But it wasn't until it hit 110 that it absolutely purred like a contented kitten.

I almost purred myself as I caught Chandra's taillights just ahead of me on the 95. It was only a couple miles more to the boneyard, and I was determined to get there first. I waved as I passed her, the surprise and fury on her face worth more to me than the car itself, and floored the gas pedal, using superhuman senses to dodge obstacles as expertly as a ten-year-old with an Xbox. I came to a stop alongside the boneyard's prison-style brick wall and climbed from the car. I didn't need to glance at the sky to know that dusk was splitting. I could smell the ozone ripping and air molecules disintegrating around me. Chandra's cab revved in the distance.

By the time she appeared like some vehicular demon, dusk's back door was wide open and I was standing in front of the wall where our crossing always took place, feet spread shoulder width apart, hands fisted on my hips, smile plastered firmly on my face.

Without reducing her speed, Chandra smiled back.

"Fuck!"

A mortal wouldn't have made it. Three steps and I dove to the side, the nose of the cab so close I could feel the bumper whizzing by my shin. The sound of the car slamming through—through, not into—the brick wall was mere background noise, the scream of twisting metal nothing but screeching musical notes as my backpack wrenched my shoulder, causing me to flail as I hit the ground. The loudest sound by far was the snap of my arm as the rest of my body landed squarely on top of it.

I yelled out in pain, curling into myself as dust and smoke billowed around me, obscuring the wreckage Chandra's crossing had wrought, myself included. If a mortal had happened to be standing there—a variable we normally checked for before barreling into the next reality—he'd have seen nothing more than a vehicle smashing into a wall. If he bothered to call the police or an ambulance, unlikely in this part of town, by the time help arrived there'd be nothing to see but a fine layer of dust over an empty lot. By then, dusk would be firmly on the side of night, the wall again whole and closed, and people would undoubtedly wonder what that person was smoking.

It was that thought—the passage of dusk, not smoking—that brought me struggling back to my feet. The pain in my arm was already subsiding, I could actually feel the muscles and tendons separating enough to allow the bones to knit back together, and I winced as I grabbed my bag with my good hand and staggered to the opening in the wall. The dust was already swirling and milky, a muddy congealment that would soon cement over, making it appear as before. I'd seen Warren walk behind the cab after it'd created an opening between the two realities, so I knew it could be done. Taking a deep breath, I dove through.

I should've paid closer attention to the timing. As I reached the place where the wall should and would be the densest, I choked on the thickening air. I tried moving faster through the muddy no-man's-land, fighting for another step, another breath, but the congealing concrete was sticking to me. It seeped through my lips and began lining the inside of my cheeks, inching its way backward and down my throat. I gasped, quickly abandoning that effort when it only encouraged the wet concrete farther into my throat.

I backpedaled, fighting for breath once I'd cleared the perimeter, wiping the concrete from my mouth with equally coated fingers. Back where I started I could only watch as the veil of the wall rose again, the last of the day's light saluting the valley in a sunless wink off the cyclone wire, before solidifying back into solid brick. The rest of the smoke dissipated, the grit settled, and I looked at the ground. Mine were the only footprints marring the dust. There were no tire marks from Chandra's homicidal attack, no broken bricks piled at my feet. By this time I had enough breath back to curse again, and did so freely since there was no one around to hear me.

There was a final ripple to come, similar to an earthquake, but without the sound, and only the walls surrounding the boneyard were affected by the shocks. As light played over the concrete, similar to the way heat shimmers off an asphalt road, the aftershock snaked along the wall counter-clockwise and disappeared around the first corner. It would eventually return to the point of origin where I stood, panting, pained . . . and thoroughly pissed.

Forgetting my surroundings, forgetting everything but that final triumphant look on Chandra's face, I lifted my conduit from my bag, and when the rippling appeared, traveling down that fourth and final wall, I fired into the shimmering oasis until the chamber was empty of arrows.

Childish, I know. It was wasteful and pointless, and I was already turning to leave, already thinking of how to spend the ensuing hours until dawn, when the rippling stuttered, then stopped short of the original mark. The passage incomplete. I could see through to the other side where rusted and toppled signage with burned-out bulbs and busted tubes of twisted wire littered the boneyard floor. I saw the old HACIENDA sign, and in the distance, like a beckoning mirage, the Silver Slipper.

Closer still, I saw the yellow cab.

Then the uppermost part of the wall began to harden, brick by brick, dropping lower to the ground, gaining in speed with each section. I dove, the weight of an entire wall crushed down on my ankles with the speed and density of a boulder falling from a cliff. Rolling, I came up on the other side missing a shoe, left leg scraped from mid-calf to ankle, but safely inside the boneyard.

It took a moment for that to sink in, then I laughed aloud, as I studied the newly constructed wall. My left shoe, lost during the dive to safety, was stuck, a permanent fixture with a large chunk of cement dried around it. My bag was half caught, half free, but the opening was on this side of the wall. Good thing, I thought, stooping to examine it, because if the clothing, comics, and mask inside were found next to the Porsche—found, more specifically, by a Shadow—my identity as Olivia Archer would be known by all. But they weren't, it wasn't, and I was safely inside. I gave another small hoot, and started pulling at the bag.

Some of the clothes were bound to the wall and had to be left, and one of the manuals was glued about three-fourths down the page, but I ripped what remained and tucked it under my arm with my disks and the rest of my belongings. After wiping the remaining grit from my mouth and ears and blowing my nose on my favorite tank, I couldn't help but laugh again. I was in the boneyard, right where I was supposed to be, if not exactly when. And feeling rather smug about the whole incident, I set out with one shoe . . . in search of Chandra.

9

When I'd first learned about my troop's super-hero hideout, a.k.a. the sanctuary, the only image I had to compare it to was the Batcave, a subterranean grotto filled with all the things a hero needed to become strong and super and invincible; unusual weapons and eccentric instructors and a diet that most likely consisted of Wheaties. I thought of a place of respite, a haven where agents could rejuvenate, train, and return refreshed to mortal reality, ready once again to face off against the Shadows.

And would you believe I was mostly right? See, that's the thing: most of the superhero stories are true, though when presented as fiction in a form most widely read by children, they're often dismissed as nothing more than some nerdy writer's fanciful imagination. And that's key. Skepticism is a far more effective deterrent to the determinedly curious than the best effort at concealing the truth. Nobody really thinks a man who dresses as an oversized bat is going to live beneath a mansion in a damp, high-tech cave.

And nobody thinks an entire troop of superheroes fighting to save Las Vegas from evils worse than Donald Trump's arrival actually bide beneath a glorified junkyard, their sanctuary accessed by the giant heel of a dilapidated silver slipper.

I intended to head straight to the fifteen-foot slipper, slide from the heel directly into the toe—and the chute leading to the sanctuary below—and take up with Chandra the issues I had with vehicular manslaughter. I wore a mask to shield my Shadow side from getting fried by the light when entering the sanctuary, and was already fixing this over my eyes when I heard the laughter. Dropping it and my battered belongings next to a giant letter G, I followed shouts of encouragement and genial chatter to the center of the boneyard. As I peered around a rusted star, my mouth dropped open.

There, where I'd last seen the carcasses of the original SANDS sign and a handful of truck-sized silver dollars, was a garden of stone walls. From my slightly higher vantage they created an intricate pattern, like one of those fabled English mazes made of tangled hedges and turf. This one, however, was made of concrete slabs, six feet high and about as long, with gaps of about a half a foot in between.

In front of this strange garden was the entire Zodiac troop, as well as a young girl I didn't know, and a half-dozen children sitting off to the side. On second glance, I saw Warren was missing, and so was Tekla, but Micah was there—which meant this was important enough to pull him from his precious lab—and so was Gregor, my errant cabdriver. Chandra was next to him. She'd replaced the murderous look on her face with one of perplexed innocence, shrugging as she explained something to Vanessa, our Leo of the Zodiac, and Felix, the Capricorn. They shot one another a questioning look, and my gut tightened in response. She was clearly talking about me. Saying I'd missed the crossing, perhaps, or that I hadn't shown up at all.

"Bitch," I muttered, and was about to step forward when Hunter strode into view, passing out an armful of guns.

"All right, guys. Warren wants this done before full dark, so let's get started. Losers exit the game immediately. If there's no winner declared tonight, the game will resume tomorrow."

"Why can't we finish it in the dark?" This question came from Riddick, a troop member almost as new as I. Built like a diver, all sinewy muscle packed tightly together, he came from a long line of accomplished Aquarians, and had taken up the sign after his aunt died of supernatural causes the previous fall. Eager to prove himself, he was a welcome member to the strengthening Zodiac.

The only less experienced member was the petite woman next to him. Jewell had unexpectedly inherited her star sign when her older sister was killed last winter after the sanctuary had been infiltrated by a mole. Jewell had lived her entire life within the confines of the sanctuary and believed she always would. Until her sister's death, she'd operated as a sort of glorified valet for her stronger sibling, and she still hadn't seemed to have reconciled herself to this new fate— that she was a heroine, expected to succeed where her sister had failed—but here she was all the same, the troop's new Gemini.

"Because the object isn't to stumble about until you happen to run into somebody, that's why," Hunter replied coolly, handing him a weapon. Riddick swallowed hard, his Adam's apple bobbing beneath his ginger goatee. "The idea is to make it to the center of the labyrinth without detection, or at least without being struck by anyone else."

"Yes, but why?" Micah asked, sounding like a petulant five-year-old. It was that question, however—perpetually asked—that made him such a damned good scientist. "What does a game have to do with battling Shadows?"

"The Tulpa, if you haven't noticed, is extremely fond of games, especially puzzles. Particularly those on a grand scale." Hunter replied, handing Micah a gun. "We've found blueprints of such a maze, and we think it may be located in his troop's hideout."

"And at the center of this labyrinth is . . . ?" Gregor trailed off, accepting his own weapon with his good arm. The new girl, beside him, took her gun from Hunter with a nod of her dark, bobbing curls.

"Some say that's where the Tulpa sleeps at night, where he gathers enough energy around himself to reanimate the following day. Others claim there's an object those seeking the Tulpa's destruction would covet, which we most certainly do."

"The original manual?" Felix asked, cocking his weapon with a loud snap.

Hunter shrugged in reply. "The only thing known for certain is the Tulpa holds this place, and whatever it contains dear to his nonexistent heart. No one has lain eyes on its core before, and if he's hiding it that thoroughly, you can be sure we want whatever's in there."

"Meanwhile, I'm assuming the maze is rather complex," Micah put in.

Hunter smiled coolly. "That's an understatement. And it is deadly to the player who enters, but does not exit, in less than twenty-four hours." Hunter motioned to two of the children, who'd apparently been waiting for his signal. Clamoring down from a giant genie's lamp, a boy of around eleven rushed to Hunter's side, followed by a girl. He handed them both a gun, and positioned them back-to-back. "Our version, however, won't be quite as fatal."

In a maneuver they'd obviously practiced for this demonstration, the two children counted off ten paces, and froze. Hunter snapped his fingers, and they pivoted, turning the weapons on one another. It was unclear what happened to the boy's shot. He'd obviously fired, but let out a startled yelp, eyes winging from his opponent to the gun in his hand. He took her shot, clean and true, directly in his midsection. Day-Glo green spread from his core like a poison, color seeping through every pore, up his neck, coloring his face all the way to the roots of his spiked hair like a baby Hulk.

The girl who'd won the contest began to point and laugh, as did the other children, hooting from the sidelines, and calling down from their perches atop the nearby signs. Green Boy held his arms out in front of him, studying his hands and palms, flipping them back and forth, before he looked to his friends and shot them a wide grin of blinding Day-Glo teeth.

"Okay, Landon. Elena," Hunter said, nodding to the children. "Show them how to exit the game."

Roaring, the boy dropped his weapon to the ground, bent his knees, and was suddenly arcing through the air, arms cycling wildly as he directed his descent to land directly in front of his victorious enemy. Once down, he growled again. Elena squealed, dropped her own gun, and bounded to the top of the Slipper in an impressively elegant leap, ducking for cover behind her ward mother's robes. I watched the horseplay and smiled. At least some things were normal around here.

"How long does that shit last?" Riddick asked, meaning the paint. The jump was something we all could do, and yeah, it came in handy.

"Twenty-four hours," Micah answered, confirming my suspicions as to the paint's origins.

Hunter crossed to the front of the concrete maze. "I'll sit out so we have an even number of players—"

"Chicken," Felix said, shooting him a boyish grin. Vanessa supplied the clucking sounds.

"Another piece of advice," Hunter said, ignoring them both. "And this direct from Tekla. Sight is actually the least valuable sense here, so use your hearing, your sense of smell for tracking, but most importantly, use your sixth sense. That's the only way to get out of this alive.

"As this is the first time running this, Warren wants to know operative times and where we all place, so remember the purpose of this exercise. There's a way to get to the center of this maze in seconds, without detection. The Tulpa knows it, and he's mastered it, which means you must as well."

I looked at Riddick and Jewell, and could practically see nervous energy rising off them in waves. Riddick's knuckles were white as they gripped the butt of his gun, and Jewell had hers pressed against her heart. They had yet to encounter even a Shadow agent, so the mention of the Tulpa had gained their full attention. Then again, I'd run headfirst into the Tulpa, and the memory still had me waking up in cold sweats.

"Now, the guns won't fire until I press this button, and in order to give you each time to spread out, I won't do that for sixty seconds from . . ." Here he looked at his watch. "Now."

They all stared at him.

Hunter stared back. "That means go."

They scattered, pushing into one another, scrambling in effort to be the first into the maze, and looking less like a troop of superheroes than a gang of unruly schoolyard kids.

"Bang! Bang, bang, bang!"

I whirled, heart in my throat, to find two sets of fingers pointed like guns and trained on my midsection. I lifted a brow.

Little Marcus raised his own six-year-old brow in response. "We got her, mother Rena!"

How embarrassing. Caught snooping by a couple of rugrats. Linus, the one who'd shot me with his index finger, waved me out from behind the busted star, and into the clearing where I could be seen by Hunter and Rena, the only adults left in the boneyard.

"Someone wants to talk to you," Linus said, maintaining his tough-guy stance, legs spread the way he'd seen the agents stand thousands of times before. "And she doesn't take no for an answer."

"Yeah," Marcus said, clearly not wishing to be left out. "So we can do this the easy way or the hard way. It's up to you." They looked up at me expectantly, and for a moment I saw twenty years into the future when these two would take up star signs and hunt Shadows. Then, keeping one hand trained on me, Linus reached down and yanked up his drooping pants.

My lips twitched. "Uh . . . the easy way, please."

"All right," Marcus said, like he was doing me a grave favor. "But take it slow, sister. Any sudden moves and we'll drop you like a used-up ho on the corner of Fifth and Bridger."

"Marcus!" Rena chided from her spot in the clearing. She was standing now, head tilted our way, though her eyes weren't trained on us. Probably because she didn't have any. "I heard that!"

"Shit," Marcus muttered.

"She probably heard that too," I said, grinning at him.

"Silence, prisoner!"

"Gentlemen," came another voice, this one as deep as they were imitating, and I reluctantly shifted to face Hunter. He nodded at me, then at the boys. My two guards trembled in their Keds. My knees were often weak in Hunter's presence too, though not usually from awe. "What do we have here?"

"An intruder, sir!" Linus answered, prodding me forward with his gun finger. I stumbled a bit, and snickering erupted behind me.

"I see," Hunter said, giving my disarrayed state a quick once-over. "And how did she get inside the compound unnoticed?"

"We don't know," Marcus admitted, but quickly put the troubling question behind him. "Should we kill her?"

Hunter did smile at that. "Not just yet."

"Thanks," I muttered, and heard Rena laugh from her perch on the Slipper. She might not be able to see, but her other senses were razor-sharp.

"Don't thank me yet," Hunter said, before turning back to my captors. "I propose we throw her into the game with our brave and noble agents, see how she fares against the finest of the Light. Hand her over to me now, and I'll make sure she receives due justice."

By giving them a choice, Hunter had made them co-conspirators in determining my fate, and the two boys looked at each other like they could hardly believe their luck. Besides, there was only so much more they could do. Their fingers weren't really loaded.

"Into the maze with her!"

"Yeah, let the agents of Light have their way with her!" And Marcus's face began to glow, literally, like a globe lit from within. Hunter and I turned away as rays of light began to shoot from his face. Once I was secured at Hunter's side, the boys went whooping and hollering back to Rena, who congratulated them on their catch and got Marcus to stop glowing like an oversized firefly so they could all settle in to watch the competition.

"Do I even dare ask what happened to you?" he said, plucking a chunk of cement from my hair.

I winced as it came free. "I'd rather you not."

"Chandra said you didn't make it over," he said, leading me to the playing field. I shot him an irritated glance, knowing he found my ongoing spat with her amusing.

"She was wrong," I said shortly. No way was I going to let him know I'd nearly gotten stranded at the Peppermill, run down by Gregor's cab, and trapped in a brick wall. So I waved at the block maze instead. "When did this get here?"

"The museum cleared the space to make room for some new signage. It hasn't arrived yet, so we thought we'd take the opportunity to run some outdoor drills."

Opportunity, I thought, inhaling deeply. I located Chandra easily. She was left of the center of the maze, deep in the thick of it. Pulling my conduit from my waistband, I headed that way.

"Hold on," Hunter said, and yanked my bow from my hand, replacing it with a bright plastic squirt gun. "No missiles more deadly than the paintballs."

"I wasn't really going to kill her. Just scare her."

"The look on your face alone should do it."

"Fine." I cocked a fist on my hip, trying to look tough despite the toy in my other hand. "Any other rules?"

"One. You have twenty seconds." He pumped a cartridge into another gun's chamber, and his eyes narrowed meaningfully on mine. "Then I'm coming after you myself."

Linus and Marcus began to yell enthusiastically from the side. No questioning who their favorite superhero was.

"You said you were sitting out," I said, shooting them a nasty look.

"That was to keep the numbers even." He flashed me that feral grin. "With the two of us they're still even."

"But the rest of them have had an entire minute to spread throughout the labyrinth."

"And you have the element of surprise on your side."

"That's not fair."

"Nineteen, eighteen . . ."

"Asshole." I yanked off my other shoe and entered the maze on the run. And as I pulled back the safety on my gun, I momentarily forgot Joaquin and Regan and my evil, murderous father. It'd almost be worth getting run down by Chandra . . . if I could run her down in the end.

My heart was slamming against my ribs by the time I'd counted off the final fifteen seconds, and I knew if I didn't settle my nerves soon Hunter would scent me out before I'd gone another twenty paces. I slammed into a dead end and was forced to turn around, which made me think I could double back and surprise him, though he might anticipate that. No, I wanted my shot at Chandra before taking on the troop's weapons master . . . and before anyone else could get to her.

Of course, I tended to be a little single-minded when it came to vengeance, and Hunter might anticipate this as well, enabling him to plow through the rest of the unsuspecting players like a bull through Pamplona. But that, I thought, smiling to myself, could be to my advantage. Find a hidey-hole and simply let Hunter clear the way.

I squinted through a slat between two of the erected walls. No wonder Hunter had said not to rely on sight. Every so often a player could be spotted fleeing two or three rows away, but you had to stop moving entirely to see it, and still

had to reach them once you did. Besides, the slats were too
thin to point the gun nozzles through, so shooting between
them was also out, though I was willing to bet little Jasmine
could have squeezed through them in Gumby-girl mode. All
I could do was be alert. And creative. I thought about climbing over the walls, but then I'd be a target from all sides. I
didn't want to leave here green.

I glanced at the sky and hitched my gun higher. Full dark
was another fifteen minutes away, give or take. So how did
the Tulpa manage to get to the center of the maze in mere
seconds? Could I be lucky enough that the ability was hereditary? Because that would be the way to do it. Get to
the center, win the game first, and battle my way out from
within.

Right now I just had to concentrate on avoiding Hunter,
and so I moved quickly, silently, and took calculated risks in
charging around corners. Finally I scented a mild thread of
warming honey on burned toast. Keeping low, I turned the
next corner . . . and nearly bumped into Jewell.

"Wha . . . where—?" She was green before she could finish the sentence.

"Sorry," I said. The whites of her eyes tinted over as she
rolled them. A second later she shot upward and out of the
maze. One down, eight more to go.

There was a grunt, then an outraged howl from my left,
approximately three feet away, and Felix jumped into the
air, though it was more instinctive than any sort of attempt
to leave the maze. I used the intervening seconds to whip
around two corners in quick succession, and ducked into a
pocket of darkness that had already bloomed with the night.
A second later Micah yelped in surprise, and turned to glare
at me. Felix sauntered around the corner as I straightened,
and gave me a grin as green as the grass in springtime.

"How's it feel to get a dose of your own medicine, you
green fuck?" Felix said, giving Micah a semiplayful shove.
Micah shoved back, and they both vaulted into the air, Felix
calling out behind him, "Good job, Olivia!"

"Thanks a lot," I muttered as cries of "Olivia?" and "Olivia's here?" went up around the maze. So much for the element of surprise. Refocusing, I settled my energy back into myself and stepped forward, not a second too soon. A paintball splatted right where my head had been. I rolled and dodged two more pellets in quick succession, then aimed without sighting, and fired behind me. Hunter lunged back into hiding, and I squeezed off another shot before fleeing around the corner.

I needed distance. Hunter was right on top of me, but I might be able to lose him if I made a few right choices . . . and if I got lucky. Sucking in a deep breath through my nose, I again tried to relax. I was about to let the air out through my mouth when I had a thought. Holding the thought—one of Hunter—and breath in my mouth, I turned to the wall I was pressed against and pushed the air out through the slats, sending my pheromones, my nervous energy, and my thoughts of him out with it. I pressed my eye against the slat, and within seconds saw a figure skulking through the shadows. Smiling, I headed in the opposite direction, deeper into the yawning maze. Closer to Chandra.

Three more times I blew through the slats, and three more times I sent agents on meandering chases. I doubled back twice to make little green men out of Gregor and Riddick. Vanessa got away, though a half minute later I heard her cry out, and up she went, a green blur of cursing fury. Quickly, silently, I counted the players who'd exited the game. Seven. And none of them Hunter, I thought, setting my teeth, which meant he was still somewhere behind me . . . and only Chandra remained ahead.

I was getting closer to the core of the maze. The zigzagging paths were getting shorter, even the dead ends. I still got stuck; for every corner I turned I had to navigate two dead ends, and I finally gave up trying to retain even a remote sense of direction and just concentrated on moving quickly. I stumbled, falling to my hands, and though I barely made a sound, it sounded like a cannonball to my ears. Picking up a rock, I catapulted it over the nearest wall, into the next row, where it clattered loudly, hoping that'd alleviate some of the damage.

And then my diligence was rewarded.

She'd been heading my way, and pulled up as the sight of my gun landed between her eyes. "Next time you try to run someone over," I said, backing her up, "check the rearview mirror to make sure they're down for good."

I motioned with my head for her to throw her own weapon down. She did, and it clattered harmlessly to the ground. "Go to hell."

"You'll go first, and you'll go green."

"Just get it over with, Malibu Barbie."

But I backed away instead. She frowned, watching me with mistrust. "It wasn't really fair that you didn't know I was here, so I'll give you another chance to get as far away as possible. On my count. One . . ."

She didn't have to be asked twice. She readied herself to run.

"Two," I said. Knees bent, she rocked on her tiptoes, waiting for my final count. I shot her. Then I smiled. "Three."

"Bitch," she spat, and green-tinted saliva landed on my bare foot. It refreshed the image of a cab hurtling toward me, so I shot her again, not just twice, but four times, nailing her the last time on the fly as she vaulted into the air just to get away from me. She wobbled mid-air, and I smiled as she disappeared.

The smile dropped as a muzzle settled cool and firm on the back of my neck. "Should have saved one of those for me."

Oops. At this range I'd be green for a week. I shifted, knowing I'd been bested, but still wondered how much distance I could get between myself and the gun if I took off now.

"Uh-uh," Hunter said, grasping my shoulder with his free hand. "Throw your weapon down, and make sure it's out of reach."

My gun skittered away and was quickly eaten by the shadows creeping up from the dirt floor. It was almost full dark now. Outside, the voices of the disqualified players rose and fell in muted chatter, but we were deep in the labyrinth, well out of their sight line. Hunter turned me into him and backed me against the wall, so I was pressed against the cool concrete on one side and the hot warmth of his body on the other. He paused to look me over.

"Better hurry. A few more seconds and you'll have to call game." I tried to breathe easily, trying not to reveal fear or intimidation, trying especially not to reveal that it came from the nearness of his body and not the gun pointed loosely at my side. *I am not afraid,* I repeated over and over in my mind, but it was a lie. I was trembling in my Wonderbra.

"Well that's the thing about being the one to make the rules," Hunter said, his voice low and filled with something that alarmed me even more. "You get to break them any time you want."

Even with night settling around us, this close to mine his face was clearly defined. His brown eyes pooled with depth, his black hair was slick with shadows, and his breath was like the stream blowing in off the gulf. Desire usually smelled earthy, but Hunter's was dense, musky with heat. He smelled dangerous . . . and I liked my men dangerous.

"Break the rules?" I asked, meeting his gaze directly. "Or change them to meet your needs?"

"Same difference." His eyes traveled down to my lips, then back again.

My eyes did the same. "You're complicating things."

His brows quirked philosophically. "Life tends to be complicated."

"So we should just consider this a training exercise, then?" I asked, swallowing hard. "For life, I mean?"

He hummed in the back of his throat, inching closer. "Not all life lessons are unpleasant."

I leaned into him, my eyes fluttering shut. Even humans

reacted to pheromones, though they were unaware of it, but when you could *smell* them—really scent every molecule and particle making up a particular chemical compound—well, it was like walking into a hothouse on a blustery winter day. It flooded the senses . . . and made you want to undress. Blood raced to places in my body that weren't supposed to have a pulse. I groaned, releasing my own pheromones into the air, and pushed his weapon aside so nothing lay between us.

Hunter closed the gap with his body.

We'd kissed once before. I'd possessed the aureole that first time, and in order to keep him safe I'd passed it along to him, exhaling the power of temporary immortality into his mouth, a chaste kiss turned torrid as his body responded to it, to me, even while unconscious. Unfortunately a bit of my soul or essence or *something* had been passed into Hunter as well—and we now knew things about each other no other person alive knew. He had lost his parents to the Shadows, I my sister. He had a child he'd die to protect; I had one I didn't even acknowledge. I blamed our sense of shared intimacy on this bartered knowledge, just as I blamed this moment on the circumstances, telling myself that any woman would have to be dead not to feel a modicum of sexual attraction to a six-foot-three, rock-hard superhero. And while that first kiss had been a gift given out of duty rather than passion, it wasn't until now that I realized I'd stored the taste of him inside me.

It was shocking to find a gentle, restful place on his warrior's body, and I slipped my tongue along the edges of his lips—only a quick taste, I thought—just to experience the vitality behind all that softness. His immediate response flooded me, my brain numbing as his lips pressed against mine so that I was unable to process scent and taste, thought and reason, longing and touch, all at the same time. That kiss was like swollen storm clouds ready to erupt, and when he moaned into my mouth it was dewy and thunderous and zinging with ozone.

"What the hell is going on in there?"

We broke the kiss, both of us pulling back at the same time, and I blinked hard to get my bearings, to stop my head from spinning and my heart from slamming in my breast. Hunter called time, his voice so hoarse and deep it could set off car alarms, and I glanced up to find that not only had it grown full dark, but the sky above the maze was roiling with cloud cover. The haze was thick and low like an orchard of vaporous hanging fruit, laced in mist, sweet and ripe in the moist heat. I swallowed hard.

So this was what happened when two superheroes made things complicated.

And goddammit, it was too much. I felt like I'd just gorged on something rich and fine, and now—even after only a swift taste—I felt weighed down, like I was buried beneath boulders. Being this open and vulnerable felt like I was digging my own grave. I didn't want any more pain squeezing at my heart. I'd had enough for one lifetime.

And that was what truly made Hunter dangerous, I thought, wiping a hand across my mouth. He made me forget he could hurt me.

I shifted my gaze, breath shaky, to find him regarding me just as warily. I cursed inwardly as his powerful aura snapped white and gold sparks around him, like he was a sparkler on the Fourth of July, and I was the darkness. It reminded me of the differences between us; male to female, his pure, unadulterated Light to my half Shadow, but instead of that complementing me, it made me feel bereft and lacking. But then I glanced at his lips again before I could stop myself. They were parted and still moist from my kiss.

Stop it, Jo, I told myself, slamming down the mental shields that would keep my secrets even from myself. And so I did.

The gun was lolling in his fingers, and I moved swiftly, firing downward so the pellet struck somewhere in the buttocks, or perhaps the thigh. He jolted, grinding closer, making me immediately wish I'd chosen another tactic, and remaining too close, he didn't release me. And he didn't turn green because he'd already called time. In fact, he didn't turn anything but mad.

"You set me up," I said as his eyes flashed betrayal. "You sent me in here knowing the others would either take each other out or be too surprised to see me to react. You followed because you wanted this."

I ignored the fact that I'd wanted it, too. Because of our once-shared power he knew I hungered for him, and that one kiss was enough to leave me raw and aching and vulnerable. So I refused to feel guilty under the weight of that steady stare. He'd made this happen, even knowing there was a place inside me he couldn't touch, a bruised spot already occupied and fiercely guarded where Ben lived, and always would. That wouldn't change just because Hunter lured me into straying mazes, made storm clouds roil above my head . . . and caused my heart to pound like the thunder fueling it all.

"You're treacherous," Hunter whispered, giving me the space I wanted, the jaw I'd just been caressing clenched hard in the dying light.

"You're an opportunist," I replied, letting Ben's image fuel my indignation.

Hunter shook his head and gave a mirthless laugh as he turned away. "I'm just a man," he said, and the soft vulnerability shocked me into silence. I swallowed down the lump that'd suddenly grown in my throat, and resumed breathing as I watched him leave, thunder rumbling along the already thinning clouds above. Once alone, I slumped against the wall, and let the cool concrete seep into my skin. I remained there until the sky was again arching and wide, spread out above me like a blank slate. Then I went to join the others like nothing had happened. As if I was fine.

As if storm clouds and superheroes weren't complicated, treacherous, tempting things.

10

"What, in this particular Universe, were you thinking?"

I'd been back in the sanctuary just long enough to take a shower before my reaming began. Warren stood before me in the astrolab, a dome-shaped room with a ceiling of stars, though right now the bright lights were whitewashing the galaxy into oblivion. The room was scattered with books and papers and maps, pencils, rulers, scales . . . all more mathematical than mystical. This was Tekla's office, where she mapped out her natal charts and made her predications. Currently, though, she was observing Warren and me from a stool in the corner like a bird on a perch, and damned if she wasn't the most watchful, calculating creature I knew.

If she *were* avian, though, she wouldn't have been a bird of prey. No, she was small and brown, like a malnourished sparrow; and though she'd lost some of the gauntness she'd possessed when I'd first met her months before, she was still sharp-featured, with lines of perpetual worry and fatigue webbing her eyes. The others assured me she'd always looked this way; that her son's death last year had only accented what was already there. The lines were a product of knowing too much of fate's design . . . and being able to do too little about it.

I looked to Tekla for help, but it was clear we weren't going to have any sisterhood moments right now. Her eyes were trained on me just as narrowly as our leader's, and I swallowed hard as I looked down and picked some dried cement out from under my fingernails.

Okay, so it'd been stupid. My shoe was stuck in the boneyard's perimeter, and while that could be taken for a mason's mistake—if you didn't look too closely—the backpack that'd half made it into the boneyard with me was clearly made of material, zippers, leather, and lacing. Apparently bits of it were showing on the outside of the boneyard wall as well, but the bigger problem was that its presence there had kept the barrier separating the sanctuary from the rest of the world from fully closing. Oops.

"I'm sorry," I said again, but I was having trouble keeping the contriteness in my voice by this point. Warren heard it, which only furthered his tirade.

". . . and to use a conduit of Light to purposely destroy a wall meant to protect your troop from the Shadow's harm is not only irresponsible, but borders on the treasonous!"

"The barrier's not destroyed," Tekla said from her corner stool.

Now he whirled on her. "It's compromised!"

"I was angry!" I said in my defense. "I just saw the cab through the dust and took aim. Besides, *you* cross over on foot all the time."

"I follow the route set by Gregor. And I make sure the barrier's closed behind me!"

"Enough." Tekla stood and began walking toward me. I automatically shrank back. It wasn't that I didn't like her; I did. She was the troop's Seer, and a bit off because of it, but she was powerful. So much so that her deep lavender aura was visible to me even with my diminished abilities. If I stared at her too long, her outline burned beneath my lids every time I blinked. I held my breath now, anticipating the worst. "I'll work with the Archer on rebuilding the breach—agents should know how to repair walls if they're going to tear them down." I swallowed hard at the censure in her tone, looking away. "And then we'll work on controlling her temper."

My gaze swung back to her suspiciously.

Warren screwed up his face, just as perplexed. "That's it?"

Tekla tilted her head at him. "It's timely, don't you think? There's the maze in the boneyard representing the Tulpa's labyrinth. And other walls that need to be constructed and deconstructed at will . . ."

Warren's expression immediately cleared, and he smiled as he looked back at me. "The barrier . . . among other things."

"Hey, I enjoy cryptic banter as much as the next girl," I said with mock cheerfulness before letting my face fall. "But someone wanna clue me in here?"

Tekla turned her sharp gaze on me again. "You're going to remain within the sanctuary until we're sure you can't be goaded into jeopardizing our troop's security."

"I haven't—" I was about to say I hadn't jeopardized anything, but I had. Never mind the wall . . . I'd let a Shadow initiate live in hopes she'd feed me more information about Joaquin's whereabouts. I'd then met him in neutral territory the next day. Wait until Warren and Tekla found out about *that*.

"I haven't hurt anyone," I said instead, which was true. It just happened to include Regan, a mortal enemy. So I changed the subject. "And what about Chandra? She tried to tattoo skid marks on my chest."

"Which you'd have recovered from." Warren blew the issue off, and waved away my gaping protest. "Chandra's going to be a different color than the rest of the human race thanks to your hijinks in the practice maze. I think that makes you two even."

Sure, because a two-ton vehicle and a paintball were sooooo similar.

Warren read my thoughts and smiled thinly. "But what

Tekla's saying is this: the second sign of the Zodiac says that Shadow and Light will square off on a cursed battlefield. In the Zodiac mythology *battlefield* is often equated with *playing field*."

"Yeah, 'cuz war's just so much fun."

Warren ignored me. "The maze out front is a mockup of the Tulpa's labyrinth based on blueprints seized at Valhalla. We need someone to learn how to get to the center of that maze in record time, and this is the perfect time to train for it. The paranormal world is quiet, the Shadows have been in hiding since your accession—"

I snorted before I could help myself.

Warren froze. "What?"

I bit my lip, trying to keep my face straight. "Well, you don't really think they're in hiding, do you? Quivering in their shadowy little lair?"

"You know differently?" he asked shortly.

"No," I said, because I didn't. Not for sure. But Regan had hinted at some evil plan, so I did too. It eased my conscience a bit at having let her live. "But I doubt they've just given up wreaking chaos and destruction in favor of another hobby."

"Oh, but they have. At least for the time being. It's clear the Tulpa wants you to switch sides, so he's pulled back, probably hoping to lull you into thinking he's not all that bad, that they're just like us." He rolled his eyes, and Regan's words again skittered through my mind. *You think we're wired differently than you,* but it's not true . . . we're like you. Oblivious to my thoughts, Warren shot me a stubbled grin. "As long as the Zodiac is balanced—twelve of them, twelve of us—then there's peace in the mortal world. That's all I care about."

It was true; Warren wasn't one of those, myself included, who thought the best way to save humanity was to annihilate the Shadow side. No, he believed the entire Universe was one giant scale that needed to be kept in balance, that even he was just ballast to be positioned at a fixed place and time to keep his troop, his valley, and his mortals safe.

I gave up trying to argue with him on that point. "So an entire troop of habituated bad guys is going to stop causing mayhem and pain just because one dude wants to win me over?"

"Yes."

"Well, I don't think so." I muttered, shaking my head as he dropped into a swivel chair next to Tekla's desk. "It feels like the calm before the storm to me. It feels like they're coming after us."

"And you have so much experience in these things, do you?" He leaned back, lacing his fingers behind his neck.

Now my voice was hard and loud. "Hey, I may be relatively new to this game of paranormal hide-and-seek, but I've spent my entire adulthood on the offense against danger and attack, and my gut is telling me something's going to happen, and that we won't know what it is until it's too late."

Warren gave his head a sharp jerk, causing his lank hair to sway against his shoulders. "It doesn't work that way, Olivia. As long as our numbers are equal, there's cosmic balance in the city. There's no way they can attack us directly. We're too strong."

I had to admit it seemed far-fetched, even with Regan's warning. How could they wipe us all out in one fell swoop? They had no leverage. We were stronger than we'd been in years.

Tekla, who'd returned to her perch and had been observing all this with a sort of detached scrutiny, cleared her throat. "Perhaps Olivia's objections have more to do with a personal desire than any intuitive hunch."

I stiffened, and the room got very still, very quiet. "I don't know what you're talking about."

"I'm talking about Xavier. The Tulpa. Joaquin." Her smile didn't reach her eyes. "You're saying we should destroy them before they have a chance to do the same to us, but what else do you want? Vengeance perhaps? We'd understand if you did."

My jaw clenched involuntarily, and I forced it to relax before whispering. "No. You wouldn't understand."

She tilted her head to the side, still birdlike. Still watchful. "I too have lost someone dear to me. And at the hands of the Shadow Aquarian."

Yes, I wanted to say, but after Joaquin murdered your son you'd been safely cocooned in this sanctuary. I'd had to go it alone in a world of Xaviers and Joaquins and Tulpas.

"Are we done here?" I asked Warren, heading to the door before he could answer. I didn't look at Tekla at all.

"Olivia. Olivia!" His voice followed me out and into the hallway, and I heard the uneven gait of his limp, a pronounced slap-and-drag, as he ran to catch up to me. "Jo."

My real name stopped me. I turned to face him in the sterile hallway, my face as blank as the concrete walls. "Why?" I asked him harshly. "Why wait for the Shadows to strike first? Why not head them off?"

Warren suddenly looked as tired as he did grave. "I want peace."

"And I want them all dead." The words shot from my mouth, and I looked away before Warren could see how much I truly meant them.

He ran a hand over his face and sighed. "If you just trust me, and wait, I swear you'll have your revenge. Xavier's a mortal, and your hatred of him is petty, and must be let go. But," he said, before I could protest, "the Tulpa will pay. Joaquin *will pay.*"

I searched his lined and sunburned face, and inhaled deeply to be sure he was telling the truth. I'd have taken him at his word months before, but Joaquin's words had wormed their way into my brain, and now I had to wonder.

He lies to you. He doesn't want you to know the extent of your powers. He thinks you'll turn on him.

And I looked at him then, really looked at him; seeing past the lank and greasy hair, the face that was usually grime-streaked and the body normally draped in a beggar's clothes, and I saw the man who led this city's fight against evil, one who'd tricked me into this lifestyle because it suited his troop's needs, but who'd also held my hand in those early days, saved my life, and told me about my fucked-up parentage.

Including the fact that my mother was still alive.

But he asked too much, I thought, turning away from him so he couldn't see the tears stinging my eyes. I'd joined his troop, learned the truth about my mother, and took up the star sign she'd abandoned in order to keep me safe. I'd accepted that she didn't want to be found, and agreed not to look for her. For now. I'd given up a life that may not have been perfect, but it'd been mine. I was dead to all those who'd known or ever loved me, and the things I loved, like photography, were dead to me.

I'd even stayed away from Ben.

And even if Warren was right about the Tulpa—and he'd really stopped targeting the agents of Light because of me—he was dead wrong about Xavier. He hadn't seen the way the man had treated me, or the rampage he'd gone on after my mother had left. Warren didn't know about the piles of clothes he'd burned, the jewelry he'd given to the maids, or the pictures he'd made Olivia and me cut up while he watched.

And he'd especially watched me.

Because even though Xavier knew nothing of superheroes, portals, and paranormal battles, the timing of my mother's disappearance hadn't been lost upon him. His eyes burned hard and hot into mine as he slammed album after album down in front of me, studying my reaction like I might know where she'd gotten to. Like it was my fault she'd gone.

"Not like that, Joanna!" he said, wrenching the scissors from my hand so the photo I was halfheartedly holding fluttered to the ground. "If you want people to respect you, and not walk all over you"—because, of course, the rape had been my fault as well—"you have to destroy them utterly! You have to obliterate them from this earth. Like this." And he cut and cut until my mother's face lay like confetti at our feet.

Joaquin had nearly killed me just because I was Zoe Archer's daughter.

Xavier had made me feel guilty because of it.

And the Tulpa had been behind it all.

So they'd all pay, I thought, smiling in spite of myself. With their lives, their money, their power. With whatever they valued most.

"Okay," I finally lied, turning back in time to see the relief flooding Warren's face. "Tell Tekla I'll start tomorrow."

He nodded, satisfied with that, and turned from me to limp away. I watched him disappear back into the astrolab, and waited until the door shut behind him. I'd stay in the sanctuary and train like he wanted, but I'd do it for my own reasons. I needed to be stronger and smarter from now on, so I'd push myself, study my lineage and the legacy of the Kairos, and I'd learn what I needed to from Tekla. So that soon, very soon, I could go after Joaquin myself.

The smart thing would be to retire to my room for the rest of the evening. It would give me a chance to calm down, give Hunter time for a cold shower, and nullify the possibility of running into Chandra . . . which was the last thing I needed right now.

Naturally I did no such thing.

Instead I slipped along a corridor where a red neon stripe skated along the floor, lighting my way, marking my forward progress while simultaneously dimming behind me. I ran my hand against the wall, letting symbols for horoscopic glyphs, planets, polarities, and the four elements appear and disappear beneath my touch. With the floor glowing beneath me like I was starring in some old Michael Jackson video, I halted in front of a solid concrete wall, flicked my wrist, and the wall folded back to reveal a gilt-glass elevator. When something sleek rubbed against my left calf, I jumped and looked down to find a tawny feline glaring up at me, poised on her back haunches, eyes locked on mine.

"Come on, then," I said, and the furry little warden followed me in before the doors whisked shut behind us.

I glanced down at the cat once the elevator started its descent. She was sitting primly, facing forward like me, her tail curled tightly about her, as self-contained as if she were alone in the steel box. "You don't think I'm acting like a rogue agent, do you?" I asked her, because of course that's what had been left unsaid in the astrolab. It's what Tekla meant when she claimed I was jeopardizing the troop, why she'd insisted I stay in the sanctuary. It was the reason neither of them wanted me out there on my own. They hadn't needed to say it in order for me to feel it. The possibility was as real to them as my joining the Shadow side, and they were constantly on guard against both.

Thing was—and I'd never say this aloud—I wasn't entirely unsympathetic toward the plight of the independents. Most, I'd discovered, were simply agents displaced by unrest and unbalance in their own cities. Well, I certainly knew what that was like. And often they were all that was left of a troop decimated by the opposing side. I mean, what were you supposed to do—where were you to go?—when life as you knew it no longer existed? When the family you'd been raised with had been targeted and murdered, one by one? I knew what that was like as well.

So it didn't seem fair to me that every independent was labeled a rogue and forced to retreat to towns or suburbs too small to warrant concentrated attention. Not only was that mind-numbing for a cast-out urban dweller, but to take on and survive enough opposing rogue signs to make a name for oneself? Those were odds even the most hardened Vegas bookie wouldn't touch. Gathering enough allies to build another troop? Near impossible. Most small towns didn't have enough of a human population to warrant one. And though it was possible for independents to join a city's already established troop, it was rare. Most Zodiac signs had been ancestrally filled for generations, and the battle to keep the signs within a given family's lineage was fierce.

Warren, I thought wryly, would know that better than most.

My feline companion and I stepped out into a passageway facing a set of smoked-glass doors. I held one open, let the cat saunter in ahead of me, and followed her into a dimly lit room that arched around us like a steel womb.

And it *was* a womb of sorts. Cavernous throughout the middle, with an echoing concrete floor, the high ceiling looked to be drawn upward to a single prick of light, a bright star holding together the sides of the room. Though the walls curved elegantly into a 360-degree circle, length after length of paneled sheets gave the illusion of an octagonal shape. There were twelve emblems, two per sheet, and each individual panel represented one of the twelve zodiac signs. Grouped in pairs as they were, they looked like they were eyeing the entrance I'd just come through with great suspicion.

There was also another pair of eyes trained upon me, but these held surprise rather than mistrust, and—if I wasn't mistaken—a healthy dose of awe.

"Hello," I said to the young woman I'd seen earlier in the boneyard, feeling free to regard her with as much curiosity as she was showing me. She was petite, at least five inches shorter than I was, and slim-boned, though that meant nothing in the world of supermechanics. Pretty in the way of Victorian debutantes and romance heroines, she had a head of cascading mahogany curls Botticelli would kill to paint, and guileless eyes that sparkled with hope . . . a handy trait for a hunter of conniving, vicious, and deadly supernatural beings.

"You're the Archer," she said, the awe seeping into her voice.

"And you're . . ." I couldn't think of a polite way to say it. "Very green."

She grimaced, revealing green gums. "Micah says it'll wear off sometime tomorrow. It's kind of embarrassing, but at least I'm not alone. Marlo," she said, and held out a hand.

"Who tagged you, Marlo?" I asked, the question echoing through the room as we shook hands.

"Vanessa."

"She's a good shot," I said sympathetically.

"I was just lucky to be included. Initiates aren't usually invited to train with the troop, but Tekla prophesied dangerous trials ahead for me, so Warren said it was okay to start my advanced training early."

I wouldn't have sounded so joyous about grave tribulations in my future, and told Marlo as much.

"Oh, but it's an honor," she said, wide eyes going even wider. "Tekla usually only forecasts the fates of full-fledged star signs. All the initiates she's ever cast for—Hunter and Zoltan and Mace and Stryker—have gone on to do great things. I'm the youngest yet."

Hunter was certainly accomplished, but Zoltan and Mace were before my time so I didn't know anything about them. Stryker, though, had been ambushed and murdered in the process of metamorphosis—no longer an initiate, but not yet a star sign—and I wondered if she'd thought of that.

Instead of mentioning the dubious honor of being aligned in fate with Stryker, I changed the subject. "So you must be the Libran initiate, am I right?"

Marlo nodded enthusiastically. She was only a couple of years younger than I, but her sheer excitement made her look much more so. "I've been training for a few weeks now. Hunter says I'm making great strides. He's already designing a weapon he says will play on all my strengths."

I raised a brow. You didn't need super senses to tell she'd already developed a super-sized crush on our weapons master. She'd probably grown up idolizing all the older troop members, I told myself. Plus she and Hunter had both been born and raised in the Zodiac. They might make a good match in the future, probably a great one. Libra and Aries were opposites on the Zodiac wheel.

So why was jealousy shooting through my blood like warmed quicksilver?

"That's great," I told Marlo, and quickly crossed to the panel with an outlined rendering of a centaur on it. It glowed, reassuringly bright, and the tension drained from me as I looked up at it. As I glanced around at the eleven other emblems circling the room, most lit like mine, satisfaction coursed through me. Most of these signs had been dark when I'd first come to the sanctuary, dead like Stryker's. The troop had been systematically "depleted" by the Shadows . . . Zane's fancy way of saying murdered. But we were back up to ten members now: the Libran sign waiting for Marlo to mature enough to undergo metamorphosis, and for Tekla to either take up the Scorpio sign or pass it on. So far she'd refused to do either, and Warren seemed content to let her contribute solely from within the sanctuary.

I pressed the button next to the slats just below my sign, and spoke my password clearly and directly into the opening. Nothing happened.

"Wha—?" I slapped my palm against the metal panel, and cursed. "Not again."

Repeating my password met with the same results. I sighed. The panel, actually a door, and the words, really a combination, were the only thing between me and the panel's contents. Sometimes I hid things in there, and every once in a while I opened it to find a gift—some small trinket like a photo or article of clothing—though nobody could explain how or when it'd gotten there.

More often than not, however—especially lately—this happened. Which meant it now contained some important object, one that would eventually be helpful to my fight in the Shadows, if only I could get to it.

I went ahead and pushed the disks I'd carried with me through the slats, waiting to hear them thunk to the ground on the other side. I was met with only silence. "What kind of superhero can't get into their own locker?" I muttered blackly, jiggling the latch below.

"Try giving it an offering."

I turned to Marlo, who was busy spoiling the cat splayed on a stamped concrete star. She'd kept her distance, but was watching me carefully. "Sorry?"

"An offering," she said, standing, wiping cat fur off her black trousers. "They can be testy sometimes. You might have to bribe it."

"I've already put something in there."

"Yes, but that was probably to keep it safe, right?"

"That's what a locker's for."

She shook her head. "You need to give it something that's the opposite of safe. These things are tools. You must be approaching a growth spurt in your education. Feed it something it can use to assist you in the future, and it'll trade you whatever's inside for that info."

I'd have to go back down to the barracks and find something there. "I don't have anything."

"Here," she said, turning away. "Try this."

I watched her stride over to the Libran locker, and cocked my head. "You have a locker already?"

"Yeah . . . sort of. Well, no. It doesn't really lock yet, or recognize my imprint, or respond to my voice . . ." She ducked her head like she was afraid I'd laugh, but I didn't. I knew just how she felt. She pulled out a pad of paper and a pen from a duffel bag at the foot of her locker, and handed them to me. "So, anyway. Just write something about yourself and stick it in there, but make sure it's something you wouldn't want anyone else to know. Maybe a secret hope or desire. Something worthy of trade."

"Worthy of trade," I repeated, looking at the pad she'd pressed into my hand.

Her head bobbed rapidly. "Whatever's in there is important enough that you have to work for it. The harder it is for you to access, the more useful it'll be to you later."

"Then why make it so hard to get?" I muttered.

"Because that's how life works," she said, shrugging it off in a way that made her appear even younger. "The most vital object lessons are the only ones worth striving for."

I narrowed my eyes at her. "You've been talking with Tekla, haven't you?"

"Just try it," she said with a shy smile. When I didn't move, she started. "Oh . . . right. Uh, let me know how it goes."

"I will. Thanks." I waited until she'd gone and then glanced at the cat. It returned my look before lifting a leg to clean itself.

Turning back to my locker, I slapped the pad against my thigh. "Something worthy of trade."

Well, there was the way I'd broken into the boneyard, but Warren already knew about that, or my run-in with Regan, but I wasn't about to admit that to *anybody* just yet. I thought of the jealousy that'd rushed through me when Marlo spoke of Hunter. Hm. That was certainly nothing I'd ever admit; it'd be mortally embarrassing if either of them knew. Was mortal embarrassment enough?

I wrote the admission down, folded the paper, and slipped it between the slats of the locker. Nothing happened. So I wrote another note—*Fuck you*—and slipped it through as well. A second later it was spit back out.

"Just testing," I said. I kept thinking. Something I wouldn't want anyone else to know. Well, that was easy. All my secret thoughts revolved around Ben Traina. How I didn't want anyone to know how much he still occupied my waking hours. How my body warmed at the thought of him. How I'd broken into Warren's cabinet in the record room and reviewed the file I knew he'd keep on Ben because of his past association with me.

I smiled bitterly at that last thought. Warren kept tabs on every aspect of his agents' lives, easy since he watched most grow up in the sanctuary, and assigned them their identities once they began working on the outside. But then there was me. He was still puzzling out my past piece by piece, slow going since he didn't trust my account not to be influenced by emotion, or some other agenda he didn't name. And digging into my past meant digging into Ben's.

After the attack on me, after Ben decided he was at fault for being unable to stop it, he responded by marrying someone safe—someone who wouldn't sneak across the desert on moonlit nights—then blamed her for not being me. Warren's notes indicated he'd been repeating his childhood, treating his new wife as his father had treated his mother, though I could've told him that.

I remember thinking I'd have argued with Ben as I studied those files. But the six-year-old records Warren had filched from a mortal shrink's office indicated that this other woman hadn't. *I don't handle breakable women with care*, Ben had told the doctor . . . and there was a postscript that showed the psychiatrist believed him enough to be worried for the woman's safety.

So Ben gave his sweet, breakable wife a divorce—even though she said she didn't want it—and also gave her half of what he owned at the time. Fast forward a few years, and she was remarried—a banker this time, not a cop—and living in southern California with three dogs, two kids, and another on the way.

But this wasn't about Ben, I reminded myself, tapping my pen against my bottom lip. This was about me, my neuroses. So I slid my back against the cold, unyielding metal, dropped to the floor, and began to write.

Dear Ben,

I have a photo of you, but I can't seem to bring myself to look at it. I know exactly where it is, of course, tucked between an old picture of my mother when she was my age—looking expectant and smooth-skinned and impossibly fierce—and another of all the Archer women taken before the summer that changed our lives forever. But just because I don't look at your image doesn't mean I've forgotten you. I don't need a two-dimensional print to bring back the memory of our skin burning the sheets beneath us, or the scent of rich musk

*as you slept beside me, or the need that curled inside
me every time you looked at me. The real me.*

Remember her?

*Sure, she was slightly damaged, chipped even, and
cynical and tough enough to really resemble her
mother there at the end, but you knew her intimately
and loved her deeply, and you were nestled deep inside of her only moments before that photo was taken.*

*That's the thing about that photo. I know that little
half smile is on your face because of the broken, damaged, cynical, tough—and impossibly happy—me.
And now that you're gone—or I guess what I mean to
say is now that we're gone—looking at that photo is
beyond me. I can barely look in the mirror anymore.*

*And it's the not looking that makes me restless. I
wander our sinful city like a ghost of my former self,
seeking enough distraction to keep from giving in to
the temptation to drive past your house. And if nothing in the gilded and grimy streets can do so, I head
over to my sister's high-rise condo where I climb out
on a ledge far above the city, where the air presses
against me even on the calmest of nights, and I close
my eyes, feel the ribbons of light spinning on the other
side of my lids, and wonder . . . will you ever smile
that way again? Have you smiled that way since?
And, if you have, who brought that smile to your face?
The one reserved for me. The Joanna-smile.*

*I never try to answer that. I block it off in the same
way I tuck away that aging photo. I just let the wind
press me against the ledge until I begin to waver, and
I open my eyes so the question fades in the glare of
the electric river flowing below me. Then I climb back
inside, avoiding all mirrors as I cross that palatial
loft, and when I let myself out I'm balanced again. I
can tuck you away and tell myself I'm ready to move
on. But in truth I would give it all up and let him walk
free . . . if only I could return to you.*

Usually I kept missives like this in a keepsake box near my bedside. I figured it was as close to sleeping with Ben as I'd ever get again. But this time I stood, tore the page from the pad, and folded it before sliding it through the open slat. A buzzing rose from inside the locker, like a hive of bees growing closer. I took an involuntary step back, but there was only a sudden stillness pressing down on the room, and then the latch clicked softly open.

"Next time," I said wryly, swinging open the door, "just give me a knife and ask for a vein."

So what was this thing that'd required so much of me, demanding an admission I hadn't even allowed myself to study too closely? It was small, for one. In fact, it fit in the palm of my hand; a gilt jewel box with a gold clasp, and velvet the color of the midnight sky cushioning what was inside.

"My precious," I hissed, unable to help myself as I lifted the ring from its cushion. Holding it, however, all humor drained from me. I'd seen this ring before. It'd been years, and I couldn't be sure when it had disappeared, but my mother had disappeared along with it.

It was too heavy and wide to be considered feminine, but the sheen off the metal—not gold or silver, and certainly not platinum, though it had that heft—was so muted it was nearly opaque, light catching only in the dual grooves hedging a cloudy gray stone. I tilted it back and forth in the light before slipping it on. It was too large for the ring finger of my right hand, but it nestled nicely against the knuckle of my middle finger and, I was pleased to see, looked like it belonged there. And when it began to glow, a gentle pulse in the dim, cavernous room, I knew it did.

"I hope you don't think one ancient piece of tin makes up for leaving me."

I was talking to my mother now, and because I could do that anywhere and garner the same result, I shut the locker and headed back to the elevators, careful not to leave the cat stranded behind me. But I thought about my words. My mother had turned my life upside down by leaving, and even though I now understood why, sometimes I couldn't help but wonder: did she even feel an ounce of the guilt and shame and ineffectiveness that I had after failing Olivia? Because that's what she'd done by leaving. She'd failed me. No matter the reasons, she'd abandoned me when I'd needed her most.

And if she came to me with tearstained eyes and a face I barely remembered, would it be enough? Would it make up for my having to go it alone in the world—both of them— while she knew where I was, what I was going through, and chose to stay hidden anyway? I couldn't answer that. My feelings for her were muddled now. She'd gifted me with weapons, power, strengths I had sought ever since someone had tried to make a victim out of me, and she was apparently still giving gifts. Everything, I thought sourly, except herself.

"And what kind of mother does that?" I whispered, rubbing the ring with my thumb.

I couldn't answer that question. I had no maternal instincts. Whatever soft feelings I did possess had been reserved solely for my sister, Olivia, who was long gone. And for Ben, I thought. Though the only way I could show my love for him was to stay far, far away. So unconditional love was foreign to me now, and I didn't even know if I'd want my mother to open up that part of me again. What if she left a second time? Would I be able to survive hurting that much again?

These questions occupied me so completely that it wasn't until I was back in my room that I realized the sacrificial note I'd pushed through the slats, as well as the disks I'd deposited for safekeeping, had been nowhere in that locker. Like they'd never existed, I thought, studying the odd ring. Like they'd been eaten by the darkness.

The bloodline of both sides of the Zodiac is matriarchal. The lineage of the star sign runs through our veins. So generation after generation, women took up the mantle of power and responsibility for the troop's succession, making sure even if they died, their house's legacy continued. But it was the first-born women who were most powerful, and some star signs—both male and female, both Shadow and Light—spent lifetimes attempting to make up for that lack.

Brynn DuPree, Regan's mother, inherited her star sign after her three older siblings died in quick succession, what the Shadow manuals described as "mysterious and dishonorable" deaths. All had used their conduits to take their own lives, though there had been no perceivable impetus or inkling that any would do so. I'd have thought suicide was what made the deaths dishonorable as well, but that wasn't it. They'd died outside of battle, and in the Tulpa's judgment, that was a far graver offense.

Brynn, meanwhile, had been killed by her opposite on the Zodiac, a much younger and surprisingly handsome Cancer of Light, Gregor Stitch—our superstitious, one-armed taxi driver—who'd lured her into a confessional, heard her out, then gave her five Hail Marys before burying a flanged-bladed mace into her core. But it was as I read about her life, not her death, that I found the best explanation for her daughter's actions the day before.

Regan's father had been a mortal priest. The human element didn't weaken anything, the bloodline still passed through the mother, but unlike the Light, Shadows didn't fall in love with humans. They hunted them.

The Shadow manual Jasmine had found for me described Father Michael as ascetic, pious, and deeply committed to the Church, his greatest passion helping those in his flock attain immortal life. Brynn's definition of immortal life was obviously a bit different from Father Michael's, and *her* greatest passion was leading good men astray. Once Michael had fathered Regan, Brynn held his life in ransom. Blackmail was just the leverage she needed to involve him in some of her more heinous crimes, not only giving her a mortal ally to cover her own tracks, but ensuring he'd keep his big mouth shut about his own multiplying sins. By the time he was caught stalking a schoolyard five years later, the man in the mug shot hardly resembled the kind young priest who'd started out with such hope at the beginning of his clerical service.

And that might explain why Regan had kept my true identity to herself when she discovered I was masquerading as Olivia. Like her mother, she possessed information she could use to her sole advantage. It also explained why she thought I could be so easily "turned" to the Shadow side when she'd allowed me to kill Liam. Unlike her father, I hadn't even taken vows.

But what about her warning not to return to the sanctuary? Was it a ploy meant to try and draw me to the Shadow side? And why would a woman raised in the Shadow lifestyle really turn against another Shadow, give a sworn enemy the aureole, and hand that enemy complete control over her own life?

To gain my trust, she'd said, but that was foolish. If she was caught by the Tulpa, no matter her reason or excuse, she'd be dead before she saw another splitting dawn. Besides, would a woman ambitious enough to murder her own troop member really be content sitting at my "right-hand side"? I sincerely doubted it. There was a deeper motivation there, I thought, studying the pages detailing Brynn's life. A dark passion inside her rivaling that of her mother.

So the question remained. What was Regan really after?

I couldn't answer that yet, but that wasn't enough to keep me from using her . . . and not just for the information she might provide about Joaquin. At least that's what I told myself.

Our mythology tells us the second sign of the Zodiac will soon be fulfilled.

And . . .

The Tulpa has found a way to wipe you all out in one fell swoop.

I didn't believe either of those things, but Regan did, and

that's what mattered. I'd play on those beliefs so that Regan DuPree remained useful to me. But she was useful and dangerous, I thought, tucking the manual into my bedside drawer. And *smart*. Because it was a good scheme to play both sides. And I'd go ahead and let her live as long as I could do the same.

11

Saturn's Orchard, located at the top of a stunted and narrow staircase, reminded me of my Krav Maga dojo in the mortal world. Nondescript, spartan, and clean; if I closed my eyes and inhaled deeply, I could pretend I was back in that heated little room, learning to protect my own life . . . rather than the Las Vegas valley as a whole.

Of course there were differences. For one, the paranormal version was also a mood room. I don't know if being pyramid-shaped had anything to do with it, but the room reacted to emotion. The whitewashed walls acted as a blank canvas for dueling agents—and when engaged, glyphs soared over a colorful universe, indicating who was winning.

To get there I had to pass the children's ward, where the sounds of high-pitched laughter and chatter floated down the hallway in a cacophony that was like nails on a chalkboard to me. I stuck my head around the corner, peering in the direction of the noise. I knew nothing about kids. I was rarely around them, and my own childhood had been blotted out by the trauma endured in my teens. I knew they ate a lot of mac and cheese, that play was the focal point of their day, and most had limited impulse control, which made them do things like scream their little heads off for no reason. In truth, they kind of frightened me. Almost more than the thought of chasing Shadows.

"They don't bite, you know," an amused voice piped from behind.

I turned to find Gregor, his wide eyes crinkled with humor as he looked at me. Other than a subtle green cast to his skin from the exercise in the boneyard the night before, humor was the one thing that saved Gregor from looking fierce. Okay, that and the rabbit foot hanging from his belt. And while the symbols worn around his neck didn't soften his image, they did speak of his superstitious nature; a cross, a Jewish star, and a crescent moon all clustered together in unlikely harmony. His warden, Sheena, was tucked beneath his good arm as usual, clearly unimpressed.

"Some of them do," I replied, barely containing a shudder.

He grinned more widely. "That's called teething. Only the little ones do that, and they're long in bed. The others have been instructed not to bite the star signs."

"Comforting that they had to be told," I said, leaning over to stroke Sheena behind her ear. She pressed into my touch, trusting Gregor to keep her balanced. "Listen, have you been keeping up with the papers? Or the scanner? Anything going on that looks like Shadow activity?"

He shook his head, which gleamed even in the dim light. "I get the dailies first thing in the morning, local and national, and nothing's popped. Nobody has a clue what the Tulpa's up to, but we're as balanced as we ever were, that's for sure."

I thought about that for a moment, and though his certainty was probably warranted, asked, "Do you think you could save them for me at the end of the day? At least the front page and the metro section? Warren wants me to stay in the sanctuary. Again."

Gregor shot me a sympathetic look, showing me he'd already heard. "Sure . . . looking for anything in particular?"

I thought about lying, then reconsidered. It would cost me nothing to tell Gregor about the lab—he didn't need to know about Liam and Regan, or the information that'd led me to Joaquin at Master Comics—and if anyone could help me discover the mystery of what a scientific laboratory was doing in a casino, it was he. So I told him about the portal Hunter had pushed me through at Valhalla, and what I'd found behind it. "So I was wondering if you'd heard of any missing person cases in the last, say, three months."

"I wonder what they're up to . . ." All the humor was absent from his gaze as he squinted in thought. "I could go through the archives. Look for a missing doctor, scientist. Maybe a professor of science out at the university."

"Yeah, someone like Micah. A lab rat."

"Better yet, I'll just ask him when we get to the Orchard," he said, motioning up the stairwell.

I frowned, surprised. "That's where you're going?"

He nodded, and Sheena stretched to nuzzle his chin. "Same as everyone else."

I'd thought my training session with Tekla was private, and was surprised to find he was right; the others were lounging about the room in varying degrees of green-skinned glory. Most had faded to a light jade by now . . . all except Chandra, I noted, with more than a little satisfaction. She was still a dazzling Day-Glo emerald, and I gave her a little finger wave from across the room. She merely returned a finger.

Micah, as large as a sumo wrestler and as tall as a basketball player, was stretching lithely on the floor, and Gregor dropped down beside him to fill him in before Tekla arrived. I remained standing, though I shot him an apologetic smile. "Sorry about the hit yesterday, Micah. Good job on the color, though."

"Thanks." He smiled wryly, examining his fading forearm. "Next time I'll try to concoct something a little less durable."

Micah and Gregor were the only senior troop members in the room. Warren was absent, and the rest of the star signs were juniors; Vanessa and Felix, Riddick and Jewell, and me. The training we underwent—such as the maze out in the boneyard—was a good way for those in the middle to jockey for position, and the initiates who were raised in this subterranean grotto started that practice young. Scoring kill spots against enemy agents also gained you more power within the troop hierarchy, and the foiling of a Shadow plot was a good way to earn brownie points too. But everyone knew their place at any given moment.

Everyone, I thought wryly, but me.

"Monkeys?" I heard Micah say, and turned back to find him gazing up at me questioningly. "Primates are generally used for more complex research . . . combating disease, testing transplantations and vaccines, new surgeries."

"Things that would eventually be used on humans," Gregor said, and the two of them looked at each other in the long stretch of silence. After a moment Gregor rose again and left the room. I knew he was headed to speak with Warren.

I swallowed hard. "It's serious, then?"

"It's probably nothing, but you were right to say something." A swift smile flickered over his face as he motioned around the room. "Ready for class?"

I narrowed my eyes, wondering why he was changing the subject, but let it drop as I noticed all the training paraphernalia—heavy bags, pads, ropes, and mitts—had been put away, and the spongy mat with its opposing sparring circles had been removed to reveal a naked slab of concrete.

Micah explained that the mat's removal deactivated the mood room, and in its place was a single mirrored panel propped vertically beneath the apex of the whitewashed pyramid; colorless, stark, and somehow intimidating.

I stepped forward, studying my reflection in the shiny slab, hands on hips, feet splayed wide, a stance that looked a hell of a lot more assured than it felt. "So . . . what? We gonna practice our scariest superfaces on each other?"

Micah gave a shrug of his giant shoulders, and stood with a grunt until he towered at his full seven feet. "Probably another lesson on energy. We'll find out when Tekla gets here."

"She's always late," I grumbled, still peeved at the way she'd dug at me the day before. "You'd think a psychic would know we're all waiting for her."

"It's an affectation," Micah said, smiling sympathetically and ruffling my hair. "The troop's Seer is allowed her eccentricities. Just look past the quirks, and you'll learn something despite yourself."

I was about to say that *quirk* was a nice way to word it, but Marlo walked in just then . . . followed by Hunter. I got that funny feeling in my gut again, and quickly looked away. Fortunately, Tekla's appearance saved me from having to question why.

She wasted no time on niceties, instead heading straight to the center of the room, where it turned out today's lesson would be on yet another of Tekla's favorite subjects: controlling our thoughts.

"This wall beside me is made of glass, better to reflect the clearest sense of your goals. But beyond that, like the labyrinth in the boneyard, it's made from thought." She looked at each of us, and the room fell unnaturally still. "I created both walls with nothing more than the strength of my mind. I dreamed them into being. Does anyone recall what else had been wrought into being by the whim of a powerful mind?"

Her eyes landed on me, though we all knew the answer to that question. "The Tulpa."

She inclined her head. "That's right. A living being who moves, breathes, eats, shits, and sleeps." And now she began to pace, her black salwar-kamiz flaring about her ankles. "A being who's dedicated his entire undeserved life to destroying you. How much easier, then, to create a mere wall from the ether." She waved her hand, and the air shimmered about her fingertips. A second wall materialized, rippling, before solidifying into one identical to the first.

"Whoa," Riddick said, awed. I had to agree. The most awesome thing about it, though, was that the wall's appearance hadn't seemed magical or miraculous at all. It was as natural as if someone had just walked in a door.

"Your thoughts create your reality," Tekla went on as we all crowded closer. "What you believe is true and real becomes true and real for you."

She paused, then looked at Felix, just as he was opening his mouth to speak. Tekla's stare had nothing to do with her being psychic. We all knew Felix would be the first to ask a question, and he caught the look and laughed self-consciously. "We know that . . . but that wall's not going to disappear just because I say it's not there. It's tangible. It's a wall."

"I agree," Jewell said, clearing her throat nervously. "You can't just lie to yourself about things already in existence."

"Not lie and actually believe it," Riddick agreed.

Tekla raised her brow, a subdued challenge. "You don't think so? What about this: I'm not too drunk to drive. He's just working late. The glove doesn't fit." Tekla allowed her mouth to quirk. "People *do* lie to themselves, and they get away with it because every action affirms and reaffirms their perception. That's the power of the human mind. That's the power of thought, which is nothing more—and nothing less—than energy. And when you have a particularly powerful mind, extraordinary things can happen."

She made another wall appear, effortlessly, then turned back to us and smiled.

"So what's the practical application?" Riddick asked, moving forward first to touch the wall, then knock on it loudly when he found it solid.

"Good question," she said, automatically folding her arms before realizing she wasn't wearing her robe. She linked her hands instead. "One answer is the element of surprise. Say your back is against a wall, literally, and a Shadow makes a move against you. Instead of making the choice to flee or fight—"

"I never flee," Felix said, cocking his fists on his hips.

"We know, Felix," Tekla said, and he wilted slightly. "Thus the Shadows already know how you will act when backed against that wall."

"Except you don't have a choice in that instance," I said in his defense. "You fight or die."

She smiled like she'd been expecting me to say that. "Ah, but you always have a choice. It's like dropping a footprint on the moon. Once you take a step, the landscape of your life is forever changed.

"So the question I pose to you today is, what do we want that landscape to look like? Which direction do you want that footstep to lead? What walls need to come down before you reach your goal? Once you have the answers to these questions, the Universe will conspire to bend to your wishes."

She inclined her head and folded her hands together like a Jedi knight. Impressive, it was. She then shifted her gaze to Riddick, motioning him to the wall. "You first."

He swallowed hard, but strode forward with determination.

"What were you thinking yesterday when you were all scattered in the labyrinth?" she asked him. "What was your intent going into that maze?"

"To win," he said, running a hand over his rust-colored hair. "To kick some ass."

The rest of us laughed, but Tekla's smile was close-lipped as she motioned to the wall in front of him. "Focus that on the wall now, projecting that intention, and will it away."

Riddick squared his shoulders and stared at the wall like it was a mortal enemy. For a moment nothing happened, and I thought that's what Tekla wanted us to see—that nothing happened when we faced our obstacles with the wrong intent. Instead, the base of the wall shimmered briefly, setting the length of it to swaying, and looking as though the whole thing would topple. I felt myself go cross-eyed as I stared too hard at the spot, and had to blink. Beside me, Vanessa shook her head. When I focused again, I'd found that another wall had appeared instead, thickening the first.

"A second thing you might want to remember," Tekla said wryly, "is that the wrong intention can generate the exact opposite of your desired effect."

Riddick scowled. "What's wrong with wanting to kick ass?"

"Nothing. But it's not a strong enough motivation to create lasting change. It needs to be linked to a higher reason." She jerked her head at Felix, who immediately clapped Riddick on the shoulder, backed the frowning man up, and smiled broadly at the rest of us as he rubbed his hands together.

"My intention was to have green friends," Felix said, grinning. There were snorts and scattered chuckles—none from Chandra, I noted—but they died down as he turned his focus on the second wall. Felix was close to being a senior agent, and I had no doubt he was keyed in to a "higher reason." We all held our breaths as the entire wall began to shimmer, then shake. The unmistakable scent of burning wood rose in the air, and a low whirring sound ebbed up from beneath Felix's wide stance. It died down when a fourth wall materialized out of nowhere.

"What the fuck?" Felix said, disbelief in his face and voice as Riddick thumped his back in mock sympathy.

"Humor is one of your gifts, my boy, but I doubt you'll be winning over any Shadow agents with wit alone." Tekla raised her brows until he acknowledged her point with a meek nod, and stepped back with the rest of the group. Then she turned to me. "Olivia? You were one of the last players standing. What was your intention yesterday?"

"Why don't you ask Hunter? He's the one who pulled me into the game."

"Thank you." Tekla didn't even blink. "But I'm asking you."

I sighed and reluctantly shuffled forward. This was going to be bad. I couldn't lie about my intentions. This group would scent one out quicker than a coyote tracking a jack-rabbit. So I focused on the wall, where my image stared back at me—beautiful, but defensive and dark eyed—and told her the truth. "Vengeance."

The explosion was deafening. The wall shattered, sharp missiles flying to pelt every corner of the room. I had time to duck, but not cover, and yelped as a shard bit into my right cheek, feeling the same knifelike stings on my legs and arms, and hearing the others cry out like soldiers dying on a battlefield.

Over as quickly as it began, the silence that followed was punctuated only by labored breathing, and I peeked from my hunched position, felt tentatively at my wet cheek, and came away with blood. The others were doing the same, some still gasping in surprise and confusion, others cursing freely and shooting me steel-plated glares. Only Tekla, standing as she'd been before, remained untouched.

Because she'd known what was going to happen, I thought bitterly.

"Another fine example of what not to do."

That made me see three different shades of red. "You wanted me to break through the wall," I said, crossing my arms. "I did."

"Look around you, Olivia. Look what you've done to your troop."

I didn't need to look to know what she was really saying. If we'd been on a mission in the real world, my actions would have wiped out my whole troop. They knew it too, and their eyes were on me, as heavy as their silence. Because the single unspoken question winging through each of their minds was the same one that'd dogged me since joining the troop. *Will you give up your quest for vengeance for us?*

And goddamn if that didn't make me want to dig in my heels even harder.

"So I'll have my vengeance, kill Joaquin, and then I'll stop."

"Well, that's the thing, Olivia. There is no final action." Tekla pursed her lips and turned to address the others. "All your deeds live within, piling up to create your life. So revenge isn't just a step in the wrong direction, it's an A-bomb that will flatten everything around you."

I stared at Tekla as the silence drew out around us, gradually scenting new emotions in the air; my defiance, sure, and anger at the way Tekla had ambushed me, but there was sympathy there too—I didn't know who that belonged to—and regret, which would have soothed me if not for the sudden loamy whorl of fear emanating from Marlo's direction. That hadn't been there before, and I gritted my teeth—resenting its appearance now, blaming Tekla—though I refrained from looking at Marlo. I didn't want to frighten her further. My eyes, I knew, were as black as tar.

"I'm doing the best I can," I said between clenched teeth.

"I don't want your best. I want you to break through that wall—"

"Then show me how!" I yelled, and had the satisfaction of seeing her jerk in surprise.

Her eyes narrowed immediately. "The rest of you leave us."

The troop filed out in silent singles and pairs, as I stared at Tekla, she at me.

"Focus," she finally said when they were gone, "and do it again."

"No." I folded my arms over my chest.

She blinked. "What?"

"I said no. I want you to show me." I hesitated, wondering if the rumors were true and she really could trap a person in her gaze, though it was too late to back down now. I pushed back a sweaty tendril of hair and squared on her. "Take me out onto the streets where this shit can be put to practical use. *Show* me."

She looked at me like I was speaking another language. Maybe it was just that people didn't talk to Tekla that way. Maybe it was because I was pissed enough to momentarily forget that fact. "I can't."

"You mean you won't."

"I mean I *can't*."

"Sure you can. All you have to do is fire up the Scorpio glyph, put on a kick-ass outfit, and get in a Star cab."

She didn't answer, just stared a moment longer, before turning away to sail toward the door. Lesson over. But I'd finally pushed Tekla's buttons, and I was bitter enough to want to keep on doing it. Let her get a taste of her own righteous medicine.

"What could be so powerful that you'd rather leave our Zodiac empty than take up the Scorpio sign?" I called out, knowing part of the answer was grief, but pushing for the rest. "Have you lost your powers? Your nerve? Your drive?"

"You *dare* question me?" she asked, voice barely a whisper as she pivoted to face me. Her lavender aura began to glow now, like it was shot through with gas. "You, who don't even know your own power? Who can't control her simplest thought? Who mistakes base impulse for drive?"

"Don't do that," I said, shaking my head. "Don't take that mystical, imperious, overbearing—and, by the way, bitchy—tone with me. Not when I've been so honest with you. Not when you use my weaknesses against me every day."

"You've been honest, have you?" She strode over to me so fast, I took a step back before I could stop myself. "Then what's the dark spot in your aura that means you've a secret you're telling no one? What's the dream you had last night that caused those circles beneath your eyes? What's keeping your focus so weak and dull you can't even crack a mirror?"

Nope, it wasn't lack of power keeping her from claiming her star sign, that was for sure. I crossed my arms and lowered my chin. "You're trying to distract me, and it's not going to work. I want to know why you never leave this sanctuary."

"My duty is here."

I shook my head. "Not good enough. The man who murdered your only child is out there, stalking others. His entire purpose in life is to spread hate and dissension and pain . . . all the things you preach so vehemently against, and you're doing nothing about it."

"I'm training this generation's Zodiac how to defeat him using tools that will balance—"

"Blah, blah, blah!" I'd heard it before, and raised my voice so it overtook hers. "Joaquin destroyed someone noble, good, and entirely of Light, attacking him when he was supposed to be safe, murdered him practically in your lap, and did it before Stryker even had the chance to—"

"I was there!" Tekla screamed, and the remaining mirrors around us shattered, falling like glistening rain. I rocked back on my heels, ducking for cover as the walls of the pyramid rumbled too, bowing in on themselves. A weight crushed down on my skull and chest, like the pressure in an airtight cabin was about to give with a violent pop, or someone extremely large was sitting on top of me. As I dropped to the ground I saw Tekla standing with clenched fists, her eyes wide and furious, hair snapping from its bun to swarm, Medusa-like, on a current that didn't exist. I tried to cry out, but it was soundless, my windpipe crushed beneath invisible fingers. All I could do was lie in a fetal position, black spots dancing before my squeezed eyes, and suffocate.

By the time I realized I could open my eyes again, the room was noiseless. The screaming wind had scuttled to a gurgle, and the vacuous white walls of the dojo were back in their original slanted shape. I sucked in a breath so deep, it was like I was breaking the surface of the ocean, and it cut through the silence like shears through silk.

Chest heaving, I looked up and saw Tekla standing amid the debris of glass and ceiling plaster, looking like a disheveled statue. She blinked and said softly, "I was there."

Oh Jesus, I thought as I slowly gained my feet. What had I been thinking? Just because she gave off an aura of invulnerability didn't mean she didn't have deep pockets of regret eating at her insides. I, of anyone, knew how deeply such emotions could be—and needed to be—hidden. Legs wobbling, I licked my lips and found my voice. "I'm sorry. I shouldn't have said . . . I don't know what got into me."

But she stared through me like I was just another wall that had to be knocked down. And right now, I wouldn't have stopped her if she'd tried. "Every breath Joaquin takes is a betrayal to my son's memory," she said, big bird eyes solemn, face drawn. "I curse every morning the sun still shines on his head, and relive Stryker's death every night in my dreams."

"So why don't you do something?" I asked quietly, taking a step forward.

Her eyes focused and found me, halting my forward progress. "You mean go after him before it's time? Force the Universe to bend to my will? Or give you leave to attempt it so I can watch you die as well because I haven't had time to pass on the tools you need to fight him?" She shook her head. "I don't want vengeance at any cost, Olivia. Losing one more life to Joaquin's depravity is a price too dear to pay, no matter what I might desire."

Because she seemed to have reached into her vast reservoir of control again, I approached her. "Lives are being lost anyway. He's not out there playing . . . Parcheesi."

A slim eyebrow lifted, and I shrugged. It had been the only thing I could think of.

"No, I know he's not." She sighed, and she looked more human, vulnerable and soft than I'd ever seen her before. "But I can't take up my star sign again. I'd get in my own way."

"Like I do, you mean." Which was why she got so angry with me. Her way of controlling herself was to hole up, push away the impulse to go after Joaquin, and teach us all to do the same. At least now I understood why.

"You lack control, Olivia." She gazed at me for a heartbeat before adding, "That's dangerous for any agent, but as the Kairos your every action is loaded with meaning, charged with energy. When the second sign of the Zodiac comes to pass, you must be prepared."

"But what does that have to do with breaking through mental barriers?" Literally, I thought.

"What is the mind," she retorted, "if not the ultimate battlefield?"

I swallowed hard because I suddenly saw what she was saying. A weak mind was a cursed mind. *A cursed battlefield.* "And if I'm not prepared?" I asked, my voice small.

"It will kill you."

But not today, I thought, looking around at the devastation caused by Tekla's emotions. And that's all I could concentrate on. If I constantly relived the past, as Tekla did each night, or worried about portents yet to be fulfilled, I too would have trouble climbing from my bed.

"Well," I finally sighed, motioning around the room, "at least now I know you're human."

Human-ish, anyway.

"Don't let it get around," she said, and shot me a sad smile before waving her arm through the air in a way I was becoming accustomed to . . . and sick of. A complete wall of sheer unmarred glass appeared in front of me. I sighed, then stepped forward as she began rambling again about focus, desire, and intent. Tekla observed, commented, even encouraged me as I attempted to dissolve it with my mind. And then she yelled some more.

This time I let her.

12

After a few days of nothing happening—and I mean nothing, no reports of Shadow sightings, no paranormal activity threatening the balance of the mortal world, not even a hangnail to bitch about—I sank into a relatively boring routine of waking, training, eating, and sleeping. Nothing nefarious had happened after my return to the sanctuary, and after a week, I put the run-in with Regan out of my mind, knowing nothing would.

I still scoured the papers for odd events, but if Gregor and Micah and Warren were worried about Valhalla's lab, they weren't sharing their concerns with me. I got Vanessa to bring me the new manual of Light the day it came out, and though none of the agents could bring me the Shadow manuals, I did, at length, become confident nobody but Regan knew what had happened in Valhalla's aquarium. She was supposedly keeping my hidden identity to herself, so I saw no reason to mention our encounter either.

It was true that I'd let a Shadow initiate live, but Regan was virtually harmless as an initiate, and as long as she continued to believe I might be persuaded to the Shadow side, I didn't think she'd jeopardize that hope. Besides, Cancers metamorphosized in June and July—less than a month to go—and I figured I could kill her in good conscience after that. After all, she had spared my life. Letting her live until she'd reached her third life cycle was fair enough.

So I stopped worrying about lying to Warren and the rest, grew less paranoid about my compromised identity, and as the days veered from the warmth of late spring into the full furnace blast of high summer, even Regan and her dark machinations seemed like a dream.

Meanwhile, my relationship with Hunter was heating up as well. Or I should say my *non*relationship. I tried to avoid him, but my awareness of him was so great I knew almost to the minute when he returned to the sanctuary. And his presence there, I was finding out, was ubiquitous. He left only to put in his shift at Valhalla, returning each evening as dusk split the summer sky in two. Unlike the rest of us, he didn't seem to occupy an address outside the sanctuary; that, or he preferred his tiny room in the barracks to any dwelling that lay on the outside. I didn't dare ask why, fearing he might construe my curiosity for romantic interest.

Not that I could avoid him completely. He was too integral a part of the troop. Hardly a day passed when someone didn't recommend asking the advice of the weapons master, or lauded the weapons master, or raved over the latest design of the weapons master. If the Shadow agents only knew that our beloved weapons master was planted as security in Valhalla, like a renegade bee from another hive, they'd shit bricks. And slay him on his very next shift.

And a part of me couldn't help but think this was exactly what drew Hunter to his job. Hiding among the Shadows must give him a rush. He toed the line between disguise and discovery more closely than any of us, though it didn't seem to frighten him. Not the need to be ever-vigilant and keep every emotion under control, not the discussions about infiltrating more deeply . . . not even me when I tripped out and inadvertently showed him my Shadow side. In those moments, just after the ebony iciness had left my gaze—when everyone else was still trying to get their glyphs back under control, incrementally backing away at the same time—he just tilted his head in that steady way he had, languidly expressionless, and flexed.

So I reconciled myself to the momentary need to remain where I was, played my game of sexual cat-and-mouse with Hunter, tried to bait Chandra whenever nobody was looking—a girl still has to have her fun—and almost began to believe Warren was right, and the Shadows had forgotten us completely. That the world was as our troop leader envisioned it: balanced, peaceful, and destined to remain that way.

That's why I was so relaxed the night of the Valhalla event, perched alone atop the Silver Slipper, drinking directly from a bottle of Chablis because I'd forgotten to bring a glass. The wine slid into me like liquid peace, a cool sensory contrast to the lights I could see glowing along the Strip like a burning oil slick. Early June still had cool nights, but another month from now the concrete jungle would retain the heat of the day like a banked coal, waiting to spark again with the coming dawn.

A flash of light rocketed into the air in the distance, then burst into a bright bloom of raining purple color. That first colorful explosion was followed by a well-choreographed, and costly, display of fireworks, and as color bloomed in the sky, I leaned on my palms to watch the show. It wasn't as exciting as New Year's Eve, when every major hotel on the Strip fired a series of identical blasts into the air in perfectly synchronized choreography, but Xavier Archer was no slouch in the self-promotion department. I lifted my bottle high, saluting his masturbatory display of self-indulgence, then jolted when my cell phone rang in my pants pocket.

"Shit," I said, wiping wine from the front of my shirt. "Hello?"

"Olivia? Can you hear me?" Cher's voice came over the phone, the boom of fireworks sounding over the line before it reached me in the boneyard. I smiled. I'd known she'd be in the thick of it.

"You seem to be having a hell of a party," I said, raising my voice as the first whiff of gunpowder wafted my way.

"Oh, we are! We are! Xavier showed up to start the fireworks show himself, and he ordered a whole round of champagne for everyone with balcony views. That's us."

"Of course it is," I said, but frowned at the mention of Xavier. He may have had an ego for days, but was an infamous recluse. This, along with the bachelorette auction, would make two appearances in as many weeks. Virtually unheard of. "He must be celebrating something special," I said, toying with my ring, which pulsed gently in the dim boneyard. "Probably a hostile takeover of some poor publicly owned company."

"Maybe," and I could imagine her shrugging as she said it. "He gave some speech about long-held plans coming to fruition. Said sacrifice is required to achieve utopian dreams."

"Whatever that means," I heard Suzanne add in the background.

Leaving the wine bottle where it sat, I rose and stared hard at the city, the light in the sky now bright enough to eclipse those blazing from the ground. The scent of sulfur was stronger now, almost noxious as the potassium nitrate began to assail me. I covered my nose with my free hand. Meanwhile my mind raced. I'd known of no big deals closed, and if there'd been plans to expand or take over another property, I'd have heard about it before now.

"It means we all get free Dom P.," Cher said, her giggle drowned out by another round of starry blasts.

"Cher? I—I can't hear you," I lied, choking as the boneyard grew thicker with smoke and scent. "Call me tomorrow after you've gotten over your hangover." And I hung up without waiting for her reply.

Meanwhile the debris in the boneyard floor had disappeared into a misty haze, black fog rising to claim the signs, dragging them into a proper grave. From my perch I could see beyond the walls and cyclone wire to where the streets were disappearing as well. Filmy clouds continued to rise, swallowing the terrain until the streetlights glowed like eerie beacons.

"What the fuck?" I said, and nearly choked on the sharp, peppery toxins.

My phone rang again.

"I seriously can't talk, Cher. I'm busy . . . getting a massage," I managed, before choking off into a fit of shallow coughs. My eyes were watering, and the lining of my nose itched, making me sneeze.

Laughter, tinkling like bells, sounded over the line. "You don't sound like you're getting a massage . . . but if you are, you're missing all the fun."

"Who is this?" I asked, but the answer came to me before another word was uttered. "What do you want?"

"I already told you that, Archer," Regan said, derision seeping over the line. "I want you to come to the Shadow side and live happily ever after."

I snorted. The Brothers Grimm had nothing on her fairy tales. "So come and get me."

"Uh-uh-uh," she sang, and I could practically see her blond ponytail swinging. "You made a bargain with the devil when you let me go. I told you where Joaquin would be, now you have to do something I want."

I squinted into the boneyard as if that would bring Regan into view. "You knew he'd be untouchable at Master Comics. That's the only reason you told me he was there."

"Untrue. For example, I know where he is now, and it's not neutral territory. In fact, I can see him from here. He's standing right in front of Valhalla, watching a blond woman take in the fireworks . . . you see those, don't you?"

"I see them," I said, looking into the sky, my voice a near whisper.

"Good. Well this blond looks . . . well, she looks a lot like you, actually. He's been stalking her through the crowd. I recognize that look in his eye, and his scent is on the wind, despite the stink of the fireworks. It's sweet and earthy at the same time, like caramel charring on the barbecue, and fat worms tunneling up from the grave."

I closed my eyes. It was a good description. He smelled just like that.

"You can probably stop him if you hurry, Joanna. You can save this girl from being another headline in tomorrow's paper, and do it while exacting your own revenge. But you should hurry, he's already talking to her. She's smiling up at him, forgetting the show in the sky, even forgetting her friends beside her."

But I couldn't hurry. Not only was I not supposed to leave the boneyard, it was past dusk. And by the time dawn arrived, I knew that woman would be long dead. Regan knew it too. So, as the fiery crescendo of the show's finale erupted above us, all I said was, "Fuck you."

Regan responded with false surprise. "There's only one reason I can think of that an agent of Light wouldn't try to save an innocent. You went back to your sanctuary, didn't you, Joanna? Even after I told you not to." She clucked into the receiver like she was scolding a young child. "Well. Now you've done it. Though I suppose you still have a chance . . . if you get out of there as soon as possible."

"What's going on?" I asked, watching the sky like the answer was being written out there.

"Meet me outside Valhalla at dawn. I'll tell you then."

"I can't," I said, and felt a very unheroic sense of relief at that. It was all I could do not to add, *I won't.*

"Ah well." Regan sighed dramatically, before that tinkling laughter sounded over the line again. "That's all right, Joanna . . . we're already in."

And the connection went dead.

I blinked and looked at the phone, then slowly dropped it to my side. The fireworks had stopped, and long wisps of smoke, like dragons' tails, were all that lingered in the sky. Even the haze along the streets was fading away. But as I stared out into the warm, bleary night, I swallowed hard and let out an audible moan.

What had I missed? I wondered, covering my mouth with a shaking hand. *Worse, what had I done?*

13

The sanctuary exploded with sound just before dawn. I took a jagged path toward awareness, fits and starts of comprehension battling the fatigue brought on by my sessions with Tekla and the alcohol I'd drunk earlier. Footsteps pounded in the hall, and the strobe light above my door fired light in half circles across the concrete walls of my room, left to right, then back again, while emitting a high-pitched whine that had my teeth clenching hard. As soon as my feet hit the floor, the screeching mercifully stopped, but if I were to lie down again, it would start right back up.

Not that I would. The strobe was a part of an emergency system notifying the troop to assemble. Something had happened on the streets of Las Vegas, something bad enough that those on patrol tonight weren't able to contain it alone. I lifted my chemise over my head and yanked on the tank top and jeans I'd let drop to the floor only hours earlier, pulling my hair back without brushing it. I did take the time to pull on sneakers, then grabbed my conduit on the run.

The briefing room was at the mouth of the barracks, its location chosen for emergencies such as this, and as fast as I'd been, most of the others were already there. Nobody else, I realized, had bothered to get dressed. Warren stood at the front of the room, barefoot and in sweats, along with Micah and Tekla, who—though robed as crisply as ever—looked like she hadn't slept a wink. They were bent together, obviously arguing, so I joined Vanessa and Jewell at a table near the back, while Felix and Riddick sat hunchbacked in front of us, heads close, whispering back and forth. Hunter was working the grave shift tonight, I remembered, catching myself scanning the room for him, and Gregor was on patrol in his cab, but a moment later the door opened again and Chandra entered. She seated herself directly across from Jewell, running her hand over her short, uncombed hair, and turned to Vanessa without glancing at me.

"What's happened?" she asked, before I had a chance.

"Multiple attacks on innocents," Vanessa said, lifting her head to the front of the room to indicate she'd been eavesdropping. She was still in her pajamas, long curls springing from her head in a thousand opposing directions. It made it difficult to concentrate on her face, though her words were dark enough to make me. "All in different parts of the city, but same method, and nearly in unison. Warren thinks it was timed. The attacks all began after dusk."

"How do we know it's the work of the Shadows, and not another mortal?" Jewell sagged against her chair, and nervousness had her knotting her fingers together. This would be her first real test as the Gemini of Light since her sister's death. I too looked to Vanessa for the answer.

"Because it's too widespread . . . and they're dying in groups, mostly pairs."

"Pairs?" I said, speaking for the first time. "Has that ever happened before?"

"No," Warren answered loudly, and that was how he called the meeting to order. Micah took his seat, and Tekla moved to the right of Warren's shoulder, watching him gravely. "It seems the Shadows have been saving it all up for this one go."

Warren's eyes flickered my way, then quickly away, though I'd been careful to keep my expression blank. Now didn't seem like the time for *I told you so's*.

It seemed Gregor had gotten a blip on his police scanner after dusk the previous night. It sounded like nothing more than a domestic dispute at first; a husband and wife had been killed in their bedroom, and police were sending in a forensic unit to investigate. Gregor changed the channel. About fifteen minutes later, another call came in.

"He thought it was the same call," Warren said, "a man and woman found dead in their bedroom, but then the dispatcher said it had a similar M.O. as the one on Bridger, and *that* was the one he'd heard earlier."

So the mortal police suspected a serial killer, and Gregor began to as well, though one of a different sort. He drove past the site of the first incident, but picked up no scent of Shadows, and was quickly shooed away by police. Ditto the second crime scene.

"So what convinced him he was right?" Jewell asked, looking up from the pad where she'd been taking notes.

"The scanner itself. Homicides began being reported almost like clockwork, every quarter of an hour, then every five minutes, then one right on top of another. All were at residences in the core of the valley. Then the reports began coming in from the clubs."

"Strip clubs?" Felix asked. Under different circumstances I'd have teased him about that—masquerading as a frat boy, he was most familiar with those establishments—but there was nothing joking in his tone, and I glanced back at Warren to find him just as serious. Exactly how many victims had been found? I wondered.

"Mostly, but a few dance clubs and ultra-lounges as well." Expression distant, he bit his lip. "The Palladium alone had three attacks in one hour."

"Jesus," Riddick said, sitting up straight in his chair. "They're everywhere."

"But they're not. Gregor wasn't able to pick up the scent

of even one Shadow. Whatever they're doing, they're doing by remote, and they've been planning it for a long time."

This time Warren did look at me, and it was I who averted my eyes. A *told you so* looked like it would have killed him.

"So how are they attacking?" Riddick said, stroking his goatee. We all looked back at Warren.

"That's what we have to find out. How are the victims being approached? How can they catch so many people off guard, couples especially, without one of them getting away, or fighting, or at least one victim left alive to report it to the police?"

"And no one's seen a thing?" asked Chandra, tucking a chunk of hair behind her ear. It sprang back out immediately.

Warren shook his head. "That's the strange thing. Nobody's reached for a phone, called out to their neighbors for help, nothing."

"Maybe they didn't have time."

Warren inclined his head in Jewell's direction. "Except the victims show signs of dying silently *and* slowly, and by that I mean hours, painful ones at that. It's like when the exterminator comes to your house. The next day there are roaches belly up on your floor. That's how these people are being found. All over the city."

"Cause of death?" Vanessa asked, grimly.

"Also unknown. Gregor's still monitoring the ETS scanners, but the only thing they're reporting openly are the location of the victims and that they all seem to be burn victims."

"Like in a fire?"

"A fire with no flame, no smoke, and no ash," Tekla said from her corner, her voice taking on the lyrical cadence of prophecy and prediction she was so famous for. We all turned to her. "A flash fire. People incinerating for no reason."

I winced, the visual coming unbidden.

Micah turned back to Warren. "Sounds like a chemical fire."

Warren shrugged to show he just didn't know.

"Definitely Shadows," said Chandra.

"Duh," I said, earning a glare from her but getting to the point. "So what do we do?"

"*We* are going out there to investigate, find the cause, and see if we can't head off any further fatalities. You are going to stay here."

Stunned, it took a moment for my eyes to narrow. "Wha—?"

"Uh-uh." He held up a hand, silencing me with a stiff shake of his head. "This isn't open for discussion. Chandra will go in your place, and you'll—"

"Bullshit! I'm the star sign!" And I'd find a link to Regan, I knew it, if only I were allowed out.

"But Chandra can help Micah determine whether this is indeed a chemical attack," Tekla said reasonably. "And this may be the onset of the second sign."

A cursed battlefield.

My fist found the steel table, and everyone around me jumped. I wasn't in the mood for *reasonable*. "Even more reason for me to go. You *need* me out there!"

"She's right," Felix said, leaning forward as he turned back to Warren. "We don't know what this is. We need all the manpower we can get."

This earned him a stare so hard, he dropped back in his seat, face burning. When nobody else spoke up in my defense, Warren turned that same steely gaze on me. "Olivia, we've done a search since your discovery of the lab in Valhalla. A genetic scientist and an evolutionary biologist have both gone missing in the past five months. Now that the Tulpa's mole"—he couldn't even speak her name, his lips screwing up on the word—"has been banished from inside the sanctuary, he needs another way to get to you."

So *that's* what they hadn't been telling me. I looked at Gregor, who averted his gaze, then to Micah. They thought the Tulpa intended to inject me with the makeup of his genetic template, thus linking himself to me. And why not? The same ploy had almost wiped out the agents of Light just months earlier. What better way to keep track of me too—to draw me in closer, and know what I was thinking and feeling at all times—than to bind me to himself.

The Tulpa's found a way to wipe you all out in one fell swoop.

Binding himself to the Kairos could do just that. No wonder they didn't want me leaving the sanctuary.

And yet I didn't think so. What about what Regan had said? *We're already in.* And what about her claims that the Tulpa needed me to come to him willingly? I decided to try again. "Tekla . . . ?"

She frowned and gave me a small shake of her head. "Warren's right. The Tulpa will do anything to get to you. It may be that these attacks are really just a smokescreen to draw you to him. But if we think you can help after we've assessed the situation—"

I stood up, my chair toppling behind me. "But I'm the one who told you about the lab!"

"Which is how we know to take this precaution." Warren stared at me, brows drawn, face pinched, and I stifled my next comment. That look said he'd lock me up if he had to. The others saw it, too, and were glancing around uncomfortably. Vanessa put an hand on my arm. "Olivia," she said softly.

Slowly I lowered myself to my seat, and when I finally broke eye contact, Warren's shoulders dropped, and he exhaled loudly. The rest of the troop relaxed as well. "So, for the rest of you, I've designed a plan that will put us in all corners of the city, working inward." He pulled down a projection screen, while Tekla got the lights, and the others settled in to retrieve their assignments. Felix sent me an apologetic smile, and Vanessa patted my hand lightly before turning her attention to the front of the room, and I sank back into my seat, forgotten from that moment on.

They discussed and debated strategy right until the approach of dawn. I wasn't consulted, or even acknowledged, but they didn't kick me out either—at least Warren had enough decency not to do that—so I listened, observed, and learned with the others. I also put together what I knew from each of the times Regan and I had spoken, letting her cryptic remarks tumble in my mind like an ongoing craps game until I finally had enough information. After the meeting was adjourned, and the others began to prepare for dawn, I sulkily left the briefing room, making sure Warren saw me returning to the barracks.

But once back in my room, I began to make plans of my own.

Dusk's arrival found six superheroes—and Chandra—lined up on the launchpad, preparing to hurtle up the chute one by one from the steel womb of the sanctuary and into the cool hours of a predawn boneyard. They were dressed in the clothes needed to play their roles as mortals on the outside, as they'd begin this reconnaissance mission by scouring the sites most familiar to them.

Warren would crawl along the underbelly of the inner city under the soiled rags of his vagrant persona. Gregor would continue to drive his cab, Chandra masquerading as his fare. Micah would scour the hospitals as a physician, and Felix's long run as a college student would allow him into the clubs and parties where this thing had really taken off. Vanessa, meanwhile, would join the drove of reporters trying to get a bead on the sudden spike in apparent homicides, and if all that failed, they'd each work their way into the city's center, and less familiar environs.

Tekla and I were there to see them off, both of us dressed as well. She'd be heading directly to the astrolab to cast lots or run charts or whatever she thought the situation called for, so she was in her work robes, and I was wearing old jeans and a tee, a bandana covering my blond locks in that white-bread gangsta way. After the others had disappeared, the airy hiss of the tunnel swallowing them up, I turned to her in the ensuing silence.

She held up a hand before I could speak. "It's for the best, Olivia. You'll see that in time."

"I doubt it," I said sullenly.

Tekla knew I was baiting her, and she merely inclined her head, aura steady. "I can tell you're not going to be reasonable today, so I'll be off to work. You're free to remain here to pout."

"Oh, I can remain *here*, can I? Thanks so much."

"Don't get snippy with me." She whirled on me, snapping, "I've never been wrong about something of this magnitude before."

"Tekla," I said softly, shaking my head. "We both know that's not true."

The barb—a reminder of all the lives that'd been lost when she'd been usurped in the troop by a mole—struck as I'd intended. Her expression hardened, and I was careful not to look into her eyes. Right now was not the time to find out if she really could trap someone with her gaze. "You know, Olivia, not every horrible thing you say can be attributed to your Shadow side."

As much as I wanted to, I didn't call her back to apologize. Instead I waited until I was certain she'd gone, and slipped behind a pillar to snatch a slim leather satchel I'd deposited there only an hour before. Then I placed my shield over my eyes and yanked back the propulsion lever.

A whoosh of air jerked the breath from my body, then biting cold stung my skin as I hurtled up the chute, the voices of those who'd gone before me still echoing off the cylindrical chamber. Bright lights streamed past my mask, but Hunter's invention did its job, shading my Shadow side from the light so I cleared the bright spiraling tube safely, vaulting in the air with the same sort of free-falling emergence a child must feel at birth. Suddenly my limbs were free and reeling, and I was reversing direction, again the victim of gravity. I spotted my landing and dropped to a crouch on the Silver Slipper.

Backlit in the approaching dawn, perched on the highest sign in the boneyard, I was now at the greatest risk of discovery. All any member of the troop had to do was look behind them, and that they didn't revealed how much they trusted me, or how little they really knew of me. I was about to set them straight, though if all went well they'd never know it. Vaulting the fifteen feet to the dusty ground, I charged ahead, careful to keep silent, downwind, following their lead.

The exact moment when night and day split isn't a palpable thing. I don't know how to explain it, except to say it's like entering the embrace of a familiar lover. At some point you're able to anticipate timing and touch, melding the new sensation in with the familiar experience, so that your movement from one side to the other is sure, smooth, and relaxed. So at the moment Gregor gunned his engine, wheels spinning madly against gravel and broken glass, and just before the cab shot forward like a greyhound out of the gate, I lowered myself into a runner's crouch.

He barreled ahead, and I bolted across the remaining acreage of the boneyard, eating up the ground with long, sure strides. Metal screamed through stone as the cab hit, the high-pitched tearing of the car's body muffled by the explosion of disintegrating concrete blocks. When the ripple came around the final wall—the one I'd breached before—I fired another full round into the congealing concrete, then plunged headlong into the chasm. I knew it'd be close, but when the shockwaves shuddered around my frame, and concrete pressed in, pressuring my skull, I could only hold my breath, keep my eyes shut, and work my way through what felt like a mile of concrete. The wall was solidifying at my heels so quickly it would swallow me if I stopped. My satchel took on drag, like a parachute opening after a diver, and I had to fight it—limbs wheeling madly—to power through to the other side.

The wall suddenly released me and momentum thrust me forward, so I ended up on hands and knees, concrete dropping from my face in wet chunks. It took a moment of wracking coughs, but eventually I was able to reach blindly behind into my backpack. I washed my face with a wet towel, then my hands, the towel quickly stiffening as I blew my nose and started digging out the concrete in my ears.

Senses restored, I stripped off the bandana protecting my hair and dropped it to the ground. It fell like a rock. My jeans crackled as I stood, and I glanced behind me to see a splinter in the newly formed wall, an opening, if one knew where to look. I pushed away my unease at leaving the barrier compromised yet again, and reasoned that the Shadows had to know we were looking everywhere for them. The last thing they'd do was come knocking on our front door, and I'd return and mend the small fissure before it was found . . . by Shadow *or* Light.

So, mentally apologizing to the God of Fine Vehicles, I clicked open Olivia's Porsche and climbed into the driver's seat with brittle chunks of cement falling off me everywhere. First stop, home to change. It didn't matter how fast Gregor and the rest were. They had seven stops to make before they could begin their investigation. I had two. And in this car, I'd make them both in record time.

14

If you don't count the traffic, Vegas is an easy town to get around. It's laid out like a grid, one flat street bisecting another, north to south and east to west, with a swirl of interstate looping psychotically about the middle. There wasn't much traffic this early in the morning, and I reached my second destination in five minutes flat.

This time I drove my other car. I'd bought the old clunker last winter, and nobody knew about it, not even Warren. This was what I used for my late-night hunts, when taking a Porsche into the city's underbelly would be like taking Pam Anderson into a high school boys' locker room. I kept it in a remote corner of my high-rise's garage, where the shadows ate up most of the chipped paint and dented bodywork, and while the community board didn't like it, I paid them enough in association and parking fees to keep them quiet. Besides, I always kept it covered.

As manic and peopled as the site of the first attack must have been a dozen hours ago, it was deserted now, all the cops back in the shop typing up their reports, all the curious onlookers locked safely behind closed doors, thanking their lucky stars that whatever ill fate had befallen their neighbors, at least it hadn't visited two doors down. I sat in my beat-up two-door, dressed in black fatigues, a dingy wig covering my hair as I waited for the others to make their way into the core of the city.

As I waited, I listened to the scanner I'd had installed in this car, a page out of Gregor's book, though this one was tuned to the station the troop used to communicate. Even expecting it, I jolted when the static burst into syllables, straightening from my slouch so quickly, Wild Turkey sloshed over the scarred leather seat. It was Gregor's voice, and I upped the volume to make out his words and code.

"There's been a mix-up at Sky-Chem, Inc. Two tests have been tampered with, though one has gone missing."

Warren's voice returned immediately. "Has the technician made contact with the other concerned party?"

"Affirmative. Second party is not currently in residence, but en route from California. Expected at Sky-Chem's downtown office, First and Ogden, ASAP."

In context, the dialogue made sense. Chandra worked at Sky-Chem laboratories doing drug tests on city employees. She had found another victim. She'd moved the body and was now a short distance from the California Hotel. The crossroads had been given as a reference point. The remaining agents would scent her out from there.

And with a body to examine, there was a biological template to work from. Since said body was also just four blocks from here, I yanked my keys from the ignition and immediately took off in that direction. If I waited, the others would close the perimeter, and I wouldn't get close enough to see or learn anything at all. So I needed to get there first using a route none of them would use, remotely possible only because I'd already legged countless hours on these streets.

Most of the roadways in this area were short but wide, trapped between railroad homes built in the early 1900s, now renovated office buildings, with a spattering of new construction. A few blocks over, downtown Vegas teemed with slot machines, dollar-ninety-nine breakfasts, and a multimillion-dollar canopy of lights, but on this side of the metaphorical tracks, cheap thrills were the thing of dreams. As was, it seemed, indoor plumbing. There was so much urine on the walls of the alley I veered through that I could see the stains even in the moonlight.

I paused when I reached the alley's end to peer around the corner, covering my nose as I studied the building across the street. A brick affair that'd seen its best days about three decades past, it was shrouded in darkness, its business day long concluded. The building adjacent to it had been renovated into a bank, which meant security, sensors, and cameras. In comparison, this one looked like a neglected dog. Even a break-in would be welcome attention. Happy to oblige, I skirted across the street.

There was a dim alcove with dual glass doors, and I peeked through them into the lobby, redesigned to look edgy and modern, though stripping the yellowed linoleum had apparently been beyond the budget. Black tape along the floor showed where the cattle—or customers—were to line up, and walls of half brick, half glass, probably bulletproof, held cages where clerks served their time. The place was otherwise windowless.

Only one place to go, I decided, sticking my head out from beneath the portico to survey the rest of the building, and that was up.

A good rock climber can wedge fingertips and body parts into the smallest of crannies, stem from the most unlikely of places, and defy gravity with nothing more than flexibility, confidence, and strong thighs. I wasn't a good rock climber . . . but I was a heroine, and if I wanted to hang on to a measly piece of brick, I could. It helped that I had no fear of falling, but it would have helped more if I could've just leaped the thirty feet to the roof, which I *hypothetically* could. Hypothetically being the key word. Down was one thing; you just aim and let gravity do most of the work. Up was quite another.

All in all it took me a little over a minute to scale the wall, long enough to be spotted if someone had been approaching from a westerly direction. I still had the presence of mind to glance around before swinging myself onto the crackling, dilapidated rooftop, sidestepping broken tiles, bottles, and newspapers in a crouch, wondering how so much litter found its way onto the rooftop.

According to my calculations, and the death scent growing stronger with every advancing step, the opposite wall should look down on the alley where Chandra had stashed the body. I took a full minute to center myself, making sure my breath was even, then peered over the side.

It took a moment for me to spot them, eyes running over the various bumps and shadows protruding from the alley floor, but then Chandra's bulky, loathsome silhouette lumbered into view. She bent over what I assumed was the body, examining it with careful attention until softly running footfalls caught her attention. She tensed, shoulders squared, then relaxed as Micah rounded the corner. They whispered in half sentences and medical jargon, a conversation born of familiarity and long hours spent together in the lab, and the few words I caught were difficult to follow.

Half a minute later Warren stumbled up the opposite side of the alley, still immersed in his character. His walk gradually straightened, though he still possessed the authentic limp, and his head came up, scouring their faces before moving on to the rest of the surroundings.

I jerked back from the ledge, because if anyone was going to discover me, it was Warren. He had an uncanny sixth sense, especially when it came to me. We'd been linked with a binding agent months before, and though he swore the compound had been dissolved, I sometimes felt twinges in my breastbone when he was near, like a second heartbeat. And if I felt that, I'd decided, Warren probably did too.

I waited another minute, then chanced another look over the ledge. There were six silhouettes now assembled around the body as if about to perform some sick act of satanic worship . . . or as if they'd just finished. Jewell arrived just then, moving quickly, and the others made room for her, falling back to allow her in, and giving me my first good look at the ravaged body.

It was a woman, painfully ordinary in every way. Height, weight, hair color . . . even her state at the time of death could be termed average. After all, plenty of people died naked. Some even died with a horrific and pained expression on their face, eyes sealed wide in the final throes of fighting off the Reaper. But I doubted many others died with burn marks blackening their lips, shriveling their skin so that their death mask was frozen in a grotesque parody of a grin. I also doubted too many people had the same burn marks charring their fingertips, incinerating skin and tissue all the way down to the bone.

But this woman had pulled a triple-hitter. The burns extended to the entire area nesting between her spread legs, a charred and blackened void now, still smoldering and unrecognizable. The rest of her body was marble white, pristine and untouched against the filthy ground.

"What the fuck?" I pulled back, unable—indeed, unwilling—to process what I'd just seen. It looked like nitric acid had been poured over her body. Except there were no splash marks. And who burned only in three distinct and entirely separate areas of the body? And how had her attacker gotten away without discovery, without the victim—who looked like she'd died in intense agony—even making a sound?

Worse, was this what all the victims looked like?

I leaned back over the ledge to hear the other agents wondering the same thing. Hearing the word *prostitute* gave some clue as to how she'd gotten naked, why she'd been vulnerable to attack, but no one could guess at what had caused such painful mutilation. "How does a person burn to death with most of their body untouched?" I wondered aloud.

"They don't," came a voice from behind. I whirled, blood pounding in my ears because suddenly I smelled her— smelled the lack of her—and it was too late. Regan stood a handful of feet away in a flowered summer dress, looking young and completely out of place on a dilapidated rooftop in a neighborhood that looked and smelled like it needed to be flushed. For someone with supersenses, I sure was getting snuck up on a lot lately.

"How did you—?"

"Evade your detection? Again?" Her face was guileless, but her voice teased. Seeing the way my eyes narrowed, how my shoulders squared defensively, she answered her own question. "I'm an initiate. I'm losing my human odor because I'm no longer mostly mortal. I haven't metamorphosized yet, so the Shadow pheromones can't be scented on me. Basically I'm in an olfactory no-man's-land. We often send out older initiates to do reconnaissance work because of that. It's good training, and we can't be tracked by the agents of Light. Didn't you know?"

I hadn't—*we* hadn't—and I was peeved to find it a good idea. Warren would never go for it, though, in part because he'd have to get through Rena to do so. Shit, I thought wryly, they didn't even allow full-blown agents to leave the sanctuary if they thought it unsafe. Thus my position on the rooftop.

"That's another opportunity you had to kill me," I said in a whisper. "And you didn't."

Regan shrugged the words away and crouched beside me like we were longtime bosom buddies. "You're starting to owe me big time."

And my sense of right and wrong was just fucked up enough to believe that. Almost. "You're not going to kiss me again, are you?"

"Believe me, once was enough." She leaned forward to study the drama unfolding below.

"What did you do to that poor woman?" I finally asked.

"Nothing." She tilted her head prettily. "She did it to herself."

"Because she was a prostitute? Because she made her living off the streets?"

"Now, Joanna," she sang—she seemed to love saying my real name. Shooting me a sly smile, she blinked twice. "You know we don't play favorites when it comes to harming mortals. Besides, how could we be in this alley as well as at the other hundred and eighty-seven places at the same time this brutality was occurring?"

"A hundred and eighty-seven?" I repeated faintly. That was more than in the past . . . what? Five years combined?

"That's what the preliminary reports have confirmed," she said, and I was sickened to hear a note of pride tinge her voice. If there was any doubt she was Shadow, it was gone now. "Who knows how many have yet to be found."

All I could think to ask was, "Why?"

That little laugh tinkled out of her, subdued given the other agents, but infused with delight. "Chalk it up to collateral damage, Joanna. We had to cast our net far and wide. I told you we had something big planned for the agents of Light. The real question is *how*."

I didn't know. How *did* a person burn to death with marks on only ten percent of their body, at most? How did it happen all over the city at approximately the same time? How were the Shadow agents doing it seemingly from remote? And how was this to affect the troop? The same gnawing sense of anxiety I'd had when talking to Regan on the phone came over me, that unease as I'd watched the fireworks from the boneyard, feeling I was missing something so obvious it was staring me right in the face.

I gasped and looked up to find Regan doing exactly that.

"It's a virus," I said softly, and watched recognition dawn mockingly on her face. She tilted her head slightly, a silent indication to go on. "It's airborne, released with the fireworks from atop Valhalla. The spores needed time to drift, to settle, to infect. That's it? That's the plan? To make thousands of people sick just so you have a chance of infecting one or two agents of Light?"

I couldn't think of anything more heartless and inhumane. I recalled the way the gunpowder had possessed a peppery note, how the sky had filled with smoke—God, with disease—and the ground in the boneyard had disappeared in a haze of filmy, infested clouds. A cursed battlefield. *The second sign of the Zodiac.*

I swallowed hard, pressing a hand to my lips. I knew my thoughts were flashing across my face like a ticker on television, but I couldn't stop them. I'd stood in that boneyard, breathing deeply, trying to scent out the irregular notes on the wind . . . and that had been just what the Shadows had wanted.

I imagined myself in the place of the woman sprawled carelessly and obscenely on the ground below me, imagined what had to occur inside the body to end up that way, and I couldn't help but shudder.

"Don't worry, Joanna." Regan leaned forward until her eyes found mine, and she smiled reassuringly. "You're immune."

Then she blew me a kiss, and lifted her brows as if to say, *See what I mean?*

I didn't . . . and then I did. The ground swayed beneath me so suddenly, I had to grab on to the ledge to steady myself. The air left my body in a relieved and astonished whoosh, and I closed my eyes, remembering the way Liam had reacted in the aquarium when Regan had kissed me.

"You infected me," I said, faintly.

"I protected you," she corrected, and when I opened my eyes she smiled again. "I gave you immunity. Looks like you owe me another one."

"I owe you?" I asked incredulously. "For setting a deadly virus loose on the valley?"

"Don't be dramatic," she said, and rolled her eyes. "Only a small percentage of the population is susceptible to this strain, and even they had to be in the infectious range when the spores fell."

So the agents below couldn't contract the virus by touching the corpse . . . and they'd all been safely ensconced in the sanctuary the night of the fireworks. So that was a relief. But still. "The valley's almost two million strong!"

She winced, seemingly sympathetic. "Urban living's a bitch."

I looked back down at the woman on the ground, knowing that whatever her occupation, whatever her reasons for being out on these streets, she didn't deserve this. No one did.

"They don't appreciate you, you know," Regan said, mistaking my pained expression for the agents, who were packing up and getting ready to move out. "You should be down there with them, not up here squatting, having to do your job from afar."

A small flicker of resentment stirred in me at those words, but I smashed it down, refusing to open my mind to it. "They're just doing what they think best."

She made a falsely considering note in the back of her throat. "And look where it got them. Had they been more proactive in the past six months, like you, this might have been stopped."

I looked at her sharply. "Could it have been?"

She shrugged. "We'll never know, will we? You should cut your losses, Joanna. Come with me and I'll show you all that's truly possible. As your ally I'll make sure you're never lacking in knowledge, assistance, or friendship. We'll be the best in generations, you and I. The strongest, the most powerful."

"The most evil."

"Tomato, to-mah-to." She flicked a pebble she'd been toying with over the ledge, then grinned. "At least come and see how much fun we're having watching your buddies chase their own tails. We have a pool going . . . how many mortals will die before the first agent of Light figures out how to stop it? I'm taking the over." She laughed again, this time louder, and I knew the sound had been heard because there was a tensed shuffling below us, then dead silence.

I didn't care. I was ready to haul her giggling ass over the side of the ledge—discovery and punishment be damned—

and she must have sensed it, because before I found my feet she was away, positioned in the middle of the rooftop, the ancient air-conditioning unit safely between us. From there she pulled a slip of paper from her bosom and held it aloft.

"What is it?" I whispered sarcastically. "More protection?"

"Joaquin's home address."

My eyes went from hers to the paper and back again. She stared at me knowingly. "Gotta protect myself as well, don't I? You stay there long enough for me to put it on the ledge behind me, and it's yours. Deal?"

I didn't want to make any more deals with this psychopathic bitch, but I didn't have long to make a decision. The agents were active again below, disposing of the body, dispersing to their next locations, most likely heading back to the sanctuary. I had to get there first . . . but what to do about Regan? I'd let her live once already, and look what had happened.

Then again, she'd let me live twice. I bit my lip, thinking fast. I'd already be in a heap of trouble when my deeds in the aquarium were found out, but that wouldn't be until next Wednesday, another five days. The question was, could I find Joaquin and exact my revenge before Warren read the new manual? Because one thing was certain: once he found out what I'd done, he'd never let me exit the sanctuary again.

I glanced back at the paper between Regan's fingertips. An address. Well, it didn't get much easier than that, did it?

A shout sounded below me, and I knew I had to move quickly. I nodded, then settled back into a docile crouch. Regan backed up, scooping up a shard of glass without taking her eyes off me, and secured the note with it on the opposite ledge. Then, without glancing, she stepped backward, dropping from view.

Her gleeful yell followed her descent.

I launched myself forward as alarm rose in the alley, yanked the paper from beneath its weight, and vaulted to the rooftop across from me. Somersaulting out of my landing, I kept sprinting until I ran out of rooftops, then leaped to the ground in a blind freefall, feet bicycling madly in the air. I landed in a crouch and took off from there. I didn't dare look back, or stop, and by the time I reached my car I knew no one had followed.

Sliding into the seat, I closed my eyes and took a moment to catch my breath. Then, under the feeble light of a flickering lamp, I opened the slip of paper. No name . . . just an address I memorized immediately. After burning the note with the car's cigarette lighter, I smiled to myself and gunned the engine. All I had to do was help the troop realize the second sign of the Zodiac had come to fruition, that it was a virus plaguing the valley, and do so without letting on how I knew. Then I'd go after Joaquin.

And after that I'd turn my attention to Regan.

Because she was wrong, I thought, heading back to the sanctuary through the dark web of decaying streets. I didn't owe her shit. Hundreds of innocent lives lost made us more than even.

15

The others didn't return to the sanctuary that dawn, the next day, or the day after, and by the time they dragged in half a week later, I was desperate for news. I'd combed through all my manuals and gone over Regan's words in my mind, and was itching to add another corner piece to the puzzle of how this thing was being spread—but when those of us left behind gathered to greet the returning agents, I could tell from their slumped shoulders, weary and loaded, that they were no closer to knowing what had caused this plague than when they'd left.

That's what it was being called. A plague. Newscasters and reporters nationwide had jumped on the story, and the sensationalism only increased as the number of victims continued to rise. Regan has said only a small percentage of the population was susceptible, and if those numbers were right, those who'd survived the initial onslaught were somehow passing this virus on to others. The latest official update from the television had said a few hundred deaths, but as horrible as it sounded, that number was manufactured, a blind meant to keep public panic down. So my first question when the others stumbled in was going to be, *How many?*

But one look at their collective faces and the words dried like dust in my throat.

Warren was in the lead, as usual, but he held up a hand to stall whatever question had been about to pop from Tekla's open mouth. She snapped it shut quickly, brows drawing tightly together, her hands white-knuckling in front of her as Gregor walked past shaking his head.

Jewell looked like a survivor of a natural disaster, a lone human barely standing while everything lay flattened around her.

Hunter looked pissed.

Vanessa had red-rimmed eyes, and Micah had his arm around her waist, like he was afraid she'd topple without his support.

I'd never seen Felix without at least a small spark of mischief glinting in his eyes.

Riddick looked small despite his bulk and size.

"Jesus," I whispered, when they'd all passed. Chandra hadn't even registered my presence, and that more than anything else made fright knot up beneath my breastbone. Tekla, Rena, and I automatically drew together. Marlo, who'd come late to the launchpad, pulled up short when she saw the others' faces, and was now clasping my hand tightly. I didn't blame her. Superheroes weren't supposed to look inconsolable.

Tekla sighed heavily. "Give them time to find their equilibrium. Let the balm of the familiar, and the safety of sanctuary blight the images they've brought back with them. There will be time enough for questions tomorrow."

"But more people will be dead tomorrow," I said, unthinking, and was immediately ashamed. Of course the troop needed rest. But I needed to tell Micah about the virus, though I still hadn't figured out how to do so without tipping him off to how I *knew* it was a virus.

"More will die anyway," Tekla said, and wandered away, her robes and then the hallway swallowing her up. I shuddered, watching her leave. That wasn't pessimism. It was prediction.

With a muttered good-bye, Marlo followed Tekla back to the astrolab. I swallowed hard and turned to discover Rena already facing me. Tall, she wore a shapeless, long white robe similar to Tekla's, hazardous considering her occupation. Still, she never seemed mussed, untidy, or ruffled. Her hair, which must have been a vibrant red at one time, had faded to a soft copper, gray wisps threading away from her temples to the bun lying just above the base of her neck. Her only adornment was a pair of gold disks circling her ears, and those appeared larger than they were simply because they winked so close to her sunken and scarred eye sockets. The rest of her face was lined only with the normal evidence of age. She'd been the troop's senior ward mother for a long time now.

And, I thought, swallowing hard, if she'd had eyes, I'd say she was glaring at me right now.

"What?" I said, resisting the urge to look behind me.

"Maybe you're the one who should be answering a few questions," she said, and harsh anger sharpened her words.

"What do you mean?"

Her expression tightened. "I know you left, Olivia. Not just the sanctuary, but the boneyard. I went searching for you, and followed your scent all the way until it disappeared into a solid block wall."

Oh shit. I'd forgotten that despite the cross-hatching of scars marring the lids where her eyes should have been, Rena could see better than most people with 20/20 vision. Superheroes included.

"I have a good reason," I started, but she waved the words away impatiently.

"There's no good reason to ignore the direct orders of your troop leader. Ever."

And nothing I said could change her mind. Rena Hightower was charged with raising the children of the Zodiac until they entered their third life cycle, so every troop member that'd just passed us by had been, and in a way still was, her child. All except me.

I glanced around to ensure we were alone, then stepped closer. "All I did was follow them to the place where they found their first victim. Then I came right back. I just had to see."

"Imagine the trouble I could get myself into if I *just* had to see?" she said, so bitingly I had to wince. "Restrictions are put on us for a reason. You were told to stay here and you should have done just that."

"But—"

"Don't *but* me, Olivia Archer," and I knew I was in trouble because she'd never used my full name before. "You disobeyed a direct order, and as soon as Warren doesn't act like another disappointment is going to crush him, I'm going to tell him."

"No!" My voice came out louder and harsher than I intended, and I grabbed her hand without thinking. She jerked back with more strength than I knew she possessed, and I'd already started apologizing when she grabbed my hand again. "Where did you get this?"

I should've known Rena would be the first to notice the ring, even without eyesight. I considered lying for a moment, but the question had been asked with more curiosity than anger. "My locker," I said, causing her to nod to herself as the metal circling my finger warmed beneath her touch. "It was . . . waiting for me when I came back this time."

Waiting was the only way to describe the way the locker proffered its occasional contents.

"She must've left it for you," she said, and her expression softened as she rubbed the ring with her thumb, then smiled. She sighed it away almost immediately, and dropped my hand. Louder, she said, "It's a special ring, Olivia. One you're obviously meant to have."

The discovery had taken some of the venom from her voice, and that relieved me enough to have me regarding it anew. "Yes, but why?"

"That's up to you to discover, but I can tell you what it does . . . or at least what it did for your mother." She reached for my hand again and lifted it high, tracing the grooves around the cloudy stone. "Though it's beautiful, it's not only an ornament. See how the slits carve up and under the stone?"

I nodded before realizing she couldn't see the movement. "Yes," I said.

"If you follow those grooves and pull up on the stone, it'll unhinge. Depress it again, and in that moment, you'll have the power to call anyone to you, no matter where you are, and no matter what the circumstances."

I'd known there was a way to call enemy agents to you, though *call* was a deceiving term. Invoking an enemy's name would reveal your location by loosening your scent on the wind, so we trained to dampen our emotions and keep this from happening. It'd never occurred to me to draw them to me on purpose. And, I thought, studying the ring with renewed interest, it'd never dawned on me that there might be a way to call allies to your side as well. "You mean . . . like a get-out-of-jail-free card?"

She almost smiled at that, and inclined her head. "All you have to do is think of that person, and they'll be there."

"That's awesome," I said, studying the ring with new-found awe.

"Yes, but . . ."

I sighed, dropping my hand. "There's always a *but*."

And now the smile came. "And this time it's also a condition. You can only use this ring once. After that it loses all powers and must be passed onto someone else."

But one shot was all I'd need. I knew exactly who I'd call . . . and Rena did too. She shook her head and gave me a sorrowful smile. "Your decision cannot be made lightly, Olivia. You were given this ring for a purpose, and regardless of what you want, that purpose must serve the troop and the citizens of this valley. It's a great honor to be gifted with a physical totem. You must choose wisely."

I sighed, my heart sinking. Why'd there have to be a friggin' lesson in everything?

Glancing back up at Rena, I saw some of the tension had left her body. Obviously if the locker was showering me with gifts of this magnitude, she'd trust I was still doing my best for the troop. Now to convince her that keeping silent would do the same. "Please, Rena. I need a little more time."

Rena's look was both patient and critical. She'd been a mother for a long time. "You keep doing things on your own and you're going to find yourself with all the time in the world. Alone." She took a symbolic step backward, and I suddenly felt just that. "I know you've had only yourself to depend on in the past, but you have to learn to work within the structure of this group. You can't keep going off on your own because you have a hunch you think might help."

"I'm *trying* to work with the group. If you haven't noticed, I'm the one who's been left behind."

She said nothing, which I found encouraging.

"Just . . ." I blew out a long breath, trying to figure a way to explain myself without giving anything away. "There are things I know . . . or not know but *feel*, because of my Shadow side. Warren wants me to pretend it doesn't exist, and Tekla wants me to stomp it down until it really doesn't, but if restrictions are put on us for a reason, Rena, then so are abilities. What good is such a skill if I don't use it for Light?"

Rena's lips thinned as she searched for an argument. "We've always gotten by without the help of Shadow intuition before. The power of Light has always been enough."

"Yes, but have you ever seen anything like this before?" I said, throwing an arm out to the chute, and the world above. I didn't say the second sign of the Zodiac had been fulfilled, but I decided to hint at it. "You know we're the real targets, don't you? These mortals are only collateral damage. They're coming for us, they're coming *here* to the sanctuary, and they won't stop until every child of yours burns."

Rena gasped and I winced, knowing she was putting the scent that lingered in the air together with the faces she'd traced beneath her fingertips every day.

"Shouldn't we use any tool available to see that doesn't happen?" I said, softer now that I saw her wavering. "Even an instinct derived from the Shadow side?"

She made me wait for her answer, but finally heaved a sigh, causing her gold hoops to jangle. "All right. I'll keep silent," she said, before holding up a finger. "But only because I scent a grain of truth in what you're saying."

And because of the ring, I thought, though I wasn't about to question it. I opened my mouth to thank her but she held up her hand. "And only for a short while longer. After that—"

"I know," I said, nodding. "You'll have to tell Warren. I understand."

"Oh no. You don't understand." She shook her head, and that fierce resolve returned, her voice hot in warning, fear, and the frustration of finding herself stuck. "After that, *you'll* have to tell him. He'll decide what's to be done with you and your instincts."

Another day passed before Warren told the rest of us there'd been nothing the troop could do to help the mortals of Las Vegas. They'd spent their days easing the suffering of those victims found still alive, and hid as many of the bodies as they possibly could.

Why hide them?

Well, first, each body the troop stumbled on had to undergo a thorough examination, and it wasn't of the open-your-mouth-and-say-ah variety either. If unofficial autopsies started showing up all over the valley, it would send up red flags to both the mortal authorities and the Shadows. Additionally, if we could keep the perceived number of deaths below the expected tally, maybe it would draw one or more of the Shadows from hiding to see what was going on. But that hadn't happened. And knowing what I did about the use of initiates in such situations, I knew it wouldn't.

But what was most discouraging was the number of victims.

"How many?" I gasped, when we'd all finally gathered back in the briefing room. Hunter was missing—he'd been out in the field twice as long as anyone else, and seen so much he didn't need to be briefed—but everyone else seemed rested, showered, and calmed, if not exactly chipper.

"Two thousand, seven hundred, and thirty-one," Micah said tersely. *A cursed battlefield.* He then flipped open a notebook and began to read from it, putting whatever was written there in laymen's terms so the rest of us could understand it. "Basically, it's an extremely rapid breakdown of the body's tissue upon contact with something else. Food, maybe, because of the mouth. Or it could be some sort of flesh-eating disease, but I don't think so."

"So not burn marks?" Felix asked, leaning on his back chair legs.

Micah shook his head. "From what I can see it looks more like the decaying process that occurs after death. There's a systematic breakdown occurring in the tissue in three distinct areas—mouths, hands, genitalia—though that alone shouldn't be fatal."

That made me pause. Strange that the virus would affect only three parts of the body. Why hands? Was it symbolic because we didn't possess fingerprints? Because the Shadows didn't want the mortals to discover this anomaly if an agent of Light were to fall? Whatever it was, I needed to speak up now, let Micah know it was a virus so he could focus on answering these questions himself . . . and work to find a cure.

But how to let them know without giving away what I'd done . . . and without jeopardizing what I needed to do next?

While I wondered, Chandra spoke up. "What about a biological attack?"

My head shot up. Yes. Closer . . .

"You mean like anthrax or ricin?" Micah shrugged and flipped his notebook shut. "Something like that could certainly affect a large group of people, but it would start in a contained area. Or at least have a point of origin we could trace it back to. These victims are spread all around the valley. Different social classes, workplaces, lifestyles. Nothing to unite them at work, play, or socially."

"So nothing other than they all live in Las Vegas?" asked Felix.

Except that they were all gathered outside Valhalla the night of the fireworks . . .

Micah ran a hand through his hair thoughtfully. "There is one thing, actually. A similarity in DNA, a strain of chromosomes that might indicate a propensity toward mutation of sorts. I haven't had time to study it further, but my bet is the answer lies there. I'd have to get back to the lab to know for sure, though." And his legs twitched beneath him, indicating he wanted to do just that.

"Wait!" I said as he began to rise. They all looked at me and I bit my lip, thinking fast. "Um, what about motive? I mean, maybe if we discover *why* the Shadows have suddenly decided to begin mass murdering innocents it'll lead us to how."

"They're Shadows," Chandra snapped. "Do they need a reason?"

"They don't need it, but they probably have one," I said, snapping back before turning away from her and addressing the rest of the room. "I mean, even if you're right and they're trying to draw me out in the open, it still seems a little extreme. What if it's a trial run for something else? Something bigger?"

"That's not how they operate, Olivia," Warren said, squashing the idea immediately. "Humans are sometimes affected by our paranormal battles, and it's our job to keep those individuals safe, but the Shadows don't target groups of people. Otherwise, why not wipe out the entire city? Why not do it years ago?"

I crossed my legs, my foot bobbing impatiently. "You're operating on the premise that the Shadows seek balance, like you do. What if that's changed? What if they want a greater influence over the valley? What if the Tulpa wants annihilation?"

Chandra scoffed. "You can't annihilate an entire city. Without mortals the Shadows would have no one to influence, to carry out their schemes and autosuggestions, to create chaos on their behalf."

"Not the *mortals*, Chandra," I said bitingly. "Us. What if it's a trial run for us?"

An unsettling silence fell over the room as they each considered my words. Even Warren was listening, eyes fixed on me as if seeing me for the first time.

"I'm just saying if I were—" I was going to say *Shadow*, but I was half that, and wouldn't be doing myself any favors reminding them of it. "If I were a Shadow agent and I was going to do something this big, I'd test it first. Make sure it would invade or infect the way I thought it would."

"Test it on monkeys," Micah murmured, mind working.

"Test it on mortals," I corrected, because the whole of the valley had become a part of the Shadows' experiment. They all were silent after that.

"Maybe we should . . ." Chandra trailed off, her own gaze far-off and thoughtful.

"Go ahead, Chandra," Warren said to her.

"I was just thinking maybe we should all give blood samples to Micah. You know, in case it is a biological weapon. Then we can rule out for sure that none of us are . . ."

Infected. The word she couldn't speak was on everyone else's faces. Vanessa and Felix looked at each other. Riddick and Jewell did the same. Warren cleared his throat, and all eyes returned to him as he reluctantly nodded his agreement. "It's a good idea. Everybody hit the lab so Chandra can take a sample of your blood. I doubt we've anything to be worried about, but it's best to be safe."

I swallowed hard, realizing what I'd just gotten myself into. If the virus could show up in the blood, then couldn't the immunity do the same? After all, what was immunity but a sampling of the toxin turned safe? If I gave blood, would it send me into further lockdown? Would biology give up the secret I'd worked so hard to keep?

But if my blood did possess the immunity—and all I had was Regan's faithless word on that—then I owed it to my troop, and the city, to offer it up. And studying the samples would take time. If Micah hadn't discovered my immunity himself by morning, I swore I'd tell him myself. But dawn was fast approaching, and Joaquin's address was flashing like neon in my mind. Warren could lock me up in the sanctuary for as long as it took to find a cure, but I wanted, and *needed*, to end Joaquin's contemptible life tonight. Talk about a cure for the world's ills. So I left the meeting and headed back to my room in preparation for escaping the boneyard one last time.

"That you, Olivia?"

I jumped, automatically feeling at my hip for a weapon that wasn't there. A chuckle came at me from the darkness, and my heart settled enough to make out the shape of the man coming at me from an adjacent passageway. An orange ember was brought to his lips, flared, then obscured again in a puff of smoke.

"Shit. Hunter." I put a hand to my chest and inched closer, joining him in the shadows. "What are you doing loitering in the dark?"

"Is *that* what it looks like I'm doing?" That laugh again, a sound void of humor, then another deep inhalation on his cigarette. I hadn't even known he smoked. "I'm not *loitering* in the dark, dear, dear Olivia. I'm reveling in it. I'm bathing in it. Fuck, I'm . . . I'm one with it." He motioned widely around him, then leaned his head back against the wall and closed his eyes. He wasn't bathing in the darkness, I thought, sniffing as I approached him. He was drowning in it . . . it and the bottle both.

"I thought you were sleeping," I said, alarmed because

Hunter never, ever drank. I'd never learned the reason behind that, but the fact he'd abandoned one of his most stringent personal mores had me biting my lip in worry.

"Sleep?" His head rolled forward on his neck. "Nooo . . ."

I gingerly tipped up his chin, and saw it wasn't just drink that kept him from focusing on my face. His eyes looked burned out, like they couldn't bear letting in another appalling sight, and his breathing was shallow . . . and reluctant. That's why I hadn't sensed him there. He was almost devoid of anything that passed for human life.

"You're very drunk."

"You're very right."

"C'mon, Hunter," I said, taking his hands. "Let's get you to bed."

"Absolutely. Bed is where I need to be." He let me shift him to his feet, but his acquiescence was more surrender than agreement. We maneuvered down the hallways, his cigarette hanging from the side of his mouth, the smoke making my eyes sting. Though he was moving his feet, I got the feeling he didn't care whether he came or went, stayed or left, lived or died. Bone-deep didn't even begin to describe his fatigue.

"This is it, right?" I asked, steering him to a nondescript door off the top of the Z-shaped barracks.

"Home sweet home," he agreed, and blew the air out of his nose while dropping his face against the wall. It was as close as I'd ever heard Hunter come to a giggle. He fumbled to get his hand aligned with the palm plate, and nearly fell inward when the door swung open. We stumbled in, and I jumped as a clap of thunder split the room in two and rain began to hammer on the window opposite the door.

A holograph, I thought, sighing. We had the option of programming three-dimensional images onto the walls in our rooms—a green meadow, a streetscape, anything to further personalize our space—but I hadn't activated the feature in my room, forgetting it even existed until now. A holograph of a soft summer shower might be relaxing, one with light from a far-off street lamp playing over slowly streaking walls, and headlights from cars ferrying souls unlucky enough not to be tucked snugly in bed adding to the comfort and security of being nestled inside.

But this wasn't womblike and warm. This assaulted the senses, an angry attack from the heavens that ripped through the bruised sky to punish the pane.

"God, no wonder you needed to get out of here. This is . . ."

"Atmospheric," he finished, opening his arms wide to throw himself off balance again. I let him stumble since he was headed toward the bed, but he righted himself again in an exaggerated sway and offered me an equally overstated grin. I smiled back weakly. Seeing a heroic man this drunk was like seeing a rhino tottering about after receiving a tranquilizer dart. You really didn't want to be near it when it fell.

"I was going to say depressing."

"What? You don't like rain?" He maneuvered over to the wall, touched the faux window, and came away with wet fingers. A water wall too, I realized, as he rubbed his smooth fingertips together. "I love rain," he whispered. "It makes me feel small. It feels like baptism."

The note of loss in his voice bored a hole straight through my chest, and another sharp bolt of light cracked through the room, lighting the hollows under his eyes. I felt the air escape me as his shoulders slumped, and crossed the room quickly, putting my arm around him again, this time in comfort rather than support. He turned into me, and heat leached from my body into his and back again. I imagined it driving the cold spots from the crevices of his heart, held him for a long minute, then squeezed him hard before pulling away.

He pulled me close again.

"Hunter," I said, my voice muffled against his chest. God, but his skin smelled good, even with the alcohol and sorrow permeating his pores. Still. "Let go of me."

He released me enough to stare down at me, eyes so dark his golden skin appeared whitewashed in contrast. "I'm sorry, Olivia, but you're being a tightass, and this is for your own good."

And he kissed me. And that's when I realized that whenever he did so, I thought of violence. Sure, it was tempered with warmth and the softness of his full lips, but there was a firmness in his embrace, a determination to infiltrate, overpower, and conquer that made some primal need in me rear up to do the same.

My hands were on him before I could stop them. We overbalanced—he was drunk and had an excuse; I simply had a sudden and blinding need to taste and feel more—and we crashed against that wall of water, the pane shaking beneath our combined body weight. He could match my strength, so I wasn't gentle, concentrating solely on my hunger as lightning scorched the sky behind him. In the brief illumination I saw water sluicing over the sides of his silhouette, plastering his hair to his skull, his T-shirt to his back, molding his jeans to his ass. I lowered my hands, pulled in close, and he dropped his head back on a rich, musical moan. A single trail of water coursed over his left cheek, and I caught it at his neckline, stroked upward with my tongue, found his ear, pressed closer.

His hands were on my waist then, beneath my shirt, printless fingertips gliding along my sides. They dipped to the small of my back, met there, and I quivered as they lowered, cupping me from behind. He was towering over me now, head bent, his lips so close to mine, I scented his breath on mine.

"Joanna . . ."

My name, whispered, brought me to my senses. It wasn't supposed to be paired with his. Not in my dreams, or in my life, not even surrounded by a punishing rainstorm bested only by his heart against my own. It was supposed to be Joanna and Ben. The way it'd always been. The way it always would be.

So what the hell was I doing? This wasn't a flirtation, or a game, or fun. This was a wild bid to escape whatever had buried itself in his mind. I pulled away despite a desire to curl up into his core, knowing there was no epiphany to be found in his arms. Or mine.

"How altruistic of you," I managed, when I got my breath back. I licked the taste of him from my lips and met his gaze. "Now let me go."

His mouth quirked, like I'd told a joke, but he let his arms drop. I felt unbalanced; free, but fettered at the same time. Hunter seemed to know it. Letting out a deep sigh, I shook my head and headed to the door. His voice stopped me halfway across the room.

"Jo."

I turned back warily. As the only member of the troop outside of Warren and Micah who knew my true name, he also knew not to use it. But he used it again now that we were alone, tongue silky over the single word. "Jo. You think I don't know how you want me? That I can't see what's going on inside you? Or feel it?"

I gave my head a short jerk. "I know you know."

"Because you know me too. Because when you gave me the aureole we became joined." He took a step forward, steadier now. "You've already let me inside of you."

I swallowed hard. "Not on purpose."

Another step. "You don't have to be alone."

I looked over his shoulder to the wall of glass and falling rain. What he meant was *we* didn't have to be alone. Me, him, and the emotions that'd lain him flat tonight. If I stuck around I'd learn about them all, and I wasn't sure I wanted to know. I had my own failures to be haunted by, my own epiphanies to seek.

"Hunter, I—"

"Need an ally," he interrupted, as sober as he could manage. "Someone who knows your secrets and has seen into your Shadow side . . . and still stands by you. Warren won't, you know. You don't want him to know about your daughter—"

"*Not* my daughter." I was getting tired of having to remind people of that.

"The child who carries your lineage in her blood, then," he said sharply, and that somehow sounded worse. Maybe because it was the truth, and someday soon I was going to have to face it . . . and do something about it. I dropped my head, saying nothing, and a moment later the warmth of his palm glided up my arm, sending chill bumps along my side, while he rested his hand on my shoulder. His weight against me was solid and reassuring. "Warren can sense you're not telling him everything. He's waiting for you to make even one false step. If anything reminds him remotely of the Shadows he'll name you a rogue, just like his father."

I jerked away, my hands automatically clenching into fists. "Thanks for lumping me in with a murderer."

"I didn't. I lumped you in with the other person Warren loved and still killed out of duty." His eyes were half shut with fatigue and drink, but what I saw of them was calculating and too knowing for my liking.

I looked away, staring at the storm flailing at his false window. It suddenly felt like I was out in it. Warren wasn't doing that. Was he? Look for faults, waiting for me to screw up?

"Look." Hunter sighed. "I want to help you. I'll keep your identity, your daughter, and your moves against Joaquin hidden. I can do that, you know. I can be your secret keeper."

He said it like he meant *love slave*. Damn those lips, that voice . . .

"In exchange for what?" I managed, falling back on my trusty sword of sarcasm. "My bed?"

Because the mention of Warren's rogue father had been a veiled threat. So had the reference to Ashlyn, whom Hunter knew about because of the aureole, but Warren did not. Venom coated my words, anger boiling in my core. I thought my Shadow side must be peeking through; there was just a hint of smoke rising in the thundering air, possibly a deepening of my eyes, though I'd have to look in a mirror to know for sure. I didn't want to do that.

And I didn't want to admit Hunter would be a great ally. He had more patience with me than Warren, and seemed able to face those black holes in me that even I could not. Like now, I thought wryly, watching him stare at me. Even at a time when I was afraid to face a mirror.

"I didn't say you should barter your body," he said carefully, reading my mood. Then he licked his lips. "Just . . . share it with me."

Don't you just love semantics?

I studiously kept my eyes off his lips . . . and his hands, and his eyes. And the rest of him too. Because even though I could use an ally, what I didn't need right now was a lover. Unfortunately they were being offered as a package deal. I lifted my chin and steeled myself against the offer, the need. The understanding.

"I still love him," I said flatly, and had to watch Hunter wince. He didn't recover as quickly as he would've were he sober—a stab of pain, then disappointment blazing in his eyes as the next arrow of lightning flashed through the room—but eventually his expression closed.

"Which is why you should let him go."

He knew all about Ben, of course, had learned about him and more when we'd swapped memories and emotions through the magic of the aureole. And I could see why he wanted to feel it again. I'd never felt more understood than in those brief moments. I'd never been less alone than when Hunter had seen the Shadow in me and hadn't shied away, but accepted it and my thoughts as his own. I knew, in exchange for helping shoulder his own mental burdens, he was offering to do the same now.

But he was in a self-destructive mood.

"And letting you into my body as well as my mind is going to help with that?" I said, forcing a note of detachment into my voice that I didn't really feel.

He shrugged, offered me a rare if lopsided grin. "Can't hurt."

"You know *that's* not true."

But I swallowed hard. I'd enjoy having him inside me, that much was true. You didn't have to know Hunter when he was sober, and in save-the-world superhero mode, to know there was a world of possibilities waiting in those arms. Even now, with him smelling of booze and staggering slightly, his focus was like the sun through a magnifying glass.

And me, I thought, shifting my feet, just a little ol' bug.

"Sleep it off, Hunter," I said, my voice more callous than I intended as I turned from him and opened the door. I escaped into the light and sterility of the hallway, blinking hard, because this was what felt unreal. It was a too-abrupt end to the violent music of the thunderstorm, and the heated tension between Hunter and me as we faced off in the near dark. I turned back a second too late. He had followed me to the door, and when I looked up the lust in his gaze had been shuttered, and all that remained was the cold depths of the emotions he was trying to escape.

"Look, I'm sorr—" I started, but the door clicked firmly shut in my face, and the silence of the hallway rose to a buzz in my ears. I finally got my feet moving, my footsteps filling the silence. By the time I reached my room, I was breathing in time to them, a steady beat despite my own erratic heart, as the possibilities Hunter had spoken of died around me.

I made my move on Joaquin the following night. I'd have gone the previous dawn, but I slept badly after fending off Hunter's advances, dreaming of making love with Ben while another man watched through a rain-streaked window. I dreamed I was back in my old body, which would've made me happy if I hadn't realized someone else was inside my dreaming flesh as well, curled around Ben, sharing it—and him—with me.

It also seemed poetic to attack Joaquin in the hours he'd first attacked me. It was the same time of year, and the same desert sage rose to perfume the air in the predawn hours, when decent people were still sleeping off the hangovers of the night before.

So I used my daylight hours to rest, and to plan. There were detailed maps of the city archived in the record room adjacent to Tekla's astrolab, and I spent half the day there, poring over photos of street maps, imagining and reimagining scenarios of approach, infiltration, and escape, and staring at the home of the man who'd affected my life more than any other since the one who spawned me.

I used the photocopier to make duplicates of the residential streets and his home, and sat down to study them, thinking I really should make more use of this room. I knew the arteries and thoroughfares of Vegas as intimately as I knew the veins webbing my wrists, but there were other Vegases in the journals and books and registers here—line-drawn depictions of the original settlements—Indian, Spanish, Mormon—and those primitive roads lay like ghosts beneath the alternately beautiful and stark streets I knew. Someday I'd like to know them all.

"Later," I said aloud, and shut off the lights as I exited the room. First I had another man to make into a ghost.

16

If you head away from the Strip on the I–95, past the old wash and the clusterfuck known as the Spaghetti Bowl, you'll end up in a tony and relatively new suburban master-planned community, where housing prices reflect the desirability of the area, and residents make sure the distinction is known. As you make your way up Summerlin Parkway, the mountain ranges that once lay so far from the center of town begin to butt up against rows of communities plotted to provide developers with the greatest return per square foot. The uniformity of the houses also provides neighbors with added anonymity; nobody knows exactly who's being rude when they drive directly into the garage of the house looking much the same as theirs, closing the door with nary a how-dee-do.

It was in one such neighborhood, pressed against a mountain—a hill compared to the ranges hovering over the valley, but mountainous nonetheless—that Joaquin's nondescript home rested. Of course, Joaquin would like that. The blending, I mean. Physically he was that way as well. Most people would pass right over him; just a tallish man with shadowed eyes, pale skin, and hair a bit too long to be fashionable. But just as the bones beneath that benign exterior were blackened with decay, what lay in that house was coiled and waiting to strike.

I pulled up half a block from his lot to study the darkened windows of a detached home, light beige and single-story, with shuttered windows and a security gate over the front door. The front yard was xeriscaped—what a good little environmentalist our Joaquin was—and it blended perfectly with the houses on either side of him. I'm sure he enjoyed walking among the mortals he stalked, waving to a future victim on his way back from the mailbox, or petting the dog of a man whose wife he'd already marked as his own. I winced to see a tricycle trapped next to his mailbox, the thought of Joaquin living next to children instantly icing me over.

Stepping from my car, mask fixed firmly over my eyes to conceal my identity as Olivia, I had an arrow already notched in my conduit, held ready at my side. The street was deserted, but I'd already decided my approach would be from the hillside. The desert side, I thought, peering into the darkness. Just as he'd once approached me.

Nothing smells as fresh and clean as the night-laden desert air. The dusty floor was packed solid under my feet, the star-flecked sky swung wide overhead, and I moved lithely among bramble, boulders, weeds, rocks, skirting the jutting cacti poised like spiny sentries all along the hillside. As a kid I'd taken many such forays into the desert night, the complete dark and stillness adding to the thrill of the illicit outings. Joaquin probably thought of this hillside as his own, but that didn't faze me. I'd always considered the whole of the Mojave my home.

The brick wall separating his house from the untamed desert was my first hurdle. I vaulted it in a quick, single motion, watched only by the half cast eye of a slivered moon. Landing in a worn patch of grass, I darted beneath an overgrown pepper tree, where I remained for another minute to temper my thumping heart. I'd dreamed of this day too long to let my emotions overtake me now.

I approached the house cautiously, struck by the complete stillness. It was summer, and though the birds had retired for the night, chirping crickets should have softened the silence. Yet not even a blade of grass rustled in the breeze ferried from the hillside behind me: It was like the air too had abandoned this lot, run off by Joaquin's predatory scent in the same way pesticide kept insects at bay.

Or killed those who didn't obey their instincts, I thought, swallowing hard as I slid up the back porch. Reaching into my utility belt, I opened a compact mirror and peered into it to gauge the angle needed to reflect the home's interior. Even in baggy black fatigues, my face half covered by my mask, I had to admit I looked fabulous. Whoever it was who said, "Die young and leave a pretty corpse" was probably a fan.

Flicking my wrist toward the window, I did a swift sweep to detect any movement inside. There was none. So I tilted the compact slowly, making out a couch and coffee table in the dim room, a television perched on a small rectangular stand, and shadows—the normal kind—layering one another in varying degrees of density, banished near the left corner where a dim utility light, probably the bulb over a stove in the kitchen, had been left on.

I moved back from the window and followed the wall until I reached the sliding glass door. Putting the compact away, I gripped my conduit in one hand and a heavy-duty flashlight in the other. Something told me Joaquin was so confident nobody would dare enter his private domain that he didn't bother with an alarm system. What I didn't expect was for him to neglect locking the door as well. Surprise, then wariness, held me back when the door slid smoothly open, not even a squeak to break the oppressive silence.

Arrogant bastard, I thought, widening the gap. In one quick movement I'd breached the threshold and whipped my flashlight over the room like a spotlight arching over the night sky. There was nothing here but the objects I'd seen through the window, so I clicked the light off and let my eyes adjust to the interior, sliding the door shut behind me.

On closer inspection I saw the flotsam and jetsam that occupied Everyman's household—newspapers stacked neatly
to one side of the sofa, four different remotes to operate one
TV. Typical man. Next to an oval glass-top table I spotted a
large water bottle, like the ones delivered door to door in big
green trucks, brimming with coins.

How about that? Joaquin saves his pennies.

Another smaller jar rested on a wooden chair that looked
to be sized for a child. At first I thought it contained the
overflow coins from the first, but these weren't the right
shape or size, and coin didn't gleam in the moonlight like
broken seashells. I reached into the jar.

I knew even before touching them that they weren't seashells. Running my tongue along my top row of teeth, I
paused over the smooth surface mirrored in my hand, minus
the root. At least he'd washed the viscera from each tiny
trophy before depositing it inside. Fastidious, I thought,
clenching my jaw. Then I wondered which of the hundreds
was mine.

"Stop it," I ordered myself, depositing the tooth back with
the others. I wasn't going to start playing victim just because
I was finally facing the man who'd tried to make me into
one. But I wondered what he planned to do when the jar was
brimming. Something significant, probably. Something to
mark the occasion. Or maybe he'd just start another jar.
Maybe he'd simply go on killing.

"Not after tonight," I swore, and turned with more determination, if less care, to search the rest of the house. "Not
ever again."

Thirty tense seconds later I had the kitchen canvassed, as
well as the laundry room leading to the empty garage. That
half of the home searched, I turned my attention to the hallway, and the bedrooms I knew lay beyond. My feet were silent on the living room carpet, and I paused only long
enough to affix a bugging device beneath the cheap metal
coffee table, placing the bug to track it in my inner ear. I

wanted to know if he entered the living room while I was in another part of the house.

Away from the kitchen light, in the pitch of the darkened hall, the scents of charred candy and rancid flesh grew stronger. I caught myself breathing shallowly through my mouth, trying not to let too much of the stench in. The front rooms had been for show, with all the charm of a third-rate sitcom set. This, though, was where Joaquin lived. His stench was imbedded in the walls.

Inching along until I came to a trio of closed doors, I studied them all, then raised my conduit to the door on the right.

Let's see what's behind door number one, I thought, swinging it open. I crouched, prepared to blow the shit out of a secondary bedroom that had bare floors, naked concrete lying in spotty patches of light from the streetlights leaching through the vertical blinds. It was a workshop of some sort, I saw, straightening. All the tools were normal enough; jigsaws and cordless drills, pegboards anchored across an entire wall filled with hammers and wrenches and screwdrivers, aligned according to purpose and size. Drill bits lined the workbench in neatly arrayed plastic boxes, and I was willing to bet the locked drawers were equally well kept.

So, I thought, the anal freak liked to do his work away from the prying eyes of neighbors and passers-by. Interesting, as it didn't appear he was much for home improvement.

I returned to the hallway, leaving the room open. Door number two was positioned on an interior wall, too small to be anything but a utility closet. I told myself I was being thorough as I moved toward it, and that I wasn't avoiding what could only be Joaquin's bedroom directly across from that.

I whipped the closet open to find nothing but a bare lightbulb, the string used to turn it on swaying from the ceiling. I pushed that door open as far as it would go, just as I had with the first, then turned to door number three. Joaquin's bedroom. God, I did not want to go in there. But if I could catch him unaware, blow off his head in his sleep while he dreamed of murdering little girls in the desert and taking their eyeteeth home as a prize . . . well, isn't that what I'd come for?

The memory of the jar in the living room mobilized me, and I took a deep breath of Joaquin-soaked air, filled my lungs with it, and held it as I reached for the handle.

A noise on the other side stopped me.

It wasn't a snore, or the rustle of bedclothes as someone shifted positions, but a pleading sound, a soft whimper followed by ragged breathing, and in the brief silence I was sure I could hear someone struggling to crawl across the bedroom floor.

Like I'd once struggled to crawl across the dusty desert floor.

Thinking of tiny bodies, crushed spirits, and airless desert nights—and all those goddamned teeth in the living room—I expelled the tainted air from my chest and yanked the door open. But there wasn't another young girl looking up at me with bloodied limbs and pleading eyes. That was just me, my mind. A memory. Instead there was something else.

And boy, did it look happy to see me.

"Uh . . . good doggie?" I said, taking in the sight of an animal with the muscle of a bear and the angular ferocity of a wolf. He let a warning rumble loose in his throat, and the deep reverberation jarred through my immobile bones like a jackhammer through concrete. His ears were pricked forward, eyes bright, and I had no idea what kind of dog he was beyond "not friendly." Those eyes narrowed as I took a small step back, flashing scarlet, though that could've been my imagination. One thing was sure. If dogs could speak, this one would be saying, *Yum.*

No wonder the back door had been unlocked. Who needed a security system when Cujo lurked inside? Those hadn't been whimpers of pain I'd heard from the other side of the bedroom door, but cries of longing as the beast sensed an intruder. I swallowed hard, shifting my weight to take another step back, and pulled from my mind the only word I could remember from a long-ago documentary on the Discovery Channel.

"Stay," I said in German. Or so I thought. I'd probably said *Puppy Chow* because he launched from his back haunches so fast my vision blurred.

I raised my weapon arm too late. I couldn't clear the beast's bulky weight, and his front paws—flashing wickedly sharp claws—sank into my shoulders, mouth open and snapping. It was all I could do to wedge my forearms between us as I bowled over backward, footing lost, the stench of matted fur and stale dog breath washing over me as I hit the hallway floor.

My head slammed into the baseboards, and black dots threatened to swallow my vision, but I squeezed my eyes shut, lowered my chin, and crossed my arms over my face. He was reaching for my nose, but found my left arm instead, and I cried out as dozens of razors punctured the skin, and again when he reared back, pulling flesh and tendon and muscle with him. If there'd been more room for him to angle himself in the narrow hallway, the bone would've snapped. As it was, the space created between us was only wide enough to get one knee up, and I rammed it into his midsection, turning feral growls into a savage howl.

Great. Now I'd pissed him off.

He lunged again, but this time I caught his throat, fisting the fur there to yank him toward me. As I scissor-kicked my legs simultaneously, he flew over the top of me like a vulture swinging over its prey, twisting in the air to launch another attack even before he'd landed. But I found my knees as he crashed to the ground, and when that great muzzle snapped open again, I centered my conduit in that throat and fired inside.

The beast jerked as if puzzled, his jaw snapping shut on a bubbly whine. He shuddered as if he was swallowing the arrow, then blinked. Shuddered again. And his mass expanded by another foot.

"Shit," I said, realizing too late what I'd done. This beast was to Joaquin what my cat, Luna, was to me, a warden. It couldn't be killed, maimed, or reasoned with by an enemy agent. Wardens were trained from birth to defend their owners and territory, to recognize and attack whomever took the risk anyway. If it seemed like an unfair trade—the Shadows had dogs while we had cats—well, you hadn't seen Luna shear the eyesight from a Shadow agent in one wicked swipe. Not wanting to see what this hound could do given the same opportunity, I leaped over him, batting clumsily against the narrow walls like a pinball machine on full tilt.

Instinct had me darting right, into the workshop, and I kicked the door shut just before the dog barreled into it with a jarring thud. The door shuddered under his weight, and I didn't bother with the lock. A few more hits like that and the entire frame would split in two.

I raced to the window, shoving the blinds aside only to find a barred-up alcove. A fluorescent bulb burned down on me in a mocking echo of the streetlights outside, bricks plastering the frame where the window used to be. He'd rigged it, the bastard. No window. No exit.

Conduit ineffective, I searched the room for another weapon, and had just grasped the handle of a screwdriver when the door crashed in. I whirled to find twin rubies of hate fixed on me, a muzzle bared and rumbling, and teeth as sharp as pokers visible in an oversized jaw. Knees bent, I braced myself as the dog lunged again.

It saw, or sensed, the screwdriver in my hand, and dodged my stabbing motion, barreling into my body, flinging my arm wide. Our howls mingled as he latched on to my bicep this time, and I head-butted him before he could rip it open. He snapped at my face once, twice, saliva dripping to pool on my chest, and I backpedaled, lurching into a defensive position again.

"Bring it, you mangy, flea-bitten prick!" His ears flattened at the growl in my voice. This time I waited until he'd committed, his jaw plunging precariously close to my unguarded neck. I took a risk, one that would cost me a hand if I judged wrong, and let my fist disappear into that great mouth, felt the barbed teeth skimming the soft skin at my wrist, then wrenched the screwdriver upright, lodging it between the lower jaw and palate. Eyes bulging with pain, the dog's frenzied growls snapped off into whimpers and I fled around the workbench, knocking it over before barreling through the remains of the shattered door and out into the relative freedom of the hallway.

Whimpers followed me. No wait, I thought, tilting my head. They were growls.

No, they were whimpers.

And growls.

Forcing myself to turn slowly, like the moon circling the earth, I shifted my attention back down the hallway and into the living room. Where another dog inched slowly forward, head lowered, eyes bright.

Fresh out of screwdrivers, my left arm still throbbing from the first dog's assault, I lunged for the next nearest door. Almost human in their outrage, cries sprang up in the hallway. I pulled the closet door shut behind me, and stood shaking in the dark as ramming, accompanied by furious howls, escalated outside.

I fumbled for the light above my head, my hand shaking so violently the string slipped through my fingers twice. Finally I snapped it on with a quick jerk of the cord, and blinked in the unrelieved wash of the bulb. Sucking in a deep breath, I held it before slowly forcing it out. The dogs could scent my fear in the air, and it drove them into further frenzy. I straightened my mask calmly enough, until it sat firmly on the bridge of my nose again, yet my heart skipped a beat when I started taking inventory, eyes falling to my left arm.

So that's why it hurts so much, I thought, studying the saliva and blood-coated limb. The bones were miraculously intact, but a flap of skin the size of a baseball fell open when I lifted my arm, exposing muscle, tendon, and a vein that had somehow escaped assault. That pumped merrily along like a beautiful string of red licorice. I was grateful, but it wasn't something I especially needed to see.

Using my right hand, I unhooked my utility belt, letting the pouches slide onto the floor before securing my left with the thick leather. It was awkward, and took a bit of time to fashion something both secure and flexible, but it gave me something concrete to focus on, other than the numbness that was quickly shifting into agony. By the time I finished, my hands had stopped shaking, and the dog had ceased beating at the door.

It would never look the same again, I thought, with real regret. Wardens left scars; they were as deadly as conduits in this way, though perhaps Micah could smooth over the worst of the damage with another extensive surgery. Provided I lived long enough to undergo one, I thought, flexing my fingers. Meanwhile intermittent whines and scrapes at the door broke the otherwise eerie silence.

I leaned back, cursing my stupidity. I should've waited to confront Joaquin outside his lair. Now the element of surprise had been wrenched from my grasp by fur and teeth and glowing eyes, and that gave me a reason to snarl. Joaquin would love the idea of me squirreled away in his closet, anticipating his return in the hours before my death, and I'd just decided I'd rather be a chew toy than provide him with any such satisfaction when the wall behind me shifted.

I jerked upright, my first thought, *Earthquake*. That, or they were detonating something at the nearby nuclear test site, though I quickly realized neither of those things would've caused this wall alone to move. I whirled, flattening my palm against the drywall where my head had been resting, and pushed. Nothing. I pushed again, lower this time, putting all my weight into it. There were no corner seams that I could see, no markings to differentiate the wall from any other.

I pivoted to face the door, and leaned back again.

This time, when I felt the wall shift, I went with it, pushing with my weight. Apparently I didn't know my own strength. The top of the wall flipped backward while the bottom scooped me up, like a seesaw extending the length of the closet.

In retrospect, it would've been a simple thing to let the panel fling me back, my legs arching overhead so I could somersault off the platform before the wall swung back into place. Instead I panicked, stomach lurching as my limbs flew out, a leg nearly getting wedged between the ceiling and the opening created by the pendulum's motion. I bent my knees just in time, but the movement threw me forward, and I slid from the tilted entrance into a heap on the floor, head first.

"Ouch," I said, my neck making adjustments that would've made a chiropractor cringe. I untangled myself, rose carefully, and felt for my conduit as I looked around. There was nothing to see . . . literally. I felt my eyes widen, I felt them blink, but the void was as complete as if I'd been dumped into a black hole. Joaquin could've been standing inches from me and I'd have never known.

That thought, plus a healthy dose of paranoia regarding a third dog, forced me into action. I might be blinded, but I had no intention of returning to that closet, or the set of razor-sharp teeth waiting for me beyond that. Using the wall as a guide, I took a step forward, then another. With the third came a telling rustle in the air. Of course, it registered too late. As I shifted my weight forward, the floor dropped from beneath me, a gaping mouth upturned to swallow me whole. I freefell, arms pinwheeling as I plummeted, ambushed yet again by something I didn't know.

I was beginning to feel picked on.

It wasn't a long fall. A child could've managed it in a playground. But I had no idea how far this rabbit hole went, so when the floor reared up seconds later, the impact jarred my bones and I crumpled like a wadded-up paper doll.

"Ouch," I said again, really meaning it this time. Pushing myself up with my good arm, I held the other lightly to my forehead. Pissed-off fireflies danced before my eyes, and I watched with a shiver of alarm when they coalesced into two slim lines, like they'd been giving their marching orders by the U.S. military. My head screamed, and my arm took up the echo in a pulsing beat, but I sent up a silent prayer of thanks once I realized the lights weren't just a trick of my battered brain, but a path leading deeper into this residential underground.

I hadn't found Joaquin, I thought, taking a cautious step forward, but I'd somehow stumbled upon something he valued enough to keep hidden behind attack dogs, secret passageways, and a simpering urban veneer. So I followed the glowing snake of lights along its subterranean path, not looking back as I traced the twisting coil deeper underground.

My eyes gradually grew used to the dim underground, and I could make out shapes and symbols along the smooth walls, like the hieroglyphics of a lost tribe long before the written word came into existence. Some characters I knew, others I recognized by sight but still didn't understand, and more were entirely new to me. Though they made no sense to me, I knew enough of Zodiac mythology to figure they probably told a story the deeper they progressed.

Deeper, it turned out, didn't mean lower. As my attention returned to my footing, I was surprised to feel the path shift again to the earth's surface. Into the mountain, I thought, suddenly realizing why Joaquin had chosen this location. I increased my pace, and after one more S-curve the footlights ended. I paused outside a carved entrance covered by velvet curtains so heavy and black, I'd have thought I was about to fall into another void if I hadn't seen the edges. Taking a deep breath, I drew the curtain aside . . . and stepped into the most gorgeous room I'd ever laid eyes on.

"Well, look at that." Ignoring the fact that it was an underground cavern, everything looked like a scene right from *Architectural Digest*. Well, if *AD* crammed their "best of" issue into one room, that was. There was no rhyme or reason to the stash; Art Deco chairs with bright orange seat cushions held court next to statues of African kings. A vintage Asian china service was displayed primly on a tortoise-patterned tabletop, while a gold-leafed floor lamp sent soft light blooming across a makeshift vignette of white ceramics and glazed coral. And that was just one corner of the jam-packed room. Elsewhere, Oriental rugs draped the dirt-packed floor in vibrant patterns, and a gigantic bed loomed dead center, where a giant oak headboard and a virtual mound of bedding rose in a luxurious wave of stripes and prints and color. And then I looked up.

The ceiling was made from the desert floor, though centuries of baking in the unrelieved sun couldn't keep out the shell-backed, shiny-skinned, and multilegged vermin that had survived the ages as well. Snakes and lizards, wasps and worms, and vinegaroons—a particularly foul cross between a spider and scorpion—festooned the ceiling like living chandeliers, macabre creatures twisting in the lamplight, their movements played out on the walls in triple size.

Desert predators, all of them. It didn't matter how much gilt was in this room. This was still Joaquin's home. And he, I thought, watching a snake fall headfirst from ceiling to floor, was the largest predator of them all.

I cocked my head, listening to the pressing silence in this underground tomb, realizing that was exactly what this could be. If something went wrong down here, chances were nobody would ever find me. I'd remain deep underground, sealed beneath the hillside, Joaquin's home marking my grave. But I couldn't return the way I'd come. Even if I could vault up the pitch-dark incline back onto the platform at the false closet's back, there were still the dogs to consider. And Joaquin's return was growing imminent. Maybe he'd hole up in the Shadow sanctuary, passing along with the dawn into that reality. That would give me at least twelve hours to figure a way out of here.

But, looking around, I didn't think so. The ornate bed told me he slept as much down here as he did upstairs—probably more. Why share a street and a neighborhood with others when you had a mountainside all to yourself? And Joaquin was a loner. He preferred to work alone, live alone, kill alone. Besides, the lights had been left on. I don't care how forgetful or apathetic, nobody left the home fires burning if they were going to be away more than twenty-four hours.

And, I thought, pushing through the room, nobody as cautious as Joaquin had a bunker without a secondary escape.

The crunch of hard little bodies sounded beneath my boots as I crossed the dirt-packed floor. I jerked back heavy wall hangings, looking for hidden doors, and lifted rugs for trap doors that led even deeper. Dusty carcasses of roaches and abandoned snakeskins littered the undersides. "Sweep it under the rug" was apparently a maxim Joaquin took literally.

As I straightened, my eyes flitted to the far wall, where a large black curtain matching the entrance was fixed like an inkstain over the carved earthen walls. When I yanked it back, however, I had to pause before my feet would move in the right direction.

Joaquin might have spent his downtime in the previous room, but this was the one he loved. Starkly different from the first, almost Zen-like in its austerity, it had a simple wooden trestle centered and spanning six full feet, and a candelabra picketed at each end. None of the wall hangings or adornments I'd woven my way through, in what I now realized had been a small antechamber, were evident here. Instead, the garish lights were replaced by thick black tapers, set at precise distances apart, none currently alight. This floor was bare too, but stamped firm and worn smooth with use and time, and obviously great care. The most startling thing, however, were the crevices pocking the bare walls, like eye sockets following my every move.

I tucked the curtain behind a wrought-iron wall sconce, picking up the scent of champa as I ventured further inside. For a moment I thought I was standing in the world's largest wine cellar. It was certainly cool enough. And, I thought, looking up, the surface creatures hadn't breached this section of the mountain cavern. Spotting a gold-plated lighter on the table, I picked it up and put it to the taper closest to the door, then lifted that eye level to peer into one of the cylindrical holes. Visions of tarantulas and rattlers filled my head. No way was I blindly sticking my hand in there. But the holes didn't contain bugs, and they didn't house wine.

I slipped my hand inside one and came out with a stack of papers, puzzled until I lifted the front page to the light, and read the heading there. *"Twilight Alliance,"* I said aloud, my finger tracing a drawing of two Shadows grasping forearms. I frowned, pushed it back into its slot, and pulled out another. This one was called *Black Fire* and featured a Shadow agent named Quentin Black, a pyromaniac who liked to send the fire department into fits every spring by torching distant areas of the valley simultaneously. A third depicted a woman who seduced mortal men into doing her bidding—theft, rape, murder—then set them on the paths to their own suicides directly thereafter.

They were Shadow manuals, rows and rows of cubby-holes filled with them, some two and three to a crevice. I spotted a ladder with a rail that slid along the perimeter about fifteen feet up. Joaquin's own private Shadow library, I thought, as Regan's words at our initial meeting shifted through my head.

He likes to be the first to read the Zodiac manuals.

"So Joaquin has himself a little hobby," I muttered, opening a manual. A scream, followed by a harsh, rattling laugh, bounded from the pages. But was it more than that? Because a setup like this seemed excessive for a mere hobbyist. I knew collectors who kept their comic collections in plastic sleeves and behind glass cases . . . but in underground mountain chambers in a cathedral-type setting? That didn't just border on strange, it tipped into full-blown obsession. An obsession, I thought, putting the manual back, that Joaquin either didn't want to share or didn't want anyone else to know about. Interesting.

I pulled out another manual, and though I immediately recognized there was something off about the cover, it took me a moment to realize this one wasn't the work of Zane and Carl.

Philly's Penumbra, set in Pennsylvania. Backdated a week. Joaquin must have them overnighted to his home, but if so—I looked up again at the cavernous height of the ceiling, manual slots soaring all the way to the top—he was doing so with every Shadow troop in the country. Which meant the accounts of the Shadows' dealings in each major city in the United States were archived in this room. A quick tour around the perimeter confirmed this suspicion, though it didn't explain why. He couldn't interact with or influence the balance of troops in other cities as far as I knew. So what was the point of all this? Was he picking up tips from the manuals? Incendiary techniques from Quentin Black? Or just a simple diversion for those nights when he wasn't out raping, murdering, and otherwise victimizing the women of Las Vegas?

"Except . . ." I muttered, tapping my fingers against the cool earthen wall. Except there were too many of them, stacked too precisely, protected too well, and collected too obsessively. I crossed to the trestle table and the sole manual lying there, opening it to a page that'd been bent, marked because it was obviously meaningful to Joaquin in some way. I saw only a panel depicting a street fight between agents of Light and Shadow in a city with a river winding through the middle of it.

He was studying it. But for what? "Why?"

As tempting as it was to stop and investigate further, I couldn't risk it. Today was Thursday. The new manuals came out every Wednesday, and after Joaquin had committed whatever crimes and melee he could happily manage in a twelve-hour period, I'd bet another eyetooth he'd be back here, poring over pages that would bring this shrine to life with sound and color and light.

A plan began to assert itself. If I could find a place to hide, somewhere I could burrow in so deeply that Joaquin would never intuit my presence, I could stalk him from down here. I could take him in this room, which he felt was a safe and hallowed refuge. One moment he'd be leafing through pages of violence, incense burning the air, and the next he'd be sitting, stunned, in the afterlife. I smiled. There was a lot to be said for the element of surprise.

The crowded anteroom would be my best bet, I decided, snuffing the black taper and exiting the room after one final look. There were dozens of niches and crannies where I could bury myself; an old English wardrobe, a sliver of space beneath the giant bed, or a leaning bookcase piled with old tomes, though that might be tricky to wriggle my way out of later. I rejected a large trunk as being too uncomfortable—plus if Joaquin carelessly threw the lock, I'd have sealed myself in my own tomb—and studied the rest of the room, kicking off a scorpion as it scuttled across my boot.

Somewhere on the hillside's surface the day was being born. Now that I was more than human, I felt the nascence of dawn and dusk the same way consciousness slipped into me at the start of every morning. I'd known coming into this I probably wouldn't be heading back to the sanctuary at dawn, but I still had to fight back a wave of regret. It disappeared entirely seconds later as a noise sounded from the bug I'd planted in the living room. It was a lock snicking, a door being opened, then keys tossed on some hard surface, probably the coffee table, as the sound thudded jarringly through my earpiece. I looked around with renewed resolve. The evidence of my run-in with the hounds of hell would probably send Joaquin scurrying to his hidey-hole to make sure for himself that nothing had been tampered with.

Which meant I had to hurry.

I yanked the device from my ear as my gaze landed on a space I'd dismissed before as being too narrow. But it was deep and would provide easy access to the other chamber, and I could slip behind Joaquin when he ventured inside. So I slid in sideways, angling to nestle back as far as I could, and cocked my conduit in front of me as I made sure my mask was firmly in place. Then I slowed my breathing until the air around me was as pristine as glacier wind, and waited.

I'd been standing still a full thirty seconds when it occurred to me to wonder: if daylight couldn't seep underground, why was it growing brighter in here? With a gasp, I looked down to see my glyph alight, then an arm like a crowbar yanked me against a body I knew all too well. My wrists were grabbed, torqued expertly in an unnatural angle, making my dog bite throb anew, and my conduit clattered uselessly to my feet.

"Regan said you might be stopping by," Joaquin whispered in my ear.

I'd have sighed if I had any air to spare. Instead I choked on fear and adrenaline. As I said, there was a lot to be said for the element of surprise.

17

With no conduit, no leverage against his superior physical position, and having received a few sharp blows from Joaquin against my face and kidney—warning shots; he wasn't trying to hurt me yet—I was easily subdued. I quickly found myself in the center of the room, trussed up to a sturdy, high-backed chair, which Joaquin happily assured me was an original Louis the Fourteenth. Oh goody. I'd hate to die bound to something from IKEA.

I looked around for something I could use as a weapon, but I was tied up so tightly, I might as well have been wearing a straitjacket. There was nothing I could do but wait for an opening and hope Joaquin released me, or made a great mistake. Like the one I'd made.

For now, he was simply scrutinizing me. He hadn't removed my mask—I think my identity was yet another treasure to be mulled over later—but gone was the lascivious smirk he usually wore—I'd long ago become more to him than a mere conquest—and in its place was a thoughtful gaze, like I was a puzzle he'd yet to solve. Of course, when he saw me watching, his demeanor shifted, and a cagey gleam returned to his eye.

"Still looking for buried treasure, Archer?"

"You seem to have plenty," I said, indicating the room with my eyes, as everything else, including my neck, was too tightly fastened to move. The ropes dug in uncomfortably, and the glyph on my chest was beginning to feel like a severe case of heartburn, though I tried to let none of this show. It irked me that his glyph was significantly less pronounced, the smoke rising from his chest in scant tendrils, like incense recently burned out.

"Oh, this?" he said lightly, looking about as if seeing his cavern for the first time. "This isn't treasure. It's . . . creature comforts, that's all."

"And the mini-cathedral you've built next door?"

"Ah, yes. I was wondering how you liked that. You spent enough time in there," he said, and I could see it bothered him. "I almost left my hidey-hole to find out what you were up to, though I could see where my reference room would be of interest to you. Perhaps you'd like to borrow a few manuals, do some light reading of your own . . . though I'd have to insist you return everything back to its proper place. It took me ages to organize."

"No, thanks," I said dryly. "You know why I'm here."

"Yes. Hunting me," he said, eyes widening dramatically. He laughed then, and I couldn't blame him. I'd have done the same were our positions reversed. Sometimes irony sucked. "You've done so well too. Without Regan's help I doubt you'd ever have found me."

I bristled at that. "Maybe not here. Not now. But I'd have found you."

"Oh sure," he said, crossing his ankles as he leaned against a pine farm table crowded with Civil War–era dust catchers. "After your entire troop was massacred by disease. After the valley's population was decimated, though that could be any day now." He leaned close to me, so close my eyes nearly crossed, his soiled breath warming my cheeks. "By the way, whatever damage was done to my dear pets upstairs will be done to you, tenfold."

The thought of screwdrivers made me swallow hard, and picking up the emotion, Joaquin inhaled theatrically. I smiled back and let my Shadow side flare, sending up the scent of fresh ash to mingle with the cloying scent of burned honey and rotting fruit. Joaquin jerked back at the reminder of just whose daughter I was, and for the first time, looked as if his back was against the wall.

Perhaps I did have a weapon after all. "My father—"

I was going to say, *My father has ordered me not to be killed, hasn't he?* but Joaquin didn't give me the chance. His expression hardened into stubborn lines, and it was even more frightening in this gilded, infested room than it'd been on a moonlit desert night a decade earlier. I snapped my mouth shut, knowing I'd pressed too hard, but it was too late.

"Fuck it."

He came at me like a bull, fists clenched, and I tried to push away, but ol' Louis had made some seriously fine furniture. Joaquin was on me instantly, my hair clenched so tightly in one fist that tears watered up in my eyes, nails from his other hand digging into my shoulder as he pressed me back so the wood of the chair sent arrows up my spine. Then his lips were on mine, thin and slimy and demanding as his tongue fought entrance past my teeth, an intrusion that reminded me of the lizards wriggling above us, the worms writhing in delicate peril, the serpents sliding through earthen roots and sun-baked grit. I gagged on a combination of panic and revulsion as juices from his mouth entered mine, his death stench seeping down the soft lining of my throat.

He finally pulled back, a curious mix of triumph and fear twisting his features into an uncertain blaze, all wiped away with a frown as he watched me hack and spit. His sewer-water saliva was fouling my mouth, and noxious fumes rose to burn the membrane lining my nose. I needed a glass of water, pronto. No, I needed a tetanus shot. Better yet, a shot of pure alcohol to cleanse my senses . . . and something to cool the ember on my chest where my glyph was scorching through my shirt. Fuck, but it hurt! I focused on that, and used the pain to anchor me.

"What?" I demanded, as Joaquin continued looking at me expectantly. I spit again.

His eyes narrowed, and he leaned forward slightly, but his mouth only twitched, holding the words back as he waited for . . . something.

He's waiting for you to die.

I stilled, before letting a curious, cautious look sweep over my face. I exaggerated it since he couldn't make out most of my features beneath my mask, then started gagging and choking, alternating back and forth . . . just for good effect. Joaquin did lean forward then, hungrily taking in every spastic twitch of my body, the saliva pooling at one side of my mouth, and the way my eyes rolled back into my head, showing only white as I let my head loll forward. I heard a choked sound coming from him, though not one of regret or sympathy, but one of climax, like he just came and was reveling in the aftershocks . . . or was just about to.

I straightened. And smiled. "I'm such a tease."

Every feature on his face sharpened into angles and points, his nostrils flared, and the ripe scent of anger and embarrassment flooded me. His recovery wasn't as quick this time. His glyph was smoking again, and I saw his right hand shaking as he backed up, trying for nonchalance as he reordered his thoughts to take in this unanticipated development. Regan might've told him I was coming for him, but she'd forgotten to mention my immunity to the virus.

"See the obits lately?" he asked conversationally, leaning back again. Picking up an antique letter opener, he began to clean beneath his nails. My eyes darted to my conduit lying next to him, my own fingers twitching behind my back with the need to curl about it. I jerked my eyes away too late, and Joaquin's full smile returned, though he pretended not to notice. "Fascinating reading, really," he went on. "Couples, young and old. Lovers, gay and straight, black and white.

We've created the great equalizer in this virus. The greatest, even, as mortals and superhumans alike are susceptible to this strain."

"But not you."

"No, not me. Nor you, it seems." He raised a brow, inviting me to expound on that. Why not, I figured. Talking might keep him from other activities. Torture, rape, and murder came immediately to mind.

"Regan kissed me," I said, without emotion.

"That whore." Joaquin shook his head, almost sadly. "You know, Regan won't tell me who you are behind that mask. She wanted to keep that little nugget of information to herself." His eyes lingered on my face, though he didn't try to remove it right now. He was going to save that for later, I knew, when it counted. When it would best serve to make my humiliation complete. And, of course, he had all the time in the world for that.

I swallowed hard, but managed to keep my voice even. "Yes, she seems to keep all her bases covered."

"She's a devious bitch. Manipulative. Conniving. A perfect Shadow-in-training." He pursed his lips, like a proud father bemused by his offspring's latest antics. "Yet you have something extremely interesting in common with her."

If he expected me to prompt him as to what that was, I was happy to disappoint. I'd been taken in by Regan's act hook, line, and sinker, and didn't particularly want to hear about our similarities. Which Joaquin also knew.

"You're both puppets," he went on, tapping the letter opener against his thigh as he approached me again, slowly this time. "And neither of you know it. Of course, that just makes it more fascinating to watch. A tragedy of Shakespearean proportions. Or is it a comedy?"

He straddled my legs and sat, nestling in close, not bothering to lessen his weight on my behalf. Shit. He was going to start.

I can survive this. I did before and could again. Even if he got inside me physically—which seemed probable at the moment—he wouldn't get inside my mind. Not this time. So I clenched my teeth, and even though my stomach knotted at the thought of his scent and rot invading my body, I kept my chin lifted high.

"Miss me?" he whispered, giving me the once-over, eyes lingering on my chest. My heart skipped a beat. My glyph pulsed painfully.

"Like a urinary tract infection," I said, through gritted teeth.

He drove the letter opener into my wounded arm. When my screaming stopped he said, "Of course you didn't miss me. How could you? After all, I'm always there, aren't I? In your mind, behind the lens of your eye when you look in the mirror. Your first thought when you wake in the morning . . . the last when you go to sleep at night."

Oh God, how had I gotten here? After all my training, my preparation—my metamorphosis into something super, for God's sake!—I'd still ended up back where I'd been a decade earlier. Pinned beneath all this evil. Helpless. Again.

No! I told myself, fear worming itself into my thoughts. *I'm not a victim! And no matter what he did to me, I wouldn't be made to feel like one.*

So why did I suddenly wish I was dead?

A whimper escaped me at the thought.

Joaquin heard it and bent to me, pausing for a long moment before licking my face, starting below my jaw and ending on my cheek just below my mask. His tongue toyed with the edges of it briefly, as if seeking entrance.

It was all I could do not to scream. *Not again! Not again! Not again!*

He pulled back, but there was no reprieve as he pushed his groin against mine. I'd already known he'd be hard. "Tell me," he said, almost lovingly, "in those deepest, darkest hours, when nobody's watching, and there's only you and the singular, compelling thought of me . . ." He paused until I looked at him. "Do you touch yourself?"

I jerked away, giving him the reaction he was looking for,

and his laughter washed over me like a violent summer storm, beating against my skin, and me with nowhere to take cover. Oh God, I thought. I should have listened to Warren. I shouldn't have left the sanctuary. I should never have tried this on my own. I'd wanted vengeance at any cost . . . but now that it was too late, I realized the price was too dear.

"I do love it when you're predictable, Joanna," Joaquin said, still chuckling as he caressed my arms with his fingertips. They felt like worms and snakes, and all the crawling things that lived in this underground grotto. Despite myself, I started to shake. "The predictable ones are so much fun. Less challenging, true, but then I was never one to do something simply for the challenge."

No, he'd done it for the joy he derived in seeing his victim beg and scream and cry, and especially for the humiliation. If I hadn't known that before, I knew it now by the way he worded his thoughts, singling me out, then lumping me in with the rest of his victims, like I was nothing special to him. Just another body, another tooth in the jar.

One thing he was right about, though. I was predictable. And that's what Warren and the others had been saying, what Regan had capitalized on, and the hubris that, even for a heroine, could only lead to one place. Capture.

So I concentrated on not crying or screaming or begging . . . and ignored the question: why couldn't I have realized all this five minutes earlier?

"The Tulpa will kill you," I whispered, mouth as dry and parched as the desert ceiling above as I played the only card I had left. I closed my eyes when I said it because I'd never thought I'd have to use it. I didn't want to admit it now. But it was true, and Joaquin knew it.

There was no response. Unnerved by the silence, I opened my eyes again, and found Joaquin staring at me ruefully. "My life," he finally said, "is about finding out exactly what hurts people most. And when I find it, that one thing that'll break the human soul, I use it to make those people beg me to hurt them. It's like a giant chessboard, really. You position yourself just so, bide your time, wait until your opponent has committed, and then watch the surprise bloom on their face when they realize they've ended up in exactly the place they *claimed* they wanted to avoid."

He ground against me in demonstration, a slow and sensuous dry hump, taking something meant to be beautiful and turning it inside out. But it was his words that had my breath quickening. *Dammit, Jo, don't let him in!* But it wasn't an order anymore. It was a plea.

"Your Tulpa is no different," he said, continuing. "He knows who I am, what I am, and what I'd do if I got my hands, my cock, on you." He ran his fingers over my hair, pausing at my mask, caressing my face. "His precious Kairos."

He paused here, stilling to hold up a finger. "Let me clarify. He doesn't just know this, he expects it. That's why he's kept me in his organization all these years. That's why he didn't kill me as soon as he discovered the girl I'd attacked all those years ago was his daughter. In a way, he wants me to finish what I started. That way he's absolved, you see?"

A tear slipped from the corner of my eye.

"And then there's you. That beaten and broken little girl who grew up to be a woman with a chip on her shoulder that spans the Strip. You may not have known it before now, but you sought this out. You want me to hurt you. You expect it. And you'd be disappointed if I didn't."

"That's not true," I said, but my voice was barely a whisper, like I had no conviction left inside me. Like I didn't even know who I was anymore. Or had never known myself at all. Oh, God . . .

"It is." He smiled serenely and rocked into me again. "That's why you're here now. You *need* to feel the pain because beneath all this peroxide and silicone and shit," he said, flipping a blond curl from my shoulder with disgust, "pain forces you to remember who you really are. It lets you know why you exist, why you wake every dawn and retire each dusk. I anchor you to this existence, Joanna. I give your days meaning and purpose."

I tried to shake my head, but the bindings held me fast, and the invisible ones—the ones he was talking about—held my tongue. Don't let him be right, I pleaded silently. I *don't* see myself as a victim. I never have.

Had I?

"When I hurt you, Joanna," he said, his soft whisper at odds with the hand that had lifted to twist my nipple between ironclad fingers, "when you think of me hurting you, it puts you in your place beneath me . . . and that, my dear, is where you feel most safe."

I cried out, unable to stop myself, eyes tearing with the pain of both his actions and his words, and cried out again when I realized I was pissed at myself for doing so. Like it was my fault, and the blame for his actions lay solely with me. And anything was better than that. So I wished for unconsciousness, I wished for death . . . I wished, as he wanted, that I'd never survived this the first time.

Those wishes rose like noxious fumes escaping the earth . . . only they'd been stewing deep inside my core all these years, rich, like emotional deposits lain down one atop the other, waiting for the right person to come along and mine the vein.

This, I suddenly knew, was the real me. Me, giving Joaquin exactly what he wanted.

As he scented it all, his throaty laugh rose in tandem with my voice, and he twisted harder, his amusement reverberating through his body, joy in every noxious breath.

I shut my eyes, the only movement I had left to me, and there was a gusting boom, like a cannon going off. I looked up to find spiders and worms and vermin and rats and reptiles all slamming to the floor in a explosion of dust, followed by five bodies dropping to the ground like precision-guided bombs, chests glowing like beacons.

Goddamn, I thought, choking on a cry of relief as Joaquin's weight disappeared. I loved having superhero friends.

Joaquin made the only offensive move he could, lunging

for my conduit still lying on the pine table. Hunter's whip flicked out, the tail knocking the conduit from reach, sending a stinging barb into the soft tissue of Joaquin's palm. He yelled in rage and pain, and I was gratified to see his glyph now puffing away like a teepee's smoke hole. Hunter yanked back on his whip, but the barb had only caught the fleshy part of Joaquin's hand, no bone, and it ripped away, freeing Joaquin again.

Vanessa rolled beneath the table, flicking her steel fan open as she came to her knees, the barbed claws on the end swiping through the air at Joaquin's ankles. He jumped, avoiding the strike, but she caught him on his way down, as she lifted to a crouch, while he simultaneously darted from the path of Felix's double-edged boomerang. Joaquin yelped as one of his Achilles tendons was torn, and I did too, as Felix's boomerang came precariously close to shearing my skull on its return flight.

"Watch it!" I yelled, struggling against my ropes. Felix scowled, leaped on an ornate credenza, and came up behind me.

"Hold still," he said, and with a flick of his wrist cut through the ropes at my neck with the boomerang, before working his way down. I wriggled free, bindings falling from me to mingle with the reptiles now slithering across the floor, and Warren handed me my conduit as I stood. I cocked it, looking for Joaquin.

"Where'd he go?"

"That way," Vanessa said, pointing in the direction of the reference room. I bolted forward, though the others had already beaten me there, skidding to a halt before a thick steel door. The black curtain had been rent aside.

"No!" I pushed past them all, pounding on the door, then pushing against it with my good shoulder. I wasn't going to lose him now. *I wasn't going to let him get away with saying, or making me feel, all those things.* "No!"

"Shit!" I heard Vanessa say.

"We gotta go!"

"Olivia!" Warren yanked at me, as I continued to pound at the door. "The ceiling's caving in!"

I looked up to see sun streaking in through the crumbling hillside, then back at the door, where I knew Joaquin was breathing and alive and safe on the other side.

"No," I whispered, choking on dust-filled air, as I raised my conduit and fired into the steel door. I'd rather die than let him live. An arm curled around mine and yanked me back, causing a misfire, but my indignation was cut short by a solid crack against my skull. My vision fled immediately, and I felt myself falling as if in slow motion. A set of arms curled about me, softening my landing, then everything drowned in black.

I wasn't awake. I was floating in memory, drifting along echoes of forgotten sound. Like the emotions Joaquin had laid bare, I was buried deep in my past, and even though I recognized it as a dream, I felt and saw and smelled all the things that'd assailed me after that first attack. And like the first time, I couldn't escape any of it.

Beeps and readings from complicated machinery surrounded me, and voices intermittently spewed from an intercom in the hall with words I'd long stopped hearing. I was lying on a bed, body aching because I'd been there for weeks. I looked down, past crisp white sheets, and tried to count on my fingers just how long I'd been in the hospital. But I couldn't concentrate. I was distracted by the brace on my right hand, holding my fingers straight and aligned, like the Boy Scouts' three-fingered salute. My eyes wandered, drawn to the blackened nail beds poking from beneath the dingy gauze, where the jagged fingernails had only now begun to lengthen, finally long enough to cover the tender flesh beneath. Proof that I was healing. That my body was fighting even as I remained not moving, not speaking, trying not even to think.

I wriggled my fingers, then tentatively twisted my wrist when that provoked no real pang or ache. I lifted my entire arm shoulder height, and frowned when there was no smarting response. I repeated the action with my other arm, the one sealed tightly in a cast. There. A sliver of white-hot pain shot through me, and I dropped it again, letting the ache wash over me, ringing through my core before it ebbed and faded away. I closed my eyes, and rested.

When I opened them again, it was dark. The streetlights outside my window had come on, and I could see the headlights of passing cars as they sped down Flamingo Road, each in a hurry to reach a separate destination, all unknown to me. All unimportant.

What time was it? I wondered, my mouth dry as sandpaper. For that matter, what day was it? I glanced at the wall across from me with a giant number twenty-five emblazoned, black on white. That couldn't be right. That meant it'd been only one day. Twenty-four hours since the doctor had sat next to my bedside, face solemn and concerned, voice soothing and low, tanned hands patting my own as he told me I wasn't merely healing. I was growing life.

But he was wrong. They were all wrong. Because I was broken. You couldn't go five inches up or down my body without running into something that was fractured, shattered, or bruised. Me and Humpty Dumpty, I thought, biting my lip till it bled. Never to be put back together again.

I licked the blood away, surprised at the metallic taste, then frowned as I thought, *That's not right.* Bleeding means the vessels were working, and the heart was pumping, doing its job like nothing ever happened, like it hadn't been stomped on and bruised and stopped. So why did the fucker keep on ticking? I felt my betraying heart skip a beat, before it started slamming against my chest, faster and harder with each progressive beat, and my head grew dizzy and light. I opened my mouth to suck in a lungful of air—because that's all I had left, one lung—and still the panic attack snuck up on me, an A-bomb detonating right in the middle of my chest.

I wish.

I swallowed hard and tried to slow my breathing, ignoring the button beside me that would call the nurse who would provide the drugs that would numb me to the world. I fumbled for the remote, pushing it behind me, deep beneath the extra pillows I'd been given, before fishing out another hidden treasure. My own call button. My own form of medicinal relief. I was my own nurse.

The razor had come from the guy in the bed next to me. They'd let him shave before he left the hospital, and he'd tossed it in the bin between our beds, and left without saying good-bye. The adventure from my bed to the trash can three feet away had been my first since fleeing across the desert night, and I'd almost ruined it by sitting up too fast. I passed out and flipped the wrong way on my bed, but luckily the nurses had been in the middle of a shift change, and never noticed a thing.

Now I curled my fingers around the razor I'd nicknamed Tonto after the Lone Ranger's loyal sidekick, and lifted the bedsheets to reveal the pale, freckled length of my good thigh. The marks from the day before were already scabbed, healing. And that just wouldn't do.

"You'll get better, Joanna," my mother had said, smoothing her hand over my face, drying my tears after the doctor had gone away. "You'll see. You're going to heal, the pain will stop, and you'll go on to live a happy, full life. I promise you. You will survive this."

I sliced, once, twice, and her voice receded. She finally shut up. I shut her up. I shut the doctor up. And the screams and cries in my head, the ones that woke me up in a cold sweat each night, the ones that caused these sudden attacks of panic, finally shut up, too.

I sliced again, watching the blood well, a thin black line in the dim light. Cars continued to race by outside, but it didn't matter where they were headed. My thighs burned.

The pain anchored me. It gave my life in this bed meaning and purpose.

When I was in pain, I felt safe.

I came to in a place very similar to the one I'd left in my dreams. Curled on my side, I first saw the machines, all turned off and silent in the corner as there was no real emergency here. Not on the surface anyway.

"He got away, didn't he?"

I didn't turn or look around, but I knew someone was there. I could smell them in the corner. I inhaled deeply and caught something close to brewer's yeast and Axe aftershave. Felix.

"He did. Who's Tonto?"

I did turn my head at that. "What?"

"You were talking in your sleep. Who's Tonto?"

I dropped my head back on my hands, facing the wall again. "An old friend," I whispered, and touched the bandage on my left arm, wondering, as a reassuring flash of pain shot through me, what else I'd said. "How'd you find me?"

"Your glyph," he said, coming around the side of the bed so I could see him. He looked odd without a smile touching his face or eyes. I looked away, touching my chest. The ache was gone now, the fire doused, but the tenderness was still there. "Light finds Light."

"A tracking device?" I asked, lifting my head.

Felix mistook my awe for annoyance, and crossed his arms over his chest. "You're lucky Joaquin likes to keep his victims conscious while he toys with them. If you'd been unconscious, or dead, it would've been impossible to locate you down there."

Because the glyph would have gone dead as well.

I turned away from his accusing eyes and sat up, realizing I was in the same room I'd recovered in after Micah had turned me into Olivia. It was a hospital just outside Vegas that served as the troop's cover for medical emergencies and recovery. Since it was after dawn—both too late and too early to return to the sanctuary—I gathered we were biding our time until the next crossing.

I knew why Felix was here, of course, just as I knew someone else was stationed outside the door. The rest had probably gathered in one of the conference rooms to discuss me, and while it rubbed to be the topic of conversation again, they had just collectively saved my life. Besides, the thought that I'd failed them all once again shamed me, adding to the misery brought on by my capture. And my dream.

So instead I turned my thoughts to Felix's words, how he thought me lucky to have been conscious while under Joaquin's thumb. *Toyed* was such a benign word for what he'd done. He'd revived shattered memories knowing that's what had driven me all these years, through my young adulthood, into superherodom, and ultimately into that dank and infested hillside. Just the way he'd wanted, I thought, sighing. Just as he'd intended.

"Why do you have to make it so hard on yourself?" Felix asked, and I drew my gaze up to his in surprise, then found I couldn't hold it, the sympathy in his eyes too much to bear. I turned away, but knew as soon as he moved to my side, his breath stirring my rumpled hair, his body warming my bare shoulder as if his hand were hovering just there. I curled back up on the bed and closed my eyes, a sigh lifting from behind me as I did it. "Every time you act alone you make it harder to trust you. It's like you go out of your way to remind us that you're not really Olivia Archer . . ."

That I was someone they really didn't know.

"And still we help you. It'd be nice, for a change, if you'd do the same."

But I couldn't even help myself.

Felix sighed, as if I'd spoken aloud. "You can start by working with us, as a team. That's what a troop is, you know." He hesitated—I heard the catch in his voice—but plunged ahead when I remained unmoving. "You want so badly to exact your revenge that you're going to get us all killed."

I half whirled at that. "You didn't have to come after me!"

Felix's eyes narrowed as he began shaking his head. "Haven't you heard a word I said? Yes, we did."

Because we were a troop. I swallowed hard, but couldn't form a reply, and when he realized there'd be no tantrum or argument, he huffed and turned his back on me, probably thinking me a lost cause.

Probably thinking they should've left me underground.

I'm sure it was against direct order, but he left the room after that, locking the door behind him. I was glad. The stagnant scent of his disgust made me want to hide my face.

18

I took the meal they brought me at noon, the other they served at five, and waited as patiently as possible while I counted the minutes until dusk. Finally, even my guilt and lingering sorrow burned off like morning fog along the left coast, and by six I'd had enough of cooling my heels. I stormed over to the door, intent on plowing through whoever was seated on the other side. A good confrontation would get me feeling more like myself.

The door swung open just as violently as I'd meant it to, but I had to jerk back to avoid getting beaned in the head—again—then froze when I saw the faces of the five heroes assembled there. A slew of magazines struck my chest with enough force that I stumbled back a step. "What the fuck is this?"

I glanced down at the floor, and realized Warren hadn't thrown magazines, but manuals. There were multiple copies, but only two editions, and they each had my image emblazoned on the front. The first was titled *The Archer: Ambushed*. The second, *The Boneyard Breach*.

"Umm . . ." I said, when what I meant to say was, *Oh shit*.

Warren's brows grew together in fury. Micah, who'd come in behind him, crossed his arms, his gaze equally heavy on my face. Hunter cursed and shook his head, while Vanessa only stared. Felix didn't look at me at all.

I'd known this was coming, of course. I'd had two weeks to prepare an answer, longer than I'd thought since everyone had been so occupied with the virus that reading comics had been the last thing on their minds. Someone, however, had concluded my appearance at Joaquin's home hadn't sprung up out of nowhere, and they'd gone to Master Comics to do some investigating of their own.

"Okay, I know how this looks—"

"No," Warren's voice was a whip as he stepped into the room. "If you knew how this looked, you'd be backed against that far wall, prepared to fight your way past the five of us or die trying."

Taken aback, my explanation died on my lips, and I looked from Warren to the others, searching for some sign that he was exaggerating. But their expressions didn't soften or change. He waited until my gaze had returned to his, then raised a fist before pointing one finger in the air. "You hunted down and killed a Shadow—one who knew about your hidden identity—and didn't say a thing—"

"But have you read it? Did you see why?"

He ignored my question, and ticked off another offense. "You gained the aureole without telling any of us, and were therefore off our radars for a twelve-hour period. A period in which we may have needed you."

"I'm perfectly safe when I possess the aureole," I said, immediately regretting it. I only sounded arrogant.

Warren held up another finger, his middle one, which, I was sure, wasn't by coincidence. "You arranged a meeting with Joaquin at Master Comics, and discussed this troop—"

"I did not! I was told by a reliable source he'd be there, and I'd have done more than talk with him if it weren't a designated safe zone!"

Warren held up his entire hand now, stepping forward as

he did so, and I stopped talking. Very quietly, in a voice so faint you wouldn't have heard the individual words without superstrength hearing, he continued, "And after I gave you a direct order to remain in the sanctuary, you breached the hole in the boneyard's walls, leaving the sanctuary vulnerable again, so you could meet with that same *source* on a rooftop above a crime scene where your entire troop was gathered . . . and could be picked off one by one."

I hadn't thought of it that way.

Which was, of course, Warren's point. I hadn't thought at all.

Micah stepped forward, an expression of pure hurt staining his eyes, and shame overran my anger. "You've known all along what we're dealing with, haven't you?" he asked.

I closed my eyes, knowing an admission would be more damning in their eyes than all of Warren's points put together. I rubbed my hands over my face, trying to think of a way to spin this so they'd understand, but that was futile. My troop thought in terms of black and white. Right or wrong. *Shadow or Light.* Opening my eyes, I found Micah next to me, and though the truth was already reflected in his face, I knew he wanted me to say it.

"I've known since the night of the attacks."

His face contorted, so many emotions passing over it at the same time that I winced seeing it, then winced again as he cried out, simultaneously driving a syringe into my good arm. I yelped and tried to pull away, but he wrapped his other arm around me to steel me in place, and I whimpered as he roughly drew the blood from my arm. When he was finished, he pushed me away so that I stumbled, careening into a wall with a small grunt. Nobody moved to help. I rubbed my arm, but knew that wouldn't elicit any sympathy either. The needle mark was already healing.

I'd given a blood sample before leaving the sanctuary, but apparently Micah hadn't gotten to it. Probably because he'd rushed out with the others to come and save me. I swallowed hard as he pulled a white, palm-sized cassette from his pocket and injected my drawn blood into one side. Then he held the cassette still, watching the other side for a reading.

All the blood left in my body drained away. I could reason with them to read the manuals, convince them I was ambushed by Regan and Liam, but all I could do while Micah scrutinized my blood was wait, breath held, even though I knew what the results would be before he lifted his head and addressed the rest of the group.

"Positive," he said, voice rasping. "She's immune."

"You knew," Warren said, stepping toward me, and the look on his face was the same that'd been there when he'd reached for Joaquin. Micah reached out to grab me again.

"No, no," I said, panicked now, jerking away from Micah as my words tumbled out. "Read the manuals! You'll see. She kissed me . . . I didn't know that's what she was doing. The Shadow agent who was with her was surprised as well. He thought she meant to kill me." And as I heard myself defending things that were indefensible, I wondered how I could have been so taken in.

"Who is 'she'?" Warren wanted to know.

"Regan . . . uh, DuPree is her last name. She's an initiate; the Shadows use them to track agents of Light, and that's why she doesn't show up in the manuals. She gave me Joaquin's address, then told him I'd be coming. I trusted her because . . ." Because she'd lied, I realized, doing a mental head slap. She'd lied about wanting me to come to the Shadow side, and her desire to sit at my "right-hand side," and I'd believed her.

God, had I wanted to believe her?

Warren backed up a step, his body language no longer quite as threatening, though he didn't let up with his words. "And this Regan lured you to the aquarium and told you Joaquin would be at Master Comics?"

"I wouldn't say lured—"

"She's the one who followed you to that downtown rooftop, where we were all gathered below, sitting ducks—"

"She was alone," I protested.

"No, Olivia. You were with her."

And I had nothing to say to that.

"She knows who you really are doesn't she?"

It was the first time Hunter had spoken. I glanced over at him, surprised. I'd almost forgotten he was there, leaning near the door, one foot propped on the wall in a pose that looked relaxed, almost benign. How deceiving.

I bit my lip, but it was in the manuals anyway. And I was done lying. "Yes. For months now."

"And you let her live?" Disbelief swam on Felix's face.

"She's an initiate. I thought she was harmless. She—"

"She had information you wanted," Warren interrupted, taking up the interrogation again. "She bribed you with the one thing she knew would convince you to spare her life. Bread crumbs leading to Joaquin's door. Meanwhile she lied to you, betrayed you, and persuaded you to betray us."

"I haven't," I said. "I swear."

Warren looked at me like I was a mentally incapacitated two-year-old.

"I swear I didn't," I said again. "I didn't know there was a virus until I saw that woman in the alley, and I have no idea how it's still being spread among the mortals. The initial exposure came with the fireworks off the roof of Valhalla, but Regan said those susceptible to infection had to be within falling range of the spores for it to take effect. That's all I know. I swear on my mother's life."

There was silence as they contemplated my words, weighing them as a group while scenting the air to test my sincerity, checking for lies as they studied my face. I knew if they decided I was lying, I'd never leave this room alive. Finally a sharp inhalation.

"Give us a minute alone," Warren told the others without looking at them. When nobody moved, his mouth tightened. "Alone!"

His voice was barbed, with the ruthlessness that made him the only choice for troop leader. He played the fool, sure, but a truly foolish man wouldn't have done it so well.

"I warned you of this, Joanna," he said, using my real name when the room had emptied. "I told you this vendetta against Joaquin would be used to harm us all—"

"It hasn't! Not . . . yet."

"But they've found a way to exploit it, haven't they?"

I shook my head. "Regan's working alone, I'm sure of that. If she weren't I'd already be dead." *We all would*, I thought, remembering Warren's anger about the rooftop.

He joined me on the edge of the bed, though there was nothing companionable about it. I resisted the urge to inch away, and found I couldn't meet his eyes. "Let me tell you something about initiates, Joanna. You don't know this because you came to us late, but for those raised in the lifestyle, there are certain things that can never be done. One of those is disobeying a senior troop member when given a direct order. If Regan's been contacting you regularly, drawing you along on a wild-goose chase, it's not by her own design. Somebody's pulling the strings behind the scenes. She's merely—"

"The puppet," I finished for him, Joaquin's face looming in my mind as he'd been, smirking and sure, hours before. We'd both been played like puppets. I ran a hand over my face. "But she said she wanted me to join the Shadow side; that's why she let me live. Zell or Sloane or any of the other Shadow signs would've killed me on the spot. That's what Liam intended. They all want me dead."

"There's one who doesn't. And he's the one who cannot be disobeyed."

I shook my head. "No. The Tulpa doesn't know who I am. If he did he'd have come after me himself. He thinks he has a right to me, like I felt I had a right to Joaquin." I looked up at him now, eyes imploring, desperate for him to see I'd never intended to injure my troop. "I've searched him out for so many years, Warren. And I have both more to gain by his death and more to lose with his existence than anyone else—"

"But—"

"But I was wrong," I provided, and saw surprise bloom in his expression. "You were right and I was wrong. I disobeyed and unwittingly put you all in danger, and I did all those things you said . . . except one." I placed my hand over his, ignored the stiffening muscles beneath mine, knowing the contact would strengthen his ability to read my sincerity. "I never betrayed you. I never even thought of it. I defied you, but I swear there was no malice in it. And I promise, if you'll just give me another chance, I won't be taken in again."

Warren jerked his hand away, and now it was he who wouldn't meet my gaze. "It's more than that. Awe at some unidentifiable power can easily mutate into admiration. Especially if a person's been convinced that power is theirs for the taking."

Trouble or not, anger surged at that, and I catapulted from the bed's edge, whirling to face him. "Feeling the Tulpa's power last year in Valhalla didn't make me hunger for it, Warren! It made me realize how much I'm lacking, and how much more strength and experience I need if I'm to survive it again!"

"So you decided to seek it out for yourself."

"Damned right," I said, and hell would freeze over before I apologized for that.

"And did you stop to consider there might be a reason we're going slowly with you?"

"I did."

"And?"

"And you still don't trust me." He opened his mouth to protest, but I stopped him with a shake of my head. I'd thought a lot about Regan's words and decided they made sense. It was a lot to ask a man who was uncomfortable with shades of gray to fully and immediately accept a troop member who was both Shadow and Light. "You never say it outright, but you ignore the talents that side has gifted me with, the things I can do and see because the Shadow lives inside of me, and refuse to use them for good."

He shook his head. "Not true."

"Then look me in the eye and tell me you haven't sat up at night worried your precious Kairos was going to start pinch-hitting for the other side." My mouth was dry, my heart pounding, but it felt good to finally get it out in the open . . . even if it might get me killed. I forced him to meet my gaze, eyes fierce as I pleaded with him to listen to me. "Because that's what you're saying, isn't it? That I'm going to be so enamored of the power promised to me by dear ol' dad, that one day I'm going to wake up and take all the training and knowledge and power your troop has gifted me with, and start using it against you?"

His answer came in the emotions bleeding through the molecules between us. They were torn, sullied things, sharpened by a confusion he'd never felt before. Warren had only ever had one job, to lead this troop against beings who operated under the same restrictions but refused to play by the rules. While we fought fairly, they looked for loopholes. We acted defensively while they played offense, and a mean one at that.

Was it any wonder that the way I bucked at my restraints was seen as a rebellion? Or the way I questioned everything was interpreted as devious? Shadows were not to be trusted—as I'd just found out the hard way—and here was one, half one anyway, living in their midst, sharing their thoughts, emotions, training, secrets. I'd be just as cautious in Warren's shoes, but how many times was I going to have to prove myself for him to stop frowning when he looked at me? Or wondering about my motives? Or fearing my growing strength?

Warren's sigh broke into my thoughts, and for the first time since he entered the room I really looked at him. He had a gash on his arm the length of two fists, and though his lids were heavy with fatigue, his hair even greasier than usual, he wasn't in his hobo attire. He was just an exhausted leader in a war that showed no sign of ending.

"You underestimated this Regan woman," he finally said, standing.

"I know." My glyph nearly started pulsing at the thought of it. "It won't happen again."

"It shouldn't have happened at all," he said sharply, though before my hope could ebb, added, "but we'll start over from here. You're going to tell us everything that happened from the first time she contacted you. If you can convince me that she's the only one who knows about your hidden identity . . . then we'll see what can be done."

He meant he wouldn't take it from me. Yet. And I nodded because it was as much of an accord as we were going to reach . . . and as much of an apology either of us was going to get. He was still angry with me for endangering them all, but at least he no longer thought it purposeful. And, I thought, rising, I was back in the loop again. Back in the troop. For now, anyway.

We crossed back into the boneyard at dusk, and I spent the evening piecing together everything that had happened since I met Regan. It was strained at first; Warren would barely look at me, ostensibly busy taking notes, while Micah stiffly directed impersonal questions in my general direction. But after an hour or so of answering their questions as fully as I could, they began to understand the how and why of my actions.

Not that Warren would ever admit as much. He kept his head bent over his notepad, but Micah's eyes softened when I revealed Joaquin's words to me while I was trussed up in his mountainside. Gregor was present, as he could best piece together a timeline between my account and the events he'd been logging from the front seat of his cab, but everyone else had been told they'd be updated in the morning, and to get some sleep before our next group move. I had to admit it was nice being on the inside for a change, and I fought off my own fatigue in favor of being a central part of the planning stage. Besides, I owed them.

We talked well into the night, taking our dinner in seclusion, and I discovered during the course of the conversation that Warren and the others hadn't spontaneously realized I was gone. Rena's conscience had gotten the best of her and she'd told them about my disappearance the week before. I'd also been spotted entering the archive room the day before, and a closer look had revealed a map still positioned in the photocopier there . . . a map of Joaquin's neighborhood.

Tekla, meanwhile, had retired to the astrolab to meditate, draw up a new chart based on all current information, and study the sky via the cam she'd hidden on the highest hotel in Las Vegas. I was secretly glad for her absence. As hard-nosed as Warren could be, Tekla was doubly so. Nothing was middle ground for her. She epitomized the polarities she studied so fervently, and I knew no degree of explanation would ever sway her.

Warren finally threw down his pen and leaned back in his chair. "So there's an antivirus out there somewhere. All we have to do is locate a vial of it, and Micah can mass produce it. Spread it among the mortals."

"Can't we just draw it from her?" Gregor asked, because it'd be great if we could whip up our own concoction of magical whup-ass, but the Shadows had used science to develop a weapon to be used against us, so we had to do the same. "Use her blood to isolate the . . . thingies?"

Micah smiled at Gregor's scientific prowess. "We could, and will, but that'll take time, and we don't have that."

"What about the lab in Valhalla? Let's break in again and steal whatever we can get our hands on." I flipped open the latest manual to the page where Hunter and I stood talking in the casino, garish lights blaring behind us, pulsing up from the page like neon hearts. Hunter towered over me, which took me aback a bit. Did we really look like that together? It was a bad drawing, surely exaggerated, but it reminded me of the way he'd looked in his bedroom, taking up all my personal space, eyes dark as raindrops and lightning slashed over his cheeks.

There'd be no more stolen kisses now, I thought, thinking of the hard way he'd regarded me tonight. Or invitations to a room with a rain forest view. I sighed and shook the thought from my head.

Micah's big shoulders drooped as he took the manual from my hands. "Sure. It'll be that easy."

"Hunter can do it," I pointed out.

"He can help," Warren corrected, rising to pace. "But we need his identity to remain a secret."

"I'll do it," I said, earning a trio of blank stares. I scowled.

"I'll send Jewell and Riddick. They're not well-known faces yet. Felix can provide backup."

To be honest, I was almost relieved at not being included. My failure with Joaquin had shaken me more than I wanted to admit, the nightmare afterward sealing the deal. My confidence was shaken. I needed to regroup and, yes, learn some more. But first I had to see to one more thing.

"I have to know that he's safe," I told Warren after the others had left, and I told him what I needed to do. I held up a hand even before he opened his mouth to protest. "You want me to stay away from Ben, not even think about him, but I can't do that unless I know he doesn't have this virus."

He looked at me for such a long time, I thought for sure he was going to say no. So when he agreed, even going so far as to say he'd take care of it himself, I was relieved. And suspicious. Warren wasn't beyond saying what I wanted to hear in order to get his way. But I nodded to let him know that was good enough for me . . . and silently vowed to find a way to double check his work.

Meanwhile, I needed to mollify Tekla—if she'd even talk to me at all—and apologize to Rena for putting her in the middle. Mending ties within the sanctuary would have to take precedence for now.

We adjourned around one in the morning, heading back to the barracks with a semi-plan. Yet as soon as the door to my room snicked shut behind me, I took one look around at the sterile and safe surroundings, and knew I'd spend the rest of the evening wondering about things I didn't have the power to change.

I was overtired, and the thought of a little something to settle my nerves seemed like a good idea, so I swerved back down the hall and toward the cantina. But if I'd known the response my appearance down that steep stairwell would elicit, if I'd had the power to see what swinging through those doors would do, I wouldn't have gone in there. Instead I would have run screaming the other way.

19

♈   ". . . with reports of at least a half dozen other plague-related deaths at one area hospital, though officials have declined to officially comment on that number. Authorities are asking residents to refrain from drinking tap water, saying only bottled water should be consumed until local reserves, including Lake Mead, can be cleared as possible contaminants for the deadly outbreak . . ."

The television was on when I entered the cantina, and I shot the perfectly coiffed, disease-free anchorwoman a glare as she cheerfully segued into a piece on the secret lives of showgirls. Onscreen, the scene shifted to an explosion of color, brightening the room, playing over the walls so the cantina looked like a movie set. Then the scene shifted again, darker now, so that all the color was stripped from the deep velvet furniture. Music was also playing, clashing with the voice-over onscreen, probably forgotten by whoever had been watching their nightly ration of bad news.

The room was unlike any other in the sanctuary, plush rather than spartan, and similar to the über-lounges on the Strip that charged membership as well as admission before allowing you the privilege of buying a twenty-dollar drink in the confines of their swanky interiors. Velvet couches in cubes of midnight blue were parked around stainless steel tables, matching the appliances in the corner bar, while the table lanterns that could be ignited at a touch were currently off.

The constellations punctured the ceiling in a rendering of the night sky, and the hum of a fish tank, brimming with the exotic, represented the first of the four elements. The others—fire in the candles, air in the sky depicted above, and earth anytime someone clothed in mortal flesh entered the room—gave the room an enclosed feeling. Womblike and safe, it was a place to forget you even had troubles.

"We're watching that," someone said as I reached up to switch the television off. I whirled, and their scents hit me as I did, a heady combination of happiness and lust that grew thicker the farther one entered the room.

"Sorry." I stepped back before I could stop myself, embarrassed for having come upon someone's make-out session even though this was a patently public area. I wanted to tell the couple to get a room . . . but then I saw who it was.

"Hi, Olivia." The voice was unnaturally high, even for a young woman's, and infused with excitement, nerves, and a bit of womanly pride.

"Hey, Marlo," I said, swallowing hard, before turning to her partner. "Hunter."

He inclined his head, a closed, haughty expression on his face, watching me as he let his fingers play across Marlo's knee. She giggled softly, curling closer into him, while I fought the urge to run from the room.

"I didn't know anyone was here. I was just . . . getting a drink." And I noted he was drinking again too. I refrained from offering him my version of a PSA. He didn't look like he was interested.

"So. Get a drink," Hunter said, neither expression nor voice altering as he lifted an ice-filled tumbler to his lips, sipping as he watched me over the rim. Marlo, apparently fascinated, watched him.

Okay, this was awkward. Not to mention *obvious*, I thought, crossing the room to duck behind the stainless steel bar as more giggles rose up behind me. Hunter was obviously still pissed at me for rejecting him, and probably smug about having to save my ass from Joaquin. Messing around with a beautiful initiate was just his way of getting back at me.

It's not all about you, Jo, I chided myself, and bent for the ice scoop, loudly filling a glass shaker as whispers rose like gentle steam behind me. Hunter had moved on, as one might expect of a virile, gorgeous superhero in his prime. Marlo was an obvious choice. Young, beautiful, interested . . . and available.

The scent of lust—citrusy, peppery, and warm as mulled wine—washed over me again, and I swallowed hard to keep my own pheromones locked firmly inside, barely daring to breathe lest the emotion making my face burn hot and my heart squeeze tight be released into the air. Hunter would just love that.

When I thought I was suitably under control, I rose, heart burning like a coal, and grabbed a bottle, pouring the liquor in the tumbler blindly. My back was to the room, and I shook the mixture hard to drown out the sighs behind me. I focused on the television, a commercial now, and tried to breathe in the scent of the alcohol in the bottles around me, and not the spice in the densely packed air, but my hands faltered when I spotted movement through the bar's mirrored back, and a small wisp from that banked coal inside me escaped.

Hunter's arm snaked around Marlo's shoulders, fingers coming to rest just below her earlobe to linger against the sensitive skin on her neck. He pushed the chestnut curls away from her face, and I froze, mesmerized by the sight of that strong hand doing something so gentle and intimate I could practically feel the memory playing across my skin.

Like in the boneyard, I thought, before shaking myself from the memory. *Yeah, that oh-so-romantic moment you shared right before you shot him in the ass.*

I resumed shaking my drink, telling myself I didn't care, but I couldn't tear my eyes from the mirror as Marlo slid her fingers over Hunter's chest, pressing against the hard contours outlined in his black T-shirt before curling to grasp his neck. The subtle scent of ground anise wafted over to me, smooth like soft licorice melting on the tongue, and Hunter's eyes flashed my way. I quickly looked away, fumbling for a glass to pour the now pulverized contents from the shaker inside.

I was done here. I could leave now. Yet my limbs wouldn't respond. My eyes seemed to lift of their own will from the icy glass in my hand to the mirrored scene playing out behind me. I don't know who reached for whom first—they seemed to draw together simultaneously as all well-matched couples do—and my own mouth parted as their lips met, a sigh like a caressing breeze escaping Marlo, her eyes closing as if going into prayer.

Hunter's eyes never left mine. I saw the play of his tongue over her mouth, I saw her bite his top lip, the seduction extending into a full-mouth kiss so passionate the air burned around them. I swallowed hard, realizing too late I'd released some of the jealous bile giving me heartburn; I smelled the soured emotion and knew Hunter would too.

I wasn't going to care about this, I told myself as I brought my drink to my lips, only to find it too strong and harsh and bitter. I drank it anyway. And over the rim of my glass Hunter pulled Marlo against him, his hands and lips demanding on hers, eyes fastened equally hard on mine. A wisp of smoke rose between me and the mirror, my jealousy and the Shadow side of me playing together to lay open my feelings, and Hunter saw it. He kissed Marlo harder, eyes victorious, and—unable to stand it any longer—I whirled away from the mirror to leave.

But the smoke was still there.

"Hunter! Stop!"

He thought it was my jealousy protesting. His other arm snaked around Marlo's waist, pulling her into his lap, but perhaps it was her weight that told him there was something wrong. She slid over too lightly, too limply. Or maybe my glass shattering on the marble floor was what finally brought him around. "Stop!" I screamed.

He pulled away, confusion and alarm settling in his normally stoic features as Marlo's head lolled back, and she hung limp in his arms, like she'd never giggled, smiled, or kissed in her life. She looked like a life-sized doll, broken, but with smoke rising like steam from her mouth. I flew across the room in seconds that passed like days, and lifted Marlo's head, shaking her as though she were only in a swoon. Passing out, however, didn't cause blood vessels and capillaries to break around the eyes. It didn't make the soft flesh around your mouth blacken and start to shrivel back from your teeth.

Hunter put a hand to his mouth, wiping it with the back of his palm, eyes as wide as coins as we laid Marlo flat. I slid a pillow under her head, and as I did she momentarily came around, uttering one strangled, questioning word. "Hunter?"

Hunter covered his mouth fully then, hands shaking, eyes tearing up above them, and I wanted to tell him it would be okay, but I caught sight of my own horrified face in the mirrored wall behind him, pale and desperate and horrorstruck, and knew that was a lie. None of this was ever going to be okay again.

By the time we woke Micah and moved Marlo to the sick ward, it was too late. She was still breathing, but it was a shallow, halting exhalation, the kind I'd once seen in a puppy that had developed parvo and lay limply in my palm before expiring. I didn't even have to look at Micah's blighted expression to know Marlo would soon do the same. I wanted to leave the ward and go back to my room, alone, so I could shower away the scents of anise and burned flesh, and try to make sense of the equally scorched thoughts bubbling in my head.

Warren, however, made Hunter and me return with him to

the cantina, and had us walk through the scene over and over again, though now the lights were on high, and the music and television off. It still smelled like scorched spices, though, and Hunter shuddered as the scent washed over him. I reached out to touch him, but he jerked away and wouldn't look at me. We spent the next hour exhausting Warren's questions, but came no closer to finding out how Marlo had been infected. She'd never left the sanctuary, so the most frightening thought was that others could be walking around with this poison in their bodies, ticking bombs that would explode without warning, and—as we found out at four A.M.—eventual death.

Later, in my room, after I'd run water as hot as lava over my body and my skin was bright red, I lay back on my bed and let the thoughts, tangled like twine, unravel in my brain. Fatigue had me following each thread only so far until I drifted off, only to awaken abruptly, my heart momentarily picking up pace with a new bone to gnaw. Finally, sometime around six in the morning, an idea rose in my mind. My body went numb as the idea crystallized, growing hard as a stalactite, the sharp tip pointing down, directly into my gut. I opened my eyes slowly, blinked twice, and rose in a single smooth motion to dress.

Weaving through hallways too sterile and quiet, I shot up to the boneyard, where I knew I would be alone. I climbed down the ladder affixed to the heel of the Silver Slipper and ducked under a fiberglass champagne flute, just in case some industrious employee showed up early. Then I dialed the number stored under "Received Calls" on my cell phone. This time, now that it was too late to do anything, Regan answered.

"Yes?" she said, oh-so-sweetly. She didn't sound sleepy at all.

"You bitch," I said, voice rasping from my chest. "You wanted me watching the fireworks. You knew I'd breathe in that virus, and the curse of the second sign, and take it back into the sanctuary."

"Uh-uh-uh," she said, and I could envision her blond po-nytail swaying. "If you recall, I told you not to return to your sanctuary."

Which was a surefire way to make sure that I did. "Bitch," I repeated, closing my eyes.

Regan laughed that tinkling laugh of hers, and it rang out over the line like cracked bells. It was a sound I was begin-ning to hate. "Have an eventful night, did we? I can just imagine the panic in that place right now. I mean, what hap-pens when your sanctuary becomes a battlefield?" The ques-tion was rhetorical, and I didn't even attempt to answer, but her next words snagged my attention like cotton caught on a thorn. "You won't stop this, Joanna. It's futile to even try. This virus is going to spread throughout the valley like a brushfire, and nothing can change that."

And we didn't have a cure. I closed my eyes, leaning my head against the giant champagne flute. "And what are the Shadows going to do while that happens?"

"Take a page from the agents of Light," she said, the smile evident in her voice. "We sit back and do nothing."

The dig hit home, and my knees buckled beneath me. I glanced around like there was someone in the boneyard I could turn to for help, but in the morning light the retired signs showed their age, rust stains and naked bulb holes stark under an already unrelenting sun. It looked like an abandoned carnival, all the patrons fleeing once the illusion broke with daylight. "I'll find you, you know," I said to Re-gan, hunched over my knees. "I'll find you, and this time I'll kill you for what you've done."

She scoffed, and her mocking voice fell flat. "Give it a rest, Joanna. Your whole vengeance-till-death bit has got-ten old. You haven't killed Joaquin and you bartered away your two chances with me. Besides, I could pass right under your nose two weeks from now and you wouldn't even rec-ognize me."

"Your metamorphosis," I said, my veins icing over once again. They could turn her into a man if they wanted to. He could ask me out on a date and I wouldn't even know it was him. Her.

"That's right. Happy Birthday to me," she said, and laughed again.

"It just makes you fair game," I told her, needing to believe it myself. "Remember, I'm inoculated to this virus as well. When you finally do come out, I'll be waiting."

"Oh, no, *I'll* be the one waiting." She laughed again, and before I could find a reply, the line went dead.

20

The last time the leader of troop 175—paranormal division, Las Vegas—picked up a weapon, he'd used it to slay his father. Warren Clarke hadn't touched any weapon since, and to understand why, all you had to do was read the manual depicting the confrontation between him and his rogue father. I'd paid a near fortune to Zane to do just that, and the bloodbath that'd popped up at me from within those pages had given me nightmares for weeks. I saw firsthand how Warren had gotten his limp. And I saw how far he'd go to protect his troop, even from another agent of Light. Even from someone who was already *in*.

It was that, more than anything else, which had me waiting until near dusk to enter the briefing room where Warren had gathered the other star signs. I was the last to arrive, my face impassive under the weight of ten other gazes, my hair pulled back into a severe bun, gelled and fastened at the nape of my neck. I wore no jewelry save the ring my mother had left me, though the blank slate of my frame was marred by the bright summer dress I knew the others would immediately recognize as Olivia's costuming, the face I presented to the outside world. Not one I normally wore about the sanctuary.

Warren's eyes were narrowed, he already didn't like what I was going to say, and I let my eyes move over him impassively because I'd been ready for that, just as I was ready for Gregor's curiosity, and Micah's scrutiny. Riddick and Jewell were merely attentive, and I felt a pang of regret move through me at the thought of never knowing them better. Vanessa knew I was up to something, clear by the reservation in her posture, and the genial boyishness dropped from Felix's face as soon as I'd entered the room.

I hesitated when I spotted Rena. We hadn't spoken since our confrontation at the launchpad, and now it was probable that we never would. I glanced at Warren. "Where's Tekla?"

"She's not coming."

"I wouldn't have asked everyone to be here if it wasn't important," I said, and felt my annoyance rise enough to momentarily overtake my nerves.

"I doubt it's as important as charting our next move," Chandra said from her chair in the corner. She was leaning on the back two legs. One push, I couldn't help but think. "Not that we'd have a next move if it'd been left up to you."

"Chandra," Rena chided, and relief spun in my veins. She'd forgiven me, then. Too bad I was about to disappoint her again.

"I'm just saying, Tekla has enough to do without having to worry about this one's latest hysterics—"

"We all know what you're 'just saying,' Chandra," Felix interrupted sharply. "Now shut up and let Olivia talk."

I'd have shot him a grateful look if I'd thought he'd still be on my side five minutes from now. As it was, I just got on with my task, turning to look at Hunter for the first time.

He was a shade of his former self, and if Carl were drawing him now, it would be in charcoal, all the life and vitality leached from his image. Red pockets were smudged beneath his eyes from lack of sleep, too much drink, or both, and his face was drawn, cheeks sunken, like he'd lost weight overnight. He saw me studying him and raised a brow in mock regard, but it was clear he'd lost interest in everything around him. The spark that had once lit him from within was gone. It was my job to put it back.

"I'm sorry," I told him, and watched his Adam's apple bob. Whatever he'd expected me to say, it wasn't that. "I'm so desperately sorry and sick for it all."

He nodded after a moment, a slight, almost imperceptible move, but it was enough.

"Sorry for what, Olivia?" Rena prodded softly, and I shook myself, clearing my throat.

"For what I'm about to say," I said, and turned to address the whole room. "The virus. I know how it's being spread."

"It's not just by those who watched the fireworks, is it?" Micah sat up so straight he was almost out of his chair. I didn't add insult to injury by making him ask me any more, instead plowing forward and running myself under with my own explanation.

"Initially it was. But it's sexual in nature. It's transferred from an infected carrier by touch, through sex . . . through kissing." I glanced again at Hunter, whose face had fallen, a look of betrayal haunting the glassy indifference in his eyes. "That's why most people are dying in pairs. That's why there's no differentiation in sex or sexual orientation or race. Everyone wants to be loved. But for those who touch someone who already has the virus, it's a need that will kill them."

"Of course. The three distinct areas," Micah said, aloud but to himself. "How could I not see it?"

"That's why the deaths have been spread all across the valley," Gregor said, "and why it's usually not spouses who find the victims."

"Except for one small thing," Chandra said, and I fell silent. I'd been expecting it, but still had to control a shudder when she pointed to Hunter. "Him."

"You mean because he's not dead," I clarified.

"Exactly."

Felix said, "Well, maybe it's because he's a full-fledged star sign, and so he's protected from infection whereas a mortal or an initiate like Marlo wasn't."

I saw Hunter flinch, and decided to end his guilt before it could sink in any deeper. Even if it meant that guilt was transferred firmly onto my shoulders. "No," I said, and all eyes returned to me. "Hunter would've died along with Marlo, except he was immune as well." And here I swallowed hard. "He gained immunity before the virus was released."

There was silence as I let them work this out for themselves, and of course Hunter's expression cleared first. After all, he was the only one around when I'd kissed him in the labyrinth. The others, feeling the shift of emotion, followed my gaze to him. I didn't think his face could drain of any more color, but it had, leaving his skin looking waxen.

"You," he whispered.

"Me," I nodded, and a gasp rose up in the room.

"I'm confused," Vanessa said, looking from Hunter to me and back again. Riddick and Jewell nodded mutely, and Felix's head was tilted. He was still working it out. I glanced at Micah and Gregor, though, and could see that the older troop members had gotten it. Warren's expression was fully closed. His reaction would be a few minutes in coming. Unable to take anything back, I filled in the time, explaining.

"*I* passed the immunity on to Hunter before the night of the fireworks. It's the only reason he's still alive. But Regan called me on my cell phone that night. She wanted to make sure I was watching the fireworks. The virus was what they were really celebrating at Valhalla."

I looked at Warren and swallowed hard. "You were right. I underestimated her. I let her live because she was an initiate, but I played right into her hands. We've all been wondering why the Shadows aren't active in the mortal realm right now, why they haven't been for the past six months, but it was because they didn't need to be. After all, why risk their hides individually when they had a weapon that could wipe us all out?"

Not one of them spoke or moved, and only one was still looking my way. Hunter hadn't moved, and his eyes were cutting me with laserlike precision. "I'm the one responsible for Marlo's death. Not you. I'm sorry."

"Oh, *now* you're sorry?" Warren's voice was low, but he'd risen from his chair and looked taller than his middling height. "*Now* that disease has entered our home, our haven . . . you're sorry?"

I nodded mutely. I was sorry. And I knew it wasn't good enough. Besides, I was about to make it worse. "One more thing . . ."

"What was that?" Warren demanded, his sharp voice a stark contrast to my half-swallowed words. I knew he'd heard—they all had—but he wasn't going to let me slide through this admission, and I was almost glad of it. I could bring back the scent of charred anise by just visualizing Marlo's smiling face.

"I said there's one more thing you all need to know," and my voice was stronger, almost challenging. "The fireworks weren't just a celebration. I was in the boneyard, and I saw them. I smelled what was in them. I was there when the virus became—"

"Airborne." Micah looked at me, horror widening his eyes.

And I'd been standing on the highest platform in the boneyard, watching while dust and disease rose up around me. I'd answered a phone call from Regan.

You see the fireworks, don't you? she'd asked.

I see them.

Good . . . we're already in.

I looked again into every face in the room, and this time horror stared back at me. I swallowed hard. "I carried the virus back with me. Every breath I've taken since that day has been infecting everyone around me. I'm—"

"Don't you dare," Warren interrupted again, but this time his tone was dangerously low. He advanced on me, and I took a step back. "Don't say you didn't know or that you're sorry. There are no excuses for . . . for *this*!" He held up his hand, and I saw where his fingertips had been burned when he'd tried to clear Marlo's mouth of an obstruction that was both burning and choking her. That obstruction was her tongue.

"Wait, wait!" Micah stood, holding up his hands. "We don't know for sure that we're all infected. Maybe Felix is right. Maybe full-fledged star signs can't be affected."

"But the children," Rena said, hand fluttering helplessly to her chest, then her mouth, then back to her chest. If she'd had eyes, they'd be fixed on me just as accusingly as Warren's were.

I sighed, weariness overtaking me suddenly. I needed this to be over now. "Riddick, will you come here?"

He frowned, but didn't move. I smiled wryly and motioned him forward. "I promise. I won't even touch you."

Warren gave his consent with a stiff jerk of his head, and only then did Riddick rise to stand at my left side, though I noted he didn't come too close. That was fine because I then crossed the room, bending to whisper in Jewell's ear. She didn't jerk away, for which I was grateful, but a look of surprise bloomed on her face, followed by a fast and furious blush. She glanced up at me as I straightened, then nodded. "Okay. If you're sure."

Acutely aware that every eye was on her, she went to stand at Riddick's side. She didn't touch him, not even when she cupped a hand to his ear, but when she told him to close his eyes, he did. And when she said the rest of what I'd instructed her—things I knew she'd wanted to say to him for a while now; how much she was attracted to him, how his body and mind moved her, how she dreamed of him when alone at night—a slim wisp of smoke escaped his parted lips, evidence of the disease rising to curl about him like an entranced cobra . . . and all in the room gasped as one.

Jewell backed up against the wall, her hand covering her mouth in horror. Riddick's eyes flew open, catching on one shocked face after another. "What?"

No one answered. I turned slowly and faced Warren. "The disease is dormant until sexual contact, any one of you, save Hunter, will die from just one kiss."

For a moment he didn't move. Then he advanced on me, his limp pronounced, and his mouth drawn in a thin, sharp line. An image of a blood-splattered machete slashing through the air, over and over again, rocketed through my mind, and I began to shake where I stood.

"I am sorry," I whispered again, and got a brief flash of understanding from his storm-dark eyes before they shuttered again. Then his face took on the aspect of a squall brewing in the middle of the sea. His whole face sank into the storm erupting inside him, and his fists bunched and released, lips worked, not getting anything out . . . until he did. "Get out."

And even though I'd been prepared for that—even though I knew I was lucky that was all the leader of the Zodiac troop did, and demanded of me—I was still numb as I made my way to the launchpad. I'd already successfully retrieved the disks from my locker, and stashed my bags where I'd left my satchel a week earlier. What I wasn't prepared for was for Warren to follow me up the chute and wordlessly strip me of the mask that would allow me to re-enter the sanctuary.

Then he returned inside, leaving me to make the crossing on my own.

I shook as I waited, like some refugee victim who knew she was alive, but wasn't sure how . . . or even if she wanted to be. And when I felt dusk silently settle over the boneyard, I went ahead and created another breach in the wall, stepped through it one final time, and returned to the mortal reality. Warren, I knew, would be along shortly to shore up the fissure I'd made, but that would be out of habit. There'd be no breach of the boneyard's wall from the Shadows now. Why should there be? They were already in.

While I was on the outside. Alone.

21

The memory of Marlo's lifeless body kept me going those next few days. That and the disgust and horror on Hunter's face as he realized what I'd made him into. That last look had been a telling one. He'd never forgive me—I hadn't really expected him to—and he'd never look at me with longing or lust again either. And that was okay. If I could just regain enough trust to be allowed back in the sanctuary, the closeness we'd once held after sharing the aureole would be replaced with professional reserve, which was all I really wanted.

Wasn't it?

I was wondering about that as I parked in front of Cher's house, where I'd been staying since my ejection from the sanctuary. Olivia's home was unsafe now that the gloves were off between Regan and me, and even though she was supposed to be tucked away in some safehouse in preparation for her metamorphosis, I wouldn't put it past her to have revealed my hidden identity to Joaquin—or even the Tulpa.

"Heya, honey. What's up?" Cher said when I entered her guest room, her eyes never leaving the comic she was leafing through while lying on my bed. Not a comic—a Shadow manual. Shit. Had she gone through my stuff? Or had I left that one out on the nightstand after combing through it the night before? It had to be the latter, though I knew Olivia wouldn't have made a stink either way. Those two, I had to remember, kept no secrets from each other.

"Not a lot," I said, keeping my tone light as I toed off my tennies. "Just back from the gym."

She was propped up on her elbows, and as I tossed a few local magazines down onto the bed—weeklies that offered underground commentary on the city, politicians, and entertainers—she gave me a horrified once-over. "Darlin', did you . . . sweat?"

I hadn't actually. If I were to work out to the point of breaking a sweat I'd break whatever machine I was training on. There wasn't a free weight made that I couldn't lift a thousand times, and sparring with mortals was a total waste of time. I had been at the gym, though. The repetition of running or biking in place helped me think. My conscious mind zoned out while my subconscious pondered whatever problem I was trying to figure out. Besides, it was the last place the Shadows would think to look for me, and these days I was taking refuge where I could find it.

"Um . . ." I'd applied water to my chest after the workout to make it look a little more realistic. I should have known Olivia didn't sweat. "See, there was this girl next to me on the treadmill, and a cute guy on the other side of her, so I thought if I just went faster than her I could get his attention, but every time I upped my speed, so did she."

"That whore!" Cher threw the manual aside as she sat up.

"Yeah, so I ended up sprinting for like, five whole minutes, and when I looked up, the guy was gone."

Cher shook her head. "Next time why don't you just ask him how to work the machine? That always works for me."

Oh yeah. The this-inanimate-object-is-smarter-than-me approach. That was so me. "I'll do that," I said, and shot her a weak smile.

"What are these?" she asked, holding up one of the weeklies.

"Just local newspapers. They're free at the gym, and they have lots of good articles."

She looked at me suspiciously as she smoothed her hair back from her face. "You sure are readin' a lot these days."

Comics and angry criticism was considered reading a lot? "I'm not really reading them," I said, and her expression immediately shifted to relief. "I just look at the social events in these, and I like the pictures in the others."

"Oh, but I'm not talking about *this*," she said, picking the Shadow manual back up. "This is really good."

The lights and movement that animated the manual when I touched it were dormant in her mortal hands. Apparently it had some sort of sensory on and off switch, and it looked like any other comic as she thumbed it open. "What issue is that?" I asked, leaning forward.

"It's called *Daughter of Blood,* about Dawn, the Shadow Gemini."

I couldn't help myself. "Oh, I can't stand her. She's a real bitch."

"Yeah," she agreed, flipping through the pages. "But she dresses cool."

I drew back, studying the panel she flashed at me, unreasonably annoyed that my/Olivia's best friend would find one of the foremost supervillains in the city attractive. "No, she doesn't. She's totally hooker-fied."

"You think?" she asked, turning the page back to study it. "I don't know. I'd wear that."

"Sure, to a costume party," I said, flopping down in an oversized side chair.

Cher angled her eyes up at me, plucked brows winging high. "See, honey, that's why I don't exercise. It puts me in a shitty mood too."

"I'm not—" I stopped, sighed, realizing this could go on forever. And would, I thought, if I were still me. The good thing about being Olivia was being able to change mental direction without signaling first. Especially with Cher. "So where would someone go if they were looking to have sex with a lot of people?"

"It's *Las Vegas*," she pointed out, flipping another page.

Point taken.

Then again, that kind of thinking would mean I had nowhere to begin looking for Joaquin, which wasn't exactly true. Since I knew the virus was now being spread sexually, I had a fulcrum around which to expand my search. Las Vegas was hardly lacking in establishments meant to whet the sexual appetite.

The question was, which of the nightclubs, sex shops, lounges, or strip joints would be most alluring to Joaquin? Because he'd want to be out there, watching devastation unfold among the populace of healthy, sexual humans who had nothing more on their minds than a sweaty workout themselves. It fit in perfectly with his M.O.—causing pain through sexuality.

I mentally scratched the strip clubs from my list. As much as mainstream society liked to demonize the clubs and the women who worked there, they were fairly white-bread. How else could they flourish in every city in the country? Our culture's dirty little open secret. Besides, that was too blatant for Joaquin; the sensuality and allure of sexual desire would be lost in the transaction, money for titillation. No, he got his jollies from more unpredictable circumstances. Joaquin, I knew, liked the chase.

I reached over and grabbed one of the folded weeklies from the bed, tossed another to Cher, and flipped directly to the back where all the political rants and pseudo-articles that filled the earlier pages were replaced with ads offering phone sex or house calls or "special massag-ies."

"Help me look for a dominatrix," I told Cher, trying not to wonder where all these girls came from. I angled the paper to the side. Did their mothers know they were posed like this?

"Dang, girl," she said, picking up the magazine. "You aren't turning into a muffin bumper, are you?"

"Don't worry, Cher," I said, skipping past the ads that promised one-on-one action. Joaquin would want to cast a wider net. "You'd be the first to know."

She smiled brightly. "Why thank you, honey!"

"Thanks for what?" Suzanne asked, entering the room without knocking. In other families that could be a cause for death by stoning, but Cher made room next to her, passing Suzanne a third magazine as she continued her search.

"Olivia's trying to decide if she wants to munch rug, but first she's looking for cheap sex with a stranger and no strings attached, just to make sure."

I blushed under Suzanne's startled gaze and held up a hand. "That's not true. I'm just . . . adding a service to my web business that makes it easy for potential visitors to find what they're looking for when they come to Vegas."

"How entrepreneurial of you, darlin'," Suzanne settled next to her daughter and picked up her weekly. "Sex does sell, and it'll certainly spice up that racketeering thing you have going," she said, flipping open her magazine. I stared.

"Yeah," I said slowly, trying to shake off the image of my sister, the mobster. "Anyway, I'm looking for some place kind of illicit. Something that reeks of secrecy and intrigue. One where you have to know a secret password or hand-shake or something to get in."

"Well, you're not going to find it in one of these rags," Suzanne said, and tossed her magazine aside. I looked at her. "You're not." She crossed her legs, flashing lean thighs. "What you want is something exclusive. Invitation only. Like a sex club that meets every so often to masturbate together, or a same-sex meeting."

I wrinkled my nose. "There's such a thing?"

She looked at me like I was hopelessly naive. "Honey, there are fringe groups for anything that tickles a human's fancy, and a few things that shouldn't. Bondage, bestiality, sometimes both." I shuddered at that, and Cher let out a horrified squeal. "They don't advertise because they know society wouldn't approve. But there's a whole subculture of people who indulge in fetishes others try not to even imagine."

"I don't really want something that . . . uh, extreme. A little more vanilla. Regular people looking for a good time, but lots of them."

"Oh, you mean like partner swapping?" That sounded about as vanilla to me as a double-caramel-mocha frappuccino, but before I could say so, Suzanne went on. "What you want is a swingers' club, though they often have an interview process that takes weeks, and you'll have to send in a picture as well."

Interviewing? I thought. To be a sex partner? I began to look through my magazine again. There had to be something else.

"Of course, anyone can register for the yearly swingers' ball. People from all over the country come to those, and if you belong at a national level you're automatically allowed in to any local gatherings."

Bingo.

"How many people?" I asked, angling my head.

"What, at the big balls?" she said, causing Cher to snort. Suzanne arched a brow in her direction, but continued speaking to me. "Thousands. People plan it into their summer vacations the same way they would Disneyland, though here they don't bring the kids."

Here, I thought, where they could die wrapped in a stranger's embrace. It was perfect. Perfectly horrible, I thought, correcting myself, but perfect for the Shadows' intentions. Joaquin might even see such an event as a mass suicide. Thousands of people putting the metaphorical cup to their mouths, and him on hand, goading them to drink. "That's it," I said quietly. "That would be perfect."

"Really?" Suzanne tilted her head. It made her look younger than her years. "You'd be interested in that?"

I nodded, then quickly added, "For my website, of course. Strictly professional research."

"Of course," she said, standing. "Well, you're in luck. The

ball's this weekend, and this one's a huge to-do in the swingers' community, an anniversary of some sort. Troy's been trying to get me to go for a month now. He says it'll 'strengthen our relationship' and 'add another dimension to our knowledge of sexuality.'"

Troy was full of shit, but I wasn't going to say that to Suzanne. I made it a rule to never say anything bad about my friends' boyfriends until I was sure they were well and truly out of the picture—preferably dead. Or gay. Or both. And while her voice was neutral as she talked about him, Suzanne might still be interested in the little jerk. Though at least she didn't sound bowled over by the idea.

"Oh, I have an idea," Cher said, sitting up on the bed so fast *my* head spun. "We could all go! We could dress up like Dawn in *Daughter of Blood*, and pretend we're into the 'lifestyle.'" She made little quotation marks in the air.

Alarmed, I sat up straight as well. I didn't want these two anywhere near a place where both Joaquin and the virus promised to be running rampant. "I don't know if they let you pretend to be someone you're not," I said, thinking quick. "They probably ask for social security and health cards and everything down to your latest medical exam."

"No, they don't. Troy's already checked it out," Suzanne put in, and I thought, *I just bet he has.* Then she added, "Who's Dawn?"

"Some make-believe slut who reminds Olivia of this girl at the gym," Cher said, and picked up the manual she'd thrown aside. "See?"

"Oh my." Suzanne clasped her hands in front of her, managing to look startled and dumbfounded all at the same time.

"Isn't her outfit cool?" Cher said, leaning over so they could both look at the same time.

"Oh. My."

"Uh . . . it's a comic book, Suzanne," I said, because her expression had suddenly shifted from puzzled to alarmed.

"Y-Yes, but . . . why?"

She meant why was it here, sullying the posh, urbane feel of her house. I couldn't fault her. Most people thought they were geeky, but I'd done a lot of reading since becoming a superhero, and I'd found the plots and action to be more engaging than most thrillers. Not to mention they were based on fact. Though I left that part out when explaining this to Suzanne.

It didn't seem to help. She bit her lip, backing up even further. "But only certain people read those things . . . and you guys aren't them."

"What kind of people?"

Her pretty mouth screwed up with distaste. "Virgins."

"It's not an affliction," I said, leaning back on my palms, amused now.

"And Dawn doesn't look like a virgin," Cher pointed out. "I bet if I show up to the swingers' ball in that get-up I could pop a few cherries."

"Can you please stop talking about that woman? Here . . . try this one." I dug around in my bag until I found a manual of Light, careful to toss it to Cher so I was no longer touching it when she spotted it. I didn't need laser beams spilling out from the pages and blowing my supercover.

"*Vanessa Valen: Agent of Light*," she read, then flipped open to the first page. She shrugged. "She's pretty hot."

"She's more than hot," I said, unreasonably miffed that Cher should prefer Dawn over Vanessa. I still felt loyalty toward the agents of Light, and still saw myself as part of that troop . . . even if I was the only one. "She's tough and she's kind, and she has the coolest condu— er, weapon out of almost anyone. You should dress up like her."

"You really read these things?" Suzanne asked me, bending over Cher's shoulder.

"They're pretty good, Momma," Cher said, saving me for answering. She held out the manual to her mother. "Here, try one."

Suzanne drew back, looking from Cher to me as if we were patients in a psychiatric ward. "You know," she said, backing away from the bed, "come to think of it, I bet a day trip to a nice little sex club would do us all some good. Olivia, you in?"

I thought about it, still not liking the idea of them accompanying me, but at least I'd be around to help if anyone tried to murder, infect, or draw them into a threesome. It looked like Troy had already planted the seed, as it were, anyway. And now that I thought of it, if Troy was so interested in sampling other people's partners, what's to say he wasn't already a carrier? I could keep an eye on him, as well as my friends, plus have a pretty good cover for attending in the first place. There was power in numbers, as they say, and this time the power happened to be anonymity. Just what I needed. "Sure, I'm in."

"You, Cher?"

"Only if I can dress up like an evil, murdering whore."

Suzanne smiled, a look of great relief passing over her face. "It's practically required. I'll go call Troy now to get us some tickets."

"Okay, so when and where?" I asked.

"Saturday night, where all the great parties are held," Suzanne said, tossing the answer over her shoulder as she glided from the room. "Valhalla, of course."

I smiled wryly. Of course.

22

It was seven o'clock, just two hours before the swingers' ball officially opened. Troy had gone down earlier in the day to register us for the event—apparently you couldn't just show up and hand over your spouse—and I was preparing for an evening of blatant flirtation and sex games like I was going to war. Of course, a real soldier wouldn't be caught dead in my battle attire; a snug halter top that criss-crossed over my chest in shiny black satin, and a flowing knee-length skirt with a slit nearly to my waist, each step providing a healthy flash of thigh. This was all courtesy of my mother's abandoned closet back at the sanctuary, so the lightweight satin was made of a material stronger than chainmail, but just as important, the length and slack in the skirt allowed me to wear a flesh-colored holster on my opposite thigh, providing a place to tuck extra ammo and a steel stiletto. The only paranormal help I was getting these days was in the form of my conduit and the ring still pulsing reassuringly on my right hand, and both of those needed to be saved for just the right moment. The additional weapon, though mortal, might come in handy. I just had to be extra careful while sitting down.

After I blew out my hair and applied more makeup than Paris Hilton on an insecure day, I gave myself a critical once-over and, satisfied, tucked my conduit in my black Gucci bag. Thus armed to the proverbial teeth, I strode out of the bathroom and into Cher's sitting area to grab the mask I'd picked up at a costume store. It fit less perfectly than my shield had, but looked similar enough to make me feel more myself, and most importantly, helped conceal my Olivia identity. Joaquin hadn't discovered it while he'd had the chance, a failure I was sure he was kicking himself for now. It was one of the few tools I had left, and I wanted to keep it that way.

But my mask was missing. The antique writing desk, where I'd left it prior to entering the shower, was empty. I looked beneath it, in the wicker trash bin next to it, and in the drawer, just in case I'd put it there for safekeeping. Nothing.

"Cher!" I yelled, trying to keep the rising panic from my voice. I must've failed. Footsteps pounded down the hall, and Cher appeared in a bathrobe with her hair in rollers, face bare, eyes wide as she looked at me.

"Livvy, darlin', are you okay? You yelled so . . ." She trailed off, taking in my attire, and her face altered from an expression of alarm to one of sheer admiration. "Oh my God! Turn, baby, turn!"

I swallowed down my impatience and turned as she circled her finger in the air. The skirt swirled, my right thigh showed practically up to my neck, and the whole thing settled with a soft flutter against my skin. I posed, as Olivia would.

"Fantabulous!" she squealed, clapping her hands. "And those are muscle shoes if I ever saw 'em!"

I glanced down at my wedged, calf-high boots. Not perfect seasonal attire, I'll admit. There had to be some sort of fashion rule against wearing leather boots in the summer, but I figured I could get away with it as just another outlandish part of my "costume." There were more important issues at stake tonight than being fashionable. Like being alive.

"Thanks," I said to Cher, "but I seem to be missing part of my costume. Did you happen to see something lying on this desk?"

"Did I?" she repeated, her conspiratorial smile making me swallow hard. She reached into the pocket of her robe and produced my mask. "Here."

I sighed, taking it. "What did you do?"

"I just gussied it up a bit," she said, waving her hand in the air like I shouldn't bother thanking her. I didn't. "I don't know if I ever told you, but I'm a devil with a hot glue gun."

She certainly was. Lustrous crystals studded every spare inch of the mask, and false eyelashes were affixed just above the eyeholes. I sighed again and pushed against one of the gems. It was glued solid. "It . . . it's . . ."

"Swarovski crystals, yeah," she said, misunderstanding my speechlessness. "I decorated it Mardi Gras style. Just because you're a bit shy at the idea of anyone knowing who you are doesn't mean you can't be fashionable."

I sighed, not just because there was no use arguing with that but because I was beginning to understand her reasoning. Besides, if Joaquin were there, the last thing he'd be expecting would be a showdown with a showgirl.

"Well, thanks," I said to a beaming Cher. "What are you wearing?"

She made a show of turning around and stripping off her robe to reveal a black mini-dress cut from neck to navel, and—from what I could see—sliced in tiny bits to cover the choicest of body parts. She whirled as I had earlier, the strips of cloth flying dangerously about her body. "Is that legal?"

"It's designer," Cher said, grabbing a strand of shiny beads from the bureau and looping them over her head multiple times so that they too draped her body. She caught my eye through the mirror. "By Imitation of Christ."

I made a face. "Why, because he had such great fashion sense?"

She only laughed. "I'm going to finish getting ready. Meet me downstairs in ten?"

"Sure," I said as she flounced from the room, her stride runway perfect despite the lack of a catwalk or music. I glanced back down at my altered mask and sighed again, hoping I didn't run into anyone I knew from either of my realities.

Though that was the point, I reminded myself. Track down Joaquin. Sneak up on him. Put an arrow through his black heart. If that required dressing up like a spoiled, jet-setting porn star/heiress, then I'd do it. Still, as I grabbed my handbag from the table to head downstairs, I couldn't help but think that Carl was going to have a field day drawing this one.

"Suz, baby. I'm so glad you called . . . all of you."

Troy spared a glance for Cher and me in the back of his Escalade, a glance, I noted, that lingered a little longer than it should have. Cher ignored him completely, staring into her compact as she applied gloss on lips that already shone like waxed chrome, and I merely rolled my eyes and looked out the window as we pulled into Valhalla's long drive. We followed it past painfully manicured landscaping with bright flowers and bushes never meant for the desert, beyond fountains depicting the feast of the gods, complete with winged Valkyries serving golden goblets to fallen Vikings.

The taxi stand was full, a line of cabs waiting to be called to the front doors by whistle-carrying doormen, like restless stallions at the Derby. Limos were wedged in slots near the entrance, waiting—in most cases, for hours—for their charges to finish the night's partying. A few Hummers and exotic sports cars were showcased up front, a hefty tip ensuring they'd be there when their owners returned, but I had a feeling Troy wouldn't spring for such a luxury, even with three stunning women in his charge, and—no surprise—he didn't. Our doors swung open and polite valets ushered us beneath the arching portico.

"Shall we?" I said as soon as we were all assembled, noting the looks we were getting from the other hotel patrons, men and women dressed for dinner or shows or a night at the tables, none of whom looked like they'd done any swinging since elementary school. I already had my mask on, relatively certain the spiked lashes would scare even the most dogged security guard from insisting I remove it. A bellman, eyes wide, held the door open for us, and Troy took the other, ushering us through, making sure to touch each one of us in some proprietary way as we passed.

The good thing about spending the entire evening with Troy was his predictability. He'd keep an eye on all of us like we were his personal harem, and that was an almost comforting thought . . . at least where Suzanne and Cher were concerned. I'd ditch him at will, though I promised myself that if it came down to taking out Joaquin or protecting these two women from harm or infection or ghastly death, I'd choose them. They were innocents, and my first priority. And besides, I thought, watching the swish of Cher's skirt in front of me, they were all I had now.

Nine o'clock was apparently still early for the swinger crowd, though there were enough people in the east ballroom to begin the evening's fun. In the event that Joaquin was one of them—knowing he was never one to turn down a willing victim—I linked my arm with Cher's so we could make our first round of the room, decorated in acres of black leather just for the occasion. I hoped.

First, however, we had to register and receive our armbands.

"Got anything in pink?" Cher asked the receptionist sitting behind a long draped table just to the right of the door. Pamphlets touting regional, local, and national conferences were splayed out before her, but Cher was busy studying the red, blue, yellow, and green plastic bands taped to the table in front of us. "Pink's my favorite color."

The woman only stared.

"I'm more of a purple-lovin' kind of girl myself," I added,

smiling down into the woman's round face. Besides, purple was almost black, and I thought Olivia would consider such a detail.

The woman just blinked and turned her cold gaze on me. "What the hell is that supposed to mean?"

Hunh? "Well . . . purple is traditionally the color used for royalty. It's also really great with my coloring, though it has to be the right shade. Lilac would be best."

Troy, who'd been listening behind us from his guard post next to Suzanne, edged his way between us and the table. "I think she means what does the color signify for the purposes of this event. In this case, purple and pink mean nothing." He turned back to the greeter, and his lips drew up in pure saccharine smile. "I'll take a green one, please."

The woman blushed all the way down to her graying roots. As she fumbled with his wristband, I noted she too had a green one fastened over her own pudgy wrist. I held out my hand for one as well. She ignored me. "And your name is, Mr. . . . ?"

"Just call me Troy."

"Troy," she said breathlessly, her eyes traveling up to his lips. What the hell was going on here? Was there some sort of mental telepathy at play, or had I completely missed the nuances of a new form of speed dating? "That's lovely, but I need your full name so I can give you your name badge."

"Ugh." Cher shuddered beside me. "Name badges?"

That seemed to wake the woman from her lustful reverie. She was all business as she flicked through a box to find Troy's badge. "It makes the introductory process less inhibiting, and it's a good conversation starter. Your place of birth is printed below it as well, ah . . . Mr. Stone."

As she handed it to him I held out my arm. "Green, please."

Suzanne put her hand on my shoulder. "Um, Olivia, maybe . . ."

The woman—her badge said Mary Malone from Topeka—snapped the green over my wrist. Troy nodded approvingly. I lifted my mask, smiled at Mary again, and used my sister's sweetest tone—and the dimple I knew resided in her left cheek—to try and win her over again. "Thank you, Miss Malone."

This time she responded warmly. "You're very welcome . . . ?"

"Olivia. Olivia Archer," I said slowly, my brows drawing together at her quick change of heart. My dimple wasn't that cute. She handed me my name badge, fingers lingering over mine, and I drew back quickly. I heard a muffled snort behind me, but when I turned Suzanne's face was straight, absent of all humor.

"And for the rest of you?"

Cher held out her wrist. "I'll take—"

"Maybe we should find out exactly what each color means first, dear," Suzanne said, stilling her stepdaughter. "Mary?"

Mary blinked at us in surprise. "Oh, are you first-timers? All right then, welcome. We have a color-coded system that's used nationally, so if you attend any soirees in other parts of the country, you'll know what to ask for. It's very simple, though. A red wristband means 'women only.' Blue means you prefer to be approached only by men. Yellow means 'only couples,' and green means . . ."

My brain scrambled, trying on the remaining options. I didn't have to, though, because Troy lifted my hand high, kissing the fingers just below my own green wristband before murmuring, "Anything goes."

Before I could respond—i.e., barf all over the reception table—both he and Mary shot me meaningful looks. I ripped my hand from Troy's and lowered my mask over my own burning face. The giggle came from beside me again, and this time when I looked over, Suzanne's face was alive with merriment. She turned to Mary, still smiling. "I'll take a blue one, please."

"Red for me," Cher chimed in, merrily.

I turned to Cher. "Red?"

"Sure. Women are always easier to talk to, and if I don't want to talk to someone, I'll just stick close to you or Momma."

Now why hadn't I thought of that? I turned back to change out my wristband, but Mary was already ushering us aside for another party of four. Their eyes dropped furtively to our wrists, lingering on mine, before scanning my body. I pulled my mask down tighter.

"Suzanne! Cher! Over here!"

I glanced behind us to see a man winding past half-dressed mortals like they were an obstacle course and we were the finish line. His eyes lit on me, and he picked up his pace with renewed fervor, nearly bowling over a man dressed as a woman escorted by a man. I sniffed, scented out printer ink and nerves, and turned to Suzanne with narrowed eyes.

"I hope you don't mind," she said nervously, "but my friend Ian has been asking about you."

"Momma!" Cher hissed, and batted her stepmother with her Fendi bag.

"He's a nice guy!" Suzanne whispered, hitting her back. "and they have that whole computer expert thing in common." She turned back to me with pleading eyes. "If you just give him a chance—"

She was babbling, and though the last thing I needed was another mortal to babysit, I cut her off with an understanding smile. "It's okay," I said, as Ian—harmless and guileless and hopelessly uncool—came to a halt in front of us.

"Hi," he said, breathless, though I didn't think it was from his trek across the ballroom. He seemed like a breathless sort of guy in general. "Am I late? Sorry I'm late."

"Not at all. We just got here ourselves."

Ian seemed not to hear her, and was running a hand over his head, muttering, "Traffic, and I couldn't figure out what to wear . . ."

He had a lanky runner's body, strong, with long muscles, which made it totally incompatible with his face, lined and freckled from the sun. His head was topped with thinning blond hair that looked like chopped plumage, but knowing how deceiving looks could be, I inhaled deeply like I did whenever I met someone new.

Ian smelled like cotton and starch, and beneath that, strangely, like sand from the seashore. His cologne was soft and nutty, like a weakened almond extract, though I decided this guy was as vanilla as they came. Clashing sharply with all this was the tang of his anxiety—like a red wine gone bad—and the chalky streaks of his hope as he stared, unblinking, at me.

He was, unsurprisingly, sporting a red wristband, and I hid my green one behind my back as Suzanne introduced Ian to Troy, who greeted him curtly, and turned away to survey the rest of the room just as Ian stuck his hand out. Now I was determined to be nice to him. I beamed kindly when Suzanne said, "And this is Olivia."

"Hello Ian. It's nice to finally meet you."

His mouth opened and closed, but no sound came out. At least his babbling had been cured.

"Should we get a drink?" Suzanne asked, earning a grateful nod from Ian.

"This way," Troy said, starting off without us. There were makeshift bars stationed in all four corners of the elongated ballroom, though Troy led us toward the farthest, a ploy I was sure was meant to draw us farther into the lion's den. In doing so we had to pass the curtained stalls, which turned out to be vendors' booths touting everything from sex toys to videos to brochures for a chicken ranch located just over the county line. This booth came complete with a menu of appetizers to choose from, and two of the ladies of the house available to answer any questions. I admit I lingered there, wondering what exactly a "Hot Shot" entailed, but hurried on when one of them knowingly caught my eye . . . and the color of my wristband.

I ordered a seven and seven at the bar, trusting Ian to take care of the details, then turned my back on the others so I could fully survey the room for the first time.

It was certainly a different crowd than had been present for the bachelorette auction, and a part of me would've liked to just park it against a wall, like a fly, and watch the interactions between strangers take place, knowing that each whispered hello, every meeting of eyes, all accidental touches were gestures hoping to score an invitation to the bedroom. Even I, a born and bred Vegas girl, found it fascinating, though I suppose every bar on a Friday night sported a similar, if more covert, scene to this. But blatant voyeurism was out. I was in search of someone who had a greater hunger for flesh than all these mortals combined, so I focused on the men in the room, and began to hunt.

"These swingers seem pretty tame," Cher said, as Ian handed me my drink.

"I don't think you can use *swinger* and *tame* in the same sentence," I said.

"Says the woman in anything goes."

I scowled at her and scanned the room. There was a steady stream of new arrivals, and you could feel anticipation mounting, even if—unlike me—you couldn't scent it. But what I scented more than anything, was the increasingly familiar smell of infections, so the more I watched, the more baffled I became. This virus was being spread sexually. AIDS alone should be enough of a deterrent, but since the papers had even reported the burn marks around the mouths and private areas of the victims, you'd think that'd give people a bit of a clue. Stop swapping bodily fluids with strangers!

Yet here we all were, milling around like alley cats in heat, viruses be damned. Shaking my head, I followed the others to a booth where a woman was chained to the wall, realizing along the way that my mask idea had turned out to be a popular, and none-too-original, option. I hoped Joaquin wasn't disguised as well.

"They look like pageant contestants," I muttered, eyeing the name tags splayed like banners on clothing, but more often on bared flesh.

Suzanne, overhearing, said, "I don't even want to guess what you need to do to win Best Personality."

"Or Most Photogenic," Cher put in. We all snorted. Troy turned around and glared at us. Someone was taking his sexual prowess a little too seriously.

We wandered a bit longer, the crowd thickening around us, until Cher halted abruptly. "Oh shit!"

"What?"

"Is that Lon?"

The rest of us looked in the direction she was pointing, easily spotting the man with shirtsleeves rolled high and a gold-tipped cane that he used ruthlessly to clear his path.

"Oh shit!" Suzanne and I said in unison.

"Duck! Duck your heads! If he sees us, we're screwed."

"I'm okay," I said, as Lon expertly wove his way through the crowd. He was paying no attention whatsoever to the wristbands or the amount of leopard print and baby oil slicking the skin of those around him, but his eye caught on every face he passed, neck swiveling, mentally taking notes. "I have a mask on."

"What the hell's he doing here?" Suzanne asked, yanking Troy in front of her so he formed a solid, fleshy wall. Cher ducked behind him as well.

"Well, I don't think he's here for the edible body paint." I sipped at my drink, watching as Lon jotted in a small spiral notebook before it disappeared beneath his coat jacket again. Lon—no last name, just like Cher—was the city's gossip columnist. He could dig up dirt on the queen mother, and he was as ubiquitous as a cockroach, seemingly everywhere at once.

If Cher and Suzanne were caught trolling at a swingers' ball tonight, the whole city would hear about it in the morning. Olivia had also made quite a few appearances in his daily column, though fewer since I'd taken over her identity. I wanted to keep it that way, so mask or not, I yanked Ian in front of me and told the others to keep moving. Between the horny mortals, supervillains, and gossip columnists, this place was getting really dangerous.

"Wow," Cher said, stopping dead in her tracks in front of a booth where a woman hung from the ceiling, leather cords attached to a plastic bra right where her nipples should be. "I bet she wouldn't fail the pencil test."

"Honey, pencils are the least of her worries," Suzanne replied, taking in the woman's restraints.

"And that one over there," Cher said, pointing. "What do you think she does to stay so thin?"

"Besides pole-dance for a living? Probably ephedrine and diuretics. Now come on."

Weaving in and out of the crowd, I kept an eye out for Joaquin. Suzanne, noting my attentiveness, said, "Don't worry. Lon's on the other side of the room. I just saw him use his cane to crowbar a politician dressed as a street pimp."

"Oh, it's not him. I'm looking . . ." I paused, thinking, *Why not?* Why not enlist the others in my search for Joaquin? If anyone could spot a player it would be Suzanne and Cher. Of course, considering Suzanne's taste I'd probably have to keep her from running over to hump his leg, but I'd cross that bridge when we came to it. "I'm looking for a man who looks like a real seducer. He'll be good at it, too."

"A real Casanova, huh?"

"Sort of. He'll make you want to get to know him . . . but, you know, try not to have sex with anyone here," I added quickly.

Suzanne eyed a man wearing Dockers shorts and a fanny pack, typical tourist wear if you didn't count the body glitter. "I'll do my best to control myself," she replied dryly.

We continued our search for another quarter hour, with no luck. Lon spotted us once during that time, and as soon as he and I made eye contact, he started my way, barreling through the room like a Monday night halfback, cane swinging. Suzanne ducked, Cher squealed, but I turned to face him, smile on full blaze, green wristband aloft as I swirled my drink. He slowed but didn't stop. I blew him a kiss, and fear flitted across his face. I took a step forward, watched his eyes widen, then he pivoted on his heels and turned back the way he came. I'd like to think my brazen appearance was what had stopped him in his tracks . . . but the flash of steel at my thigh probably had a bit to do with it as well.

After that, we found some tables clustered in a dim corner, empty but for a couple necking in the corner, apparently unwilling to wait and see if better pickings came along. As we drew closer, they rose from their seats, holding hands, and headed toward a heavily draped area, curtained off by at least three layers of silver and black fabric. They disappeared inside.

"The common room," Troy said, seeing me watch them, and moving to put his hand on the small of my back. "Where all sorts of private things can be viewed in public."

I was going to puke if this guy didn't stop touching me. Seriously.

I glanced over at Suzanne, who was staring into her drink but talking to Ian, who kept sneaking glances over at us. I shot him an apologetic smile—at least I thought that's what it was; who knew what it looked like beneath this mask— and lowered myself to a chair closer to Cher than Troy.

I glanced with disgust at a threesome who disappeared behind the thick layers of curtains, all holding hands. Normally I was pretty open-minded. Whatever you wanted to do as long as it wasn't hurting someone was fine with me. But I'd just watched all three people enter the ballroom at different times, and they'd had less than a five-minute chat before heading to that back room. If even one person behind those curtains was a carrier of the Valhalla virus, this place was going to erupt like Mount Saint Helens. I wanted to prevent that if I could, but more than that, I needed to find Joaquin before chaos swallowed the best lead I had.

"Any particularly naughty thoughts going through that pretty little head?"

I turned to find Troy again leaning close. I glanced down at his mouth, curled in what I assumed was supposed to resemble a lascivious smile . . . and thought about punching the center of his face clear back to the base of his skull.

"One or two," I answered truthfully, voice dripping with pseudo-sweetness.

"Care to share?" he prodded, wriggling waxed brows.

Love to. I was thinking, when Suzanne's voice cut in. "How about that guy, Olivia? He looks pretty sleazy."

We all looked. I felt my heart drop, then quickly regulated my breathing before it could be sensed above the general lust. Even across the dim room I recognized Joaquin. The way he walked, the tilt of his head as he regarded the mortals surrounding him like vermin. Of course he was making no real attempt to disguise himself, and why should he? He was in no danger here. He thought himself immune to disease, untouchable by all, impervious even to death.

"He's perfect," I told her, and without taking my eyes from him, I put down my drink, picked up my handbag with my conduit still inside, and rose.

"Wait," Troy said with sudden alarm. "Where are you—?"

The rest of his words were lost to me as I trailed Joaquin. As I walked, conversations flowed around me, and I bobbed on the ebb and weave of words, but stopped to address no one.

"I can heal people with my penis," I heard a man say to more laughter than the comment warranted.

Then a woman; high voice, fluttering hands, thick thighs. Disease-laced breath. "When I was little I thought they meant 'sea men.' Little tiny sea men? I kept wondering how all these sea men got in the bed . . ."

Another man, talking above a group of stiff competitors— no pun intended—gathered around a woman so perfect, I'd bet a bill she was really a man in drag. "I like my women fuller, more curvy," the suitor was saying, eyeing him/her up and down. "After all, who wants a bumpy ride?"

I kept Joaquin's back in sight, unheeded and almost entirely unnoticed, until a man the size of a giant pit bull stepped in front of me.

I sighed and stared down at him from my leather-booted height. He was shaven bald, with squinty eyes parked too close together on his round face. Tattoos coiled around his neck, disappearing beneath a chain-link vest, which had to be murder on his nipple hair. He greeted me, then waited for me to fall all over myself to fuck him. I just stared.

Women, I had once read, found unrelenting eye contact trustful and reassuring. Men, however, often deemed it as an act of aggression, thus the innovative ways they devised to communicate without having to look at one another. Sports. Cars. Games. No eye contact equals no aggression equals no confrontation. This was why women got together for lunch, and men got together in bars.

The man asked me a question—a simple yes or no would've sufficed—and without changing my expression, I allowed the silence, and the eye contact, to draw out between us.

His left eye twitched. "I said, are you here with someone?"

"Yes." I moved to step around him. He planted himself in front of me again.

"Well, maybe your someone and you would like to come and play with me?" It didn't sound like a question.

"You're not his type," I said, and searched over his shoulder for Joaquin, but he'd disappeared in the thickening crowd. Damn.

"Well, maybe I'm your type. You never know till you try."

I shook my head, smelling the stubborn need oozing from his pores. Dammit. "Believe me, I know."

"Oh, I see," he said, and I glanced back over at him, wondering exactly what he saw. "You're one of those squatters, a one-trick pony. A tease who comes in here pretending to be up for anything but really looking for an easy mark and a rich husband."

Yes, that's me. Superheroine by day, squatter by night. "No. I only look for rich husbands on Tuesdays and Thursdays. Now excuse me."

He stepped in front of me again. And this time he put his hand on me. "So what are you looking for tonight?"

I stared hard at where he'd grasped my arm until he released it. Then I angled my gaze back up, meeting his head on. "A tall man with a big dick. Sorry."

He responded with the requisite "Bitch!," I yawned, but was finally allowed to move on. Thank God. Throwing him into the teeming stack of porn mags to our right would have really blown my cover.

But Joaquin was gone. I knew it before I inhaled, but tried not to let it get me down. We'd all perfected the art of masking our natural scents. It'd flare only under stress or emotion, so I either had to find him again by sight, or wait until he got excited . . . which, considering the things that excited Joaquin, meant it'd be too late. Circling back the way I'd come, I moved faster, head swiveling without making eye contact . . . and nearly ran into Ian.

"Olivia," he said, like he hadn't known I was there.

I raised my brows. It was impatient, and slightly rude, and so was the way I scanned the room over his shoulder. "Ian?"

His optimistic expression wobbled a little. "Uh . . . wanna dance?"

I thought about it. It would be a normal thing to do. Besides, I could survey the room from the dance floor, rotating him along, as Ian didn't exactly look like the leading man type. "Sure." I shrugged and followed him to an elevated platform centered in the room. Dozens of other couples were spazzing out to what must have been the music in their heads . . . because it wasn't to the music that was blaring out of the surrounding speakers. Ian joined them immediately. Watching him made my eyes ache. Had the reputation of white computer geeks not preceded him, I would've called 911.

"So, how are you?" he asked, jerking his head to the right.

"Fine, Ian. Just fine." Other than all the near-death experiences. I angled over to my right, forcing him to follow. Still no sign of Joaquin.

"Yeah, me too. Busy, of course. Lots of programs to . . . program."

"Mmm-hmm," I said, pivoting to my left.

"But busy is good, right?" He paused, waiting for my nod, before slapping his knee. "Yeah, busy is good."

We kept at this masochist little bob and weave for a few minutes longer.

"So, I know Suzanne has mentioned me, probably talked me up quite a bit," Ian said, huffing slightly. His breath was like warmed milk, but soured with nerves. "And of course I know all about you. Who doesn't, right?"

He laughed self-consciously, and I angled him so he wouldn't crash into the guy in back of him. "Your point?"

"Well, I think we have a lot in common," he said, bumping the guy anyway. I shifted again. "And when Suzanne told me that you read the Zodiac series of comics as well . . . well, I knew this was going to be a great date. I subscribe."

Uh-oh. "Do you?" I said, keeping my voice light. He nodded, banging into another dancer. She grabbed his butt in return, which sent him into a whole new set of spasms.

"Anyway, it's the strangest thing. I saw this girl . . . you know, the Archer? She, uh, looks like you," he said, even that coming out sounding like a question. "I bet that's where you got the idea."

"The idea?"

"You know, for your costume. You're dressed as a super-hero, right?"

A figure pulled up behind Ian, swaying slowly to the frantic beat, and I nearly froze in place. Oblivious, Ian continued dancing, inches away from Joaquin's leering, attentive face.

"Let's not talk about it now, okay?" I told him, backing up, hoping he'd follow my lead. He did, but so did Joaquin, eyes locked on mine like Scud missiles. Fuck.

"Okay, but I just wanted to tell you I think it's cool. Lots of people diss comic books as being, you know . . ." He stuck his finger down his throat, miming being sick, always an attractive gesture, and I managed a half smile. Behind him, Joaquin mimicked the move. Homicidal smartass. "Anyway, it takes the pressure off a bit. I can just be myself, just Ian Hanson going out with Olivia Archer, on a regular ol' date."

I nearly deflated as a smile bloomed on Joaquin's face. He mouthed the words *Olivia Archer* . . . then he left.

I fumbled at my bag, grasped my conduit, pushing by Ian, who started apologizing immediately, but Joaquin had disappeared. I caught a whiff of metallic rot—his excitement at learning my identity—and followed it. Ian stepped in front of me. I was getting supremely tired of men doing that. I flashed him a hard smile.

"Wait, was it something I said? Olivia, I'm sorry, it's just—"

"It's all right," I said impatiently. "I'll be right back. Just stay here."

"But—"

"Stay," I repeated, like I was reprimanding a bad dog, and Ian stayed.

A quick scan of the main ballroom showed me nothing I hadn't seen before. Joaquin wouldn't have left, not yet, not with so much destruction left to cause . . . or with my identity still fresh upon his lips. I swallowed hard and turned toward the common room, not even needing my sense of smell to guide me through the heavily curtained area. I heard my name called out behind me, Cher or Suzanne still sitting at the table where I'd left them, but ignored it, and pushed aside layer after layer of silver gauze and black velvet until I reached the inside.

Here the music was muted. Sensuous. The lights burned low, though still bright enough to highlight the voyeuristic activity. Large velvet-covered beanbags vied for floor space with leather beds, their centers piled with pillows, slim drink stands perched to the side of each arrangement . . . just in case one hand wasn't enough. I wove through the splayed bodies without looking, without stopping, Joaquin's scent strong in my nose. He wasn't even trying to hide. And he knew I was coming.

I pulled out my conduit, holding it in plain sight. Even if any of these swingers were paying attention, they'd probably think I was toting a unique new sex toy rather than a weapon. I notched an arrow in it, one-handed, as I pulled back a silk curtain cornering the far end of the room off in what must have been a VIP section. I saw figures seated, limbs splayed, candlelight pulsing . . . and a demon's smile as Joaquin glanced up at me.

His arms were thrown about two blondes, one on each side of him, both leaning into him and stroking the bulge in his leather pants. Disease practically oozed from their pores. He caressed the exposed neck and earlobe of one, dragging a bit on her chandelier earring—which she apparently found erotic—while fondling the right nipple of the other. Closer to me, on a velvet wedged seat, a woman looked up from between the legs of the only other male present. She rose in a sensuous shimmy, straddled him, and asked rather snottily if she could help me.

"I doubt it," I replied, eyes never leaving Joaquin's.

"This is a private party," she said, emphasizing *private*, in case I didn't understand nuance. I glanced at her out of the corner of my eye.

"So leave." And I really wished she would. She and the other man were disease-free. I wanted to keep it that way.

She straightened, stepping toward me like she was going to do more than that. Joaquin, voice amused, stopped her with a lazy wave. "As you were, Samantha. I invited her," he said, nodding when Samantha turned a questioning gaze on him. "Didn't I, Olivia?"

"Yep," I said, propping my right elbow up high, my conduit in plain view. "You're why I'm here."

He laughed and kept stroking his women. "No sense of foreplay, this one. No patience or restraint. Olivia Archer likes to get right to the point," he said, eyes moving to my conduit, then back up at me, indicating he knew it was there and had his own offense prepared.

"Olivia Archer?" the other man said, straightening from beneath Samantha to get a good look at me. "*The* Olivia Archer?"

"Nope," I said truthfully. "Just someone who looks an awful lot like her."

"Now, now. Don't be shy, Olivia. Everyone is here for the same thing, and we're all quite discreet, aren't we, girls?"

The women beside him purred their assent, one watching me closely as she flicked a tongue into his ear. If that was supposed to entice me, I thought, stomach flipping, it was having the opposite effect.

"Have a seat, Olivia," the other man said, either oblivious to or ignoring Samantha's heated glare. At least she'd stopped writhing all over him.

"Sit next to me," the blond ear licker said, spreading her legs slightly as she angled toward me.

"No," I told them both, and remained where I was.

"Yes," Joaquin said, and lifted his hand from the other woman's nipple long enough to release her hair from its messy updo. She sighed, flipping her hair to one side. He took the single chopstick that had been holding it all up, and pointed it toward the artery in her neck. I edged around the cushioned cube across from them and sat.

"What's your poison?" the other man asked me, though I didn't think he was talking about drinks.

"Don't, Lucas," Samantha warned, crossing her arms.

"Oh, Olivia likes it rough," Joaquin answered for me. "Isn't that right?"

"You've been together before?"

"We go way back," I replied, playing along. I positioned my conduit between my legs, pointed toward Joaquin. He ran the chopstick along the blond woman's neck. She purred and leaned into it.

Samantha, who was apparently of the if-you-can't-beat-'em-join-'em school of thought, perched herself on the coffee table in front of me, which put her smack between Joaquin and me. Placing her hands on my knees, she rubbed her thumbs over the insides, pushing slightly outward as she offered me a promising smile. She was blocking my view of Joaquin, and my shot. I shifted so I could see him again. He smiled knowingly.

"I think Samantha wants a kiss," he said, slowly thrusting his pelvis in my direction, as his harem started up on his pants again. I looked over to find Lucas touching himself.

For a moment I thought about shooting them all.

"Yes, Olivia," Samantha purred like a porn star, leaning forward so her cleavage was in my face, her short skirt riding almost to her hips. Joaquin's eyes flickered. The ear licker leaned forward to caress Samantha's ass. Her moan rustled my hair. "I'd love to taste those lips."

I waited until I felt her breath on my cheek, her eyes half closed, her lips parted . . . then put my palm on her face and pushed. Hard. Samantha flew backward, over the coffee table, and into the trio opposite us. The girls screamed. Apparently fond of violence, Lucas stroked himself harder. Joaquin merely laughed.

"Apparently you're not her type."

Wedged between the table and couches, Samantha looked like a sand crab struggling from its back. "Fuck you! Fuck her! I'm going to—"

Joaquin's hands whipped from behind the other two women to yank Samantha against him. I knew it hurt because she gasped and struggled as he pushed her down between his knees, so she was still facing me. Then his hands turned into a caress. "You're definitely my type, though. So beautiful. So perfect. So healthy and vibrant and strong."

I lowered my conduit, letting it point at the ground. Samantha melted under Joaquin's touch and words, ignorant of being used as a shield and of what his kiss would do to her. She shot me a haughty look, unaware the fingers playing over her flesh could snap her neck in a nanosecond.

Knowing he'd outplayed me and had me trapped—he'd

kill someone if I aimed at him, if I left, if I even moved at all—Joaquin laughed again. "Somebody suck me off."

I couldn't watch this, I thought frantically, as the women flanking him bent toward him. I *wouldn't*. I couldn't sit and watch while both these women began to burn inside. But the chopstick tapped lightly on one of their heads, and long fingers lingered along Samantha's neck.

"Stop!" I said as one of the women reached into his pants, pulling him out.

"No . . . don't stop," Joaquin ordered.

"I'll do you," I said, and Joaquin's surprise allowed me to stand without getting anyone killed. *See?* I thought, taking a step forward. *No harm done.*

"Oh, I've got to see this," Lucas said, moving closer as the blondes eased back. There was confusion and a bit of petulance on their faces, but they were willing to share. As long as Joaquin was.

"Put your *toy* down," he said, warning after warning layering his voice. I took a step back and dropped my conduit on the seat I'd just vacated. The air burned with satisfaction as Joaquin smiled. "Now come here."

I did, nudging Samantha aside with my foot, a rude gesture meant to anger her enough that she'd get far, far away, and it worked. She pushed to her feet, grumbling, and flounced to Lucas's other side. Now they were all lined up on the couch, watching me expectantly. I swallowed hard and took another step forward.

Well, what else was I supposed to do? I couldn't let him kill one more person. I was counting on his desire to own and possess and force me to do something I hated—to rape me yet again, but this time with my consent *and* an audience to watch my humiliation—to make him forget all about the potential victims around him. After all, wasn't I Joaquin's ultimate victim?

I stopped inches from him, so close I could feel the heat from his skin leaching through his pants, so close his hardon was unavoidable. Violent lust swirled in the air around me, making me dizzy, coating the walls and furniture and each of us with its filth. Even the blondes, twins I realized now that I was closer up, had backed away from Joaquin slightly, though to them it probably smelled like nothing more than body odor.

"On your knees," he ordered in a dark, silky voice. I swallowed hard and slowly lowered myself to the floor. Perceiving my reluctance as slow seduction, blonde number one giggled, while Lucas leaned back comfortably. Joaquin slumped forward and made himself available to me.

I reached up, shaking, and wrapped my hand around him. He pulsed gently in my hand, and I wanted to puke. Joaquin sensed this, half groaning, half laughing, and grew harder still. "Don't be shy," he said, folding his arms over his head. "Kiss me."

"And touch yourself while you do it," Lucas suggested.

"O-okay," I said. Bending forward, I let my free hand trail down my body, between my legs and the slit in my skirt.

"Olivia?"

I jerked, turned my head in time to see the curtains parting and Ian's head appear.

"Go away, Ian," I said, voice raspy, both hands working. He stared, unable to believe his eyes.

"No," Joaquin said, the smile a yard wide in his voice. "Join us, Ian."

"I . . . I . . ." Ian swallowed hard, looking at me, and I knew my eyes were as black as tar.

"Don't worry, Ian," I said, finally locating what I wanted between my legs. "It's not what it looks like."

And I drove my steel stiletto as hard as I could up between Joaquin's legs, pulling on his shaft like a gear stick, a primal cry in my throat as blood gushed over my weapon hand. My yell was nothing, however, compared to Joaquin's roar. His arms flailed reflexively, hitting the girl on his right in the face. She cried out, dropping her martini in his lap. He screamed louder.

Everyone else scattered. I'd have said it seemed like slow motion, their cries long and hollow and blasting through the tented area, but they weren't going slow. Joaquin and I were simply moving that much faster.

He was on the couch, up the wall, then flipped behind me in a motion so swift and smooth I lost my grip . . . both of them. I whirled, kicking out as I did, but his hand wrapped around my ankle and yanked. I was thrown across the coffee table and landed in a pile of limbs between Lucas, Samantha, and one of the twins. Hands scrambled at me; I didn't know if they were pulling me forward or pushing me away, but my head was up in time to catch Joaquin's victorious expression as he lifted my abandoned conduit and pointed it my way.

"No!" Ian's voice was stronger than I'd ever heard it as he barreled into Joaquin with his shoulder, arms wrapping around the other man's middle. Joaquin misfired, and the arrow meant for me plowed directly between Lucas's eyes. Samantha screamed. I lunged forward, eyes on my weapon, knowing Joaquin would swat Ian off like a fly. I landed on top of them both and began pounding on Joaquin's hand with my fists. One, two, three, four, five arrows slammed in the wall behind the leather couch. I heard the crunch of bone against bone, hammer punched again, twice, and Joaquin's hand disappeared.

I scrambled for the conduit, rolling and aiming at the same time, but found myself pointing at the startled face of a security guard who'd just breached the curtain wall. Cursing, I rose and pushed past him.

"Hey—!"

I threw off a second guard's attempt to stop me and pushed through the throng gathering around our tent. The scent of blood and pain led to an emergency exit, door swinging wide as a piercing wail rose up in the room. I ran outside, sprinting down a wide concrete corridor until it ended at a loading dock filled with the refuse of hundreds of hotel guests. Lowering my weapon, I slumped.

I should've been happy. Nobody had been murdered by Joaquin tonight. I'd saved as many people as I could, I'd impaled him between his anus and balls, and it had felt good. But I wasn't happy. Because as the scent of boiling blood grew fainter on the wafting summer air, so did that of starch and the seashore. Joaquin was gone, yes. But Ian had disappeared with him.

23

There were questions to answer in the days following Ian's disappearance, though not from Warren or
anyone associated with the paranormal community. The police
had been called in by Valhalla's security the night of the swingers' ball—someone had died, after all—and a masked woman
of my description had been seen fleeing the scene of the crime.
Tapes of the party were reviewed, the woman's moves tracked
as she circled the ballroom, danced with an unidentified male,
and followed another into a curtained-off area where the homicide had taken place. Witnesses—one Samantha Travis of
Milwaukee, and twins by the names of Danni and Darci—
claimed the woman had been identified as Olivia Archer,
which was why I was currently being interrogated on the fif-
teenth floor of Valhalla in my mortal father's plush high-rise
office, the Las Vegas Strip sprawled out behind me in a picture
window that overtook the entire northern wall.

I looked away from the view and blinked, letting an expression of innocence and confusion cross my face when the
lead detective placed yet another steaming cup of my father's imported coffee in front of me, and began asking me
questions I'd already answered.

"I don't know how else to tell you," I said, ignoring the coffee and pitching my voice higher than a dog whistle. "I wasn't at that party."

"Well, we have three witnesses, videotape, and a registration chart that says you were."

"No," I said, pushing out my lower lip in a pout. "You have three drunken people who *say* this woman identified herself as Olivia Archer, and you have a tape that shows a blond woman in a mask. Not to mention wearing clothes I wouldn't be caught dead in. Besides, wasn't there a contradictory witness?"

Officer Solomon glanced at his pad, then nodded reluctantly. "Yes. A gossip columnist, who claims to know you and your family well, said there was no way the woman in the mask could have been you. She was, and I quote 'too brazen, too lacking in personal morals, and too aggressive to be the sweet and refined real Olivia Archer.'"

"There you go," I said, preparing to stand.

"You want us to take the word of one against three?" This from Solomon's partner, Officer Carson, the younger and more tenacious of the two. "And the one a gossip columnist?"

"Who better to trust than Lon?" I said, tilting my head in his direction. "He knows everyone who is anyone and what they're doing at all times."

"Is that so?" Solomon retorted. "Maybe we should hire him on in the department then. We could use someone like that."

"Good idea," said Carson, playing along. "First thing we'll do is get him to tell us what you were doing last Saturday night."

"That'd be helpful."

"This is ridiculous!"

We all looked at Xavier, seated behind a mahogany desk stretching almost the length of the glass wall. He'd insisted on being present for the questioning, and what Xavier Archer wanted, he got. Unfortunately, even his considerable powers extended only so far, and his demand that the whole matter be dropped had been politely ignored. This did nothing to improve his mood, transforming his already bullish features into a mad-cow sort of mien. He glared at the two officers, huffing dangerously as he rose from his chair.

"You are badgering an innocent woman about the death of some . . . some pervert who was literally caught with his pants down, when you should be out there chasing down the true culprit!"

Time to put on the public relations face, I thought wryly, watching Officer Solomon straighten, his expression carefully blank. "Mr. Archer, we're not accusing your daughter of anything. We simply want to shut down all leads in effort to bring this case to a close as quickly as possible. The scandalous nature of this case has garnered a great deal of media attention."

"Well, sex sells, doesn't it?" Xavier answered, waving the stub of his cigar in the air. "I mean, why focus on a boring, old-fashioned plague killing off hundreds of people in Las Vegas when there's a sex story to peddle?"

The older officer recovered first. "Your daughter's name was on the guest list, sir."

"So someone made it up! Are you surprised? Who knows what sort of immoral, conniving people attend those things—it was a swingers' ball, for God's sake!"

"That's right, sir," said Carson, who had less to lose and wasn't as close to retirement as his partner. "And it was held in your hotel."

Xavier's mouth worked wordlessly for a few seconds, before he lifted his chin, drawing up taller. "My daughter wouldn't be caught dead at one of those events."

"But a man by the name of Lucas Liddell was," Carson said, throwing a photo of a very much deceased Lucas down on Xavier's desk. "And that's why we're here."

Xavier looked like he was going to argue some more, but a bell tone caused him to glance down at his desk, and he picked up his BlackBerry instead. The other two men turned back to me . . . and missed the expression of relief passing over Xavier's face.

"Your whereabouts, Miss Archer?"

"I was—"

"She was with me," Xavier said, flipping his BlackBerry back on his desk and coming around to stand in front of it. "We had dinner in my steakhouse and then came up here for drinks afterward, so we could talk privately."

Both officers looked at me. I nodded vigorously.

Solomon turned back to Xavier. "I trust there are tapes of you both entering the restaurant and the executive offices later?"

"Of course," Xavier said, dismissively, and stubbed out his cigar. Whatever message had been relayed on that Black-Berry had certainly bolstered his confidence. "Anything else?"

"Not if you can provide tapes confirming your whereabouts, no," Solomon said, flipping his notebook shut and standing. "We'll want additional surveillance of all the exits and entrances for that evening, of course, but—"

"I have a question," Carson interrupted, angling his head in Xavier's direction. "What were you talking about?"

"What were we talking about?" Xavier repeated, unibrow drawing down as if he didn't understand the question.

"Yes. When you came up here. For *privacy*," he said, ignoring the way his partner cleared his throat. Ambitious, this one. "What was so important you had to leave the comfort of your public dining room, in your hotel . . . in a city most people say you own?"

"My sister's death," I said immediately. "It's been over six months since my sister Joanna died, but we still mourn her. If that's okay."

Solomon looked at his partner like he was a total idiot. Xavier lifted his chin and folded his arms over his chest. I wouldn't have been surprised if he'd pawed at the ground and charged.

"Of—of course." Carson reddened over the starched collar of his blues, then cleared his throat and backed up a step. "Well, we're very sorry to inconvenience you. Both of you."

Solomon put a hand on his shoulder, ushering him to the door. "We'll just wait for those tapes and then we'll be on our way."

Xavier nodded curtly. "They're already waiting for you on my secretary's desk. I trust you can find your own way out?"

"Yes. Thank you." He bobbed his head again. "Miss Archer."

The younger officer mumbled good-bye, but didn't look at me. I breathed a sigh of relief as the door shut behind them. For a moment, neither Xavier nor I moved.

"What were you doing there?" he whispered next to me.

I pivoted to face him, not meeting his eye. "But Daddy, I wasn't—"

"I saw the tapes of you and Cher entering the building," he said, louder than necessary. I flinched, as I knew Olivia would. His voice softened, but remained clipped. "Now I'm going to ask you again, what were you doing there?"

"You saw the tapes?" I asked, looking into his face. Still ignoring the question.

"Don't worry. Gonzales has doctored them." And now the relief flooded his face. God, I thought, he truly loved Olivia. This emotion was real. What was next? Pigs flying? "A woman like you is seen entering alone. Cher and her mother are nowhere in sight."

I sighed, relieved, then bit my lower lip, feigning regret. "I was just . . . slumming."

He gave me a hard look, square jaw jerking high. "Slumming?"

I shrugged. Poor, silly, helpless me. "We thought it'd be fun to see what went on at those things. Sorry."

"Olivia." He drew the name out on a weary exhalation and rubbed a paw over his face. I tried hard not to gape because he almost looked human. "You have a reputation to maintain. A responsibility to the family name."

And that kept me from going all soft and mushy. The *name* was what he cared about most. "I know, and I'm sorry." The contriteness burned in my throat, but I managed to choke it out. "Cher was just trying to cheer me up. I was so down and she thought doing something crazy would keep my mind off of . . . you know." I studied him for a reaction, annoyed that I still cared enough to seek it, but old habits died hard.

Xavier turned away to face the window. "You mean Joanna."

Despite the censure in his voice, I joined him because I knew Olivia would. "Yes."

"Over six months. It's gone so fast," he said, his voice a mere whisper. I watched his Adam's apple bobble as he swallowed, but I quickly looked away when he glanced at me. "You miss her, don't you?"

"Oh." I sighed, taken aback by the directness of his gaze. He'd never looked at me that closely. Olivia, sure. But not me. "Terribly."

He put his arm around my shoulder then, and I stiffened reflexively, before relaxing into him. I knew the tenderness wasn't meant for me, but I couldn't help reacting to it. I'd sought his approval for so long, the impulse to pretend, just for the moment, was too great.

"I was too hard on her," he said, surprising me with how close he'd come to my thoughts, and I immediately wondered why he hadn't said this when he thought I was alive. I glanced up at him, but he continued to stare out over the city he ruled. "I wish—"

"Yes?" I prodded, heart thumping in my chest.

But he shook off the thought, removing his arm so quickly I swayed. "It doesn't matter." I looked down at my feet to hide the disappointment in my face. Meanwhile he opened the top drawer of his desk and cut a cigar, lighting it before speaking again. "All that matters is that you're protected. Even if it must be from yourself."

"Yes, Daddy," I said meekly, without turning around. I

lifted a hand to the cool pane of the window and traced the image I saw there. My fingertips, of course, left no marks.

Having regained his composure, Xavier shook his head, puffing on his cigar. I saw his reflection in the window. *I could kill you*, I found myself thinking. I could kill him because he was a prick and because he was the Tulpa's lackey, but also just because. I could kill him. I had that power.

Snuffing out a life is power amplified.

I shook off Joaquin's voice and turned from the glass wall to find Xavier closer than I thought. "Just think from now on, Olivia. Use your head. You can't do things other people do. Maybe . . . maybe ask yourself what Joanna would do. You know, if she were in your position. It might . . . help."

It was the first compliment he'd ever paid me. He'd never before acknowledged that I had any qualities he'd found admirable. I just nodded, swallowing hard, unsure how I felt about it. Xavier needed to remain as he was, one of the bad guys, the man who made my young adulthood hell, the one I'd sworn would pay for it with every crooked dime he'd ever made. I couldn't open up my heart to him now just because he recognized a strength in me after he thought me dead. Not when he had never spared me a kind word in life.

And not because he looked tired and almost . . . old. I hardened myself to the thought, kissed his rough cheek, and quickly left the room. That wasn't my problem. Being a pawn used by the most evil being ever created would do that to you.

In the days that followed, I wandered in and out of realities like revolving doors, searching for Ian. For Joaquin. For anyone. The paranormal world was a ghost town. With all the agents of Light in seclusion, and all the Shadows content to pull the strings from behind the scenes, there were no Technicolor streaks to light up the gritty, one-dimensional terrain.

The mortal reality wasn't much better. I walked from the Stratosphere past Mandalay Bay to Valhalla, without once getting jostled or having to veer from my path. I retraced my steps on the other side of the Boulevard, and found myself alone on the sky tram, a recorded voice telling nonexistent passengers to watch their step as they exited equally deserted platforms.

I took a calculated risk driving by Joaquin's house again, and though it looked abandoned, I wasn't about to risk another run-in with his paranormal pooches. After that, all my leads dried up. If the Shadows had still been active in some way I could have busied myself tracking one of them down, picking a fight, getting answers. But they'd left me with nothing to rail against, and that was when I was at my worst. Without an opponent, it was all too easy to turn on myself.

How could I have put Ian in such danger? What if it had been Cher who'd come after me? How could I have so stupidly allowed Joaquin to get a hand on my conduit, the one thing sure to annihilate me from existence in both these forsaken worlds?

How could I have let him get away?

Grasping at straws, I finally made a trip to Master Comics, hoping my ability to read both the Light and Shadow manuals would allow me to piece together enough clues to anticipate the Shadow troop's next move . . . or at least discover what Joaquin had done with Ian. But Zane's creative well, it seemed, had run dry. The latest manuals were backdated a week, and both told the same story of the swingers' ball, but nothing further. That's because nothing further had happened, Zane told me, and he looked at me with a crazed weariness, like he'd been kept awake in a cell for days by shouting guardsmen, flashing strobes, and Metallica.

"Don't mind him," Carl told me, once we'd retreated to the back room. "He gets like this when he's blocked. The psychic energy builds up because it has no outlet, and messes with his mind."

"He looks like he blames me for it."

Carl scoffed, waving the worry away. "He'll be fine once the images come rolling in again."

"What about the rest of them?" I asked, glancing toward the twins, who regarded me warily from behind cupped hands, and Sebastian—the little bastard—who'd smirked in my direction, making a point to display his copy of the latest Shadow manual. Only Jasmine looked happy to see me.

"Oh, them?" Carl said, gesturing back into the store. "Yeah. They totally blame you."

I sighed, thanked him, and left.

There was no next step, no place to go that was forward, and so I took a step back, and returned to canvassing Vegas's empty streets as I always did when I needed to think. And somehow I found myself in that same filthy alley I'd chased a human predator into the night I killed Liam. It seemed like years ago, not weeks, that Regan had set me up, but nothing had changed here. I headed past broken-down boxes and splintered crates, neither sensing nor smelling anything out of the ordinary . . . until I did.

He was slumped beneath a pile of broken crates, the clothes on his chest and the wood above him charred black with what appeared to be someone's failed attempt to burn the entire mess. Not that the man would have minded. Even with bloat and rot distending his face, and the maggots wriggling in his eye sockets to make the corpse look possessed, I could see the burn marks around his mouth. If I were inclined to investigate further—which I wasn't—I was sure I'd find his private parts equally seared by disease. He'd been dead before someone left him to this alley grave, tossed here like the rest of the refuse, the halfhearted attempt to burn his remains only dehumanizing him further.

I looked at the shredded skin and diseased flesh and moldering bloat that used to be a human, and my head swam with the same unhinged fury that'd had me driving a stiletto up between Joaquin's thighs. Those fucking Shadows had decided to play God, and someone who'd once cradled dreams was now splayed on the ground like he'd never mattered.

And someone else, who'd tried to protect me in what was probably the first bold and chivalrous act in his life, was now captive to Joaquin; a fate, I could attest, that was even more terrifying than this.

And a third someone—young, hopeful, and vibrant—had died while tasting what had probably been her first kiss, the one that should have been the sweetest. Instead it had taken her life before it'd truly begun.

All this destruction, and here I was, skulking in the alleys of *my* ravaged city, feeling ashamed of what *I* had done? While I was caught in limbo, neither belonging in the world I'd grown up in, nor yet the heroine the manuals prophesied I was to be, Joaquin and Regan and the Tulpa were stamping out lives for no other reason than to make a point. *You can't protect them all. You can't even protect yourself.*

My head was suddenly buzzing as I tasted decay, the *darkness* on the stifled alley air, playing the part *they'd* chosen for me. I punched the wall beside me, sending shards of plaster and brick crumbling to the ground. *Pull this string, and the Archer acts this way.* It was stupid, fruitless, but I punched again. *Pull this one, and she'll jump as you please.* They were able to do this—not just with me, but with all the agents of Light—because we held fast to a moral code that said killing was wrong, protecting human life was our highest duty, and we did it on a level playing field. But we weren't even playing the same game. And that's all it was to the Shadows.

I closed my eyes, let the rot of another human I'd failed to protect seep into my pores, and extinguished the Light inside me like a snuffed-out taper. I let all the anger and pain and helplessness I'd been feeling since Marlo's death pour out of me in a piercing shriek, a cry so raw the rats went scurrying back into hiding. The wind ceased to breathe. Shadows arched over me.

Strings snapped inside me.

How dare they make me feel like I had to hide—any of them! How dare they treat me like a rogue agent! And how dare I think the only solace I could find would be in these shadowy alleys, like I should be ashamed . . . or at least more ashamed than all those who chose not to act. Who knowingly put themselves before the innocents. All this time Warren had insinuated—and I'd believed—that I'd have to choose one side over the other, I thought, breathing hard. When really, all I needed to do was *be*.

I thought about the Tulpa, how only after he'd cut the ties between himself and his creator had he truly come into his own power. I had that ability inside me. I had self-will. And now that my ties had been cut with the troop, I had a place to start.

And so, as I slipped from the alley, I walked off the map I was supposed to follow, and strode into a void as vast and unknowable as the midnight desert. A cursed battlefield it might be, but I was done warring with myself.

And, I thought, striding down the center of the abandoned street, I was no longer anyone's puppet.

24

It was the last place I should have gone, a move so bold I was stupid to even consider it. And the first thing I noticed once inside the cool, dark enclave of Olivia's apartment was Luna's absence. She wasn't in any of her usual spots; beneath the couch, behind the fake ficus I'd bought to replace the real one I'd killed, or curled up on a dining room chair waiting to pounce on my feet as I walked by. I stuck my head in the laundry room on the way to my bedroom, knowing her penchant for lounging on clean clothes—and mine for leaving them there—but there was nothing.

"Come on, Luna," I said, peering in the closet before dropping to my knees to peer beneath the bed skirt. There was no sign of struggle, no foreign scent marring the space, and I knew a Shadow couldn't have entered without Luna ripping them to shreds, so I decided she was probably just making me pay for leaving her under the neighbor's care for so long. That's why it took a moment before I realized the shoes I saw pointing my way from the other side of the footboard belonged to a man . . . and they were on someone's feet.

I stood and swung at the same time. There was a blur as

the man dodged my blow and my follow-up roundhouse kick, and I whirled, ready, to find two pairs of sharp eyes trained on me. Only one pair was filled with amusement, and it wasn't Luna's.

"I take it this is Luna," Hunter said, stroking the spiky fur to calm the cat until she leaned against him. Her eyes closed, and a deep purr resonated like distant thunder in the dim room.

"You're an asshole," I told him, relaxing.

He kissed Luna on her little egg head. "You shouldn't let her talk to you that way." The cat purred louder.

I narrowed my eyes. "What are you doing here?"

"Waiting," he said, leaning against the dresser. He looked odd propped up against the frilly knickknacks and toiletries littering the vanity—a dark smudge against a sea of white and pink. "By the way, you're out of milk."

"Waiting for me?" I asked, mimicking the pose, minus the cat, on the four-poster bed.

He shrugged. "For you, for a Shadow to stop by and try to kill you. For anyone. Anything." He bent and gently dropped Luna on the bed, where she immediately began grooming herself. When he lifted his gaze back to mine, the answer was plain on his face.

I put a hand to my mouth to withhold the gasp. "They kicked you out, too."

"No," he answered, with a quick jerk of his head. "I left voluntarily."

"But why?" *Please don't say it was for me*, I thought silently. Not when it was the only home he'd ever known. The place he loved above all others. "They're the ones infected."

"But I'm the one who got Marlo killed."

"Unknowingly."

"Well, you know Warren. Even if he didn't say it . . ."

He blamed Hunter. Anger rose in me at that. Mr. Black and White. Mr. Right or Wrong. Mr. Light or Shadow, and nothing in between. "Yeah," I finally said on a sigh. "I know Warren."

Hunter began brushing Luna's hair from his clothing, careful not to look at me as he spoke. "Have I ever told you why I don't drink?" he said abruptly.

I quirked a brow. I'd seen him intoxicated twice in the past week. He looked up as my silence lengthened, read the thoughts on my face, and chuckled darkly. "Before all this, I mean. Why I haven't allowed myself a drink in almost ten years?"

I shook my head. Nobody'd told me, and I couldn't imagine what his not drinking had to do with anything now.

"You should know," he mumbled, then swallowed hard as he ate up the distance between us. His hands were shoved in his pockets, like he didn't know what to do with them, and he shifted from one foot to the other, a nervous gesture for Hunter Lorenzo. "It would all make a lot more sense if you knew."

Something making sense. That would be new. I gestured to the bed, and when he sat—sinking a good few inches into the downy comforter—I took a seat on the white bench at the bed's footboard. It was both firmer and closer to the door. Hunter, of course, knew what I was doing, and he let me, which went a long way to helping me relax further.

"Okay," I said, wrapping my arms around one up-drawn knee. "So why don't you drink?"

"Because whiskey nearly killed me a decade ago."

I drew back, startled, and Hunter let out a humorless laugh, pulling his ankle up to cross his knee, looking large and dangerous and tough, even surrounded by eyelet and lace. "Well, it wasn't just the whiskey," he said, and told me the story.

He'd just come off a mission, rescuing a commuter airliner from the Shadows, who'd hijacked it and were flying it right over Nellis air base. It was going to be shot down in seconds, as close as he'd ever come to being killed, and he said he'd never felt the passing of time so acutely. I could imagine. Agents couldn't be killed by mortal weapons, but if you happened to be blown to smithereens? I shuddered at the thought. Even if he'd lived, it'd take some doing to put those pieces back together again.

"Anyway," he said, shaking his head, "chalk another one up for the agents of Light. But I was ready for a little vacation after that, which I took as soon as I got back."

In the form of a shot glass and a bottle.

He sighed at the memory, and when he spoke, it almost sounded apologetic. "See, I'm not like Warren. I don't believe in a greater cause, or in the troop as an institution. I believe in people. Individuals." He looked at me, and I knew that's why he had tested me so greatly in the beginning, why he'd remained on my side since I'd proven myself to him, and why he kissed me even after I revealed the darkness living in my core. He knew my Shadow side and he still believed in *me*. "There has to be a deeper involvement for me. I . . . feel more if it's personal. I feel alive." He snorted. "And if there was anything I needed to feel that night, it was alive."

So when the raven-haired siren with the lush lips and the body that wouldn't quit asked if she could join him, he welcomed the company, ordered another shot glass, and drove away the Reaper with some hard-core XXX flirting.

"In retrospect, I knew something was wrong," he said, rubbing the back of his neck, wincing. "I scented deceit on her, but didn't want to admit it. I tasted guile in her kiss, a smoky heaviness that found harbor inside me. You possess the same flavor, though not as strong. I recognized it when we shared the aureole."

I licked my lips self-consciously, and he hesitated, but I motioned for him to go on. If he really believed in individuals—in me—then I didn't have to apologize for who and what I was. So, he continued, even though his instincts told him something was off, he'd ignored them and took the woman home. He shook his head thoughtfully. "I don't know how I woke up when I did, but she was straddling me, naked but for a tomahawk bowing toward my heart. I killed her in the bed that still smelled like our lovemaking."

I was about to say, *So?* when he cut me off with a shake of his head.

"I'd . . . been with her only minutes earlier. I know the alcohol was clouding my senses, but it also slowed every moment so that her death seemed to take years, not minutes. So even as her last breath rattled in her chest I was still seeing her in a lover's light. If I let myself, I can see her even now."

And he looked at me like he hoped I might understand that.

What I understood was that in telling me this he wasn't only explaining why he didn't drink, but that he knew how I could allow a Shadow to live. That even those of us who should know better sometimes mistook them for human.

"What was her name?" I asked softly.

"The Shadow woman who so ruthlessly seduced me?" he said, but the teasing note couldn't mask his shame. I nodded. He shrugged self-consciously. "It doesn't matter. She's gone." And he stood, turned his back on me, and headed out the room. Topic closed.

I was about to pursue it anyway when I noticed something else not quite right. "Oh, my God."

"What?" Hunter was back in the room in a shot. I'd probably injected more alarm in my words than necessary, but as I crossed to Olivia's desk, I said it again. Louder.

"The computer's missing."

"What computer?" Hunter turned, eyes falling on the empty desk.

"Exactly," I said, whirling on him. "You haven't left the apartment in three days?"

"I've been here the whole time."

So before that . . . not that it narrowed things down much. I'd been gone from the apartment for almost three weeks. Yet Luna wouldn't have let a Shadow just waltz in here and walk out with Olivia's computer. Not without putting up a fight, and there was no sign of struggle, nor—I confirmed—had there been when Hunter arrived to make himself at home. Still, this didn't sit right. A random break-in at a guarded, high-rise condo . . . and nobody noticed someone leaving with a desktop computer they hadn't walked in with?

"I'll have to report it," I said, mostly talking to myself. "Maybe they'll let me see the building's security tapes."

"You think it's a lead." He stated it as a fact, and I turned back to face him.

"It's something." I didn't add it was all I had to go on. He could probably see that for himself.

"Let me help," he said, lifting his chin.

I didn't have to say anything. He knew my thoughts. What about the second sign of the Zodiac? What about Marlo's death, still lying between us like an unbreachable river? Even the most understanding guy in the world, and Hunter certainly wasn't that, couldn't erase all that.

"It wasn't fair to let you take the blame for everything that happened." His voice, steady now, had lost the thickness it'd possessed while relaying the past. "I kissed you too, but I was in shock back at the sanctuary, and before that I was just acting like a hormone-crazed teen. Chasing you into that maze. Pouting when you said no that night in my room. Kissing another girl just to make you jealous." He shook his head, sighing with the movement. It was a look he usually reserved for Felix, and I would have smiled but for his next words. "Marlo died for no good reason, and I want to right that. I want to make it right."

"So . . . coworkers?" Skepticism coated each syllable, as much for myself as for him. Was that possible? "Nothing else?"

"Scout's honor."

"You were never a scout," I muttered.

"Okay, but I swear it. You don't want me, and that's okay—"

"It's not that, it's just—" He silenced me with a finger to my lips, looking down at me from his great height, and my voice died away with the touch. It was gentle, the scent of him warm and spicy on my lips, but it was firm too.

"It's okay," he said, lifting his finger away. "Besides, I was getting tired of being cooped up in that oversized shoe anyway."

Now he was talking. "All right," I said, like I had any other option. But my relief was evident in my smile.

He smiled back, cracked his knuckles, one fist, then the other. "So where do we start?"

"Well, I thought someone might show up here, but if you've already been here . . ." I trailed off, looking around.

"Three days, yeah," he said, sighing. "Besides, if we were just going to sit around and wait we might as well be back at the boneyard. I called work, said I'd reconsidered quitting my job. They told me to come in tonight for the swing shift. Apparently they're short-staffed at the moment."

"I can imagine," I said, nodding. "So you go back to investigating things from inside Valhalla. We need to track down that lab again, see if the antibody to this thing is still on property."

"That's easy enough. I'll make an excuse to patrol the building. If that doesn't work I'll find a portal somewhere—they're constantly moving, though. It might take a couple of days."

"Well, everything in its time," I said, half to myself. "Meanwhile I need to figure out who broke in here and why."

"My guess is they wanted the computer," Hunter said, earning a steely look from over my shoulder. He grinned in reply. It looked wolfish—and I fucking loved wolves—but if he could make an honest effort at sexual restraint, so could I. "What was on it, anyway?"

Every secret Olivia ever had, I wanted to say. The passwords and logs detailing her cyber life, the information she'd collected in folders, journals, notes . . . everything about her that wasn't girly and pink and expected. *Something worth knowing*, I thought, looking around at the rest of the room, as pristine and untouched as the day I left it.

"I don't know," I told him, before bending down and scooping up the handbag I'd let fall beside the bed when he'd appeared. I took out the disks Cher had given me weeks ago, and tapped them against my other palm. "But I'm going to find out."

25

I couldn't turn the fucking thing on.

With the Shadows on vacation and the Light side in hiding, I'd arrived at the shiny new Net café just off the Strip without worry or problem. I'd taken a seat in a dimly lit booth with my back to the wall so I could watch the rest of the crowd, mostly tourists buzzing in to check their e-mail. A few students were thrown in the mix, backpacks tossed at their feet, earphones hijacking their heads and necks with whatever music made them do that collective bobblehead dance. A homeless man was slumped in a corner booth, snoring away, apparently getting better rates here than he would at the Holiday Inn, though I'd have gone to the library if I were him. At least that was free.

Meanwhile I'd already wasted a quarter of my hour's bought time staring at the unresponsive screen, pushing every button on the machine that looked important, and inserting my disk in the only slot where it would fit. I didn't understand.

I glanced through the clear glass separating my console from the next, but the guy there was a gamer, and looked and smelled like he'd been parked there for the last twenty-four hours. There were empty sandwich wrappers, crushed Coke cans, and a bevy of cellophane candy wrappers scattered at his feet. If he couldn't tear his eyes away from killing mutant alien giants long enough to clear off his table, I doubted he'd be too anxious to help me. Olivia's looks could only influence men who liked their action three-dimensional.

I scanned the rest of the booths for some sign of life. Everyone was hunched over their rented computers, islands unto themselves. Same with the frosted glass-top tables set up in the middle of the room for laptops; each person a planet orbiting around their own sun, unaware of and uninterested in existence outside their personal universe. I'd never seen a café with so little socializing going on.

Meanwhile, with a newly enforced quarantine keeping visitors from leaving the valley in effect, what the place really needed was a revolving door. There was a wall of people lined up waiting for a booth, and I glanced over to find one man giving me a particularly hard look, so I went back to randomly pushing buttons on the machine in front of me. After five more minutes of expensive and wasted time, I finally cried uncle and headed back to the front desk, where yet another college student was getting some studying done while getting paid to be an electronic babysitter.

I waited for the desk jockey to acknowledge me. When I saw this wasn't going to happen voluntarily, I placed my hip on the desk, and my palm flat on his opened physics book. He looked up.

"I need help," I said.

The kid let his bloodshot eyes run from my face down to my hand, still perched on his homework, and back up again. Then he flipped a lock of greasy hair from his forehead and rose reluctantly. "Of course you do," he muttered, coming around the desk.

Pretending I didn't hear, I followed him back to my booth, thinking that if I'd turned up here six months ago as myself, he probably wouldn't have taken that tone with me. There was something about Olivia's looks, though, too bright and bold and unapologetic, that made some people unable to resist striking out at her. Never mind that she could probably outprogram anyone in this room.

"Well, somehow you managed to turn it off," he said, hands moving so quickly over the machine, I couldn't be sure what he'd done. "It was already running when you sat down."

"No, it wasn't."

He ignored me, fingers flying. "You also need to wait to boot the disk until after the system's stabilized." He snapped the disk from its drive, and it was all I could do not to wrest it from him physically. He must have sensed my anxiety, because he tossed me an inquiring look over his shoulder, then continued to punch at the keyboard. "There. Try not to touch anything but the keyboard."

I touched him, none too gently, when he turned to leave. "My disk."

And that's when he saw past the designer dress, the glossed lips, and retro powder blue eye shadow (Cher swore it was making a comeback), and found *me*. I didn't pull any paranormal hoo-doo on him. That'd be too easy, and unfair. No, I just let him see me, Joanna Archer, pissed-off computer illiterate who might not know a pixel from an axel but who'd kick his ass if he so much as gave me a reason. The guy mumbled something unintelligible and handed me the disk before beating a hasty retreat. I settled back in my booth to warily face the greater foe.

I began by scanning the disk's contents by filename alone, hoping to come upon something that said "Olivia's secret life" or "Hey, Jo! Look here." Unfortunately, most were coded numbers, and the lettering might as well have been in Greek. The disk obviously didn't contain the entire contents of Olivia's cyber life, but as she'd given it to Cher for safekeeping—like giving a hen over to a fox if you asked me, but no one had—there had to be something on here that required special backup. Whether the break-in at the condo was a reflection of this, or whether it was just an uncanny coincidence, I couldn't yet say, but I'd learned to always expect the worst-case scenario. That way I was never disappointed.

When the filename search came up empty, I started from the top and began to work my way down. I'd just begun scrolling through the first file when a chime sounded from the computer, and an additional screen popped up. I jerked back, wondering what I'd done. Then, words appeared:

Hey, baby, what's your sign?

You've gotta be kidding me. The computers were linked? I clicked on the icon to fold the new page shut, and leaned forward to continue my work. There was a file called JO.12.12.00175 that looked somewhat promising.

Don't you want to know who I am?

"Some ballsy SOB," I mumbled. I resisted searching the room and typed:

No. Fuck off twice and die.

Okay, so it wasn't very Olivia-esque, but now I could work in peace.

Dirty mouth for such a pretty girl. Where'd you learn that . . . from your sister?

My heart took up residence in my throat as I jerked my head up, left hand automatically moving to my handbag, where my conduit lay hidden. The gamer across from me had disappeared at some point, replaced by the man who'd been glaring at me, though he spared no notice of me now. The homeless man was still racking up his minutes, and there were three laptops lying open on the center tables. I zeroed in on the one person I couldn't see, a man hunched so low behind his screen it had to be on purpose.

I rose just as his screen lowered, and found Ben Traina grinning at me like he used to when we were kids. I grinned back, forgetting for a moment who I was supposed to be, surveying him for sign of injury, age, depression. Infection. Watching me watch him, Ben dropped his chin onto one fist and crooked a finger with his other hand. And just as I had the day we'd met fifteen years earlier, I dropped everything and went to him.

But not before I went to the bathroom. Locked in a tiny stall, I spritzed myself with an entire bottle of masking phero- mones, conscious all the while of my voice sounding from some far-off place, repeating over and over again, *Please, please, please.* I don't know what I was pleading for. That my emotions wouldn't leach through and twelve Shadow agents wouldn't swoop down on the café to kill the only man I'd ever loved? That there'd be no scent of death or ill- ness on his breath to mark him as infected? That he wouldn't recognize me, the love of his life, beneath Olivia's beautiful skin?

Or that he would?

He was smiling as I returned to the table. My booth had been given to another customer, I was paid up, and I dropped into the chair opposite Ben, where a steaming cup of coffee was already waiting for me.

"I didn't know how you liked it," he said, indicating the sugar and creamer in front of us. "Jo took it plain, so I thought . . ."

"It's fine, thanks." And I took hold of the coffee cup like I was grabbing for a life preserver, careful to keep the pads of my fingertips hidden. I had to force myself not to down it so fast I scalded my throat, and, sipping, I also drank in details about the man across from me. The sun streaking in the café windows caught in the richness of his hair, deeper than any shot of espresso, and longer now that he'd left the police force. He wasn't as pale as he'd been the last time I saw him, but it was summer, and he'd always tanned easily. A scar below his hairline stood out as a silent reminder of less healthy times, and a tribal tattoo was just barely visible beneath the sleeve of his white tee. I didn't have the nerve to study his eyes. Besides, they were trained too closely on me.

"What brings you here, Traina?" I said, before he caught me watching.

"Indulging my geeky side," he said, with a grin so crooked and perfect it stole my breath away. Ben didn't seem to notice. "It's an old hangout, actually. I used to write here when it was nothing more than a smoky, airless room with concrete floors and a friendly pothead for a barista. Most addictive mochas you'd ever had."

I couldn't resist. "Do the guys at the station know you like girly drinks?" I said glibly.

But he was suddenly stone serious. "The guys at the station don't know much about me at all anymore. I'm not there, remember?"

I did remember. Mostly because Ben had once told me his police badge was, appropriately enough, his shield. It filtered the world's filth and danger and corruption through a second pair of eyes, he'd said, insulating him so he could perform his job more effectively.

So what kept those horrors from climbing into him now? Because even though he was no longer a cop, he hadn't stopped seeing, or studying, the darker side of life. The hard glint glazing over those chocolate depths told me that much.

"I forgot," I lied, drawing a finger around the lip of my mug, simultaneously crossing my legs as I flicked a gaze up at him from beneath my bangs. "Still playing lone wolf, then?"

I actually felt the tension rise around us, and his shoulders rose a degree and knotted there. Christ, if he were a wolf, he'd have hackles. "Who's playing?" he said, jaw clenching as he leaned back.

And those two little words brought reality crashing back down onto my own shoulders, reminding me of the last time I'd seen him, hunched over the grave he thought was mine. I'd been trying to get him to stop his search for the man he believed had killed me, trying to keep him safe.

He's disappeared. I told him. And Ajax had. I'd made sure of that.

That's okay. Ben had said, his mournful look turning cold. *There are others.*

No, I thought, watching him now, he certainly wasn't playing. And though my mind wanted to jet back to the past when I could practically finish his sentences for him, my responsibility was to the present. I was no longer Joanna. I was Olivia. And he was dark-eyed, tense, and self-contained. A Ben I didn't know.

I'd give him leeway, though . . . a courtesy I wouldn't extend to anyone else, mortal or not. Ben had come to this place in his life because he'd lost me twice, and I knew the pain of that loss . . . what it took just to get out of bed every day. I'd let this slide, I thought, because the one thing Warren hadn't put in the files he'd amassed about me and Ben was the most important information of all: I was to blame. If not for my death the second time, he wouldn't have thrown off the constraints of his badge, his shield, to become a P.I. And there'd be no shadows shellacking his gaze, turning it into a cold, hard thing.

"So, working on anything interesting?" I asked, clearing my throat.

Ben shrugged, glancing down as he toyed with the edge of his napkin. "A couple things. Sometimes I help the department on an auxiliary basis, act as another pair of eyes on a stakeout or share some information gleaned on one of my cases. But mostly it's just run-of-the-mill stuff. A missing person. A depressing number of people wanting me to trail their spouses. An old woman desperate to find her miniature poodle."

"That one sounds like it'd tax your abilities."

"You have no idea." He rolled his eyes, and almost looked boyish.

I laughed, and felt a shiver run down my spine despite the warm cup in my hand and the heat beating on the café from outside. Chemistry was such a strange thing. I'd be willing to bet even Micah couldn't tell me why hundreds of men could leave me cold, while this one could string me along forever with only a smile. My laughter faded at that thought—at its futility—and I stared down into my cup. Ben noticed my abrupt mood change.

"So how are you, sweetheart?" he asked, his voice soft, like he was talking to a child, or someone very fragile. I glanced up in time to see the specter of pain passing behind his eyes, the ghost of the man who'd loved and lost me flickering, before disappearing into the past again. I nearly cried out in response. Fucking chemistry. "Still seeing that guy . . . Lorenzo?" There was a snapping of fingers. "Hunter Lorenzo, wasn't it?"

"Yes, it was." Ben's stellar memory made him a good cop, annoying at Trivial Pursuit . . . and extremely dangerous to an ex-girlfriend/superhero. He'd run into Hunter and me last winter at Valhalla, after reports of strange activity on the property. He'd thought we'd simply been out partying all night, so while it wasn't surprising he remembered Hunter's name, it was curious, though perhaps he was just making small talk. "And yes, I still am."

"Must be some sort of record for you. You used to say they got clingy after a while."

Had I? She? "Well, he's persistent."

"And big. Where'd you meet, the Mr. Olympia contest?"

Superhero training camp, Ben. He wrapped a barbed whip around my arm, and the rest was history.

"Valhalla," I answered, which reminded me that I needed to put in a call to Hunter to see if he'd found out anything further on his shift before we could plot out our next step. Maybe he could make some progress with the disk. I was so busy considering this that I almost missed what Ben was saying.

"—met someone too. I think."

"What?"

He jerked his head in a short nod, a movement I knew. One that spoke volumes. He *liked* this girl. I leaned forward before I could stop myself. "Yeah, her name's Rose. One of the guys convinced me to try one of those online dating things. I did it, kinda as a joke, but our profiles matched up pretty well."

"Well . . . well." That was unexpected. And . . . great. Healthy. It sounded like progress.

So why did I suddenly feel so abandoned?

Ben smiled sheepishly at my lengthening silence. "I know. Internet dating. Corny, huh?"

"No, it's just . . ." I swallowed hard, and even though I didn't want to hear it, asked, "What's she like?"

"Well, I've only seen a photo of her so far," he said, leaning forward eagerly. "But we've been talking on the computer every day for about a month, and the phone a couple of times. She likes Thai food and long walks on the beach, so we might get together and see if we have anything else in common, you know?"

I stared straight ahead, jaw clenching reflexively. *I* fucking liked Thai food.

"What do you think?" he finally said, clearing his throat in the lengthening silence.

"Are you asking my permission?" I asked shortly, and immediately wished I hadn't. He leaned back in his chair, folding his arms over his chest. I grimaced apologetically, but it was too late.

"You know, Olivia, for a long time I thought Jo was someone I couldn't have. All those years she was still alive I would substitute women in my bed for her. I fought for my victims at work, substituting them for her as well. I just didn't have the . . ." He was going to say *balls*, I could see the word forming in his mouth, and he caught himself, remembering who he thought I was.

He cleared his throat. "Anyway, when I had to get used to

the idea of her really not being out there, of a world without Joanna Archer . . ." He let his eyes close for a long moment and whispered, "I almost died. There was no reason to keep struggling any longer. She was gone. I lost. Why bother, right? All those women . . . I'd be substituting them for a ghost."

I momentarily lost the ability to breathe. That's exactly what I felt like sometimes. Casper. "So . . . why bother, Ben?"

"Because Jo would want me to. She kept living and fighting and moving forward in her life. She'd want me to do the same."

I couldn't bring myself to affirm that or say the words *move on*, but I nodded because it was the right thing to do. Just a few months ago this man was on the verge of going apeshit; he'd lost his job, his hope, and was doing a good job of losing his mind. I also nodded because he was a mortal, and it was my job to protect them. Getting on with his life would certainly do that.

And I nodded because I still loved him. Ben needed something, someone, good in his life. If there was such a thing anymore. "So when are you meeting this Rose?"

"Next Saturday," he said, expression clearing. "I thought I'd take her to dinner, then maybe the show at Valhalla? What do you think?"

For God's sake, why did he have to ask me? I didn't like it, and not just because I had to lie. Asking meant he cared. It meant this might be serious. "I think it sounds great," I lied. "Just . . . take it slow. There's some weird stuff going on in this town these days."

"I know." He nodded, shifting in his chair. "That's one of the cases I'm working on, actually."

I snapped to attention, frowning at that. "What do you mean?"

He balanced on the back legs of his chair, dropping his hands to his knees. He thought he was on safe territory now. "The department called me in as a consultant. They think the plague might be related to my missing persons case. He's a scientist; his field of study was in vitro and viral replication."

"So how's that related to this plague?" I asked. Playing dumb was such a good strategy. I don't know why I hadn't realized it before.

"Well, they don't want to say anything yet, but evidence leads them to believe the killer might be infecting the victims while having sex. He injects them with a syringe or compound that fries them from the inside out. They're dead within hours."

"He?" I said, letting disbelief bleed into my voice.

"Well, there's more than one, obviously. A gang of some sort. A cult. Maybe some religious fanatics determined to smite the wicked of this world."

"That's just . . ." Wrong. Stupid. Way off. "Freaky."

"So don't go around kissing strangers."

"Take your own advice," I said a little too vehemently, and suddenly I had to get out of there. Warren had been right. I needed to stay away from Ben. He was moving on, but I was stuck and until I got unstuck, it only meant more pain for me.

"Sure," he said after a pause, watching me fumble for my disks and bag and wallet. "Don't worry about me."

"Worry?" I said, standing, and tossed my hair over my shoulder as I shot him a flashy smile. "Now when have you ever known Olivia Archer to worry?"

I kissed his cheek in parting, and he held my hand until I promised to call him soon so we could get together for lunch. Then I swept out the doors, pretending to be as carefree as I looked. But I couldn't resist one look back. And as I left the café, I saw Ben turned in his chair, watching me walk past the plate-glass window just like every other guy in the shopping center. I smiled as I waved, but let it drop after I'd turned away, still feeling Ben's eyes pinning me from the back, like he could see through me and knew what I was thinking.

And what I was thinking was, *Fuck Rose*. Because no matter what he said, Ben wasn't finished with Joanna Archer. And he knew who I really was, I thought, touching my hand where he'd caressed it. He knew it . . . even if he didn't know he knew it.

26

Every person I've ever met believes, to a varying extent, that everything happens for a reason. Sometimes the reason is as simple as you made a bad decision, you were a dumbass, and now you've got to pay. Other times the reasons go deeper, and you can feel in the soft grit of your marrow that there are other, greater powers at work in life. That's how I felt as I returned to Olivia's apartment after my meeting with Ben. No, I hadn't discovered anything incriminating or surprising or even useful on Olivia's disks. But if the computer hadn't been stolen, and I hadn't taken Olivia's backups to that particular coffee shop, I would've never run into Ben. I would've never heard about his involvement in the missing scientist's case or known about his date the following Saturday.

Thus I would have never known to follow him.

I only considered this option because he was obviously so helpless. A man dependent on the police's misinformation about a sexual virus was going on his first date with someone since his love—his one true love, dammit—had died. Someone needed to look out for him. Someone needed to protect him from what he didn't know . . . not to mention this Rose woman who had contacted him out of the blue, without knowing anything more than noodles and beaches turned him on. Surprisingly, when I shared this with Hunter—and I had to; he could sense my agitation the moment I walked in the door—he agreed.

"He was clean in the café, right?" he asked, taking a bite out of an apple as he perched on the kitchen countertop. "You didn't smell any disease lingering about him?"

Reaching into the cabinet to pull out a wineglass, I shook my head. I felt odd about drinking in front of Hunter after what he'd told me of his past, but he insisted it didn't bother him. And I really wanted a drink right now.

"Then it's your duty to make sure he stays that way," he said, gesturing with his apple. No sign of jealousy, interest, or care either way. *Partners, remember*, I told myself.

"How?" I gave myself a healthy pour of Sauvignon Blanc and swirled it in the glass as I turned back to him.

He shrugged, and with his mouth full, said, "Kiss him."

I froze, glass halfway to my mouth. "You mean . . . infect him?" I asked, my voice high.

"I mean *protect* him." He slipped from the counter where he'd been sitting, reached into his pocket, and held a small white disk out to me.

No, not a disk, I saw, flipping it in my hand. A cassette, like the ones Micah used in his labs. I looked back up at him, my question plain upon my face.

"Your blood work," he explained, taking another bite. "I couldn't steal the paperwork from Micah's lab, but the physical evidence is there. You're not immune to the virus because that initiate kissed you. You're immune because you're part Shadow."

I glanced back down at the cassette, and saw my hand was trembling.

"See, I got to thinking after you were kicked out. Even if I were a Shadow bent on infecting innocents and agents of Light, I'd still want to get my groove on now and then."

I quirked a brow in his direction. "Poetic."

"Isn't it?" he said with a twist of his lips. "But it would be a bit of a mood kill if your partners went up in flames every time you laid one on them."

"Definitely hard on a relationship," I agreed.

"So I decided there had to be some kind of fail-safe built into this virus. I'm willing to bet all the Shadows can have sex without infecting their partners. They're genetically excluded, which means you can still—"

"—have sex with anyone I want," I finished for him. And imbue them with immunity, as I had Hunter.

He smiled bittersweetly at the thinly veiled excitement in my voice. "He'll still need to stay away from this Rose, or anyone else who might be infected until then, but with one kiss from you, the love of his life . . ."

He won't even want to kiss someone else. My heart began to pound madly in my chest. And that might just buy me enough time to find the serum that could save us all.

So I decided Hunter was right—not that it took much convincing—and plotted aloud my plans to save Ben from himself, ignoring the sarcastic voice in my head sneering, *Aren't we noble.* "He's taking her to the show at Valhalla. I thought I'd follow at a safe distance, see if I could scent the virus on her, then figure out a way to separate them if I did."

Hunter shook his head, targeted the trash can beside the counter with his apple core, and shot. Two points. Wasn't living with a man fun? "That'll be too late. What are you going to do, jump out of the bushes when he walks her to her door? Push her aside so he kisses you instead?"

I frowned. "I'll figure something out." Probably.

Wiping his hands on his pants, he gave me a hard look. "Not good enough. You can't take any chances, so cut her off at the pass. You have to kiss him first."

"How am I supposed to do that looking like this?" I waved a hand down my very Olivia, very little-sister-to-Ben body.

Hunter shrugged and pushed himself off the counter.

"Not my problem . . . and I don't need to know all the gory details. Just . . . protect him. Trust me. You'll hate yourself if you don't."

And that was personal experience talking, but before I could get into it further, he turned his back and headed down the hallway leading to the guest room.

"What about Cher and Suzanne?" I called after him.

"I don't know, but if you end up kissing them, call me. I wanna watch."

I reached in the fruit basket and threw an apple at him, but he ducked, and the apple exploded in a thunderous splat against the hallway wall. "Perv."

I stood in Ben's living room four hours later, telling myself I was just doing as Hunter suggested, and taking care of my own. The room was neat, if sparse, everything in its place but for a bowl and spoon lying in the kitchen sink, and a baseball cap thrown on a ratty old couch. The only thing marring this almost anal-retentive tidiness was the plants. I don't know why, but Ben liked to nurture varietals that shouldn't even be combined in the same sentence as *desert*, showering them with the time, love, and patience they required to grow in 110-degree heat. And under his care they not only grew, they thrived. He was a badass P.I. who'd beat down the meanest street thug without a second thought, but he sure loved his green things.

I grabbed a beer from the fridge as I looked around, searching for photos or letters or clues to the man I knew, but like me, he'd tucked most of his memories away. But if I could find some sign of the man I'd left sleeping soundly in his bed only months earlier, I knew my plan would work; I'd find my way back into his heart and mind. Cruel, maybe, but it'd keep him safe.

I wandered into the bedroom, where I leaned close to the dresser mirror, staring hard at my reflection. It and the room were tinted the faintest violet hue. I placed my bottle down on the dresser and jerked my head, an almost violent motion that left a smudged outline where I'd been standing. The outline filled in like smoke in a form mirroring mine, then snapped to mold itself back to my frame. In that brief moment I saw Olivia's face, clear as day. Then my own dark, serious eyes were back, filtered through to the outside world, encased in Jasmine's aura.

"Are you sure, Jasmine?" I'd asked the changeling at least a dozen times after she'd consented to helping me. "You don't have to if you don't want to."

"Oh, I do," she assured me, gazing up at me with eyes that were both questioning and trusting at the same time. "It's just an unusual request. I've never heard of binding to an agent who wasn't in danger before."

"You think it can be done?"

"I don't know," she answered honestly. "Zane has warned us not to extend our auras to anyone outside of the shop. But I think that's just because he likes to keep an eye on us, you know. Make sure . . ."

She faltered, trailing off, obviously afraid of offending me.

"No one takes off with your aura?" I guessed, and she answered with a small nod. I patted her shoulder. "I don't blame him."

"It's just very important for the changelings to live on. For the good of the Zodiac, I mean."

"And for you," I said, sweeping her bangs from her forehead. "You have a whole life ahead of you. I promise, I'll take care to see that you grow up."

"Oh, but I don't want to grow up," she said earnestly. "Grown-ups don't get to hang out in Master Comics. And if I grow up I'll have to forget all about you!"

She wrapped her little arms around my waist and clung to me in a more natural fashion. I patted her head awkwardly, then returned her embrace, silently swearing to cocoon her lifeless body as safely as was possible.

"And don't get in any fights, okay?" she warned once I had her tucked in safely at Olivia's apartment. "You may be immune to mortal weapons, but a knife through my aura will kill me just as readily as if I was standing there."

"I promise. And Luna will make sure no Shadows get anywhere near you," I said, and bolstered the pillows on the day bed like a mother bird plumping a nest for her eggs. Nothing was going to happen to her. "Thank you, Jasmine."

"Anything I can do to serve."

Then she changed from that smooth-cheeked girl into the monster, and finally the smoky, elongated shade that all too eerily mirrored my own. It was like the sun was hitting me from behind and casting my shadow up in front of me. I stepped through it, and all that remained of our two images was a singular pale face, one I'd taken for granted for twenty-four years, and had been missing these past months.

"Welcome back, Joanna," I said to myself, then pushed away from the mirror.

There was nothing in Ben's bedroom to indicate he still thought of me, which I supposed was healthy. If he had possessed some artifact, a lock of hair or something, he'd probably be unhinged by now, and I definitely didn't want that. I'd already promised myself to do everything in my power to make sure there was no lingering psychological damage from this visit, but as I rustled through his bedside drawer, finding nothing more interesting than an empty holster, I was mildly disappointed.

I found what I wanted in the study, though, tucked inside a vertical wire rack marked "Unsolved," and a thick folder with my initials on it. The photo that had run almost constantly in the papers and on TV during the week after my apparent death was stapled to the inside flap, and a notebook filled with scribbled notes and theories was lying on top. It was fascinating, if disturbing, to see the way Ben's thoughts, early on, had been a rambling jumble of conspiracy theories and conjecture before cooling more recently into a practical timeline of events and hard facts.

Strangely enough, the earlier entries were the closest to the truth, and I saw that he'd initially thought Olivia was the next target, which explained why—in those early days—I'd caught the edge of his shadow trailing me, a whiff of sorrow and desperation preceding him. I couldn't remember exactly when that feeling had tapered off, but it had, slowly, until it was noticeable only by its absence. That's when his mind must have cleared from the muddied disorder of his grief, and he was able to function again . . . which was how I knew he'd never know the truth. Reason was the last thing needed to understand what had happened to me. A healthy imagination and a full bottle of Scotch would have served him better.

I yelped when the phone trilled next to me, putting a hand to my heart. I'd completely lost track of time. I was calm by the time the answering machine picked up, but Ben's message caused my heart to speed up again. I reached forward to play it again, just so I could hear that cool, clear voice, but the beep sounded, and then *her* voice piped into the room.

"Hey, Benny. I'm just calling to chat, no great emergency or anything. Uh, but I guess you're not there. Anyway, I'm looking forward to Saturday. I hope you're hungry. Call me later, all right? 'Bye."

I glared at the machine like it was a mortal enemy. "Benny?" I said bitingly. My heart was pumping, my hands shaking as I pushed replay to hear the message again, but first I had to wait through another.

"Yo, B. The stakeout's been moved to L Street and it's an hour later. Bring a cup to pee in, it's an all-nighter. And munchies, dude. I'm hungry. Later."

"So that's where he is," I said. Well, he'd said he still helped out the department on an auxiliary basis. He was probably just acting as an extra pair of eyes on this stakeout. Even so, with that phone call my plans to seduce Ben in his home blew up in my face. So I strode to the kitchen and tossed my beer as Rose's voice sounded again through the house.

"I hope you're hungry," I mimicked, and relieved Ben of one phone call to return.

What? Hunter had said to cut Rose off at the pass, but now that I knew where Ben was for the night—and now that the voice, that message, had made her real to me—I was going to do more than that. I was going to cut her off at the knees.

"Benny, my ass." And I slammed the door shut behind me.

27

I was winging along L and Stone Street, trying to decide where to ditch my ride, when I spotted the first undercover cop. He was slouched in a nondescript Taurus, and I drove past him, circled the block, and came to a stop two streets south of where he was parked. Being an intelligent girl, I'd left the Porsche back at the condo and pulled out the old Vic instead. We were on the cusp of one of Vegas's seedier projects, and while the Porsche would've screamed, *Rape me!*, the Vic was more of a I-double-dog-dare-ya sort of vehicle.

Or hopefully something a little more gangsta than that.

Through the violet tint of my new worldview, I checked out my reflection again, and satisfied with my dark hair, dark clothing, and dark eyes, pushed the car door shut with a slam that ricocheted through the weed-choked lot and into the concrete buildings beyond. I doubted anyone in this neighborhood even flinched.

It was one very nervous cop in that lone unmarked car. His anxiety was as sharp as week-old sweat as he sat, hardly moving, one hand clenched around a walkie-talkie, head turned toward the building across the street on his left.

There was a portable receiver in the passenger seat, which meant whatever room in that building he was trying to maintain visual on was already tapped and live. I crouched in the gutter next to the passenger side door, praying he didn't have a partner who would be returning soon. The pocked and ill-lit street was silent and unmoving.

"Where you think you goin'?"

I jumped before I realized the voice had come over the receiver. Fortunately the young cop inside had jolted too.

"None of yo damn," a male voice returned, followed by a door slamming. The walkie-talkie immediately came to life.

"Suspect on the move. Stairwell. I'm on him."

The young cop's anxiety spiked, and the car jostled as he lowered himself further, giving me ample opportunity to raise my head and survey my surroundings. I was only using visual as a secondary sense, having already located the other four undercovers—including Ben—by scent. Visual confirmed they were all in the same locations; the first man two blocks down in a beat-up Eldorado; a second, female, standing in full view beneath the lone working streetlight a hundred yards away; another seated and seemingly dozing in a sagging lawn chair kitty-corner to the first complex, and Ben, lying beside a stack of overflowing trash cans, dressed in the same guise Warren liked to use, a street bum playing with less than a full stack.

"Suspect leaving through front entrance," I heard, and then a pop as the front door flew open. It bounced off its hinges, ricocheting back, but by that time a man the size of a small vehicle—the suspect, I presumed—had already cleared out, and the door slammed shut behind him. He began to walk, slouched, hands tucked in his oversized pockets, heading in the direction of the Eldorado.

His head was down, a black bandana wrapped around his bald skull, but every once in a while he'd lift his chin like he was looking for someone, in almost a syncopated beat, before lowering it again.

"Headed your way, Collins," my cop said.

"I see him."

The man stopped next to Collins's car, no more than a second, then bobbed his head again in that off-beat, and continued on.

Probably looking to score, I thought, watching as he crossed the intersection, past the lone streetlight and the female cop without so much as a glance at her long, exposed legs. When he'd disappeared around the chain-link fence, she began to follow. "I'm shadowing him."

"Be careful." This was from Ben.

A gnawing feeling began to grow at the base of my neck, and I couldn't have agreed more. I scented fresh blood. I pushed myself forward again, careful not to jostle the car, and peered past the front tire to the Eldorado, which lay silent and dark, Collins unmoving inside. I glanced over at the man in the lawn chair, and realized he was already dead. I wanted to jump up, tell the rookie next to me to radio Ben, but I couldn't risk spooking him so that he shot me, injuring Jasmine's aura, and I didn't want to blow his cover if he hadn't already been made. Unfortunately, the suspect returned just then, strolling down this side of the street as coolly as if it were midday, whistling under drug-soaked breath. He brought the scent of more blood with him.

If I'd had only myself to worry about, I'd have rushed him . . . stakeout be damned. But mindful of Jasmine's frail shell, pale and inanimate, waiting back home, I rolled under the chassis of the car instead, and remained silent. What happened next would haunt my dreams.

"He's heading back your way, Brown." Ben again.

My officer answered, the sweat now pouring off him in sheets. "I see him."

Brown stayed where he was. The man drew closer. I shut my eyes and fixed my mind on Jasmine's trusting face.

He was quick. That was how he'd gotten by Collins, killing him without missing one step of his psychotic beat. I smelled the steel of his gun, and that pop sounded again . . . the same I'd heard over the radio minutes earlier in the stairwell. I flinched as the bullet plowed through the floor, but held my breath. I hadn't felt this vulnerable in a long time . . . not only in the months I'd been a superhero, but years.

I swallowed as the hard toe combat boots turned from me, and a walkie-talkie clattered to the pavement. It had to belong to the guy in the lawn chair. That's how the suspect knew where everyone was located. Then the whistling began again, and trapped beneath a car with a dead cop in it, wrapped in a little girl's fragile skin, I could only watch as the killer headed straight for the trash-strewn lot and Ben.

Ben wasn't stupid. He knew their cover had been blown, so he didn't try to radio, and he was no longer slumped next to the pile of trash. Instead he'd fled to the back of the gated lot, a narrow, weed-choked strip of iron fencing separating two project houses from each other, but by the lazy gait of his pursuer, and that meandering song he was whistling—which I now recognized as some sort of sadistic death march—I knew there was no way out. So I waited until the killer's shadow had lengthened into giantlike proportions on the street, and let it snap and disappear before grabbing the radio he'd abandoned, and followed.

My choices were limited. I might be a superhero, but I couldn't be everywhere at once. I couldn't be behind the killer and still stop a bullet from entering my lover. I couldn't protect both Jasmine and Ben at the same time. "Hang on, Jasmine," I whispered.

I ran along the outside of the fence, crouched low as I leaped over bottles and cans and anything else that would give up my presence and location. I slowed fifteen feet behind my target, who stood an equal distance to the end of the fencing, and saw I was right. The fence there was high, barbed, and there was no way out.

"Know what we call this, Po-Po?" the man called out, his baritone ringing beautifully through the silent night. "This be Dog Run. 'Cause of its length and 'cause you only get out if I feel like lettin' you out."

Silence from the end of the run, but I knew Ben was there. The killer knew it too.

"You want out, you gonna have to go for a little run."

"You're under arrest."

The man laughed with his rich, deep voice. "Now I know you think 'cause you got that big ol' forty-five pointed my way that I be steppin' aside and let you on your way, but we both know I can't do that. You're what ya'll call an eyewitness. I call you a loose end, and Magnum don't abide no loose ends. But maybe we can come to some sort of agreement. Step on out here before I start punching some more holes through that back fence . . . and anything standing in front of it."

And he reached into the front of his baggy pants to pull out a sawed-off shotgun. I lifted my walkie-talkie to my mouth, and pushed the button before he could point. From somewhere in the darkness, Ben's radio squawked to life.

"You put that big bitch down or I'll show you exactly how to tie up a loose end."

Magnum jerked like a fish on a line, and swiveled to face the entrance of Dog Run. His grip tightened as he turned back to Ben.

"To your left," I told him, through the radio. He strained to peer over his wide shoulder. "Your other left, asshole."

As his head jerked away, I dropped the walkie-talkie and leaped, clearing the fence to land beside him in the space of two seconds. Despite my speed, and Ben's surprised gasp, it was about one second too long. The jittery gangster was already turning back, and I was stuck in a precarious crouch beneath him, but not so precarious I couldn't jam my fist upward in a superstrength undercut that rocked the breath from his body. I know. Such a girl thing to do. But as he crumpled, curling into himself with a strangled groan, I rose and hammered my locked fists down onto the back of his neck. Lucky for him, I didn't want him to identify me later. I'd just taken the edge off his misery.

I planted a boot on his back to make sure he remained

motionless, then looked up into the shadows at the back fence. "You can come out now."

Ben didn't move. His nerves were spiked, his anxiety and indecision sour on the still air.

"Ben," I said, knowing his name on my lips would jar him into action. "Come out."

It wasn't the happy reunion I had imagined. He emerged like a refugee, his figure hunched in ragged clothes and lank hair, stinking of garbage and sweat and whatever else he'd smeared over his body, though his eyes flashed, sharp and assessing. It wasn't a look like Joaquin's, with marble-hard orbs burning from beneath a skeleton's frame. It wasn't like any of the agents of Light either; he didn't possess the confidence of a nonmortal, or the ability to scent out danger before it was seen. No, this was an altogether human gaze, but still cold, petrified emotion. It was the look of a predator.

And I didn't care. I sucked in a deep, grateful breath. He was perfect, and safe, and whole.

"How do you know my—"

But by then he was close enough to see me.

"What's wrong?" I said, his expression making my throat tight. "Never seen a dead girl before?"

Joking was the wrong approach to take. Ben began to shake.

"Shh. Okay," I said, stepping toward him. "It's okay."

"J-Jo?" he said, his voice thin with disbelief.

Magnum began to stir on the ground. I brought my boot down, knocking him unconscious again. "Yeah, honey. It's me."

"But y-you're . . ."

"I know," I said, nodding sadly. "Meaner."

"But how—?"

"Ben, honey, there's not really time, is there? You have five dead officers out there and, I assume, a lot of explaining to do. Cuff this asshole, and get to it. We'll talk later." I glanced back down at Magnum's sprawled bulk. "He didn't see me, so whatever story you come up with will do. He didn't put up a fight, so you won't have to explain my foot-prints in the dirt. Cover them with your own and—"

I stopped, tilting my head, listening to sounds far in the distance.

"What?" Ben asked. "What is it?"

"Sirens," I said, a moment before they could be heard by a mortal.

His face cleared once he made them out, and he looked at me with renewed astonishment. "I called them on my cell while I was running back here."

"Good. Tighter time frame. Your story, whatever it is, will hold." I took a step past him toward the back of Dog Run as the first flashing lights careened around the corner. Ben stopped me, grip tight on my arm. I should have kissed him once, because once would be enough, saving him in a single instant. It was enough to make him remember me, and us, and to keep him from going on that date with Rose. From accepting poisonous kisses from strangers. From leav-ing me behind entirely.

But his eyes were warm and moist and he was looking at me with such naked longing that more adrenaline pumped through my veins than the entire short-lived chase into the Dog Run. So many people in this world, I thought wonder-ingly, but only one man who spoke to my soul. How could a superhero beholden to uphold peace and protect all the in-nocents in an entire city single out one as special, as more worthy than all the rest? How were soul mates retained when years and realities and even death stood between them?

"Don't leave," he said, and in my heart I heard what he wasn't saying. *Don't leave me. Not again.*

Tires squealed to a halt at the front of the Dog Run, and sirens and lights bathed the quiet, violent street in crimson and cream slashes. And still he looked at *me*. Not Olivia. And that made all the difference.

"Blue Angel," I said, and though it was a statement, my voice rose on a questioning note. I wasn't even sure I should be saying it.

A sigh of relief, and Ben nodded. "Wait for me. No matter how long this takes."

I reached up and put a hand to his cheek, and after a second his body heat soaked through Jasmine's aura and warmed me throughout. I smiled. "I have been."

And I stepped away, leaped, and cleared the back fence just as the first flashlights came arching our way.

28

Back in the days when cowboys still clipped along dusty one-lane roads and the test site put on expensive and lethal light shows for politicians, stars, and foreign dignitaries alike, there was a burgeoning business in Las Vegas called atomic art. Signs meant to attract attention to new establishments popped up as ubiquitously as mushroom clouds in the baby blue Nevada skies, and the Blue Angel, situated above the motel of the same name, was one of them.

When I was a kid I used to ask my mom to drive past that motel, worn down even then, save for the lovely lady twirling on her pedestal, standing guard over Fremont Street. Her robes, a powder blue, clung to her curvaceous frame, and her hair was beacon yellow as she pointed a star-tipped wand at pedestrians like she was bestowing blessings on all who passed below.

I stood below her now, gazing up at her chipped and faded gown, and realized there was more kitsch than romance to her, and that this original thoroughfare leading weary travelers downtown into Glitter Gulch was more highway to hell for most than it was yellow brick road. I sighed, unreasonably sad at being disillusioned. I'd long been aware that most people who came to Vegas never truly found what they were looking for.

So what the hell was I doing here? I should be back with Hunter, plotting our next move, kicking preternatural ass, and leaving street dreams and battered symbols to the mortals who needed them most. Instead, while the city sat embroiled in an apocalyptic-type plague, I was crouched beneath a fallen angel, trying to get my groove on.

I rolled my eyes, shifted, and placed my other heel against the wall, but I continued to wait for Ben and whatever questions and demands he brought with him. And the truth was, I *couldn't* wait. God help me, I was like a high school senior on prom night, except instead of a gown and corsage I was wearing a preteen's aura and a supernatural sidearm. How romantic.

Two and a half hours later a truck door slammed and the scent of hopeful nervousness wafted my way. I straightened, swallowed hard, and turned to face the lot behind the motel. Seconds later, Ben turned the corner of the cinder-block building and stopped, silhouetted there. We stared at each other, the Blue Angel twirling overhead, wrapping ribbons of light and shadow around our bodies so that we kept appearing to each other anew, over and over again.

I'd like to say I was giving him time to get used to seeing me again, but I was doing the same. I'd shut him off in my brain to survive this world without him, so in a sense, he was coming back to me as well. Finally, convinced that neither of us was going to disappear, we stepped forward at the same time.

A ghost of a smile flitted over his face. I felt it visit mine as well. "Hi," I said. "Again."

"You fly."

It wasn't the first thing I'd expected to come from his mouth. I'd been imagining endearments, perhaps a touch of anger or tears or silent numbness, so the words sparked a self-conscious laugh from deep in my chest, but I checked it, and it came out strangled instead. "I, uh . . . leap. It's different."

"Leap," he repeated, coming closer. "And you save former boyfriends from death by junkie in darkened lots."

I ignored the question underlying his words and focused on the facts. I smelled exhaustion and blood on him, and fresh pity coursed through me as I thought of his dead friends. "I'm sorry I couldn't save them, Ben. I was protecting someone else. By the time I realized what was happening, it was too late."

"So that hasn't changed, at least. You're still wandering dangerous streets, looking for trouble."

I wanted to bristle at that, but I had to choose my battles. "Yeah, well. You know me."

"I thought I did."

"Ben, look—"

"No," he said, holding up a hand, then extending it to brush my arm. Carefully, as if I might break. I let my eyes flutter shut, unable to remember the last time I'd been handled carefully. "I don't care. I mean, I do. I will later. But, Jo . . . you're here. I'm seeing you. I-I'm touching you. I'm not dreaming you. Am I?"

In all the time that I'd known Ben, that I'd watched and followed him—seen him joyful, grieving, strong, and destroyed—I'd never seen the toxic fusion of all those things swirling on his face at once. His eyes, however, remained steady on mine, asking, *Where have you been?*

I could either tell him, or lie. Reveal all, or remain hidden. But I did neither. I could leap from rooftops, dodge blows, and face bullets with impervious courage, but I couldn't choose between my two lives, and I couldn't allow Ben to be stuck between them, a pendulum swinging back and forth.

I shook my head sadly. "It's all a dream, Ben. It's one long night where nothing and everything makes sense. Like when you're running, but not getting anywhere. When you're falling, but you never hit the bottom." I caught myself then, how vague and unsatisfying that all sounded, and smiled ruefully. "What I mean is . . . it's complicated."

Ben returned my smile, gave a slow nod of understanding

that I didn't deserve, and said, "But it's never been complicated between us, Jo."

"Except for that whole lose you/find you, lose you/find you thing."

He brought my hand to his chest, drawing me closer. "Except for that."

And what did *that* matter? I thought, as he lowered his lips to mine, as all that was heat and hearth and home enveloped me more thoroughly than any aura ever could. What did anything matter when his lips were warming mine, when his tongue found its home in my mouth, and his arms wrapped around me to draw me deeper, both away and into myself?

Ben managed to pull away first, making me wonder just which of us was superhuman. "Unless we're going to make love in a place that charges by the hour, day, or week, I suggest you tell me where to take you. Now."

I laughed. "As tempting as the week-long stay sounds, I think I have a better place."

"Do you?"

I did, though I hadn't thought about it until now. Olivia's apartment was out because Hunter was now living there, and wouldn't *that* be fun? Ben's place would offer too much distraction—phone calls, memories, files on dead girls—and I wanted him to myself. But there was one place sure to offer both privacy and retreat from the world. I took his hand, smiling up at him as I did, and we headed to his truck. "Take me home."

If Ben was a reminder of my past, going home was a full frontal jump into a life I'd left behind. We strolled up the walkway, after making sure we were seen by no neighbors, and I fumbled for the key Xavier had given me months before. It was a gift, he had explained. I—meaning Olivia—could sell my sister's home and all its belongings, or hang on to it as long as I wanted. He'd continue to pay the mortgage, keep up the utilities . . . whatever made me happy.

I hadn't been back for many reasons, the most obvious being that I was sure it was being monitored by the Shadow organization. But the Shadows were in hiding, the streets empty, and the house was dark but for the single interior light that went on with a timer. I slid my key into the lock, closing my eyes to heighten my olfactory sense, but scented nothing more than dust, a few dead bugs, and a bunch of memories. After shutting off the alarm, I flipped on a light and glanced around. It looked like a waiting room for displaced ghosts, I thought, everything draped in sheets. There were no plants and certainly no animals. Nothing living had been here for a long while.

Ben joined me in the center of the room, looking about. "You don't come here anymore, do you?"

I thought of my darkroom set up on the other side of the house, how it called to me, and how I'd resisted coming back here even for it. For any reason. Until now. "I haven't, no."

He looked sad at that, almost as sad as I felt.

"Come on," I said, "I think there's some wine in the kitchen."

I moved around efficiently, opening drawers, and handling flatware and wineglasses I'd never thought to see, much less touch, again. I was aware of Ben's eyes following me, and I'd have risked a look in the mirror hanging across from me in the dining area, except that it had been draped as well. Instead I caught my reflection in the face of the microwave, and though blurred, it reassured me that Jasmine's aura was still holding. I turned, holding out a glass.

"Sancerre," I said. "My favorite."

"Is it?" He took a sip, though I don't know if he really tasted it. He was too focused on me. There was that predatory look I'd seen back at Dog Run, though this time I didn't mind it at all. "I never knew that. But then there's a lot I never knew about you. Here's to some things never changing."

The flash of sarcasm meant he was recovering from his shell-shock, but I merely clicked my wineglass against his, and said nothing. His expression softened.

"I meant what I said before, Jo. I don't care where you've been, what you've done. I wonder, of course, but I can see you, I can touch you. And I can see you're about to say something to try and take that away, like this is a mistake, and you must have reasons for that as well, but . . ." He paused, shaking his head, and ran a hand along his mouth. "Fuck your reasons."

I put my glass down. "Ben—"

"And fuck that reasonable tone too."

"Ben."

"That's right," he said, backing me into the counter. "My name is on your lips, something I never thought I'd hear again. So if you don't want me to start questioning all the things you're not saying, you'd better just say it again."

I was ready to argue, to bolt, but one look into his implacable face, and I couldn't help it; I licked my lips. "Ben."

"Again," he said, inches closer, watching me fiercely, seeing me as few people ever did. He always had.

"Ben," I complied, whispering, being seen.

"Again."

"God," I reached for him. "Benjamin. Ben Traina." I slid my limbs around him, wrapping myself up tight; pelvis, chest, lips meeting his, forcing him to lift me, climbing into him, losing myself. Saying his name. "Mine . . ."

He pulled back at last, smiling as he stared into my eyes. "That's all I need to hear."

He carried me to the bedroom that way, as I nibbled at his neck and ear, and the corner of his mouth, the hard warmth of his body sparking into mine. He flipped on the light with his elbow, but I reached over and flipped it back off, uncurling myself from him long enough to yank the dust sheet from the bed in a single flourish and discard it in the corner. Then I raised the blinds and opened the windows, allowing the stars and distant streetlights to bathe the room in an ethereal glow. A cricket chirped from beyond the window screen, and a night-ferried breeze swept the room like the wide caress of a cool hand. It would only last for a couple of hours, I knew. Then the scorching sun would be back, and we'd have to face each other in the stark light of day. Face those questions he wasn't asking as well. But I turned back to Ben anyway. If a couple of hours was all we had, I didn't want to waste a minute.

We filled ourselves on each other, and once we were sated, sweaty and loose-limbed, lying in a tangle in the middle of the bed, we opened our bruised and swollen lips, and simply talked. How many people get the chance to talk to someone lost to them forever?

"I knew it. I knew you weren't dead," he said, leaning on one elbow, toying with my hair with his free hand, while I passed the single glass of wine I'd brought back to the bed between us. He took the sip I pressed to his lips, and some dripped down his chin. I leaned over and licked it off, my thigh curving up and over his hip. "I felt your presence inside me, around me. Like you were watching, though not like the angels in a far-off place. Was I right?"

I nodded. "About one thing . . . I'm definitely no angel."

"Tough talk, tough girl," he said, running his hand under the covers, along my side. Chills popped up on my thigh, and he smiled. "I always liked that about you. Except . . . now you really are tough, aren't you?"

Now his hand moved to my left arm, where scars from my latest battles rose like Braille on the otherwise smooth skin.

"Find it unattractive?" I asked, dodging the question.

"Obviously," he said, slipping a hand between my thighs. I was still wet from our lovemaking, and his fingers slid along the soft skin with gentle ease. I sighed into them, my eyes fluttering closed. His voice, however, had them winging back open. "So how did you do that? That leapy thing?"

"I thought you didn't care." I sure didn't at the moment.

"I said it didn't matter, and it doesn't." His fingers explored me, brushed me open, slipped inside. We both sighed. "I didn't say I wasn't curious."

I opened to him further, lazy and unguarded. In body and

speech. "And remember what I said? All of life is one big dream. What if you're dreaming now? What if your real life awaits you on the other side of night? You'll wake and I'll be gone."

He rolled over on top of me so fast I didn't have time to save the wineglass. It tipped, spilling chilled, fermented juice between us, dribbling down my chest, soaking into the bedsheets as I stared up at Ben, startled. His eyes were wild now, and filled with the questions he was trying so hard not to ask, instinct telling him if he pushed too hard, I'd be just that . . . lost to him. And Ben wasn't going to let that happen without a fight.

"You're the only woman who's ever been strong enough for me. Did you know that?" He scraped his nails against my wrists as he pinned me beneath him, and I simply lay there, open to him, not exactly proving his point. "I like that, you know. A strong woman needing me." He lifted himself up, one hand on each side of my head, and shoved my legs open with a thigh.

I swallowed hard and traced the tattoo circling his right bicep, following the waves of pattern with my battered fingertips. I couldn't speak. I was quivering inside, and I lifted to meet his flesh, though he pulled back, smiling at me in the dim light.

"It's a different kind of strength," he continued, like he'd thought about it for a while. His erection played lightly against my belly. "Being the soft spot where a strong woman can rest." He lowered his head, hair falling over his eyes, and when he glanced back up at me through it, his smile was untamed. "I fucking love it."

Yes. Let someone else be strong for a change. I did need a soft spot. Even if only for a night.

My answer was my sigh, my breath as it caressed his cheek, my mouth as it played over his. As our tongues met he was inside me again, hard and fast in a solid stroke. I reared beneath him, wordless noises scattering across the moonlit room, my sigh turning into a needy moan.

"This is real," he said, thrusting, the impact sealing our bodies together as one. "This is all there is."

And feeling my acceptance, my need equaling his, he eased up, hooking his right ankle beneath mine, and flipped us easily, so I was on top. I gazed down and met his eyes, swallowed hard at the challenge there, and began to rock. Yes, I thought, as waves of heat rose through me, up my belly, making my head light. He licked wine from my chest, and I sighed his name into his hair. He was right. This was all there was.

After that we really did talk. I answered what questions I could—yes, I was alive, but yes, I was different too. No, I had no contact with my sister. Yes, that was in order to keep her safe. And I posed a few pointed inquiries myself. Did he miss the police force? Why wasn't he still writing? Who the fuck was Rose?

Then he led the conversation into a linear questioning about what had happened the night of my disappearance, what had happened subsequently, and what was going to happen next. I answered these with mumbled half truths about a secret life—nothing about the sanctuary, Shadows . . . and certainly not that I'd found Joaquin—and ultimately the vague responses piled up between us and we fell silent, him trying to think of ways to draw me out, me wondering where I could hide.

So I distracted him by disappearing beneath the covers, mouth too full for words, and by the time I emerged again, he was too breathless to ask any more. We sipped directly from the wine bottle after that, propped up on each other's flesh until the pastel colors of predawn seeped into the inky sky. I got up and shut the windows, knowing heat would begin bleeding into the room within the hour.

Ben watched my every move. His eyes fluttered shut from time to time, but he opened them again by sheer force of will, only letting a smile and relief pass his face when they found me again. I drifted off myself, and that was unexpected. So much so that when I did awaken it was with a jolt, breathing quickly, eyes winging open. Ben's breathing didn't change.

I rose and dressed, knowing even as I did so that it wasn't fair. I mean, here I was, a ghost lover returning to seduce my beloved, to keep him in essence from getting on with his personal life, when I'd known all along that come sunrise I'd leave him again. What I hadn't expected was to feel this soft; the ability to be fragile with another person wasn't even something I'd realized I was missing, and only the contrast between the lightness I felt with his arms around me and the heaviness that returned as I left that room made me aware of it at all. Wasn't it supposed to be the other way around?

And how the hell was I supposed to live without it now?

And still I couldn't help but think maybe I could return to him intermittently, even semiregularly, as me. It wouldn't be a normal relationship, but what was normal? The guy who went to his nine-to-five every day, then stopped by a strip club on the way home to his wife and family? The woman who waited until her husband was away on business to invite the UPS guy inside? The couples I'd seen at the swingers' ball who'd decided three was most definitely not a crowd?

Hell, I'd turned down mortals and superheroes alike just because the memory of Ben was stronger than the reality of anyone else. But if I left now—and I had to get Jasmine's aura back to her soon—at least I could comfort myself with knowing Ben wouldn't die with scorched lips and genitals.

And he won't replace your spot in bed with another woman.

I jotted down a quick note in the kitchen, telling him if he needed to get in touch with me to leave a message, unsigned, in the mailbox. Then I dropped the house key next to it before returning to the bedroom one last time. Just to look.

"It's best this way," I said from the doorway. "I promise."

As I blinked back tears, I felt Jasmine's aura loosing on

my lids, the movement echoed just a fraction of a second after mine, and knew it was time to go. Letting myself out the back door, I leaped the block wall separating my house from the next, and sprinted away from my home and lover.

Away from my real secret life.

29

Less than an hour later I was home—having driven Jasmine to her house and watched her climb a trellis into her second-story window—but home at Olivia's this time. Home *as* Olivia, I thought, catching my reflection in the entry mirror, almost surprised to see the cascade of long blond curls coming loose from their underpinnings.

Sighing, I dumped my keys on the console, my bag beneath it, and called out Hunter's name as I made my way to the kitchen. There was no answer, and just as well. The scent of lovemaking clung to my skin, and I decided to momentarily forgo food for a shower instead. I was pretty sure Hunter knew where I'd been—he'd encouraged it, after all—but there was no need to rub it in his face.

I set the spray to full heat, threw my clothes into the hamper, and was about to climb into the shower when the phone rang. I hesitated. It could be Hunter, and if he had news about Valhalla he wouldn't leave it on the machine. Then again, it could be Ben. By now he'd probably have woken up alone in a house of ghosts, and might be calling Olivia in a panic to see if she knew anything about my sudden return, and where I might be now.

But it wasn't either of them. Instead Suzanne's frothy voice followed my machine's beep, made even tinnier by her panicked voice. I'd never heard her out of breath before. "Livvy, darlin', it's me. Listen, I'm standing at the starting line for the marathon—you know, the one that ends up in Nye county?" She said this like it was a reasonable thing, and I rolled my eyes as I headed back into the bathroom. I'd listen to the rest later. "Anyway, Ian and I were supposed to meet here an hour ago, he's been talking about this race for months, and I just know he wouldn't miss this for the world.

"I know the two of you weren't seeing each other, but I was wondering if he mentioned something to you at the ball about a quick trip out of town, a death in the family, something like that? I don't know, I'm just worried is all. It's not like him. He's been missing work too—"

This is the point where I backed again into the bedroom. "—and that's not like him either. His bosses say he has a big programming project due soon, and they haven't heard hide nor hair from him for at least a week."

I whirled, staring hard at the spot where my sister's computer once sat, trying frantically to put it all into a neat time frame—the swingers' ball, Ian's disappearance, the computer's—while Suzanne's voice continued chirping along in the background.

". . . so if you happen to hear from him, or talk to him in the next little bit, would you mind giving me a ring, or tell Ian to call me himself? I just want—"

There was a loud explosion that jolted me and I looked back at the recorder, suddenly worried for Suzanne.

"Oops, there's the starting gun, honey. Gotta run. Literally. Smooches!" And she was gone.

I went back to the bath and shut off the now-steaming shower, then returned to the kitchen, not for food, but for the fingerprinting kit I had tucked behind a basket of cleaning supplies under the sink. After lightly dusting the computer desk with the fine powder, I straightened, wrists cocked on my naked hips, heart pounding as I stared at the dance of prints revealed there. Significant because I didn't have fingerprints. And neither did Hunter.

Not that I was surprised to see them. I wouldn't be dusting if I didn't think a mortal was responsible for the theft. The question was, were they Ian's? I leaned forward, viewing the desk eye level, like they did on TV. Was there only one set of prints? Or more?

"Think, think," I told myself, straightening, trying to see the larger view. Ian had been abducted the night Joaquin discovered my hidden identity, and there was a good possibility he'd questioned Ian instead of killing him, or before killing him, trying to find out how much the mortal knew about me, who my friends were. What my habits were.

I kept dusting. I wanted to see if the computer desk was the only thing touched by this intruder, or if they'd been looking for more. By the time I was done, most of Olivia's bedroom was caked in the fine, silty particles . . . and I was in even more desperate need of that shower. But I couldn't move. I stood paralyzed in the middle of the now snowy room, the sun outside beating down on the carpet and my feet while I shivered inside, and that due only in part to the air conditioning and my naked state.

Fingerprints surrounded me. They were everywhere, where they hadn't been before, and standing back, trying to see the whole picture—where the intruder had gone first, what he'd been looking for, what he'd found—I began to pick up a trail, like a train of ants leading to the nest. I followed it to where the prints grew densest.

"No," I whispered, lifting the keepsake box from my dresser, running my hands over the oiled wood interspersed with glossy mother-of-pearl. I took a moment to trace the ghostly remains of another's fingers, then fumbled with the latch until I finally managed to wrench it open. "No," I said again, but it was too late.

I staggered a bit and found the bed, dropping like the floor had come out from beneath me, like all the breath had left my body and I'd deflated to land there, a poor and pitiful excuse for the heroic woman I was supposed to be.

"Olivia!"

I heard it, knew it was my name, but I couldn't respond. I couldn't do anything but stare at the empty desk where Olivia's computer used to be, where she'd so craftily ferreted out and stored her niece's identity and location. And I let the box where I'd so lovingly, so meticulously, so *stupidly* kept all my letters to Ben fall to the floor.

"Olivia?"

The voice was closer, but it was swept away by the screams in my own head, driven back by the howls already ricocheting off the soft tissue, and the pleas I wanted to voice, if only there were someone around, up there, somewhere, to listen.

"God, you're shivering." The duvet was up, wrapped about my shoulders, then drawn in front of me, and finally I could focus. Hunter knelt before me, his face a mixture of worry and caution as he took in my nakedness, my room, my catatonic behavior.

"Hunter," I said in someone else's voice. "They know."

"Know what?" he asked, repeating it when I only shook my head harder. "Know about what, Jo?" And the use of my own name, my real name, snapped me out of my suspended state. My face crumpled.

"Everything," I said, and began to cry. "My daughter . . . on the computer. My lover . . . in the letters. Oh my God. Joaquin's not coming after me. He doesn't need to. He knows about them all."

"Who?" he asked, insistently.

"Everyone," I told him. Everyone who needed to stay hidden the most.

I didn't stay catatonic for long. I was up, dressed, and ready to barge into Valhalla itself within the hour, except that Hunter wouldn't let me. At first he tried reason, talking to me about controlling my emotions and timing and planning and a bunch of other stuff I didn't give a shit about when I thought of Ben in Joaquin's clutches. Or of the child that might be killed only because she happened, at one time, to be mine.

When reason didn't work, he sat on me. He used that big, gorgeous body to hold me down while I raged; against Joaquin, against the Tulpa, and especially against him. I told him he was no better than them. I spit on him—stupid, as I was directly beneath him—and acted like a rabid, frothing bitch. I let my bones burn through my skin, not just revealing my Shadow self, but all the rage and hate and venom that I tried so hard to hide from those in the sanctuary.

Hunter merely anchored himself more firmly on my chest, taking in the sharp bones pushing against my flesh, my eyes as black as buffed coal, the hot iron blistering the air between us. "Don't you get it, Jo?" he finally said. "I've never been afraid of your Shadow side."

And the shock of that statement, the absurdity and frankness of it, and the fucking *romance* of being accepted in all my ugliness, had me breaking down all over again. My bones sank like quicksand beneath my skin and my black eyes were extinguished by fat tears. Anyone else might have let me up then, but Hunter knew better, and he sat it out, literally. And that's how we spent the rest of the day. Until noon came and went. Until the sun fell from the sky. Until dusk crept over the valley again, and I finally slept the dreamless sleep of split realities.

30

♐   "I'm sorry."

My voice was raw and scratchy, and when I tried to clear it, I ended up coughing so hard that my gentle entry into waking hours was abruptly replaced by a scalded throat and violent headache.

"Here."

The scent of warm peppermint washed over me, and I looked up to find Hunter standing at my bedside, a cup of steaming tea in his outstretched hand. Twelve hours earlier, I would've slapped it away, sending tea splattering against the cream-colored walls along with the perfume bottles, mirrors and knickknacks I'd already destined for the trash bin. Instead, as I looked around for the remnants of those things, I accepted the tea, and took a grateful sip.

"You cleaned up," I said, as Hunter perched himself next to me. This gave me a clear view of myself in the cracked dresser mirror, and I winced at my multiple reflections. "Everything but me, I see."

He leaned back, blocking my view. I met his steady gaze. "How're you feeling?"

"Like I've been hit by a semi."

He cocked one dark brow. "I can't imagine why."

"Look, I'm sorry. Really—"

"I heard you the first time," he stopped me, though his voice wasn't harsh like I expected. Or deserved. "And it's okay."

I sipped some more tea, letting the warmth spread through my chest, and out into my limbs, pooling in my ravaged fingertips. "Thank you."

He lifted one large shoulder, shrugging off the gratitude. "Remember when we were in the boneyard? In Tekla's thought maze?"

"Hunter—"

He smiled, bittersweet, and shook his head. "Not that part. Before that. The reason we were there. The purpose of the maze."

I knew the answer—the hours spent under Tekla's tutelage, breaking down walls, had been toward that purpose. "To get to the center without detection. As quickly as possible."

"To use your *sixth sense* to reach that center," he clarified, watching me closely. I faltered under that clear-eyed gaze. "To use clarity of mind and intention to reach your sixth sense."

Yes, I knew that too. I closed my eyes and nodded. "And I had none of that yesterday. If I'd gone to Valhalla like that I'd have been dead before I hit the door."

Hunter patted my leg, warming me further. When I finally opened my eyes again, he said, "The thing is, Jo, getting through that maze was only the first step. Creating barriers out of the ether was the ultimate goal. And do you know why?"

Because the most powerful being had been wrought into the world solely by the determination of a powerful mind. "Because if you know how to build them up, you know how to tear them down."

"Valhalla is the Tulpa's house," Hunter said, nodding. "You need clarity, intention, and your sixth sense combined to enter safely, but to reach the center of his quarters, you need to be able to throw him off your trail. Create barriers of your own."

"And destroy the artificial walls he's created to throw me off of his." I sighed thoughtfully and sipped at the cooling peppermint.

Hunter nodded. "Can you do that?"

I sipped again, and this time the tea settled like a brick in my gut. I looked back at him. "No."

He nodded slowly, and to himself. "But you'll try anyway."

My response this time was a mere whisper. "I have to stop Joaquin. Find Ian. Try to find an antidote to this virus." Save Ben. Save the girl. Save myself. "I have to at least try."

"I know," he said, laying a hand over mine. It was as warm and comforting as the tea. I glanced again at Hunter. I'd never seen him like this before; gentle, understanding, almost paternal. "And as you've already made that choice, there's only one more question you need to ask yourself."

I waited.

His mouth quirked, his eyes narrowed, and there was the sexy weapons master I knew. "Who do you want walking beside you?"

"Oh, Hunter. I can't—"

"—ask me to do that," he interrupted again, rolling his eyes. "I know. But I'm the one doing the asking here. So. What's it going to be?"

"Yes." The word rushed out of me on a relieved exhale. Dying alone, after all, had such little appeal. "God, yes. Of course. If you're sure."

He smiled at me again, a grim little thing, and lifted a hand to brush back one of the tendrils hanging in my face. "You don't have to ask that either," he murmured.

Then he rose to leave, saying something about rest, that we'd leave the following dusk, but stopped in the doorway to send me a hard look over his shoulder. I pulled my eyes away from the shattered reflections of my many selves, and bit my lip. "I only ask one thing of you. Stay honest about your intentions. Anything less will kill us both."

I flushed because he felt he had to say it, even though I knew I deserved it after last night's hysterics, but lifted my chin in what I hoped was a convincingly determined look. "I want to bring Ian back. I want Ben safe. I want my . . . the child's safety ensured as well."

I said nothing about vengeance or making Joaquin pay for what he'd done to me. No request to let me be the one to kill him. I didn't say it because I finally saw those dreams for what they were: violent distractions. Finally Hunter nodded. "All right, then. Let's go get Joaquin."

He disappeared back into the living room, and I sipped my tea and let my eyes travel back to the mirror.

"Yes," I said, eyeing all my shattered selves. "Let's go get that bastard."

We found a portal a block away from Valhalla, and entered to find the world awash in a blanket of white.

"You've got to be shitting me," I said, testing the depth of the snow with one leather boot before glancing back at Hunter, still huddled in the doorway of the souvenir shop we'd come through. "We can't walk into that hotel and cross back to mortal reality with snow on our feet and in our hair. It'll be a dead giveaway."

"And the alternative is?" he asked wryly, looking at the snow like it was acid. "Walk through the front door?"

No, we couldn't do that. Now that Joaquin knew my real identity, he'd be looking for me—mask or no mask. This reality was still our best shot. "Let's find another portal."

He shook his head. "It's not the portal, it's the timing. It just happens to be snowing on this side of reality right now." He shuddered, and I don't think it had anything to do with the cold. Like me, Hunter was a desert rat. Anything this cold and white was simply . . . unnatural. "Can we wait it out?"

I glanced up at the thick blanket of clouds roiling overhead, and doubted it. This, along with the colorless landscape, was the other major difference on this side of reality. While the physical surroundings matched what one would find in the real world, the more fluid variables, like weather, were particularly unstable. Step through a portal on a bright blue summer day, and you were likely to find vicious winds circling the valley as if stalking their prey. A parched winter day might yield rainbows arching overhead, crisscrossing in shades of gray, though no less glorious for it. So while we might find a portal to enter closer to Valhalla, it would only minimize the trudge, but change nothing. Besides, this one had already sealed behind us.

"Let's go," I said reluctantly, and plodded out into the street, arms wrapped around my already chilled body. Across the road a shirtless kid skateboarded home in the dusk of his sweltering reality. I glanced back, following the dual footprints leading to the aural smears of light directly behind Hunter and me, and wished we had something to cover them with. The prints, not the smears. Those dissipated within seconds, though the vibrant colors seemed to hang longer in the heavy winter air, and I briefly wondered if the troops back east considered this a problem. Hunter followed the direction of my gaze and read my thoughts.

"Hindsight and all," he said, turning forward again.

"Yeah. I'll make a note to add snowshoes to my shopping list."

After that we fell silent, and I kept my mind off my numbing limbs by going through our plan to infiltrate Valhalla step by step. First, we had a good operative in Hunter, as he knew the property, was in uniform, and had already established the habit of varying his shifts. His colleagues wouldn't think twice at him showing up for the swing shift on a Tuesday night, though we were hoping he wouldn't have to show himself on that side of reality at all. I'd follow behind him as we tried to locate the same portal we'd found weeks earlier, and see if there was an antidote to the virus somewhere in that lab. That was our first priority.

Second, one of us had to search out a secondary portal while the other was busy in the lab. I hated to split up, but if Ian and my computer were being held in Valhalla, as I suspected they were, it was the most expedient way to conduct a search of the vast property, despite doubling the prospects of running into a Shadow agent. If that happened, and I thought that a big *if* since the Shadows all still seemed to be on their extended summer vacations, I expected to encounter only one at most. And there were still two of us.

Finally, we had to find a way to move Ian and the computer off property, and that would probably be the trickiest part. Ian was mortal and could only be moved along the natural plane, but we'd have to deal with contingencies as they came. I was ticking through the various ways that scenario could play out when Hunter suddenly spoke.

"Uh-oh."

I stopped dead in my tracks. "What 'uh-oh'?"

"I thought this might happen. You're bleeding again."

"Wha—? Fuck. No!" I whirled around myself, first one way, then the other. "Why me? Why not you?"

"Thanks for your concern," he replied wryly, before pointing at the ground where crimson-colored aura pooled around my feet. "They must have the place sensored or something, to alert them to your presence on this plane. I thought it might be all of us—all agents of Light, I mean— but they probably don't have a DNA sample for each of the agents of Light, so it must be just you."

"But how would they have a sample of my—"

I broke off and met Hunter's steady eyes, realization dawning in tandem. "The Tulpa," we said at the same time.

"They must've used some of his DNA, some skin cells or something to experiment with."

"How does an imagined being have DNA to start with?" I said, frustrated with the logic.

"How do imagined walls have molecules to keep them upright?" he countered, trudging ahead. "Besides, he's not imaginary anymore. And now we know there's something worth guarding in there. We're on the right track."

"Who cares if I'm not even allowed on the train?" I grimaced, lifting my feet higher as I walked, as if that would keep my aura from staining the pristine snowbanks. Berry slushies.

"Gonna let something like a little bleeding aura stop you?" he said teasingly.

"Easy for you to say," I almost snarled. "Your aura's packed tighter than a can of tuna."

He shrugged, turning back to trudge ahead of me, shooting over his shoulder, "All we have to do is get you inside so you can access one of the interior portals."

"Oh, is that *all?*"

"Here's what I'm thinking," he said, ignoring my sarcasm. His stride was longer than mine but I stretched to fit in his footprints, hoping to ease the chill around my ankles every time I took a step. "I go in, in uniform, and scout out the portals first. Once I have their locations, I call you inside."

"Yeah, because yelling out 'Joanna Archer' in the middle of the craps pit won't be at all obvious."

Smirking, he held out a palm-sized device. "I'll call you with this."

I halted, took the remote, and clicked the button on the side, speaking clearly into the slats. "A walkie-talkie?" My voice sounded from somewhere near his ass area.

Hunter reached behind him and pulled out its twin. "Not just a walkie-talkie, but one identical to those used by Valhalla security, in all ways but two. First, I set it to a channel only the two of us can access. Even if the signal's detected, they won't be able to locate it until we're long gone."

Okay, so I was impressed, but I had my badass superhero face on, and wasn't about to show it. "And second?"

"Second," he retorted, just as badass, "you're the only one who can use it. Anyone else depresses that button, and the device explodes, taking a limb with it."

I grinned. "Nasty."

"I take it you approve."

My smile widened. "So where am I going to be hiding with my handy-dandy explosive device while you're locating the portals?"

"Parking garage," he said, and held up a hand before I could protest. "The floors are monitored by cameras, but they only capture certain angles. The stairwell can't be viewed at all. The third level leads directly into the video arcade. I figure with all the noise and sound and color, that'll be the least likely place you and your bleeding aura will be noticed. From there, we make a quick sprint to the first portal, and we're off."

We started trudging forward again. The Strip seemed a lot longer covered in snow. "Wow, got it all figured out, don't you?"

"As best I could given time and resources."

And it sounded good. He must've been refining the details while I was doing my *Exorcist* imitation the night before. "So that's all we need," I said, sighing. "You on the inside, me with an explosive toy, and a half dozen portals to choose from."

"And luck," Hunter added, over his shoulder. "Don't forget Lady Luck."

"That fickle bitch?" I muttered, slipping the walkie-talkie into my black cargo pocket. "How could I ever forget her?"

Valhalla's parking garage was planted at the end of a road veering off from the more accessible valet entrance, and stacked like a concrete layer cake, with different colors and numbers to help guests remember which floor they'd parked on. There was nothing nefarious to indicate it was any different than any other garage along the Strip. In fact, the most ominous thing was the lack of vehicles housed within the normally packed floors. Valhalla was suffering the effects of the valley virus as much as any other property, which had to suck for the hotel's shareholders, but happily decreased my chances of being observed by mortal or agent alike.

Unfortunately, I thought as I settled beneath a metal stairwell, it also meant the casino floor would be less crowded. My red wig and sunglasses were pretty slapdash and would go only so far to shield my identity. I may have scoffed at the notion of Lady Luck, but Hunter was right. The precautions we'd already taken were no guarantee this all wouldn't blow up in our faces once it was set into motion.

I passed the time by concentrating on pulling my energy inward, finding a place of balance mortals had to spend hours in yoga or meditation to achieve. I'd learned to reach it in seconds, and hold it for hours. Within five minutes I felt like the inside of a smoky crystal ball. My exterior felt fragile compared to the power swirling inside me, like a storm was swelling, brewing in . . .

Oh, for fuck's sake. I frowned as a sound broke through my serene centeredness. There it was again. Laughter—joyous and innocent, like the tinkle of tiny chimes in a soft spring wind. I rose from my hiding spot, swiftly looked about, then darted to the edge of the parking structure to peer over the side from where the sound had risen.

Buh-bye Buddha, because there she was, a full-fledged Shadow agent, pheromones wafting from her like heated sunflowers, the power from her recent metamorphosis snapping around her in invisible sparks. Even with her back to me Regan DuPree appeared lighthearted, smiling up at a man, arm linked in his, strolling into the hotel without a care in the world. She'd changed her appearance drastically, though she looked moderately familiar . . . probably, I thought, because I'd recognize her anywhere. Her hair had been chopped short, and now framed her face in an auburn bob. She'd kept her compact build, though, eschewing the femme fatale look for something a little more streamlined.

I sighted her within the crosshairs of my conduit, and almost blew out the back of her pretty little head, but caught myself when I realized there was the issue of the mortal witness standing next to her. I tore my eyes away from the new, improved Regan, and inhaled deeply as my eyes fell on the back of the man's head. For a moment my eyes and nose warred with one another. I couldn't assign any olfactory or visual meaning to what my senses were telling me. It was like picking up a glass and expecting to take a sip of milk, only to realize too late that you were drinking wine.

But the confusion lasted only a moment. It was a long, drawn-out moment, to be sure; the longest of my life. But it would never take longer than that for me to recognize Ben Traina.

"No," I whispered, as that bell-like laugh drifted up to me again.

The exhalation cost me. Regan whipped around, and I ducked behind the concrete wall, squeezing my eyes shut against the vision of Regan clutching Ben's arm . . . and him smiling back down at her.

What was he—? And why—? And how could he—?

But I knew what, and why, and how. Hadn't he spelled it out to me in our recent night together? *Don't leave me again. I can't take anymore.*

But I had left him, hadn't I? Left him to wake alone again, with nothing but a note that essentially read, *Don't call me, I'll call you.*

And now he'd ended up with Regan. Even in my addled state I put it together easily. She had studied me and my past, and had targeted my lover. She was the woman he'd been talking to on the computer. She was Rose.

And she looked familiar, I thought, because she'd altered her appearance to look like me. The Joanna me.

"I'm gonna kill her. I'm gonna fucking . . ."

I was rising to take aim again, give chase if I had to, when a family of five stepped out of the garage elevator. As I ducked behind a red Buick while they made their way to their car; luggage, two children, and an infant in tow, the interruption gave me a moment to remember why I was there, and forced me to admit I couldn't do anything about

Ben and Regan right now. Not with Hunter counting on me, and the entire valley's survival at stake.

Later, I told myself, trying to find that Zen-like place I'd been in before Regan's laugh had broken through. I returned to the stairwell and slowed my breathing. I calmed myself, sought full enlightenment . . . and swore on my life to rip that bitch's every limb from her brand-new body.

31

"Where have you been?"

Hunter fell into step beside me as I winged past a full-sized stock car where five boys were goading each other on, bright lights and screeching wheels accompanying their raucous yells. The rest of the arcade was empty, the games huddled forlornly in the cavelike room, intermittent beeps punctuating the too-silent air in discontent. I decided now wasn't the time to clue him in about Regan and Ben. We both needed to focus, and the best thing I could do for Ben was find that serum. "Find the portals?" I asked instead.

"Three of them, one close to the last known entry into the lab. We'll start there."

By now we'd hit the casino floor. I was mildly surprised to see how much action the slots were getting, the diehards still getting their fix as the city sank around them. More surprising was the stench, a smell similar to petrol on the fingertips. I was about to ask what it was when I realized the answer was staring me in the face. Nearly every person in the casino was wearing an invisible mask of black smoke . . . invisible, that was, on their side of reality. On this side their infections were blatant. I saw oblivious people marked for death, blithely pouring money into machines while death poured from their throats, their pores, and out onto the casino floor. My aura could barely be seen through the haze.

"This is disgusting," I said, trying not to think about all the airborne diseases I *wasn't* seeing. Hunter, too busy scanning the room for agents, only grunted something about not kissing them. I grimaced and held my breath for as long as possible.

"There," he said, pointing. "See it?"

I did. A tiny pinprick of luminosity stood out even above carousels of blinking bulbs and chandeliers splintering light in a thousand different directions.

"The men's bathroom," I said, wryly. "Someone has a sense of humor."

"Maybe I should go in first," Hunter said, taking the lead. "It could be a trap."

"Right. So you can blow your cover. That makes sense," I jostled him with my shoulder to cut off his reply and unholstered my conduit, taking the shooter's stance as we flanked the doorway. "Besides, I'm the one whose aura is sliming the place like a melted Popsicle."

His mouth turned down as he watched the color pooling at my still feet, before giving a short nod, and I pivoted into the bathroom. His voice followed me back into the mortal reality. "Use the radio once you get there."

A sucking noise sounded behind me, the portal sealing shut, and just like that I was back in full Technicolor. I inhaled, whirled, whirled again, quickly ascertaining that I was, for the moment, alone. But where?

Obviously offices of some sort, I thought, once my eyes adjusted to the dimness of the windowless room. Partitioned cubicles, ten in all, stretched across the floor, with a break room smelling of burned popcorn and stale coffee, and half a sheet of uneaten cake in the shared fridge. Closed for the evening, these offices were part of the administration; marketing, accounting, benefits, something like that. I found a stack of applications, a photo ID machine, and cabinets filled with employee files. Human resources. I lifted my radio from my belt and spoke into the receiver.

"How do you feel about birthday cake?"

There was a long pause, then a crackle of static, and Hunter's voice squawked back. "Is that code for 'Help, the bad guys got me'?"

"No, it's code for 'I'm safe and sound but I'm locked in the HR office and don't know where to go from here.'"

"Coulda been worse. That's still the ground floor. I'll come and get you."

Three minutes later the lock snicked open on the front office, and Hunter appeared . . . or *almost* appeared. His outline materialized in front of me first, a gray-blue shimmer that solidified into lines with no more dimension than a stick figure's, features sketchy, like a cartoon. Or a comic book. Even as someone who'd traveled both sides of this reality, I don't think I'd have known he was there if I hadn't been expecting him.

"Gee, Hunt, you're looking a little washed out. Chin up, though. I'm sure we'll have better luck with the next portal."

He rolled his normally dark eyes, now marbles of arctic ice, and led me down the hall without reply. My wit might have been intact, but my luck didn't fare as well. Though I made it through the casino in my wig and glasses without attracting notice, the second portal was located inside the storage freezer in the kitchen of Antoine Ferrare, the famous French chef. I hid behind a crate of plates readied to be run through the industrial-sized dishwasher, waiting for the place to clear long enough to make a run for the freezer. It never did, though, and I had to settle for turned backs while Hunter held open the door, a surprised yell following me into deep freeze before the portal sealed shut behind me.

Inside I found low ceilings, fluorescent lighting and stainless steel shelving. I knocked empty cabinet doors closed with my knees, and pushed shut drawers as I made my way around the partition cutting the room in half.

"I'm in," I said into my radio, then exhaled deeply as I lowered it to my side. I'd found the lab again, but even in the gray-smeared landscape of reality's flip side, I could see there were no penned-in primates to trumpet my arrival. Both cages and creatures were gone, with only the toxic scent of ammonia to complement the sinking feeling in my stomach.

I told Hunter to wait while I had a look around, though it was more to give me time to overcome my disappointment than out of any hope I'd find anything. I slammed the doors on a metal cabinet and glanced up at the ceiling, down at the floor, and in all four corners to make sure I was missing nothing. Not a vial, not a note, not even the cap to a ballpoint pen. I bet if I dusted the place, I wouldn't find a single print.

"Well?" came Hunter's prompt over the radio.

"Fastidious fuckers," I replied, and winced at his responding sigh.

"I don't know where it is so I can't come get you."

"That's all right," I said, spotting a tiny star blinking above the exit door. "I'll find you."

I sent a final, searching look around the room, cursed again under my breath, and returned to the mortal reality using the same door I had before. This time the anteroom was dark; no alarms to trip, no armed men racing down the stairs to guard against intruders.

And this time there was a vial of etched crystal spotlighted on a coffee table in the center of the room.

I took a step toward it, studying the deep crimson liquid inside. Like blood, I thought, reaching for it. Like the serum, I knew, because I could scent the same yeasty compound now living inside me. My hand had just cleared the outer rim of the spotlight when another opposite me snatched the vial faster than I could blink.

I dropped the radio on the floor while my weapon hand came up, firing eight clean arrows into the dark, hearing some sink into fabric—the couch I'd hidden behind before—and others burrow into flesh. I backed up as I fired until I could duck behind the high desk. My breathing was ragged in the ensuing silence. Damn, not one of my senses had kicked into overdrive. Why hadn't I known anyone was there?

There was a sucking sound, followed by a rattle. A second followed. Then a third. Movement? Labored breathing? A slow death?

I glanced at the beveled mirror mounted behind the desk, which showed arrows being tossed onto the spotlit table, bloodless, though I knew they'd just come from someone's body. That someone leaned forward, and though the rest of him remained cloaked in darkness, a grin flashed like the Cheshire cat's.

"Thank you, dear," a voice said, and a single hand joined that smile, the vial flipping carelessly in bone-white fingers. "I take my power where I can get it."

"Tulpa," I whispered, mouth going dry.

The smile widened, the hand gestured. "Call me Pa."

Fuck. I tucked away my conduit because I knew it wouldn't help. The Tulpa couldn't be killed by supernatural means, as unconventional as they were. In fact, from his comment I gathered it was exactly the opposite; he gained more power from the energy expended trying to kill him. I considered making a run for it, but there was that damned mirror. I could be seen crouched behind that desk just as easily as I could see him, and right now I felt the Tulpa's gaze burrowing into me, probing behind my wig and glasses. I swallowed hard. Hiding wasn't going to help me either. He could knock this desk through the back wall with a kiss, and I was alive now simply because he willed it.

So I took a deep, steadying breath and stood.

He sat in the middle of the couch, same as before, leaning forward only enough to reveal those pearly whites, elegant hands currently splayed across his knees. He linked them as I approached, letting me know he'd do nothing to impede my progress . . . for now. The vial sat gleaming, back in the spotlight.

The radio squawked on the floor between. "Jo? You heading out?"

I stifled a sigh, frozen in place. Thank God Hunter had used my real name. Thank God he *knew* it.

"You should answer that," the Tulpa said, voice deep and deceptively reasonable.

I had to answer it. Worse than revealing my identity, Hunter might slip and reveal his own. I might be momentarily spared a gruesome death, but such hospitality, I knew, wouldn't extend to other agents of Light.

I bent, eyes ever on those hands as I lifted the radio. Not that it would do any good. I was unarmed. He was the Tulpa. I weighed the risks, decided I had nothing to lose, and held the device out to the Tulpa. "Why don't you answer it? He works for you."

For a moment I thought he'd take the bait. I didn't know how much an explosive device would hurt the Tulpa, but it'd create a powerful distraction. There was a discreet sniffing— like a hound on the trail of deer's spoor—and a disappointed sigh. He leaned back, disappearing, and when he spoke again, that calm voice had honed to an edge.

"Tell your partner to join us. All he has to do is take the south elevators to the basement floor. I'll wait."

Then Hunter's voice again. "Hey, you there?"

I couldn't tell him I was with the Tulpa. He'd tear the building apart trying to find me, and I was already past the point of rescue. I was at the mercy of a being who didn't even know the meaning of the word. I lifted the radio to my mouth and pressed the button.

"Let's abort. No more communication. Meet me back at my place in thirty." I clicked off the radio before Hunter could respond and tucked it back into my belt. Thirty minutes was long enough that whatever was going to happen to me would be a distant memory before Hunter realized I wasn't coming home.

"Willing to go it alone in order to save your partner. Admirable, Joanna. You've grown more confident since we last met."

I stared into the void where my father's face was hidden, and found the courage to speed my fate along. It wasn't that I wanted to die. I just couldn't see a clear way out of it this time.

"Scared?" I asked, my tone nearly haughty enough to rival his.

He chuckled, a big change from the last time I'd sassed him and he'd responded by nearly blowing the lungs from my chest. "Not particularly."

"But interested." I was his Achilles' heel, and we both knew it.

He leaned forward, and black marble eyes narrowed on mine. "Always that."

I swallowed hard and looked at him for the first time. Other than the creepy gaze and malleable features, he was disappointingly normal; tanned—large, of course, I'd expected no less—with a crop of salt-and-pepper hair that looked like it'd curl if it ever grew long. Damn. I hadn't expected him to be handsome. "I'd be flattered, but seeing as how the first interest you showed in me nearly got me killed, I'll go ahead and reserve judgment."

"That which doesn't kill you serves to make you stronger," he said flippantly, pulling at his cuffs. Gorgeous suit. So soft it almost looked buttery. "What I want to know is what took you so long? You entered the property almost an hour ago. Ever hear how I hate to be kept waiting?"

The bleeding aura. Not just his DNA identifying mine, but a tracking device? I didn't want to ask. I was already down, and we were in the ninth, so I just shrugged the question away, trying to look relaxed.

His voice sharpened again. "I find your reticence surprising since the last time we met you were extremely vocal about . . . what was it? Annihilating the entire Shadow Zodiac, including myself?" He tilted his head, and I saw a lock of dark hair shadow his forehead. "How's that going for you?"

"'Bout the same as your vow to hunt down and kill my mother," I said, and had the satisfaction of watching that blinding smile drop. There were Achilles' heels . . . and then there were just plain sore spots. The jab gave me confidence.

"Speaking of enemies," I said, taking another step forward. "You might want to cull your ranks. One of your newer agents seems to have taken a liking to playing both sides."

Take that, you stupid bitch, I thought, an evil sort of pleasure warming at the thought of outing Regan to the leader of the underworld. But the Tulpa just spread his hands in a helpless gesture. "Ah, youth."

My jaw tightened. "She's the one who killed the Piscean Shadow," I said, not wanting to give him Regan's name outright. It was childish, I know, but I wanted to make him ask for it. "She told me about the virus. And gave me Joaquin's home address."

I folded my arms and waited for his response.

"And what?" he finally asked, each syllable rolling languidly over his tongue. "You think it was innate talent or wisdom or *experience* that allowed her to think of all that on her own? Why, what a clever girl that would be."

I blinked and couldn't keep my mouth from dropping open. "You knew? But to allow the death of one of your agents . . ."

"A sacrifice for the greater good," he said, elegant hands linking together again, tone all too reasonable. "Regan had to gain your trust. And you had to take her bait. From there it was easy to deduce where your hate for Joaquin would lead you. Your mind is analytical and pure, Joanna."

He meant straightforward and simple. I narrowed my eyes. "You had her set me up."

He shook his head, his index finger swaying side to side with it. "Uh-uh-uh. I told her to find you"—again, that helpless shrug—"she took it from there."

Joanna. Not once had he used my cover name. And he would've, right? I asked myself. Had he known the Olivia Archer identity, he'd want me to know he knew. So maybe he was right and his brilliant little charge had taken well to her role, improvising more than a bit. Playing two sides would suit a woman seeking to make her own name among the Shadow ranks. The Kairos's identity was information she believed no one else in her troop had, and I bet she was holding that card close to her chest. It was a good theory, anyway. One I'd keep to myself for now.

"You don't look like I thought you would," I said, changing the subject.

He actually smiled at that. "Sure I do."

"No," I said, shaking my head. I'd expected him to look regal or something, literally larger than life. Instead he looked like one of the guidos who used to run this town . . . which made me think, contrary to the evidence, that his creator had absolutely no imagination whatsoever. "You don't."

"Joanna. You've been in our world long enough to realize expectations create reality."

"So?" I asked smartly, not liking the fatherly tone he was taking with me. Too late for that. Nearly killing me had blunted the appeal.

"So what exactly is it you think you're seeing?"

I drew back, knowing my surprise was written all over my face. "You're saying I'm projecting what I expect to see onto you?"

"What you *want* to see," he corrected, leaning onto his knees, giving me a clearer look. My eyes raced over his face.

"So the dirty guinea mobster before me doesn't really exist in this form outside my imagination?" I said, grimacing. That would mean it was *my* imagination that was lacking.

The Tulpa was inspecting his reflection in the mirror behind me, and sighed before turning back to me. "It's to be expected, I guess. A wop is benign for a Vegas girl. Fatherly.

I'm none of those things, of course. I should abuse you of the notion by chopping off your limbs and feeding them to my new sharks."

I swallowed hard. "Should probably leave a severed horse's head at the foot of my bed," I agreed. "But won't."

"And why wouldn't I?"

I was next to him in a flash, leaning over the coffee table before he even had a chance to lean back. He did lean forward, though, and I found myself nose to nose with the Tulpa. Up close, the similarities were startling. Up close, I thought, you could see the eyes nailing our bloodline in place.

"Because you're enjoying this conversation too much," I whispered. "And because . . . *You. Owe. Me.*"

His nostrils flared. "But you're holding up your end of this conversation just fine. Perhaps because you know I can give you more power than Warren can even dream of possessing. I can teach you the history of the Shadow side, the full legacy of the Kairos." He lowered his chin and leveled me with a knowing look. "With what I can give you, you'll drink your enemies' blood for breakfast, and sup on the bones of those you despise. I can promise that, and I never break my word."

I straightened, shaking my head, even though I knew doing so was my death sentence. "I don't want a damned thing from you."

He smirked. "Nothing?"

"Nothing."

"Are you sure?"

Before I could ask what he meant, he broke eye contact. His eyes fluttered shut, and I could see them working like minnows beneath his lids. When he opened them again I wanted to ask what he'd done, what magic he'd conjured. Where the buzzing in my veins had come from. But I didn't have to. A door slammed above us, then footsteps pounded down the stairs, and the smell alone—nauseatingly sweet— was enough to tell me Joaquin had arrived. The Tulpa was watching me for a reaction, but I only allowed my hands to ball into fists behind my back.

"You can call people to you without picking up a phone?" I said, both pleased and surprised to hear my voice was even and normal since I was now standing in a room with my two greatest enemies.

"I can," the Tulpa said, "and so can you."

"Control your thoughts and you control your reality," I said, the residual electricity from his magic still thrumming in my veins. It felt good.

"What is thought but another form of energy?" he said, seeing this, his words eerily close to Tekla's. Neither of us had acknowledged Joaquin yet, and he shifted on his feet, though he made no move to speak. It must have rankled. "As a man who was once nothing but gray matter passing through the mind of one individual, I can tell you that applied thought is enough to move mountains."

"That doesn't mean she can do it," Joaquin interrupted, revealing his discontent.

"I'm his daughter," I said, turning to him for the first time. He was wearing a suit too, though it wasn't as fine as the Tulpa's. His hands were behind his back, possibly an unconscious mirroring of mine, so all that was visible of his body was the slim neck and long face, his thin lips pressed together, not a hair out of place. "I'm the Kairos. I can do anything I set my mind to." I let loose so he could see the resemblance between dear ol' dad and me, and it must've been more impressive than it'd been in Master Comics, because he jerked back. Delight thrilled through me.

The Tulpa chuckled. "Come with me, Joanna, and I'll show you how."

I kept my eyes on Joaquin. "I already told you no."

"Come with me now and I'll give you Joaquin on a platter."

For the second time, Joaquin was jolted, and looked from the Tulpa to me and back again. I had to smile. Then I had to smother it because the Tulpa smiled in return. It was one thing for Joaquin to think we were symbiotic, it was another to let my erstwhile father believe I'd caved even an inch.

I clenched my hands into fists, arms ramrod straight at my side, and told him evenly, "If you think you can just waltz into my life after twenty-five years, you'd better apply your thought in a different direction. I don't roll that easily. I don't come when called. And I don't take from others what I intend to get for myself. Don't think I don't remember who sent him after me in the first place."

"That was Zoe's fault!" he exploded, and those black eyes flared to life, bright flames of fire dancing in the pupils, smoke pouring from his mouth. Shit, but his fuse was short. "She should've told me about you."

"Fine, it's Zoe's fault," I allowed, choking on the dusty air as I waved my hand in front of my face. Talk about bad breath. It was the Tulpa's turn to look surprised. "She's not exactly on my Christmas card list either. But, you know"— and I mimicked his shrug here—"you're here. She's not. So you get the brunt of my overdue adolescent rebellion."

"Vendettas are the most unstable form of power," he said gravely. Oh goody, a lesson in morality from Mr. Evil himself. I barely contained my eye roll. "If you proceed in this fashion you may get what you desire, but I can't promise it won't come at a deep price."

I crossed my arms and pretended to consider that, glancing from him to Joaquin and back again. "So make me a different promise," I finally said.

He leaned back on the couch, his face disappearing back into the shadows so I could no longer read his expression. It didn't matter. That movement alone told me all I needed to know. Joaquin swallowed hard, seeing it as well. "Would it be enough to bring you over to the Shadow side?" the Tulpa asked, voice disembodied. "Allow me to show you firsthand what I'm willing to bequeath to you?"

"Yes," I said immediately. "Right now."

The Tulpa straightened where he sat. Joaquin froze.

"Name it," the Tulpa said, instantly back in the light. I barely kept from smiling.

"You always honor your promises, right?" It was rhetorical, but he nodded anyway. I echoed the movement. "So allow my mother to come out of hiding. Give her your solemn word that you'll never hunt or harm her, or seek vengeance for the destruction of your maker. Let her live a normal life in peace, or return to the agents of Light to take up the Archer star sign when I leave."

Slowly he leaned back again. "No."

One side of my mouth quirked. "Not even for the Kairos?"

"You're trying my patience, daughter," he said as the room filled with smoke again. "Don't test me."

I gave as good as I got, lowering my own voice as I allowed my Shadow side to respond; I was that pissed. "Then don't lecture me about vendettas. You've got more to lose, and you'd risk it all without a second thought for a shot at Zoe Archer."

Joaquin began to choke, and even though every air molecule in the room had been flooded with our combined anger, I could breathe just fine beneath this mask of shadows. Another power I hadn't known I possessed. As for my words—and the lengthy silence coming from that darkened corner—I wasn't worried. If the Tulpa was going to kill me, he'd already have done it, and I wouldn't be able to scent him at all.

"I can see you're willing to sacrifice your life for the cause of the Light," he finally said, his voice deceptively reasonable. "And you can see I'm not willing to let you do that."

"So we've reached a stalemate. Again."

"Not necessarily," he said, and gestured Joaquin over to his side like he was a dog expected to heel. Joaquin didn't look happy rounding out our sordid little triangle, though he put on a brave face when he caught me watching.

"Sure you don't want to join the Shadows, Joanna?" he said, and I frowned, momentarily distracted by his use of my real name. An automatic response? Or hadn't he told the Tulpa of my identity yet either?

"Why?" I asked him coldly. "You want to kiss and make up?"

He managed a leer. "You guessed part of it anyway."

I feigned a yawn and looked back at the Tulpa. He leaned over and pushed the vial of serum my way. That perked me right up, and I looked up to find his gaze, dark again, boring into mine. "Go on. It's what you're here for, isn't it? Want to save the world, daughter? Risk your own life to get back in good with your pathetic troop? Give a second chance to thousands of unworthy souls?"

"Innocents," I corrected, which earned me a rueful smile. My fingers itched as I looked at the vial.

"Sure," he scoffed. "The vermin filling my casino with their death breath are so innocent. The street hookers and the pedophiles, and your fellow partyers at the swingers' ball, they're *all* innocent."

I jerked my head. "They deserve a chance. They deserve a choice."

"Hm," he said, his voice filled with false remorse. "And all they have is you."

Joaquin's gaze met mine. *What the hell was that supposed to mean?*

"And you," the Tulpa said to him, catching the movement. "I don't think even I'll live to see the day when you act out of concern or loyalty for someone other than yourself. You have all the depth of a wading pool. All the devotion of a rabid cat."

"Sir?" Joaquin frowned, swallowing hard. The Tulpa ignored him, turning back to me.

"Unfortunately," he said breezily, "you're one of mine, and she's not. Then again, she's my only blood, and you're not. Some would say her stubbornness is an inherited trait— hard to dispute—but just in case that stubbornness comes from her fucking mother's side and not mine, I'm going to give both of you a chance."

His teeth gleamed again in the sole spotlight. "It should end the way it began, don't you think? The two of you, out in the desert night." He held the cylindrical vial aloft. "The future of the valley lies in this little bottle. If Joaquin wins, he'll be credited with the destruction of Las Vegas and its inhabitants. He'll go down in the manuals as one of the greatest villains of all time."

My eyes flicked to Joaquin and I could tell immediately the idea appealed to him. He'd do anything to star in the manuals he so eagerly devoured. "I get to kill her too, right?"

"Oh yes."

I smirked. "Thanks, Pop."

His attention stayed trained on Joaquin. "Daughter or not—Kairos or not—if she can be killed by the likes of you, I don't want her."

I didn't know who was supposed to be more insulted by that, Joaquin or me. I cleared my throat. "And if I win?"

Carelessly he pointed the vial my way, like nothing precious lay between his fingertips. "You'll earn the antidote, save all the living, supernatural or not, and we're back to where we started. Balanced and even, each side fighting for dominance while we wait for the third sign of the Zodiac to be revealed."

Joaquin cracked his knuckles. "So, combat, then? Mano a mano?"

I shook my head slowly, eyes narrowed on the Tulpa. "That's not it, is it?"

Joaquin snorted. "Afraid?"

I snorted back. "Hey, asswipe. If you haven't noticed, I'm not the one making the rules." I turned back to the Tulpa. "Hand combat is too simple, too fast, too . . . pedestrian for dear old Dad's taste. Right?"

"I'd prefer it if you didn't call me old, but other than that . . ." He shrugged and began flipping the precious vial through his fingers again, bloodred and crystal flashing between the tanned skin.

Joaquin turned to stare at him. "So what then?"

"A race," he answered shortly, voice emptied of all emotion, like he had nothing invested in the outcome. "A flight among the streets you two have canvassed more thoroughly than any other agents. You're looking for this."

He withdrew another vial from his pocket, uncapped it, and waited while Joaquin and I inhaled, each fighting to make out the scent inside first. I closed my eyes, despite the immediate dangers in the room, and focused on ferreting out the olfactory thread leaking from that bottle, separating it from the others, drawing it through my pores. Almonds, chalk, soured milk, and starch. My eyes flipped open. "Ian."

If it was possible, Joaquin looked even more surprised than I. "But he's—"

"He's what, Joaquin?" the Tulpa said sharply. "Locked away? Fettered in your secret hideaway, safe from all prying eyes?"

Joaquin swallowed hard. A taut undercurrent shimmered in the air, friction between the two men, an unspoken animosity that I'd have been able to capitalize on if I'd known about it sooner. Still, it might not be too late. Shit, it might be just the thing that was giving me this chance now. I shifted, leaning on my left leg, hoping I looked like I was simply altering my stance, though inching closer to Joaquin in the process.

"So when do we start?" I asked, shifting again.

"Now."

"Now?" Joaquin repeated, still numbed by the Tulpa's hostility.

"Now," I said, and my left arm ratcheted down as my right leg whipped out, a perfectly timed sidekick containing all the momentum I could muster from a motionless position. I caught Joaquin in the side of the head and he crumpled, out before he'd even hit the floor.

The Tulpa laughed. "I assume that was for the *afraid* remark."

"Among other things," I said dryly.

My hand shifted to my conduit, but the Tulpa shook his head, making a *tsk*ing sound. "Not until you're out of the building. Until then, I suggest you use your lead wisely. He won't be out for long."

I didn't have to be told twice. I ran, taking the stairs two at a time. He was right, I thought, bursting through the stairwell door. I'd use my lead to find Ian, secure the vial, and save the known world. Murdering Joaquin could wait a little longer.

32

The Tulpa let me have my head start, but he didn't make it easy on me. I exploded into the casino and shot for the front entrance as quickly as my legs would take me. It wasn't as precarious a trip as it would've been had the casino been packed, but I still had to dodge geriatric gamblers and jaded cocktail waitresses while careening past slot banks, all of which nearly slowed me down to a mortal's pace. A woman running helter-skelter through a casino would've caught attention in any case, but I'd had the feeling of being watched from the moment I stepped back on the tacky carpeting, and my guess was that the Tulpa's telepathic skills extended to mortals. Two Valhalla guards—not Shadows, just guards—were waiting for me as I whipped through the lobby, and another pair stood at the ready, guarding the front exit.

I dodged the first, ignoring their yells as they fell in behind me, and if I'd been darting down the fifty-yard line, I'd have been home free. The second pair were more of a worry.

They expected me to dodge, or alter my direction. Instead I ducked, barreling directly into the first man's legs, flipping him over the top of me with the force of my momentum.

Releasing him, I palmed the ground and swept the second guard's legs out from under him as he came at me. Then I gained my feet and burst through the front doors, rounding a corner to press myself against the outside wall, and tried to look casual. The dozen or so people waiting in the taxi queue stared.

I smiled back as I sniffed at the air, which was too still to catch more than a skein of Ian's scent, but I determined it led north, back into the center of town. I filled my lungs and blew south. Then I waited.

"Your wig's crooked," a helpful onlooker said.

I straightened it as sound erupted behind me. Joaquin appeared seconds later, and as predicted, swung south. I raised my conduit and shot. He stepped forward, and the arrow whizzed past him. Somebody screamed. Joaquin put a hand to his ear—just clipped, dammit—and whirled my way as I raced forward. I caught him with a kick to his solar plexus, and spun to plant my right elbow in the center of his face. He went down again as hands grabbed me from behind.

Time for some girly moves. I rammed my heel into the foot of one guard, then nailed him in the temple, and when his grip slipped, spun to grasp the neck of the other. I had time to register the surprise on his face before my knee came up, his head went down, and he joined his partner in la-la land. Then, before any more backup could arrive, I ran, and this time I didn't stop.

Dodging the sirens already screaming toward Valhalla, I abandoned the main thoroughfares for little-used roadways where rock and bramble sprouted up between potholes and busted-out streetlights. At one point, when I sensed I was getting closer to Ian, but with no clear passageway to the other side of Flamingo Road, I had to skirt two chain-link fences and run along the freeway, car horns honking as they blew by me in the opposite direction.

When I finally reached the corner of Tumaric and Pollack Street, the desperate terror infusing Ian's pheromones was so strong I could practically see it. The olfactory trail broke off at an abandoned warehouse framed in concrete and chipped pink stucco, accessible by only one door.

"I know this place," I whispered, circling it twice just to make sure this was it, while drawing my conduit. I'd seen it before, but more, I sensed it. A psychic smear blanketed the building like a mental chalk outline. It was thin now, the kill spot tinny with age, but the hereditary thread of the one killed here was well known to me. "Stryker."

Was this a deliberate choice by the Tulpa? Did the location have some increased meaning or power, because Stryker died here? Or because it had been Joaquin who'd killed him? Or was it just a random building, useful because it was both central and abandoned, and nothing more nefarious than that?

I sighed. Sometimes it sucked being the new superhero on the block.

Still, super is as super does, so I kicked in the steel-plated door and ducked aside as it crashed to the ground, waiting for gunfire, booby traps, or whatever else the Tulpa had tucked in there along with Ian. The silence deafened. Not even an alarm to cut through the night. "Ian?"

Still nothing. I was sure he was in there . . . but if he was dead, if those leaky, fearful pheromones were phantom scents, I was going to be pissed. And heartsick. The Tulpa would know that, I thought with a sick twinge.

"Ian," I tried again. "It's me! Olivia!"

A scratch of movement, and if whimpers could sound hopeful, this one did. "O-Olivia?"

I sighed in relief. "Is anyone in there with you?"

"No. No, they left me alone." His voice raised an octave. "I've been here for hours. Please help me."

"I will, Ian. Just tell me . . . are there any alarms that you can see? Booby traps? Cages?"

"No, nothing. Just me, and I'm tied up. Please hurry."

Well, you'd think I'd do just that, wouldn't you? After all, I was the one who'd gotten Ian captured, kidnapped, and trussed up like a sow at the county fair. But just because it sounded like a nerdy computer geek, and smelled like one—and presumably looked like one—didn't mean it was necessarily so. Just because he said there were no agents waiting to ensnare me didn't mean they weren't there.

I took a deep breath and peered through the doorway. The dim interior matched the nightscape outside, so I didn't need time for my eyes to adjust. I stared, then stared harder, before tilting my head wonderingly. "How clever."

Besides a cement floor, concrete walls, and a steel-beamed ceiling dotted with shattered and tilted light fixtures, the building was entirely empty. Ian sat dwarfed in a room a quarter the size of a football field, hunched in a steel chair that must have lost its comfort about half a second after he'd been tied there. They hadn't gagged him, knowing nobody would hear his cries on a lonely night in a warehouse the city had all but forgotten. His face was tear-streaked, eyes wild as he looked at me from behind shattered glasses, and his shirt bloodied from a fat lip. And tousled wouldn't even begin to describe his hair. I had to get him out of here before Joaquin arrived.

But first I had to make sure this was really Ian. "Name the event you were supposed to compete in this weekend."

"You're not Olivia," he said slowly.

"Oh," I unpinned the red wig from my head, tossing it in a corner as I smoothed back the wisps of blond, sweaty hair that had escaped from my bun. "See?"

He started screaming for me to get him out of there, rattling the chair's screwed-in base with his bound hands and feet, head upturned like a baby bird's in the nest. He had about as much chance of getting free like that as I had of being the next Mrs. Brad Pitt.

"Answer the question first," I told him, raising my voice to be heard over the racket. "What's the marathon called?"

He snuffled a few times, and calmed down enough to ask why.

"Because I have to make sure you are who you say you are."

"Olivia—" he protested, and I lifted my conduit, pointing it at his forehead. He stuttered off into silence, and the smell of urine immediately joined the nervous sweat. Which answered that question.

"Sorry," I said, tucking the weapon at the small of my back. I used the light from the horizontal windows ratcheting the roofline to guide me as I hurried toward Ian. Frankly, I was already thinking of all the ways I'd make Warren eat crow when I returned to the boneyard with the cure for the virus. I'd just decided to go easy on the old guy when the world erupted in a flash of light and I was tossed backward, sparks singeing off my skin as I landed so squarely on my ass, the concrete reverberated up my spine. There was a shimmer in the air, like water flowing between two sheets of glass, and a single rectangular panel appeared before me like it'd been conjured from nothing. Twice my height, both vertically and horizontally, I didn't have to touch it again to know it was impenetrable. Gradually the glimmering lessened, and half a minute later it was invisible again.

But it was still there.

"Fuck," I muttered, rubbing my ass, and that was a sincere understatement. The Tulpa's maze was here, intact, and Ian—seemingly a mere two hundred yards away from me—was at the center of it.

"What *was* that?" Ian said, eyes still fixed on the spot where the wall had appeared.

"Not was. Is. That's your cage, honey," I said, backing up to study the layout. As much as one can study an invisible force, that is. Ian's bindings were just for show. The real hurdle was in getting to him, and I was sure the Tulpa had gotten a charge, literally, out of my running up against his mental minefield. "So that's his game."

Now I was sure Joaquin had done something to piss off the Tulpa. Because dear ol' Dad, fond of intricate puzzles and mental games, was playing with both of us. Hopefully that would unnerve Joaquin enough to have him second-guessing himself into fatal distraction. Even so, I still had to get in . . . and there was no telling how many electrified walls I had to touch just to find the entrance.

Deadly to the player who enters but doesn't exit, Hunter had said, talking of this maze. And I'd stepped into the game the minute I ran out of Valhalla. Question was, how would I make my way to Ian without getting zapped with enough volts to power a small city? The first jolt still hummed in my brain like a hive. And how would I get a mortal out of this thing without frying him like butter on a griddle?

"You jump," Hunter said, when I called him on my cell phone and gave him the condensed version of events. The urgency in my voice must have convinced him not to waste time questioning me.

"Jump," I repeated, as visions of green-faced children winging through the air popped into my mind.

"Just keep your legs together so when you land you don't straddle a wall and get the ride of your life." He paused, before adding. "By default, that is."

"Glad you can joke at a time like this."

"Was I joking?" he deadpanned. "Besides, I'm just trying to keep you loose. Relax, okay? And focus. Remember, sight is your least valuable tool. Try to tap into your sixth sense."

Focus, I thought, and took a deep breath. That's what Tekla had repeated during our sessions together—the need for clarity of mind, the harnessing of intention. Never mind that I'd never managed to break down even one of her glass walls. I swallowed hard. "You stay on the line, okay? I might need you to—"

"Talk you through it?" he finished, when I couldn't. I nodded, realized he couldn't see it, and made an affirmative noise. I couldn't tell him that I didn't want to die alone.

The sound of feet pounding across asphalt kept me from getting too self-reflective. I whipped out my conduit, fired an arrow through the open doorway, heard a halting scuttle, and fired a second shot just to buy myself a little more time. Turning back, I spoke into the phone. "Hold on."

Intention, inshmention—I just leaped. I expected the up-swing to be just fine, and was already bracing for the fall when I slammed facefirst against a barrier a good thirty feet in the air. The blow knocked me back another ten, and as I dropped, my legs ricocheted off a second wall, flinging me backward so I landed on my spine. I came to a stop against yet another wall, and scuttled away from it as its jarring power combined with the previous two. I felt like an electri-fied pinball.

The commotion, of course, brought Joaquin sprinting in-side.

"Ah. The maze," he said, looking at the three panels my graceless flight had lit up. He didn't sound surprised or im-pressed. That couldn't be good. I kept my eyes on him—once they could focus again—and as he sauntered to the right his mouth moved like he was counting, and he paced in steady, measured steps.

No, I thought again, that couldn't be good at all.

I closed my eyes, and cursed, because I suddenly knew ex-actly what the Tulpa was doing.

If she can be killed by the likes of you, I don't want her.

Those words alone should've told me he wasn't just going to give me a head start and let me waltz away with the cure for the virus. Nope, every time I touched one of these walls my power and energy were sucked back into the maze. Back, I thought, into the Tulpa. No wonder he hadn't killed me. My power would've reverted to my mother, just like Stryker's had reverted to Tekla. Our lineage was matriarchal . . . but this way he could claim it for himself.

Ian, meanwhile, had begun screaming again at the sight of Joaquin, words pouring over one another as tears and sweat rolled down his face. I tried to shush him, to let him know he was only fueling Joaquin's ego with his fear, but he was too panicked to listen. Not that I blamed him.

Joaquin finished his pacing and halted with his hands on his hips, regarding Ian sourly. "What a pussy."

I shot him a look of pure hatred as I gained my feet, steady despite wobbly knees, and checked my phone long enough to determine my connection with Hunter had gone dead when I hit the electrified barriers. "Well, what do you expect when you kidnap him, beat his face to shit, and tie him up?" I said, tossing the phone to the ground.

"But I didn't beat him at all, did I, Ian?" He blew Ian a kiss. The crying escalated. "No, I was real sweet to your boyfriend. In fact, after he decoded your computer for me, we had ourselves a real nice party. Didn't we, honey?"

Ian whimpered again, and this time I made out what he said. *Don't hurt me anymore.*

"You rancid bastard."

Joaquin smiled my way. "A couple more minutes and I'll let you say that to my face."

And he stepped forward, counting again. I didn't need a wall to light up to know he'd entered the maze. Panic must have shown on my face because Joaquin's eyes remained fixated on me as he counted off five paces, before pivoting left as he spoke again. "He always starts on the right."

And he face-planted into a stinging sheet of balled energy. I'd have laughed as his eyes rolled into his skull, except my own had probably resembled slot reels only seconds before. The energy pulled from Joaquin into the maze zipped like a current through the rest of the walls, and I followed it with my head as it crackled past me, realizing I could track it to move another few feet either way without getting zapped. Question was, which way was forward and which way was back?

"Ian. Hey, Ian!" I snapped my fingers, and when that brought no alertness to his vacant stare, clapped my hands as hard as I could. "Ian, you have to help me here. I need you to count for me. Count the number of steps I take, and remember the directions I turn. You can do that, right?"

He cocked his head to the left, but the glassy look was slowly returning to his eyes.

"Ian?" I yelled, which had him blinking again.

"I—I don't know."

My gut tightened. I couldn't do this alone. "I need your help if you want me to get you out of here. I'm going to be too dazed from hitting walls I can't see. I won't remember the path to the center of the maze, and I sure won't remember how many steps I took along each corridor. I need you to focus for me, okay?"

His brows knit together and his eyes welled up as his head jerked. No. I sighed. "I can't."

"You can, Ian. Just concentrate on the numbers." But I was losing him. I could practically feel the icy fear rending him immobile, freezing his thoughts, causing him to anticipate death. "Look, what's math, anyway, but one mental pathway leading to another? Follow the path, and you get to the answer, right?" He nodded, and I breathed a sigh of relief. "Okay, well, *you're* the answer. I'm coming to get you. Just keep track of how my footsteps add up."

And before he thought I was giving him a choice, I paced to my right, keeping my steps as uniform as possible. I hit my next wall only three paces away, and this time controlled my direction as I was repelled away from it. An ache started in my jaw, an old filling I'd forgotten was there until now. I pressed my tongue to it, hissing through my teeth when I burned the top of it. I knew I was going about this all wrong—there was another way around this maze, something I was supposed to remember or know how to do—but I couldn't jump as the walls obviously arched all the way to the ceiling, and I didn't know how to anticipate what I couldn't see.

My only comfort was in the electric snaps, followed by curses, coming from Joaquin's direction. So I stood, found the spot I'd been in right before my last point of impact, waited until Ian returned my nod, then stepped toward him, sighing with relief when I didn't fry. From the corner of my eye, I caught Joaquin watching.

"Guess the Tulpa changed things up a bit on you," I said, sounding more confident than I felt as I inched forward. Jaw

clenched, Joaquin mirrored the movement from his position.
"What'd you do to piss him off? Must have been pretty severe to have him turn on you this way."

"He hasn't turned on me," he snapped, and stepped right
into a wall.

I followed the crackle of electrical current as it arched
past me, gained another three steps, and waited until Joaquin was sitting up. I shot him a smile as I rounded a corner.
"You were saying?"

Next thing, I was staring up at the ceiling, Joaquin's
laughter echoing in my ears. "Guess blood isn't any thicker
than water, is it?"

I raised myself to my elbows, grunting. "Well, I won't
take it personally."

"He's your father," Joaquin said, clearing another foot.

"He's a stranger," I replied, standing.

"You mean a stranger like . . ." He gained two more feet.
"Your daughter?"

I bounced off another wall, and this time momentarily lost
consciousness. I awoke to find him yards closer, and whipped
myself up despite the ache coursing through my marrow. It
wasn't just physical pain, though; there was something akin
to the rush of adrenaline pouring over me, but instead of re-
ceding on a wave that left me jumpy and alert, it left me feeling sluggish and unwilling to rise from the floor. Given time,
and enough direct contact with these walls, I knew I'd be unable to rise at all. But not yet. I had enough determination left
to stand this time, but I wondered how much energy I'd already transferred to the Tulpa, and what new powers it would
afford him. It'd be nice if I could live long enough to ask.

Nicer still to pummel the sly smile snaking over Joaquin's
cruel, sneering face.

"Oh yes, I know all about little Ashlyn, thanks to Ian
over there." He shot Ian a wink and a kiss, and the mortal's
concentration faltered. I clapped my hands to gain his attention again. Joaquin seemed content to wait. When my
eyes returned to his, he smiled innocently. "She lives in the

southwest part of town. She has wavy brown hair that curls into ringlets when it's wet. She likes riding her bike and is quite the competitive swimmer."

My hands balled into fists, and I gritted my teeth to keep my eyes from stinging. I hadn't known any of that. And this man shouldn't be the one telling me. "You stay away from her," I said, my voice thick and too low. He heard anyway.

"You mean like you?" he said pointedly. "No, I could never just abandon my own child."

"I didn't abandon her," I said, knowing I shouldn't bother defending myself against him, but doing it anyway. "She was adopted."

"You forsook her," he said with genuine disgust. He looked me over, up and down, like I'd committed a crime he couldn't even fathom. Yeah, that'd be the day. "You gave her over to the care of strangers, and lost the chance for a relationship with the child of your blood. All because of the sins of her father."

I took two steps forward in quick succession, almost willing myself into a wall just so the physical pain would drown out the ache brought on by his words. An ache, I realized, that'd been living inside me for years. "You're no father," I managed, my face hot, blood pounding in my temples. Even I could smell distress issuing from me in giant bulbous waves.

"As much as the Tulpa is yours." He shrugged, unaffected, and I heard disdain in his words; for me, for the Tulpa, for everyone that wasn't directly useful to Joaquin . . . which left only himself. And men like that were the most dangerous, I knew. Unleashed from care or concern about consequence outside his own world, Joaquin was a loose cannon at best, and a suicide bomber at worst. One who'd take out as many victims as he could in the search for his own twisted salvation.

That child, I swore, wasn't going to be one of them.

"I'm only going to say it one more time," I said, spacing

my words evenly, fire burning in my core. Suddenly I found I had energy in reserve. "Stay away from her."

"The concerned mother act doesn't suit you at all," he said, and sniffed at the air mockingly as his lip curled back. "And I'll do exactly as I please with my *daughter*."

And that word, coming out of that corrupted throat, was the vilest sound I'd ever heard. I opened my mouth, ready to rage, the bones beneath my face pressing against my skin and pulling it taut when—

"She's not his daughter."

"You!" Joaquin shouted, whirling on Ian. "Shut up, puppet!"

Red cleared from my vision, and I turned to Ian to find frightened determination had replaced the stark terror from before. Joaquin snarled, strode forward, and was sent barreling to his back. I listened for the whistling of energy as it whipped past me, gained another painless few feet from it, then looked back to Ian.

"She's not his daughter," he said again, licking his bruised lips, and swallowing hard. "The blood type's all wrong. It was on her birth certificate . . . and the DNA doesn't match up either."

Relief flooded through me like a breached dam, as if something lodged in my chest for a decade had suddenly been jostled free. I closed my eyes as a shiver stole over me. *Dark hair that curls into ringlets when it's wet.*

Ben.

I remained frozen where I was, my thoughts tumbling across my mind, and from Ian's sympathetic reaction, my face as well. So Ashlyn wasn't divided evenly between Shadow and Light? She was only of my lineage? Mine . . . and Ben's?

"You're going to die, mortal! You'll bleed from every orifice before I'm done with you!" Joaquin snarled, lifting himself to his knees. "And you! Does it make you feel any better knowing you gave up a relationship with your lover's child because of me? Because it makes me feel damned fine. I took your innocence—what was left of it, anyway—and then I took your lineage. And when I finish killing you, that girl is mine."

The idea of this man's hands on my child, mine and Ben's, made my stomach pitch. I barged forward . . . and rammed directly into a wall. This time I didn't recover as fast. Even Joaquin's laughter seemed to come from a far-off place, and I felt myself shaking, shoulders jerking uncontrollably as nerves misfired inside me. But I still lifted my head. I'd endure a thousand lightning bolts into my flesh if it meant keeping him away from her.

Ashlyn. Oh God.

I sat up slowly, got my bearings, and wiped the blood from my nose where it'd begun to run. Somewhere in the soft tissue of my head, something was going very wrong. A buzzing had set up shop in my left ear, like I was losing my hearing, but I ignored it and focused on preserving my mental energy, on not being so stupid and careless, though when the time came, I knew I'd need my physical reserves too. "And you think the Tulpa would let you lay a hand on his granddaughter?" I said more evenly as I wobbled to my feet.

"Now why would I ever tell the Tulpa about Ashlyn?" I winced as he said her name, and catching it, Joaquin smiled.

"Stop!"

I whirled, thinking Ian saw something I didn't; that danger was circling me from another angle. But he was looking square at me.

"Back up a step. Be careful not to lean left or right."

I did as he said, though I asked why.

Ian licked his lips, and his breathing picked up. Excitement was rushing off him in waves now, and I turned my full attention on him, momentarily forgetting Joaquin. "I know where you are. I saw the other man leave. Turn to your left and take three steps forward."

I hesitated, but Ian couldn't possibly do any worse than I was. Nothing happened as I moved, unless you count Joaquin's growl erupting behind me. I looked back at Ian expectantly. Maybe he really had seen the Tulpa exit the maze.

He swallowed hard, distracted by Joaquin's detailed accounting of what parts he was going to rip from Ian's body first, but finally managed a nod in my direction. "Another two steps to your left, three to your right."

I followed his directions exactly. When I lifted my head off the ground thirty seconds later, he winced apologetically. "I may have gotten that one backward."

I stood up, shaking now, both nostrils bleeding, and reversed the directions. This time I made it.

Sighing with relief, Ian guided me the rest of the way through. When I was a mere ten feet in front of him, he looked up at me expectantly.

"That's it?" I asked. "I'm in?"

He shrugged as I wondered where the bells of victory were, the cheering crowds, the clouds parting from the heavens.

"That's not it," Joaquin snarled, lifting himself to his feet once again. He'd been trying to move too fast, and it comforted me that he was finally rattled. "Didn't you hear the Tulpa? You have to save him too."

And in order to save him, we'd have to wind our way back out, past Joaquin. "One hurdle at a time," I muttered, and set about freeing Ian.

Aligning my conduit with the ropes binding him, arrow pointing down through the center of the knots, I fired. Nothing happened. I made sure the safety was off, and compressed the trigger to draw back the bow again. Still nothing. Only twenty feet away, Joaquin was splayed on his back, but this time he got up laughing.

"Conduits don't work in the maze, Archer, or didn't you know?"

The answer was obvious, so my reply was a mere curse as

I bent to unravel the knots by hand. Five minutes later Ian's hands were free, but I was no closer to figuring out how to get him past Joaquin. And it seemed Ian hadn't been the only one paying attention to my progress through the maze. Joaquin was making fast progress; either he'd managed to retain his faculties while getting zapped off his feet or the Tulpa wasn't as angry with him as I'd come to believe. Either way, Joaquin would find the center in the next few minutes.

"Listen," I said, kneeling at Ian's feet, fingers working furiously over the knots there. I glanced up. He wasn't listening. He was watching Joaquin's progress with mounting terror. I slapped his leg. "Ian! You have to listen to me. He's going to take us both out if he can, but stay behind me no matter what happens. We'll circle around him, and that'll give you a chance to exit."

His eyes darted back to Joaquin. I slapped him again, harder, to regain his attention.

"Just make sure you remember the number of steps in each of the pathways out there," I told him as he rubbed his arm. "And round the corners exactly. If you hit a wall, even once, you won't survive it. Got it?"

He swallowed hard, but nodded. "What about you?"

I handed him my conduit and stood, wiping my sweaty palms on my pants. "I'm going to make him bleed from every orifice."

We lined up then, Ian behind me, both of us as far from the entrance as we could get without being deep-fried. Joaquin was moving faster, meticulously counting off steps, and I marshaled my flagging energy by thinking of a young girl I'd never known. Ben's child.

He rounded the last corner, eyes bright with anticipation as he tracked me through that final barrier. The bolted chair was all that lay between us, and Joaquin feinted first to one side, then the other; he was testing us, teasing, trying to draw us forward. Ian whimpered behind me, and I patted him reassuringly. Unfortunately there was no one to do the same for me.

Body tense, I followed Joaquin with my eyes. Neither he nor I had a conduit, but he still had an advantage. If he touched a hair on Ian's head, I'd lose this contest. More, I was sure I'd knocked into more walls than he had, and the energy loss had made me shaky. I wasn't as agile as normal, and it felt like the entire world was shuddering under my feet as I sidestepped first one way, then the other, an unwilling snake to Joaquin's flute.

Pull it together, Jo, I told myself. *If only for the next five minutes.* No sooner did I have the thought than Joaquin lunged. I dove forward, wanting to meet him away from the electrified walls surrounding us, but he did a quarterback pivot around the bolted chair, slipping away from me and reaching for Ian, who yelped and bolted. A squeal, half terror, half pain, rose from him as he scraped the invisible barrier on his left, and the scent of burned flesh reached my nose. Joaquin sucked in a deep breath, a closed smile on his lips, and lunged again.

"Run!" I yelled at Ian as I launched myself over the seat of the chair and tackled Joaquin from above. We skidded across the room, and Ian leaped awkwardly over us to clear the entry. Joaquin, struggling and swearing beneath me, managed to lift a hand and grab the other man's ankle. This time Ian didn't squeal, but stomped down hard on Joaquin's arm, twice, while I pummeled him from the top. Joaquin let go with a murderous howl, and as Ian escaped, turned the full force of that rage on me.

This time we were more evenly matched. I was grown now, my warrior skills honed first as a mortal and now as a heroine of Light. The passage into the center of the maze had taken a toll on both of us, though, and neither of us were throwing our best blows. I reached up to his greased head, fisted my hand, and pummeled his skull into the ground. My body was pressed so firmly against his that the reverberations sounded in my breast.

It sounded like a choir of angels.

Joaquin bucked beneath me, scrambling for purchase

against the ground, my body, the nearby chair. What he found was an invisible wall. Unfortunately, the maze didn't discriminate between bodies locked so closely together, and raw power shot into me, exploding in my brain in a shower of stars and pretty lights. I flew backward and crumpled against the bolted chair, head torqued awkwardly.

Joaquin, though, had taken the brunt of the blow. I rose first; grasping the base of the seat, I heaved with everything left in me. Biceps straining, lungs aching, I was rewarded only by a faint creak. I glanced back. Now he'd found an elbow and was propped up, almost sitting. I strained against the base again, and the cement ruptured beneath my feet. But the fucking chair held.

If I'd been fresh, this wouldn't have been a problem, and I wondered if the Tulpa was enjoying all the new power my stolen energy was allowing him. All that kept me on my feet was knowing he'd zapped quite a bit of Joaquin's as well, and I strained again, groaning with it, and this time was rewarded with a resounding crack. My cry turned victorious, and I steadied myself, pivoted, and sent the chair plowing into Joaquin's face.

Or where his face should've been. A hand locked on to a chair leg, then another. I pushed, but Joaquin was quicker, a forward kick catching me in the sternum beneath my makeshift weapon. Tumbling backward, doubling over, I anticipated the chair cracking over my back.

Anticipation didn't make the reality any less painful. The breath flew from my body as I ate cement, and I could've sworn I heard vertebrae collapsing in my spine. Sprawled, the line of agony concentrated in my core before burning itself out in my limbs, I screamed in pain and frustration as my hands and feet went numb and useless.

I heard the chair clatter, then crackle as it sparked against a wall, then Joaquin was on me, flipping me over.

"This is familiar," he taunted, and though he didn't exactly look fresh, he was straddling me, propping his weight on the center of my spine, bearing down. When I'd finished screaming—and that only because there was no more breath left in my lungs—he spoke, words liquid and smooth, his face glazed over in satisfaction. "Look at you. You're exhausted. Burned so badly your skin is peeling . . . probably sensitive to the touch."

He plowed his fingertips into the burns along my neck, but this time I couldn't even spare the breath to scream. Pain was a constant, but so was the rapid thudding of my heart. Which meant I was alive.

"You don't look . . . any . . . better," I told him, and he whipped his hand across my face so hard, my cheek ricocheted off the cement.

He propped himself up on my waist, sitting so straight I could've toppled him if I'd still had the use of my limbs. Instead I had to wait until I recovered, or thought of something better. Nothing was coming to me right now. "I'll never understand why you guys do that," he said, running his hand through his hair, smoothing all the ends back into place. "Expending all your excess energy protecting a mere mortal. You might've had me if not for that. And now"—he shook his head in mock sadness—"you're my victim again."

"No. This was my choice," I said, almost at peace with that. Funny, but I felt more centered and relaxed now that it was almost over. Staring Joaquin in the face was easier than avoiding him in my dreams and thoughts, the way I had all these years past. That had been a useless expenditure of energy, I knew now. And just as debilitating as the Tulpa's maze.

But that wasn't the only reason I remained still. I had one more choice available to me, something actually learned in my endless lessons with Tekla. True, I'd never been able to knock walls down with my mind, but I had become somewhat adept at building them up. Therefore, as sweat seeped down my back, I fought to imagine a single, solid wall into existence, hoping my strength would be enough to manage that much. Fortunately Joaquin was busy shooting off at the mouth, and as the air five feet to his left began to ripple, he noticed nothing.

"Ah, yes. The *noble* sacrifice." He buffed his nails on his chest, pretending to inspect them closely. "Though that's nothing new for you, is it? You did the same for your sister years ago. And now you can expect the same results . . . except this time I will destroy you."

"*I will destroy you.*" I mimicked, right down to the low baritone. It halved my concentration, but it made me feel like I still had a degree of control. "Jesus. Been practicing that one long?"

He rose, nearing the wall solidifying on his left, and I'd have cursed myself for building it too close if I had the time or energy to do so. And maybe if he hadn't kicked me in the kidney. I curled into the fetal position, my concentration snapped, but after a moment was able to take the pain and my will and center it back into the wall. Sweat began to form on my forehead, sliding along my cheeks and jawline, though I didn't dare wipe it away. If I did, Joaquin would know I was doing more than recovering from his blow. I had to keep him talking.

"I should've killed you at the swingers' ball," I said, angling myself so he was again in front of me. A second wall began to shimmer to his right.

"And I should've killed you as soon as Regan told me of your new identity." He laughed at my surprised expression, and I had to refocus as my second wall bobbled. "She did, you know. Right after she ambushed you at the aquarium. I didn't believe her, of course. It was too obvious, too risky . . . totally out of character for the agents of Light."

"And because she was just an initiate," I added, because that's what I'd thought too.

"There was that," he conceded, dropping back down on my waist, gently wrapping his fingers around my neck. He didn't squeeze, just held them there, thumbs soft on my windpipe. "For some reason she seems to hate you even more than I do." He quirked his head as if considering that while his fingers played gently over the row of vertebrae in my neck. "Of course, I don't really hate you. I desire you . . . but I'm still going to kill you."

The second wall was solidifying strangely, an amalgamation of Tekla's mirrored practice walls and the Tulpa's invisible barriers. Though I doubted they possessed the same energetic sting as the maze surrounding us, it was amazing what the mind could do once it knew what was possible. I couldn't overthink it, though, because just then Joaquin's fingers tensed, then stilled as a popping sounded from behind me, also within. The pain was momentary, the nausea fleeting. And the paralysis was immediate. Fear flooded my brain, and the third wall I was erecting behind Joaquin disintegrated. I had to refocus—I couldn't be broken or killed this way; Joaquin knew it, he was just fucking with me—but more than the physical abuse, his words had crept into my mind, and questions now warred with my concentration. I shook my head to clear it of these thoughts, the only movement left to me, but Joaquin stilled the movement with only a slight press of his thumbs.

"Regan got a real kick out of setting you up," he told me, his own nerves giving a strained lilt to his voice. He was getting excited now. "She loved that she got you to watch those fireworks, to infect your friends, chase me, lose your place in the troop." He released his hold on my neck and rose to his knees, inches from the wall on his left. I swallowed, felt my throat working painfully, and was careful not to let my eyes stray to any of the walls surrounding him. He continued to stare me down as he stood.

"I have to confess, it has been fun watching you chase your tail, Joanna. More fun than simply killing you." He kicked at my feet playfully, then stopped playing and slammed his boot down on my kneecap. I heard the crunch of bone and cartilage shattering, and even though I felt nothing, the need to scream welled up inside me. I clamped my teeth together, squeezed my eyes shut, and refused to let the tears come. That's how I caught his next words, the most telling. "I know the Tulpa thinks he can lure you to our side, but I don't. A monarchy is all good and well, especially given no choice, but nepotism rubs raw."

I swallowed down another bout of nausea, my head now pounding, which meant the physical abuse was registering somewhere, despite my numbed limbs. Voice rasping, I said, "You don't sound very afraid of your leader."

"He acts independently of his maker; we act independently of him." Joaquin shrugged, folding his arms over his chest. He was almost fully recovered now.

"The Tulpa's creator is dead," I reminded him. If I could keep him talking I could get a fourth wall up and trap him inside. And if they all held, I could heal and figure a way out of this maze. But damn, that was a lot of ifs.

"Yes, and we have your mother to thank for that," he murmured, nudging my other kneecap. I winced instinctively. "If only she'd finished the job."

I blinked, swallowed hard, and then it was done. All three walls were erected, and either my work would hold, those walls would stand, or they wouldn't. And there was no reason to prolong this any longer. Besides, his fucking stench was getting to me.

"So we have a pretender to the throne, is that it?" I said, gazing up at him. The fourth wall began to shimmer at the edges, but gave away as he stepped forward. Either he hadn't felt it or pretended not to, because he only had eyes for me. How romantic.

"I've a greater right to it than you," he said coldly.

"And I'm sure Regan told the Tulpa you said so," I said, and got to watch him flinch. "No wonder he sent you in here with me."

"No." Joaquin straddled my shoulders, forcing me to look straight up at him. "If he knew, I wouldn't be here now. He wouldn't have given me a shot at his precious Kairos. You wouldn't be walled up in a maze I've already walked through, or lying on the ground with my boot print on your spleen."

"Now why does everything you say come out like a line in a B-grade spaghetti Western?" I said, feeling my limbs start to tingle to life. Too bad, because this was going to hurt. "You're so conscious of being recorded in the manuals . . . Joaquin, the Shadow Aquarian, the big star." I scoffed as his expression tightened again. "You're so fucking wooden you make Keanu Reeves look like a method actor."

And then his expression blanked. I was beginning to recognize this as a bad sign, but as he stepped back to regard me from a distance, he unexpectedly backed into my trap. I scrambled to get the fourth wall up while there was space between us, and his face remained impassive as the air shimmered between us. Maybe, just maybe . . .

"Let me speak more plainly, then," Joaquin said slowly. "Your walls can't hold me."

Or maybe not.

And he rammed his fists outward, one to each side, and my walls materialized, shining briefly, before disintegrating altogether. In what was almost the same movement, his right fist plowed through the front wall, the weakest, and it wobbled, then evaporated. He was on me so fast—fingers around my throat, spittle raining on my face—that my gaze had barely found his before he spoke. "I'm going to rape you raw, Joanna Archer. I'm going to shove myself so far down your throat I'll tear your lungs. And after I'm done with you, I'm going after Ashlyn. Is that clear enough for you?"

A flash of fear arrowed through me like heated quicksilver, stronger than any physical pain so far, mightier than the Tulpa's walls or Joaquin's fists or even my long-held hatred, and my vision blurred—from lack of oxygen or Joaquin's words, I didn't know—but inside my head the images were clear as polished glass.

A baby squalling as it was lifted from my body.

A photo of a family I didn't know, now complete, and a card sent to me in thanks.

Ben's curls on a child's head.

All this mingled together in a collage of color and action

and sound, and then . . . nothing. Not even light. Just a blank canvas in my mind where clarity and intention finally found a resting place, and I saw what Tekla had really been trying to teach me.

That, I thought, and a way to write my own future.

"How about that?" I managed, voice strangled. "Tekla was right."

"That loony bat?" Curiosity had Joaquin's grip loosening. "I thought she stopped making predictions the night I tore her son's head from his neck."

I shook my head, my skull rubbing against the pavement beneath me, but Joaquin yanked my hair back to still the motion, though he did allow me to speak. "No . . . she saw this. You and me, here." I gasped out a strangled laugh, amazed I hadn't seen it all along. "God, how could I be so blind? I was going to get what I wanted all along. I just had to be patient and not fight it."

Joaquin, unhappy with my digression, slapped me hard. Strangely enough, that restored my vision. "And what did batty ol' Tekla say? That we'd meet again in the warehouse where I murdered her only child, both of us trapped until one of us dies? That you'd end up victorious? Because it doesn't look that way to me. Did she also see you unarmed, sprawled beneath me, unable to move?"

I looked up, blinked. "Yes."

Joaquin looked as if he couldn't decide whether I was joking or not. Then he laughed, the sandpaper sound coarser and sharper than his nails at my neck, harder than the thighs pinning me in place. It was such a strange thing to behold, a wide, delighted grin on a face I'd only ever seen hooked in a sneer, and the thought of joy penetrating the wasteland of this man's life was so startling I nearly froze. Nearly.

"It's not you on the outside," I continued speaking, almost conversationally, as the printless pad of my thumb aligned with the smooth gem sitting on my ring finger. "It's you on the inside that I want gone."

I said it like I was making a wish, and depressed the stone into its setting.

Joaquin, kneeling in front of me, sneered like he didn't already know he was dead.

"Don't give me that psychological mumbo-jumbo, or act like you're made entirely of Light. If that were true, I wouldn't have been able to string you along, using your thirst for vengeance against you."

"I know. Which is why I'm letting it go." And I pinky-swore that to the Universe. "I have better things to do with the rest of my life."

He leaned down, chest touching mine, and I stared into his eyes, startled by the sudden realization that they were actually a dark moss color, almost pretty. Crazy the things you realized when you were no longer afraid for your life. "With the next five minutes, you mean? And what's that?"

I ignored the heat of his breath, the pungent sulfur rising from his soul, and tried to read his mind, wondering when he'd realize he couldn't touch me anymore. "Helping others. Fighting for those who can't fight for themselves. Giving voice to those who can't speak."

He saw how earnest and honest I was, and doubt flickered across his face. It was fleeting, contradicted by the facts as he knew them, which he spelled out, though for my benefit or his, I didn't know. "You're pinned beneath me like a butterfly to a board. You'll never do any of that."

Too bad he didn't know all the facts.

"I already have," I said simply, and let my gaze slip past his shoulder. Joaquin turned.

She stood, solitary and small, just outside the maze, half obscured by the shadows of the warehouse. She didn't look like an agent of Light, I thought, as Joaquin's weight eased off me. In fact, right now Tekla looked like the least heroic agent I'd ever seen. I didn't know how much Joaquin could really see of her—the aura that was usually a steady soft lavender was now crackling around her in sharp violet snaps—but he couldn't take his eyes off her, and he didn't move as she stepped into a moonbeam, the light making her look ghostly and one dimensional.

So it's true, I thought, eyes flicking to the unwavering Joaquin. *She really could trap you in her gaze.*

She was wearing a robe of crimson red, a weapon like a crossbow with a chain attached to it, held at her side. Her son's. On her chest was a pulsing glyph, and with every steady beat of the Scorpio sign, the hollows of her face lit up; unsmiling, severe. Vengeful.

I spread my palm flat, moving my fingers away from the ring that had called her to me, and she acknowledged me with a flick of her gaze as I propped myself back on my elbows, pulling my legs in tight. Joaquin shifted into a fighting stance. I'd have stood myself except I wasn't sure what Tekla was going to do. But if there'd been a bunker to disappear into, I'd have ducked into it at that moment.

"Well, well." Joaquin lengthened the words, his head coming up and fists tightening at his side, like he didn't know he was moving because she allowed it. "If it isn't the Scorpio figurehead. Come to save the Kairos? Or just happen to be in the neighborhood?"

Tekla didn't even blink, and for the first time, even with two hundred yards between us, I could feel the combination of control and power that made her so revered among the troop. Swallowing hard, I wished again for that bunker. "Don't mess with her, Joaquin. You'll just make it worse."

He spared me a glance, a kind of half-amused, half-annoyed sneer that turned to confusion when he scented my own rising nervousness. It wasn't an act. The ring hadn't just brought Tekla to me. The energy used to call her was like a taut rope linking us together. The room suddenly held the stillness of a vacuum, or the eerie abandonment of a coastline right before a monsoon. What was it Tekla had once told me? About the destructive power of vengeance?

Revenge is an A-bomb that will flatten everything around you.

I curled up tighter into myself.

Joaquin frowned, then expelled the scent from his nose, nostrils flaring as he turned back to Tekla. She still hadn't moved. "I take it you've come to play, then. Two against one? Not good odds, but it's not as if I haven't raped and killed two women in one night before."

When Tekla still didn't speak, Joaquin's own nervousness mounted, though it wasn't nearly as high as it should've been. If he could feel what I felt—the raw rage gathering behind the fragile shell of that diminutive frame—he'd be on his knees already, begging for forgiveness. Instead his nerves heightened his arrogance . . . though the maze between them probably also had something to do with it.

"Or maybe you come here often . . . eh Tekla, old girl? Could this be a pilgrimage of some sort? Coming to pay your respects at the site where your son took his last cursed, gurgling breath?" He snickered, and I felt my chest tighten as the air grew thin around me. I gasped for breath, but Joaquin kept talking. "No offense to the Archer over here for the attempts I've made on her life, for the one I'll make as soon as I take care of you, but I have to admit . . . Stryker was my favorite kill."

It was like an airplane had lost its cabin pressure, and I had to put my hands to my temples as they began to pound, my eardrums tightening into a squealing ache. "Tekla," I whimpered.

But she didn't spare a glance, a thought, or an instant for me. With steps that started slowly, then accelerated, she strode right up to the point where the maze began. Then through it. And directly toward Joaquin. The electrical current that should've zipped through her body, frying her from the inside out, rose above her in noxious vapors, coalescing like storm clouds overhead. Joaquin gasped—or tried to as he backed up into me, he seemed to be having trouble breathing now as well—and I kicked at him, wanting to be as far from him as possible when this unnatural disaster struck.

Still striding forward, eyes locked on her target, Tekla lifted her arms. "Never utter my son's name again."

The cloud didn't rain. It exploded. Downward, outward, shafts of fire sheared the air in blinding arrows, careening into what remained of the maze. Those walls too flared before shattering into thousands of shards, turning the warehouse into an asteroid field of electric slabs and searing light.

I tried to lift myself to my knees and crawl from the storm's eye, but something rammed into my elbow, and the screech of living current whizzed through me. I dropped into the fetal position, crying out, but the sound was lost in the zing of live electricity. And in Joaquin's screams cresting over me in waves of unseen horror.

Tekla drew closer, and the ripping winds sagged around me as she reached my side. Calm broke around my body, like a door had been slammed, and silence buzzed in my ears, though the rest of the warehouse was still fraught in chaos. I glanced up to find her hovering above me, protecting me. But I didn't rise. Instead, I felt like I should genuflect.

The Tulpa's maze was annihilated. All that remained of the walls were flying bits, some small as ice cubes, others large as icebergs, each jagged piece visible, and careening toward a swirling vortex under which, I realized, was Joaquin. Like bees swarming, the heightening mountain enshrouded his body, only a bloodied foot or hand appearing before being attacked, and drawn back into the core. All I could make out between snaps of light was the gleam of steadily pooling blood widening on the floor. More blood, I thought, than one body could hold.

As haphazard and total as the destruction was in the warehouse, the only scratch on me was on my elbow. I gained my feet as the roar in the air softened, and straightened when it was silent enough to hear my breath rattling in my chest. Intermittent grunts came from the pile of debris, usually preceded by a sharp sizzle or crackling pop. The scent of electrocuted flesh permeated the air, and suddenly I wasn't so happy to have my breath back.

I turned to Tekla, who kept her eyes on Joaquin and the swarm until it died off altogether. I wondered briefly if she was seeing what I did, or if she was remembering as well; the night her son was taken from her, the blood that had seeped over the floor then, the weight of his severed head in her lap. Then the Tulpa's maze dissolved completely.

Take that, Tulpa.

I stepped forward, my footsteps like gunshots in the silence, until I stood over a body so mutilated and burned I barely recognized it as a person, much less Joaquin. He was still alive, though his limbs were no longer intact, severed bits lying in awkward angles, like an abandoned puppet loosed from its strings. His flesh smoldered in places where the larger sections of wall had struck, imbedding themselves to fry through skin and muscle and tissue, cracking against bone. The smaller injuries, surface ones, merely cleaved off digits, or dug themselves into organs, revealing finely sheered sections of his core where flaps of skin waved like bloody flags.

His nose no longer existed. The soft flesh of his cheeks looked like they'd been carved almost with purpose, and his thin-lipped mouth extended ear to ear, the full set of his teeth revealed in a permanent smile. His bones were black, but I knew they'd been that way before, and my eyes wandered to his glyph, still heating his ravaged chest in irregular, smoky beats. I looked at it, hating it, despite all the carnage wracked upon the rest of him.

I glanced at Tekla and saw the same nothing in her eyes that I felt in my chest, and without looking at me she held out her conduit, useful again now that the Tulpa's maze had been annihilated. Heart in my throat, I nearly reached for it before sighing and shaking my head. I'd made a vow.

I turned back to Joaquin, and his eyes, the only part of his face not completely rearranged, ran wildly from Tekla's face to mine. "You want us to hurt you," I told him, throwing his words to me back in his face. "You expect it. And you'd be disappointed if we didn't."

Okay, so I didn't need vengeance anymore . . . but I still loved having the last word.

Joaquin's lower jaw hinged open as if to speak, but blood pooled down his chin from the stub of his tongue, and Tekla fired before any sound could gurgle out. A palm-sized anchor imbedded itself into the center of his glyph. She fingered a release button, and the chain attached to the anchor retracted, yanking Joaquin's black and bloody heart out with it. His glyph snuffed out like a candle beneath Tekla's gentle breath, and a whiff of sooty smoke joined the cloying rot saturating the warehouse air. The kill spot would impress generations to come.

33

"Do you like to fly?" the Tulpa asked after I'd settled myself across from him in the stretch limo, careful not let the door latch shut behind me. We were parked in an elongated lot just off Sunset and Eastern, watching the planes take off and land at McCarran in a carefully choreographed dance across the night sky. There weren't many coming in these days, though authorities had begun letting healthy people go home once an anonymous caller had explained how the virus was being spread, and how to test for its presence.

"I wasn't aware I could," I finally said, as a jet powered into the air in front of us. The Tulpa was making me pick up the antivirus in person, and—after I'd made him swear not to kill me, order me killed, or have me followed back to the sanctuary and then killed—I'd relented, naming the time and place. I'd come to this viewing lot as a kid, and had always loved the deep rumble of power as the jets streamed, one after another, into the sky. No reason to share that, though. My childhood was none of this being's business.

"I mean, like that," he said, waving his hand to indicate the airstrip in front of us. "In planes. Do you enjoy the power of the machine as it slings you from the earth and into the sky? Does it make you wish you had wings?"

"Sure," I told him, shrugging because it cost me nothing to say it.

"What does it feel like?" he asked, real curiosity tingeing his voice.

I glanced over at him, but I'd lost the power to see auras entirely after my run in the maze, and there was no color outlining his form to indicate mood, emotion, or intent. To be honest, I didn't miss the ability that much; I hadn't been adept enough with it for it to be much more than a distraction, but it made me wonder what other capabilities he'd stolen from me.

He was in the corner right now, his face again obscured in shadows, and I couldn't help but wonder if he just carried them around with him, like an umbrella he could flip open at will. That thought was less unsettling than his prior explanation, that I only saw what I expected to see when I looked at him. So it bugged me that he was featureless now, as if I hadn't made up my mind about him yet.

Whatever, I thought, struggling to keep my expression neutral as I faced forward again. I was back in my disguise too; red wig pinned to my head, ruddy makeup, and baggy clothes to hide Olivia's form and face. I'd been hoping he'd just hand over the antivirus and we'd go our separate ways, but I guess we were going to chitchat first. "Haven't you ever flown?"

"We all have limits, Joanna."

"So you're saying you *can't* fly?" I asked, and had to wonder immediately why he was telling me this. It wasn't like revealing some pseudo-secret was going to have me softening my stance toward a wicked, mass-murdering being spawned from the sick mind of a man I was glad was dead. He had to know that.

"I can't leave the valley," he clarified, furthering my suspicion. "It's a restriction. Neither can you."

I toyed with the up and down button of my window, letting

the heat of the night air leach into the limo's cabin, and the blast of the air conditioning drive it out again. "Sure I can."

"Have you tried since your metamorphosis?" he asked, and I paused, window halting halfway. I bet he was raising a brow from his place in the shadows. And I knew he was shaking his head. A soft chuckle slipped from the dark. "Does Warren tell you nothing?"

"Warren believes—" I started, then corrected myself. "*We* believe the most important lessons are taught in the doing, not the telling."

"In other words, he'd have waited until you were on the airplane to let you find out."

I made a face. "Probably."

He laughed again, and reached out to swirl a tumbler of brandy, light cutting through the cut crystal to set the liquid glowing in amber warmth. He had nice hands, really; strong, wide, but elegant. Though I guess that could've been my imagination too. "Well, maybe there's wisdom in letting someone believe they can do anything. That way they push the boundaries of the known, test their limits, refuse to take no for an answer. I should remember that."

I stopped playing with the window long enough to nail him with a glare. I didn't need any schooling from the Shadow side. "The vial, please?"

"Impatient, aren't you?" More amusement.

"I get it from my mother," I said smartly, holding out my hand. His own whipped out, grasped mine before I could withdraw it, squeezing so tightly my arm began to go numb.

"I know," he said, and bilious smoke swelled to fill the limo's interior. It was a good thing I had the window down, else I risked suffocating on the mawkish scent. I looked down and saw his fingers through the haze; they'd turned into claws, the nail beds hinged to the bone, and slashing out in curved talons with pronged tips. I belatedly realized I should've specified not *injuring* me as one of my conditions in being here. There were a lot of ways to hurt someone and still keep them alive. Fucking hindsight.

But his grip relaxed, the pressure lessened, and by the time the fumes lessened, those honed fingertips had turned fleshy once more. A slow inhalation of breath sucked the rest of the smoke back into his body—which was weird in itself—but then he was caressing my hand, and rubbing a manicured thumb over the ring I'd used to call Tekla to me in the maze.

"Where did you get this?" he asked, his voice as soft as his touch. I looked down. The light pulsing from beneath the prongs had been snuffed as soon as I'd depressed the stone into its setting, so it was dead now, just another stone, and useless. At least until I passed it on to another. But I wouldn't do that yet because . . .

"Zoe gave it to me."

But he already knew that. He knew what this ring was, what it did, and by the tight control suddenly straining his vocal cords, I was willing to bet he'd also given it to her.

He released my hand, and I pulled it tight to my chest, rubbing it as I watched him reach into the inside pocket of his double-breasted suit and pull out the fragile vial of save-the-world serum. He didn't hand it to me, instead rolling it back and forth in his palm.

"There was a story I once heard," he said, and I'd have rolled my eyes, except I had a feeling he wasn't merely stalling. His powerful tenor was more distant than I'd ever heard it, his profile visible as he leaned his elbows on his knees and stared out the window to the sky above. "A legend about a person who would one day be born with equal parts sun and moon dominating her temperament, those planets warring so strongly within her that, unlike all others, she'd never have to bend to the influence of the stars. She would have the ability to freely choose the path she'd walk in this lifetime. Choose, also, the allies who would walk beside her. Their adversaries, so equally matched before, would be crushed beneath them. The first sign that one side would soon assume ascendancy over the other was the discovery of this unique individual."

I made a sound in the back of my throat, impatiently tapping my finger on my mahogany armrest. "I've heard this story somewhere before."

He ignored me. "The second portent that one side was finally to fall to their enemies was the sweep of a plague over their battleground, amassing casualties on both sides."

"Alas," I said wryly.

He didn't even pause in his telling. "But the third sign . . ."

I interrupted here, tired of being ignored, and wearied by a story that still seemed like some remote legacy about someone I didn't know. "Isn't written yet."

"Was written the moment the second was fulfilled," he corrected, and turned to face me as my mouth fell open. His smile flared in the moonlight splicing through his window, and he almost looked human. "The third sign is the reawakening of Kairos's dormant side. A new journey through the city she was born to, and rebirth into the troop she thought she was destined to defeat."

"Gee," I said, dryly. "You just can't trust those urban legends, can you?"

"Not always," he said easily, leaning back into the shadows, only his hands remaining in the moonlight, pale next to the bloodred vial he carelessly palmed. "But I bet I can get you to switch sides in return for Zoe Archer's life."

I froze, even though my stomach heaved. He was lying. Lying and bluffing, and I called him on it. "You don't have it to trade. She's remained in hiding through my adolescence, metamorphosis, and a virus that threatened the entire troop and valley. You don't know where she is, and you have nothing to draw her out into the open."

"There's you," he said simply, and held the vial out to me.

The straight answer so shocked me that for a moment I didn't move. And then, as squarely as a pie in the face, it hit me why he *really* hadn't killed me back at Valhalla. It wasn't because I was his daughter, or the Kairos—this legend he spoke of now—or even because he wanted to send me into his maze and steal my power for himself. He still wanted *her*. God. His quest for vengeance made mine look like child's play.

I forced myself to reach out and take the vial before he withdrew it, but because I was suddenly shaking, I had to be extra careful not to let my hand tighten around it once it was in my fist. I lifted my eyes to the inhuman ones I knew were watching me from the shadows. "I won't let you use me against her," I said quietly.

"You, my dear, don't have a choice. It'd be one thing if you'd come to me willingly, but now you've pissed me off. You want to be an enemy, daughter? Fine. I'll provide you with a worthy foe."

"See," I said, with more confidence than I felt, "I just knew we couldn't have a civil conversation without at least one veiled threat."

"Veiled?" He leaned forward then, and I saw him again, that same guido who'd promised to let me live if I could escape Valhalla, his maze, the infection coating the city. But this being gave a new meaning to the phrase *organized crime*. And I doubted any of the old-time mobsters had eyes that flared in cherry red flames from upper lid to lower, and a voice so low it could cause the earth to quake. "The minute you step from this car my vow is fulfilled, and we'll be opponents once more."

Okay, so not exactly veiled.

I glanced around at the squeaky tanned leather seats, polished decanter and glasses, mahogany armrests, and flat screen, currently off. A slim line of green neon slid around the carpeting, casting a soft glow over everything but the shadows layering his face. I sighed. "Well. It *is* a nice car."

Those glowing eyes remained unblinking and unamused. I guess I got my sense of humor from my mother as well.

"All right," I said, tucking the vial into a pocket I'd lined with foam. "Since we're telling stories, I have one for you as well." I looked up and waited until I saw a slight nod—he'd indulge me—before continuing. "Once upon a time there was a being who got off on injuring and influencing mortal lives, spreading disease and destruction in hopes that it would snowball. He wanted humans to feel chaos, to spew out soured emotions so he could feed off that negative energy, making it easier to sow evil thoughts, habits, and deeds among them. But that alone was never enough for him. He was always wanting more. And that, ultimately, would be his downfall."

"It's true," the Tulpa said, to my surprise. "Joaquin was stymied by his own aspirations. He died in that maze because he reached too far."

And because I hadn't been talking about Joaquin, I paused, leaned back in my seat, and stared.

And saw something far more revealing than any aura. I saw the puppets. And I saw the strings.

"How about that," I said, wonder spreading through me. "Joaquin was trapped in a maze before he ever stepped foot in that warehouse." I shook my head, a humorless laugh escaping me. How could I not have seen it before?

The weight of those red orbs on me told me I had his full attention now.

"You laid out a labyrinth so large and intricate, it spanned this entire city. The virus was just a diversion, sleight of hand. You weren't targeting the agents of Light as much as you were cleaning house on the Shadow side. And you used me to do it."

There was a deep breath—he was composing himself, but it was too late—and his eyes burned out, slipped back into the obsidian slate that so perfectly matched mine. "I handed you your greatest enemy on a silver platter. Where's the gratitude?"

I shook my head, scoffing at that. "I handed him to you. Of the two of us, you considered him the greater threat. But it was a win/win situation for you, wasn't it? You knew I'd go after him and you'd either score some power from me *or* stop him from looking for the original manual."

"Or both," he said baldly, no longer denying it. I suppose

he thought he was safe, that it was all said and done. That this story, the legend, was already written. He smiled, teeth flashing, and seemed to read my mind. "That is, if it were true. Right now it's just a cute story."

"And one that should be told," I said coldly, knowing it already was. Somewhere in this city, Zane was getting a buzz on. It'd be interesting to see which manual this conversation showed up in, the Shadow line, or the Light. I thought of Regan, and how she, like Joaquin, was keeping my identity to herself. It seemed the Tulpa hadn't yanked the threat to himself out at the roots. He'd merely snapped the top off a rapidly growing weed. I grinned widely, and let him see that secret in my smile. "Who knows? Someone might take up an interest in collecting."

Maybe it was the smile that got to him. His fingers twitched on his knees. "An unhealthy interest."

"Why?" I asked, tilting my head. "I mean, if the original no longer exists?"

When I realized he wasn't going to answer, I shrugged and climbed out of the car. But then I just stood there. I had a feeling he couldn't let me leave with the last word, and I was right. Seconds later, the window rolled down soundlessly. "You don't honestly believe that you can beat me, do you?"

I lifted my gaze to the clear night sky and thought about how he'd almost killed me once, how I thought I was dead again after chasing Regan and Liam back into Valhalla. And how Hunter and I had approached it with not much more going for us than a whole lot of chutzpah the night before. I hadn't really believed I could beat him then. Not any of those times. But somehow I'd survived him.

And somehow I'd do it again.

"You, of all people, should know the potency of a strong imagination."

Another plane roared overhead, and he waited until it faded in the heated night before speaking again. "Last chance, Joanna. Return that vial to the agents of Light, if you must. Fulfill the second sign of the Zodiac and put an end to the plague killing off this valley. But return to me voluntarily before the splitting of the next dawn, fulfill the third sign of the Zodiac, and I'll forget we were ever enemies."

"And if I don't? War?"

He leaned forward, and we stared at each other across the short distance, black eyes fastened on black eyes, matching resolve roiling at the surface, and the uncanny family resemblance had us both searching each other's face.

"Apocalypse," he answered, his voice a smoky whisper.

I left him then, backing away from the heat searing the air between us, the late-summer night balmy in comparison. I turned away from the offer to find refuge in the shadows, and shrugged off the feeling of blackened eyes following my heavy steps as I strode across Sunset. The taste of sulfur burned across the night, and I didn't doubt him in the least.

34

Hunter and I were allowed back in the sanctuary the next day. Tekla had cleared the way, explaining about our break-in at Valhalla, my deal with the Tulpa, how I'd saved Ian from the maze when it'd meant sacrificing myself . . . and how she had foreseen it all. We learned of all this secondhand from Gregor as he ferried us in the cab, through the boneyard wall at dusk . . . as it should be. Tekla, he'd explained, hadn't been seen since her return, and refused to come out of her room, even for meals. I knew why, of course. There was a difference between merely killing an enemy agent and torturing him up until his dying breath. I could only imagine her self-struggle as she tried to reconcile what she believed—what she taught—with what she'd done.

Meanwhile, I'd set up an appointment with Ian to get my conduit back . . . and find out who knew what about the contents of my missing computer. Fortunately, Ian saw our meeting as a date, a second chance to get together with Olivia Archer, and was gushing about mazes and conduits. I humored him long enough to ascertain that Joaquin hadn't shared the information about Ashlyn with Regan or the Tulpa, and that Ian—in a spurt of heroic behavior—had destroyed the hard drive as the contents revealed themselves. Then I got him drunk on Mai-Tais, ferried him out to the car under the relieved eye of the bartender, where Micah drove him away to mess with his memory. He woke the next morning thinking the past week's events had all been a bad, blurry dream. My letters to Ben were gone for good, but I snuck back to my old house, hoping for an answer to the note I'd so hastily scribbled on the kitchen counter days before. Given the little he knew of me, my life, and my reasoning—and how much I knew it must have hurt him to wake alone again—I shouldn't have been surprised to find only two words waiting for me in the mailbox: *Fuck you*. No wonder he'd turned to Regan.

But the antivirus was safely in Micah's capable hands, and we were planning a fireworks display of our own, though Hunter and I would probably be fast asleep before then. And while Warren made a point to specifically take me aside and apologize in private, we still weren't entirely comfortable with each other. But we were both willing to start over again, and with the Tulpa out there, gunning for blood, we'd need each other more than ever.

"I'm sorry you couldn't get your sister's computer back," Hunter said, once we'd been debriefed and dismissed. We strode the familiar corridors of the sanctuary side by side, hands in our pockets, smiling at those we met along the way, but not stopping. "I know there was a lot of . . . *her* on that thing."

There had been. But, degree by degree, I was learning to let Olivia go. "It's probably better this way. That thing was a ticking bomb. Anybody could have accessed that information."

"Information," he said, holding a piece of paper out to me. "Like this?"

I halted, eyeing it warily. "What is that?"

"Her address."

I took it and shoved it in my pocket before he could see my hand shake. "Thanks."

"Aren't you going to open it?"

I shook my head. I wasn't ready. The idea of it—a daughter, Ben's and mine—was still too foreign to me. Besides, there was one person out there who still knew my identity, and even if she was currently content to keep that information to herself, I knew she'd be watching.

Hunter and I reached his room, the rain room as I'd come to think of it, and our arrival coincided with a long silence. We shifted uncomfortably, two superheroes completely at a loss, not meeting each other's eyes . . . until we finally did. "Hunter, I just want to say—"

"Don't." He put a finger to my lips, not hard, but not gently either. "Or I'll have Micah erase your memory too."

I smiled and let it go, willing to do whatever was easiest for him. God knew I'd asked enough, put him through enough already. "Okay, but what about . . . I mean, where do *we* go from here?"

"Forward, baby," he said, and his smile was bittersweet. "Always forward."

"Not 'up, up, and away'?" I too decided to keep it light.

He winced and let out a long-suffering sigh. "You're ruining the perfect moment."

I laughed, then stopped when he abruptly bent toward me, his palm wide and warm on my neck as he pressed his lips against my forehead. I leaned into him, tears stinging my eyes. He left me after that single kiss, and the words I wanted to say died in my throat as he locked his door behind him. I swayed in the hallway, eyes shut, tingling from my forehead all the way to my toes.

Once I'd regained my sense of balance, I went to the locker room and slipped the piece of paper with Ashlyn's address through one of the slats, figuring it'd come back to me when I was ready. And when I could figure out what to do about this child, this daughter of mine, who was now burning her way through her first life cycle.

For now it was enough that I was the Archer, still one of the Light, and after fulfilling the second sign of the Zodiac, that I was one step closer to fulfilling my legacy as the Kairos. And, I thought, no matter what the Tulpa said about switching allegiances, the third portent of the Zodiac, I knew myself. My vow to topple the Tulpa's organization burned in me, strong as ever.

"Why don't you try to open it?"

I'd thought myself alone and jumped, turning to find Tekla looking gaunt and tiny and fragile, staring at me from across the room. Careful not to meet her eye, I swallowed hard and turned immediately back to the locker. "Okay," I said, thankful for something to do.

I didn't have to work at it this time. All I did was press my hand to the palm plate at the side and lift the latch. The door swung open with unexpected force, and manual upon manual spilled out at my feet. It took a moment, but I gasped when I realized they were all Shadow.

"But how—? There must be dozens!" I bent, filling my arms with them, trying to shove them back in the locker, until one title caught my eye. *Philly's Penumbra*, set in Pennsylvania. "Jesus! These are Joaquin's!"

"And there aren't dozens, but hundreds," Tekla said, stepping forward, careful not to touch any of the manuals.

"Do you think my mother left them for me?"

She shook her head, gazing down. "She can't touch them. But someone did, which means you have a responsibility to find out why."

"The original manual," I said, more to myself than her. Perhaps even Joaquin himself had left them to me. He had to know that nobody else would search as diligently and ceaselessly for the original manual as me. I could well imagine him reasoning it all out. If he were to die, he'd still want his work to live on. "These are filled with clues that will lead me to it."

And to the answer my mother sought her entire life. How to kill the Tulpa.

"So you've a new quest, it seems," Tekla said, angling her head. "Now that Joaquin's gone, I mean."

I looked at her, surprised she had mentioned his name first. She shifted under the weight of my stare, but ultimately returned my gaze. And I saw the pain living inside her. "You stepped up, Tekla. Stryker would be proud."

She lifted her chin and studied the glowing glyph on his locker, now her own. "I must seem like such a hypocrite to you. All my ramblings about intention and clarity of mind . . . but when it got down to the wire, *you* were the one who was in control. *You* put aside the need for revenge, a need that'd driven you through a lifetime. And I . . . I wasn't any of the things I teach out there."

"No," I agreed, and she sucked in a sharp breath. I put a hand on her arm. "You were just a mother who had lost a son."

She stared at her hands, studying them for a long time, before looking back up at me. "It cost you to give Joaquin to me."

"It would've cost me more had I taken the shot," I said, before asking, "Are you sorry?"

She nailed me with her gaze. "Should I be?"

"Why don't you open *your* locker and find out?" I asked, and her eyes flew from my face, her face lowering to hide her expression. "That's why you're here, right?"

She said nothing.

"Come on, Tekla," I urged softly. Then I used Hunter's words. "We have to move forward."

She pressed her hands against her cheeks, then squared her shoulders, and turned. I stepped back, giving her space and privacy as she slipped across the room and lifted her hand. She'd barely touched the Scorpio palm plate when the locker swung open, seemingly of its own accord. In fingers that shook, she lifted out a photo taped to its back. I leaned closer. It was a boy with bright eyes and a body just sprouting the strength of a man. He was tall and lanky in his youth, and had a smile brighter than all the bulbs in the boneyard. I put my hand on her shoulder, and stared with her at the boy who was strong and good and hers . . . and gone. Stryker, in his boyhood, had been the perfect initiate of Light.

"No," I whispered, when her shoulders had stopped shaking so much, and her sobs had quieted into intermittent sniffles. "I don't think you should feel sorry for what you did at all."

And Tekla cried again, with as much relief as grief, and after she'd cried herself out on my shoulder, I left her alone in the locker room with all that remained of her son.

Two nights later I had a clear shot at Regan as she and Ben dined al fresco, sitting on a bistro patio in the cooling breeze of an early fall, watching tourists weave among themselves on the Las Vegas Strip. Ben looked happy, or at least content, and I watched him with concentrated longing all the way up until he excused himself before dessert.

Regan looked content as well, like a cream-filled cat sunning herself in the late afternoon rays. She also still looked like me. But because her company seemed to satisfy Ben, I didn't kill her as soon as he'd walked away. With all that had happened to him over the past few months—hell, with what I alone had put him through—I figured he was entitled to a few moments of cheer, no matter how hollow, false, or fleeting they might be.

I did, however, pin a note to the shaft of an arrow I'd honed myself, and when the waiters and foot traffic and cars had all cleared, lifted my conduit and sent that note spinning through the air, whistling all the way until it buried itself in the wooden tabletop, half an inch from Regan's pinky finger.

She ducked for cover, then returned to her seat under the curious glances of the other diners once she realized she'd already be dead if I'd wished it. Picking up the note, her fingers trembled; and watching her lips move, I read along with her.

No matter what you think, you don't know me. You can't predict how I'm going to act. In fact, I've left everything you find predictable behind me—the broken

*young girl you studied before becoming me, the venge-
ful woman you saw searching for Joaquin, the Tulpa's
daughter—it's all scattered on the feckless wind like
the rubbish it always was. What drives me now is
love.*

And you've got mine.

*So ask yourself, as I already have, what's the worst
thing that can happen to Joanna Archer by telling you
this?*

*Then ask yourself again . . . what's the worst thing
that can happen to Regan DuPree?*

She folded the letter away and looked up. I stepped from
behind the palm tree planted on the median as the fountains
from the Bellagio soared up behind me, hidden speakers
pumping Bocelli into the air as he sang about the sun in a
language not his own. Regan swallowed hard, then squared
her jaw and raised her wineglass my way, a forced smile
playing on her new lips.

I smiled back and raised a wall of glass in front of her, my
thoughts forcing her reflection back on itself, before I let it
dissolve into smoke, like the mist drifting from the lake behind me. And while she was still considering who had whom
boxed in, Ben returned. I watched him lean toward her, ask
what was wrong. And before he could turn to see what had
her so riveted, I walked away, and left him sitting with my
enemy, who was still trembling.

Trembling in skin that was supposed to be mine.